GARMENT OF SHADOWS

In a strange room in Morocco, Mary Russell is trying to solve a pressing mystery: Who am I? She has awakened with shadows in her mind, blood on her hands, and soldiers pounding at the door. Meanwhile, Holmes is pulled by two old friends, and a distant relation into the growing war between France, Spain, and the Rif Revolt led by Emir Abd el-Krim – who could be a Robin Hood, or a power-mad tribesman. The shadows of war are drawing over the ancient city of Fez, and Holmes badly wants the wisdom and courage of his wife, whom he discovers, to his horror, has gone missing.

GARMENT OF SHADOWS

GARMENT OF SHADOWS

by

Laurie R. King

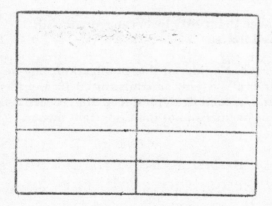

Magna Large Print Books
Long Preston, North Yorkshire,
BD23 4ND, England.

British Library Cataloguing in Publication Data.

King, Laurie R.
    Garment of shadows.

    A catalogue record of this book is
    available from the British Library

    ISBN   978-0-7505-3779-7

First published in Great Britain by Allison & Busby in 2012

Published in Large Print 2013 by arrangement with
Allison & Busby Limited

Magna Large Print is an imprint of Library Magna Books Ltd.

Printed and bound in Great Britain by
T.J. (International) Ltd., Cornwall, PL28 8RW

This book is dedicated to those who reach across boundaries with a hand of welcome.

'Let us learn their ways, just as they are learning ours.'

– HUBERT LYAUTEY

AUTHOR'S PREFACE

It should be noted that sections of this volume of my memoirs depict acts and thoughts of people that took place in my absence. I chose the God-like point of view because I thought it less distracting for a reader. In fact, those sections reflect testimonies pieced together out of disjointed segments and off-hand remarks given over the course of weeks, and even years.

If this style of narrating my memoir causes readers to interpret the following as fiction, so be it. It would not be the first time.

– MARY RUSSELL HOLMES

I have attached a glossary of unfamiliar terms at the end.

– MRH

...the breath of Chitane
Blows the sand in smoky whirls
And blinds my steed.
And I, blinded as I ride,
Long for the night to come,
The night with its garment of shadows
And eyes of stars.

– EBN EL ROUMI

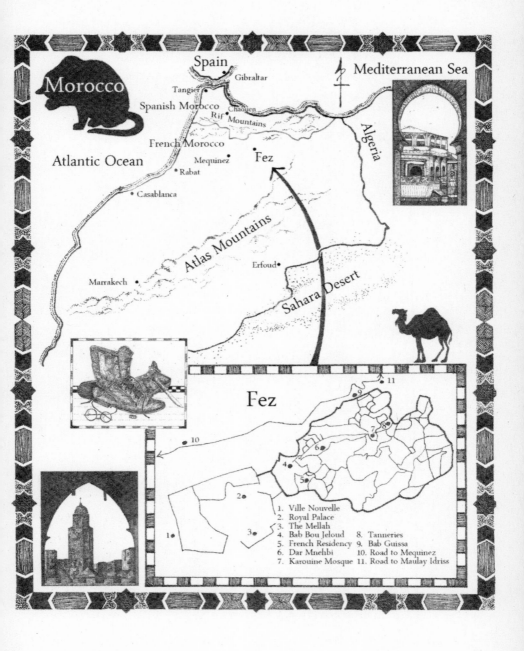

Morocco

Spain

Mediterranean Sea

Gibraltar

Tangier

Spanish Morocco

Chaouen

Rif Mountains

Algeria

French Morocco

Fez

Atlantic Ocean

Mequinez

Rabat

Casablanca

Atlas Mountains

Erfoud

Sahara Desert

Marrakech

Fez

10

11

9

7   8

6

4

5

2

1. Ville Nouvelle
2. Royal Palace
3. The Mellah
4. Bab Bou Jeloud   8. Tanneries
5. French Residency   9. Bab Guissa
6. Dar Mnehbi   10. Road to Mequinez
7. Karouine Mosque   11. Road to Maulay Idriss

1

3

PREFACE

The big man had the brains of a tortoise, but even he was beginning to look alarmed.

Sherlock Holmes drew a calming breath. Then another.

It had seemed such a simple arrangement: If Mary Russell chose to submit to the whimsy of Fflytte Films as it finished its current moving picture, that was fine and good, but there was no cause for her husband to be tied down by her eccentricities – not with an entirely new country at his feet. He'd never been to Morocco. After some complex marital negotiations, he promised to return, at an agreed-to time and place, which was here and today.

Except she was not there.

He started again. 'So she left her tent that night. After dark.'

'*Oui, Monsieur.*'

'And was still gone the next morning.'

'*Oui, Monsieur.*'

'She spoke to no one, merely left a brief note to say that she was going to Fez.'

The man nodded.

'The filming ended. The rest of Fflytte's crew came back here. No one thought this odd. And all you have to say is that my wife was last seen walking into the desert in the company of a child. Three days ago.'

17

Morocco might be a small country, but it was plenty big enough to swallow one young woman. *Russell,* he thought, *what the devil are you up to?*

CHAPTER ONE

I was in bed. *A* bed, at any rate.

I had been flattened by a steam-roller, trampled under a stampede of bison. Beaten by a determined thug. I ached, head to toe, fingers and skin. Mostly head.

My skull throbbed, one hot pulse for every beat of my heart. I could see it in the rhythmic dimming of an already shadowy room. I wanted to weep with the pain, but if I had to blow my nose, my skull might split like an overripe melon.

So I lay in the dim room, and watched my heart beat, and ached.

Some time later, it came to me that the angle of the vague patch of brightness across the opposite wall had changed. Some time after that, an explanation slipped out between the pain-pulses: The sun had moved while I slept. A while later, another thought: Time is passing.

And with that, a tendril of urgency unfurled. I could not lie in bed, I had to be somewhere. People were depending on me. The sun would go down: I would be late.

Rolling onto my side was like pushing a motor-car up a hill. Raising myself up from the thin pad made me cry out – nearly black out – from the surge of pressure within my skull. My stomach roiled, my ears rang, the room whirled.

I crouched for a long time on the edge of the

19

bed. Slowly, the pounding receded. My vision cleared, revealing a snug, roughly plastered room; hand-made floor tiles; a tawny herringbone of small bricks; a door of some dark wood, so narrow a big man might angle his shoulders, a hook driven into it, holding a long brown robe; a pair of soft yellow bedroom slippers on the floor – *babouches,* my mind provided: new leather, my nose told me. The room's only furniture was a narrow bed with a rough three-legged stool at its head. The stool served as a table, its surface nearly covered with disparate objects: in the centre stood a small oil lamp. To its left, nearest the bed, were arranged a match-box, a tiny ceramic bowl holding half a dozen spent matches, a glass of water, and a pair of wire-rimmed spectacles that appeared to have been trod upon. The other side of the lamp had an even more peculiar collection: a worn pencil stub, a sausage-shaped object tightly wrapped in a handkerchief, some grains of sand, and one pale stone.

I studied the enigmatic display. The little bowl caused a brief memory to stir through the sludge that was my brain: As I slept, the sound of a match scratching into life would wake me; the sharp smell would bite my nostrils; faces would appear and make noises; I would say something apparently sensible; the faces would bend over the light, and with a puff, I would be back in the shadows, alone.

My hand reached out, hesitated over the water, rejected it, and picked up the spectacles instead. I winced as they settled between my ears and the snug head wrap I wore, but the room came into focus.

The matches also came into focus: a cheap, bright label, in French. I picked up the box, slid it open, my nose stung by the smell of sulphur. Four matches. I took one, scraped it into life, held it to the oil lamp. A spot of warmth entered the room.

By its thin light, I looked down at what I wore. Drab homespun trousers and tunic. Bare feet. The clothing was clean, but not my hands. They looked as if someone had tried to wipe away a layer of some dark greasy matter, leaving stains in the deeper creases and under the nails.

I stretched the left one out nearer the lamp. Motion caused the flame to throw dancing shadows across the room. When it had steadied, I frowned at the finger-nails to which I was attached.

Not grease.

Blood.

The light of a candle / the sunshine smell of linen / the slope of ceiling! the soft throat of a young girl asleep / the blood on my hands–

The bolt of memory shocked me to my feet. I swayed, the room roaring in my ears, my eyes fixed on the flat, slope-free ceiling. Don't look down (*blood on my hands*) – don't think about the hand's memory of the smooth, intimate glide of sharp steel through flesh.

I ventured a step, then another, towards the shuttered window.

To my surprise, the latch flipped beneath my awkward fingers, and when the hinges creaked open, there were no bars. Why had I expected to be a prisoner?

The brilliance was painful, even though the sky was grey with unshed rain. I lifted a hand to shade my eyes, and squinted at the view: a dirty, cobbled lane far too narrow for any motorcar. One could have passed an object between opposing windows – had there been windows. I saw only one, higher even than mine, tiny and tightly shuttered. I could see two entranceways off this diminutive alley: One had been painted with brightly coloured arabesques, long ago, and comprised a small door inside a larger one, as if the carpenter had learned his craft on castles and cathedrals. The door across from it was a single rectangle, black wood heavily studded with rusting iron circles the size of my thumbnail. Around them, grubby white-wash, a fringe of grass on the rooflines, chunks of plaster flaking from walls that bulged and slumped. In one place, wooden braces thirty feet from the ground kept two buildings from collapsing into each other.

The house I was in seemed to be the lane's terminus; thirty feet away, beneath the slapdash web of braces, the passageway turned to the right and disappeared.

I pushed the shutters wider open, intending to lean out and examine the face of the building below me, then took a step back as the left-hand door came open and a woman emerged. She was swathed head to toe in pale garments, with a straw bag in one hand and a child's hand in the other. She glanced down the alleyway, her eyes on a place well below me, and I could see her brown, Caucasian features and startling blue eyes. She pulled her scarf up over her face and tugged the child down the lane, vanishing around its bend.

Arabic; French; woman in a robe – *djellaba,* the internal dictionary supplied, although that did not seem quite right. Those clues combined with the woman's Berber features suggested that I was in North Africa. Algeria or perhaps Morocco. In a *suq.*

The knowledge of *where* was just beyond my grasp, like an elusive name on the tip of one's tongue. Similarly, how I came to be here. And what had been so urgent it drove me to my feet. Or why I had blood on my hands.

Or, my name.

Who the hell was I?

CHAPTER TWO

Sweat broke out all over my body, despite the cold of the room. There was a good explanation, for everything. One that I would remember in a minute, once I could think around the pounding in my head. Or...

I turned to consider the narrow door. The shutters hadn't been locked. Yes, the window was high and the drop to the lane sheer, but perhaps it meant that my situation was not the source of that feeling of urgency. That the water in the glass was not drugged. That the door led to assistance, to information. To friends, even.

My bare feet slapped across the cold tiles. I stopped beside the bed, transferring everything but the lamp, water, and bowl into my pockets, then moved over to the door and put my ear to the crack: nothing. My fingers eased the iron latch up until the tongue came free; the wood shifted towards me. I was not locked in.

The odours that washed over me threatened to turn my stomach over. Frying oil, onions, chicken, a panoply of spices – for some reason, I felt that if I were more experienced with their names, I would be able to identify each individual element of that sensory cloud.

I pushed aside the evidence of my nostrils, concentrating instead on my vision. The scrap of corridor was no more revealing than the view from the window: the same rough herringbone on the floor, cobalt-and-cream tiles halfway up the walls, with crisp whitewashed plaster above; another door; a tidy stack of straw baskets; the suggestion of a house off to the left. I took a step out: To my right, a stone stairway curled upward out of view – to the roof, I felt, although I could not have said why. Then I heard a voice – two voices, so distant, or behind so many doors, that I could not determine the language, much less the words.

But I could hear the tension.

For some reason, I reached around to the back of my waist-band, my fingers anticipating a cold weight nestled against my spine, but there was nothing. After a moment's consideration, I drew a breath, and stepped out. Nothing happened.

I crept down the hall to the left and took up a position just before the bend, not venturing my head into the open. The voices were clearer now, the rhythms suggestive of Arabic. Cool air moved across my face and the light around the corner was daylight, not lamps, as if the walls of the house had been sliced away. Words trickled into my mind. *Dar:* a house of two or three storeys built around a ground-level courtyard, open to the sky; *halka:* its wide central sky-light; *riad:* a house whose inner courtyard was a garden.

Another brief internal flash: *clipped green rectangle / rain-soaked brick walls / figures in academic gowns / the odour of learning—*

I was gathering myself for a step towards that light when a harsh sound juddered through the house, coming from below and behind me at the same time. I hurried back into my tiny cell and

25

across the tiles to peer downwards into the narrow lane–

Soldiers!

No mistaking that blue uniform and cap: two armed French soldiers, pounding on the door below.

Aimless urgency blew into open panic: I could *not* be taken by them, it was essential that I remain free, that I get to–

To where? To whom? But while I might have given a single gendarme the benefit of the doubt, armed soldiers could only be a declaration of war. I snatched the robe from the hook, stepped into the slippers, and made for the curve of steps leading up.

The upper door's iron latch opened easily. Outside was a terrace roof around an iron-work grid, open to the house below. On one side was strung a bare laundry line; the furniture consisted of six pots of winter-dead herbs and a pair of benches. The rooftop was empty – had I known it would be? – but it smelt of rain, the drips on the clothes-line showing that it had been recent. The air was very cold.

I worked the robe over my head – it was like a sack with a hood, and to my relief smelt only of wool and soap. I picked up the stick supporting the centre of the clothes-line and brought down one slippered foot on its centre, snapping it in two; jamming the sharp end beneath the door would slow pursuit. And the rope itself– that would be useful. I reached for my ankle, but found only skin where my fingers seemed to expect a knife.

Neither knife nor handgun: not friends, then.

I abandoned the line to make a quick circuit of the rooftop, keeping well clear of the open grid, lest someone looking up see me. All around lay a tight jumble of buildings, their rooftops – squared, domed, and crenellated; brick and stone and tile; crisply renovated or crudely patched or on the point of collapse – at a myriad of levels, like the world's largest set of children's blocks. The town covered slopes dropping into a valley; higher hills, green with winter rains, lay in the distance. Here and there, tree-tops poked up between the structures, but there was no discernable break for roads, and the buildings were so intertwined that they appeared to be resting atop one another. Certainly they were holding each other upright – I had seen that from the window below. Several green-roofed minarets sticking above the architectural confusion confirmed that I was in North Africa.

As I circled the rooftop, my fingers automatically laid claim to a few small items left by the women-folk whose territory this was – a pocket-mirror with cracked glass, a tiny pot of kohl, a pair of rusting scissors too delicate to part the laundry rope – and automatically thrust them through the *djellaba's* side-slits to the pockets beneath.

The circuit ended, I was faced with a decision: The easiest descent was the most exposed; the most surreptitious way might well kill a person with a head as dizzy as mine.

I looked out over the town, where a faint suggestion of emerging sun was bringing an impression of warmth to the grey, tan, and whitewashed shapes. Weeds sprouted on every flat surface, and storks' nests. Weren't those supposed to be good

27

luck? I hoped so. The town's overall texture had an almost tactile satisfaction that reminded me of something. Something I had seen, touched – honeycomb! But not comb neatly bounded by a wooden frame: wild honeycomb, with orderly hexagons filling up the bumps and hollows of rock or tree. My eyes squinted, making the town blur; the aroma of honey seemed to rise up...

Stop: time for decisions, not distractions. I went to the low wall overhanging a neighbour's house – then ducked down as a door twenty feet away scraped open and two women came out, arguing furiously in a language I did not know. As I vacillated between waiting for this safer route and risking the other, the door behind me rattled.

Without further consideration, I scurried across the rooftop, pushed through a narrow gap, and dropped down to a wall-top eight feet below. My earlier glance had shown me a glimpse of tiled courtyard through the branches of an orange tree, with this foot-thick wall separating it from a derelict garden next door. I settled my yellow *babouches* onto the weedy bricks, fixed my gaze on the vestigial window-sill twenty feet away, then balanced like a tight-rope walker across the ragged surface to the abandoned building beyond. Fearful of pursuit, I stepped over the gap and inside – and my heart instantly seized my throat: The brick walls bled light like lace-work; the floor was mostly missing. The entire structure seemed to sway with the addition of my weight.

I stood motionless until bits of mortar and wood stopped drifting down. The breath I took then was slow, but fervent.

Moving with extreme caution, I drew the hand-mirror from my inner pocket and, keeping it well away from the light, held it up to reflect the rooftop behind me. The soldiers came into view.

Their backs were to me. I could hear them shouting at the women on the adjoining rooftop, but either they answered no, they hadn't seen me, or (more likely) they retreated inside at the first sight of strange men. The soldiers then began the same circuit I had made.

Ending up staring right at me.

I held the glass absolutely still, lest a flash of reflection give me away. They seemed ... wrong, somehow, although I could not have said why. Clean-shaven, dark-eyed, their uniforms like any others.

But French soldiers did not belong on a roof-top of that shape.

The men were surveying the tiled courtyard. One of them pointed down and said something. His companion turned briskly for the door. The first took another look around the edges, then he, too, left the rooftop.

Shakily, I lowered myself to the floor. The stable tiled island beneath me did not collapse and the wall, appearances to the contrary, seemed stout enough to support my back. Through a hole, I could see a portion of the neighbouring courtyard. In a few minutes, the military caps appeared. I listened to the soldiers berating the confused and frightened owner, whose French was clearly inadequate for the task of self-defence. Eventually, they left. I waited, the looking-glass propped against a hundred-weight of fallen plaster. Half an hour later, motion came again to the rooftop I had so hastily left.

Between the overcast sky and the dullness of the reflection, it was difficult to make out details of the two people who walked across the rooftop. I abandoned the looking-glass to stand, warily, and peer around the splintery boards that had once framed a window. A man and a woman, she in white drapery, he in a sackcloth robe over shirt and trousers, his turban a circle of cloth revealing the crown of his head. They looked around the rooftop, down the edges, into the neighbouring courtyard, appearing less angry than confused. I was tempted to call out to them, to give them a chance – but that sense of urgency had returned, growing ever stronger as I sat trapped in the crumbling building.

And, they had taken my weapons.

I was blind, no doubt about that. But as the blind are forced to rely on their other senses to find their way (*a man, in a heavy fog, explaining the phenomenon* – but the image was gone before it was there), so would I rely on what senses I had left, to make my decisions.

I did not call out.

Instead, I waited for the pair to leave. It was cold, so it did not take long. When I was alone – so far as I could tell – I stepped through the hole again and onto the wall.

And paused. A sound rose across the city, a prolonged exhortation. It was joined a minute later by another, then a third farther away. The mid-day call to prayer, a chorus of reminders ringing out across the town, muezzins declaring

30

the greatness of God, reminding the citizens that prayer is better than sleep.

I had heard it before, and yet I had not. I knew it, and yet I was a stranger. I could recite the words, yet I was quite sure they were not my own. Its meaning frightened me; its beauty moved me deeply.

And I must stop succumbing to distraction! I pushed away its spell and dropped into the derelict garden on the other side. While the sound of the *adhan* faded, I picked my way through weeds and assorted rubbish, startling a pair of cats and slicing a hole in my slippers. On the other side of the garden was a shorter wall and a heap of something that might have been unused tiles. I climbed up, and peered over.

Here was another narrow alleyway, with another pair of stout nail-clad doors, to the right and to the left. Unlike the first passageway, this semi-tunnel opened onto a marginally wider, and more populated, near-street (though even that was too narrow for motorcars). A woman in voluminous ash-coloured garments went past the opening. Two chattering children trotted in the other direction, one of them balancing on his head a tray bigger than he was, carrying loaves of unbaked bread. The children were followed by a donkey with a long wooden bench of fresh-cut cedar strapped to his back, a lad with a switch moving him along. I gathered the hem of my *djellaba,* scrambled over the wall, and dropped to the damp, slick stones.

My skull seemed to be resigning itself to the abuse; I only needed to lean against the wall for a minute or so before the pounding and spinning receded, and I no longer had to fight back the urge to cry out. When I felt steady, I tugged the robe's hood over my head and walked down the dark passageway towards the street.

For some reason, I expected to find the narrow streets bustling with activity, but the human beehive was all but deserted. Shops were padlocked. Few donkeys pressed through with their burdens. One of the lanes was so still, I could hear the sound of a buried stream through the paving stones. As I moved into the city, I began to wonder if some awful pestilence had struck my fellows as well. Was the entire populace hiding behind its shutters, infected with my same mental distress, terrified of venturing into the light? Were it not for the unconcerned pace of the occasional shrouded woman who went past and the cries of a group of boys playing in a side-street, I might have begun pounding on doors to find out.

But those residents I passed were clearly untroubled. And the air did not smell of death and corruption. It smelt, rather, of spices and meat.

I stopped, studying a building that faced the street. There were no windows on the lower storeys, but at the top, two small glass-paned openings were propped open, giving out a loud stream of women's voices.

I lowered my gaze to the ground floor: shutters on what was clearly a shop of some kind. My brain made a huge effort, and presented me with an explanation: The effect of desertion was merely because the shops were closed tight, and the men were at prayer. It was a holiday – rather, a holy day. Today must be Friday, the Moslem Sabbath.

The sound of footsteps echoed down the hard surfaces and started me moving again. I took care to walk at a steady pace, holding my body as if I not only knew where I was going, but was interested in nothing particular outside of getting there.

How I knew to do this, I could not think.

It was unnerving, as if one portion of my mind was simply frozen solid. I had no idea where I was going – where I was to begin with – yet I moved forward now as I had walked the precarious wall earlier: with the unthinking assurance that can only come from long experience. The analytical machinery of my mind also seemed to be missing on a couple of cylinders: To have had blood on my hands yet none on my garments suggested that someone (in that house?) had removed my clothing, surely noticing that I was a woman, yet then dressed me in what I knew was male clothing. Why had they done that? Similarly, I had lain in that bed for some hours with neither locks nor bonds, as if I was a guest rather than a prisoner, yet they had robbed me of my weapons – and then summoned the authorities: A pair of soldiers would not have happened down that alleyway by accident. Again, why?

I could not have given my reasons for wanting to put distance between myself and the house, but my body seemed determined to do so. And until I had evidence to the contrary, I could only trust that it knew what it was doing.

Some twenty minutes later, having come to the dead ends of four different paths, it was clear that letting my feet choose the way by turning consistently left – or right – only led to a standstill. Instead, I started looking for lanes that led uphill. And in a short time, I came to a more lively quarter with open shops. Men sat in some, all wearing the same calf-length, rough-spun robes but occasionally layered with a heavier burnoose. They wore a variety of head-coverings: Some had loosely wrapped lengths of cloth, others wore snug turbans that revealed the crowns of their heads and a single thin plait, some had the rigid caps called *tarboosh* or *fez*. The women picking over displays of onions and greens were for the most part veiled, though some went freely bare-faced. They all haggled: over the cost of lemons, the measure of olives, the quality of tin cups. Colourful displays of garments and tools spilt onto the street.

I moved at the same speed the others did; my eyes were focussed at the same distance ahead; my robes were theirs – the men even wore the same yellow *babouches*. I dodged laden donkeys and responded to the warning *'Bâlak! Bâlak!'* of their drivers and veered around displays and vendors without so much as a glance. I managed to walk past a pair of patrolling French soldiers without drawing any attention to myself. Several minutes later, I discovered that I had at some point removed my spectacles. I slid them through the pocket-slit in the *djellaba,* and when my empty hand came out again, it reached down to a display of fruit and deftly appropriated a small orange. As I proceeded through the streets, my pockets slowly filled, with fruit and a roll, a handful of almonds and a ball of twine, one decorative hair-pin, a small red Moroccan-leather note-

34

book, a fat little embroidered purse plucked from a woman's Western-style hand-bag, and a slim, decorated dagger that I kept inside my left-hand sleeve, fearing that if I put it into the pocket, within half a dozen steps it would slice its way to the cobblestones.

First an acrobat, now a pick-pocket. Had I escaped from some travelling circus?

I soon came to the explanation for this district's relative bustle: a city gate, very new and strong-looking, ornate with mosaic tile (*zellij*, the translator in my head whispered). Beyond it was clearly a more modern part of this city, with men in suits, the sign for a bank, several horse-carts, even a motorcar. And: soldiers.

I leant casually against a wall. Armed French soldiers, with the bored stance and alert gaze of guards the world around. As I watched, they moved forward to intercept a man on a white mule, who freely handed over the immensely long Jezail rifle he held and continued inside. It would seem that arms were not permitted in the city. That might explain why my hand had met a revolver's absence at my waist-band.

There was no way I could get past the soldiers without attracting attention, not in the clothes I wore now. Even were I to dress in a woman's all-concealing shrouds, I would have to take care – although as with everything else that day, I could not have said how I knew that. My mind was in a shadowy netherland, but what knowledge I did retain was crystal clear. Uncertainty and inchoate fear seemed to sharpen the essentials, helping me to read the guards as easily as I had accumulated key possessions and walked unnoticed.

Still, until I knew more about my situation, I did not feel driven to break out of this *suq*. Whatever shelter, comfort, and time to ponder I might require, I could as easily find it here as out there.

I turned my back on the outer world, and descended once more into the dim-lit warren of the old town.

On the other side of a shop piled high with caged chickens stood a pocket handkerchief-sized café with a tureen of smoking oil and neatly arranged glasses of tea. As I had passed it before, my stomach vaguely let me know that its former queasiness was fading. Now, at the aroma of chillies and hot oil, my mouth began to water and I realised that I was weak with hunger. I dug into my pockets, then stopped: Fumbling with unfamiliar money, taken from a lady's decorative purse, would be foolish. I spent a moment watching closely as a man purchased a small cornucopia of fried ambrosia, and forced myself to walk on.

At the next bit of blank wall, I surreptitiously drew out the purse, searching for the coin I had seen him use. There were two. I palmed them and put the rest away. Back at the fragrant food-stall, I nodded to the proprietor, lifted my chin at the glass case, raised an affirming eyebrow when his hand hesitated over a choice, and laid one of the coins on the tiny counter. I left my hand there until he slid some smaller scraps of metal into my palm, following them with a greasy handful of flat bread wrapped around an unidentifiable mouthful of spice. My jaws might have learnt table manners from a dog: Half a dozen sharp gulps, and the food was but a trace on my fingers – which I eyed, but did not lick: I needed to find a source of water, and soon.

In this same way, I obtained a bowl of extraordinarily hearty soup called *harira,* a sweet biscuit tasting of almonds, and two glasses of hot, syrupy mint tea.

The food did nothing to clear my brain, but it was little short of a miracle how it helped the shakiness recede.

And as if the *suq's* guiding spirit had heard my plea, around the next corner was an open area where three of the diminutive lanes came together, which in any normal town would have gone unnoticed but here was tantamount to a village green. Set into one of the resulting corners was a magnificently tiled fountain, at the moment gushing water into a child's brass pot. I waited while two women filled their jugs, then pushed forward to thrust my hands under the frigid clear water.

I could feel their disapproval, either because it was not done to wash one's hands in a drinking fountain, or because I was (to all appearances) a man pushing into a woman's realm, but I did not care. I scrubbed and clawed at my nails as if the stain were some systemic poison, and I kept on scrubbing even after my eyes assured me the skin was clean. I even splashed my face.

Finally, too aware of the waiting women, I drew back. In the centre of the open area, I held up my hands to reassure myself that the blood was gone. And for the first time, I noticed a faint indentation around the ring finger of my right hand.

I stared at it. I turned the hand over, then back, and felt a stir of rage. Take my weapons, yes, but steal a ring from my finger?

Had I been standing on the rooftop, I would have stormed the house, soldiers or no. But I had left that house hours ago; I'd never find it again.

Furious and mournful, I dried my hands on my robe and slipped back into the *suq.*

Since I was now both fed and cleansed, the next order of business was to find shelter against the night. The afternoon call to prayer had come and gone; in the short winter's day, sunset would not be far off. And perhaps if I slept, my missing past might creep back. If nothing else, a private corner would let me paw through my few possessions, and my fewer memories, and consider where I stood.

The problem was, I had seen nothing that resembled an hotel. I had seen no hand-lettered Room to Let signs propped in windows (had there been windows). I had a vague idea that benighted travellers might be welcomed in a mosque or *madrassa* school, but that was far too risky for a woman in disguise. Even a *caravan-serai,* or whatever the local equivalent might be, would be tricky. And although I spoke a couple of the local languages, I was loath to risk a demonstration of my ignorance by asking.

What I needed was another deserted building. Of which there seemed to be plenty, but I preferred one with a facsimile of a roof, and not on the point of collapse.

I kept walking, waiting for my bruised cortices to present me with an idea. A dull boom of cannon-fire shuddered over the town, startling a pair of egrets into flight, but it seemed to be merely a signal: The muezzins started up their sunset calls. More shops began to close. A wrinkled gent gave a friendly nod as he ran a chain through the iron loops on his shop's door. Farther along, a shoe-seller picked up a basket filled with fresh-made *babouches,* and with the leather odour came a vivid jolt of memory: *an avalanche of bright yellow slippers in a narrow lane / tannery smell and spice and sea-air / a donkey's bray / men shouting / above it one man's voice—*

Then it was gone, and the shoe-seller was staring at me. I gave him an uncomfortable smile and continued on.

Across the way and down a few steps, a brass-worker was closing his doors on an Aladdin's cave of gleaming metal and Mediaeval tools. His workshop opened, not directly off the street, but through a shallow arched entrance that provided supplemental display-space for his wares during the day.

My mind gave me a nudge. I walked on, bought a glass of orange juice from a man with one small basket of fruit left him, and drank it as I gazed back the way I had come, watching the brass-worker's retreating figure.

Returning the empty glass, I walked on slowly, taking great care to recall my path. I lingered in deserted streets, I passed back and forth and circled about, until the dim lanes were going dark and the darker recesses were nearly black. I waited until a group of chattering men passed where I stood, and fell in behind them until we reached the brass-worker's doorway. At the dark arched entrance, I took a step to the side.

My hands seemed to know, without benefit of sight, how to open a padlock with the straightened right earpiece of a pair of spectacles and a hair-pin. Yet another curious skill.

Inside, there were no lingering apprentices, no open courtyards to a family dwelling. A high window, gathering in the last of the day's light, showed me the room: Banquettes along two of the walls, where customers would drink cups of tea, promised cushion for my aches; two gleaming eyes from a high shelf eyed me warily, but the resident cat stayed where it was. A patch of blackness beside the faint glow of the brazier proved to be charcoal, enough to keep me warm all night.

I had not realised how utterly wrung-out I was, until I stood in that safe place.

I barely made it to the cushions before my legs buckled, and there I sat, my knees pulled up to my chest, near to weeping with relief and exhaustion. If the soldiers had knocked at the workshop door, I would have flung myself at their feet.

I sat there a very long time before the trembling stopped.

The high window had gone dark, the cat's eyes had vanished. The pain in my head, arms, and hip that I had kept at bay by movement and fear had taken over again, and it was an effort to work my hand into an inner pocket to pull out a piece of bread. I forced myself to eat it, then crawled over to add charcoal to the fire, lest it go out during the night.

By the flare of light, I examined my hands

40

again, as if the dried blood might have returned. They were clean. I looked at my right hand, with its indentation, then at the left. The left hand was where Europeans in general wore a wedding ring; however, for some reason I felt quite certain that my people – Jewish: Wasn't I Jewish? – put the ring on the right hand. That the narrow dent was from a wedding band. But why was the skin beneath it not pale? My hands were brown from the sun – much browner than the rest of my arms – and the colour was no different beneath the ring. Was I married? Had my husband died? Had he cast me out into the *suq*, for thievery?

I lowered my head to my knees, trying to think back over the day, trolling my memory for any kind of clue. I was in a North African city made up of an un-mappable tangle of tiny by-ways. Some of its buildings took the breath away with their beauty, their ornate tile-work crisp, their paint and carvings clean. Other houses were rotting shells on the edge of collapse, dangerous and stinking of decay.

One might almost think my damaged mind had created a town in its image.

Enough, I decided. I could do no more tonight. I was dimly aware that one was supposed to keep a concussion victim from sleep, but in truth, given a choice between staying awake any longer, and simply not waking up, I would take the risk.

I laid the decorative knife beside me on the cushion and tugged the hood over my face. As the world faded, again I smelt the faint aroma of honey.

CHAPTER THREE

The clipaclop of a donkey's hooves woke me. The room was black as a bowl of tar – but no: A faint glow came from one corner. Not a windowless cell, then; but where...?

Donkeys. The odour of smoke, and wool. A memory of mint on the tongue: the *suq*. I started to throw off the bed-clothes, discovering simultaneously that there were no bed-clothes and that my head strenuously objected to sudden movements. My fingers tugged at the rough wool, found it was a garment – ah, the brown robe from the hook in the small room. With that, the previous day slid into place: the dappled reality of wandering a labyrinth of dim, tight foot-paths, as if I had been set down into a world of tunnelling creatures. Into a beehive.

Shadowy streets and a shadowed mind.

Still.

I sat, pushing the robe's hood away from my face.

The concussion hadn't killed me, then. It was early: No light came from the high window. My surroundings had remained silent during the still hours, with no evidence of living quarters overhead, although after I had thrown more coal on the fire, the cat had roused itself for a bit of mouse-chasing before coming to settle beside me. And I dimly remembered a long echoing

42

prayer, or song, as if some insomniac muezzin had decided to enforce the declaration that prayer is indeed better than sleep.

Despite that interruption, I felt rested. The pain in my head remained sharp, but the rest of me merely ached. I patted around the floor until I encountered my spectacles, which had been ill-fitting to begin with and were not improved by having been used as a lock pick: One of the lenses bulged against the frame, and the right earpiece had several unintended angles. I folded them away into my pocket, and raised my fingers to the turban I wore.

Not, I thought, precisely a turban. The cloth encircling my head felt more like a bandage, although with the robe's hood up, it might look like an ordinary piece of head-gear – ordinary for this town, that is, but for a lack of the thin pig-tail many of the men wore. The part of my skull over my right ear seemed the most tender, which was perhaps related to the kink in the earpiece. All in all, I would leave the wrap in place for now.

Light would help. I dug into my garments for the box of French matches, which I had pocketed after lighting the oil lamp in yesterday's cell. They were mashed rather flat now, since I had lain on them all night. There must be some kind of a lamp here. I stood, and as I did so, some small metallic object flew away from the folds of my clothing, rolling across the stones. I stifled the urge to blindly leap after it. Instead, I felt the remains of the box: three matches.

I lit one on the second try, and held it above my head. The flame burned out before I reached the lamp it had revealed, but I felt the rest of the way in the darkness. After giving the thing a slosh, to make certain it held fuel, I scratched my second match into life and nurtured the lamp to brightness.

A myriad of gleaming shapes shone back at me: stacks of brazen bowls, trays ranging from calling card–sized to sufficient for an entire roast sheep, bowls of similar variety, a dozen shapes and sizes of lamp. But the one I carried seemed to be the only one holding oil, so I took it in search of the rolling object.

There was a hole in the floor, a drainage hole (no doubt the source of the wildlife that had entertained the cat during the night) containing sludge so disgusting, not even the Kohinoor could have tempted my hand into it. Before I made the laborious effort of climbing back to my feet, I studied the shape of the stones themselves. Yes, a carved trough led towards the hole, but a settling of the paving stones suggested an alternative route, directly towards a workbench that rested on the floor. I set the lamp on the stones and laid my cheek to the floor, the cool stones startling another snippet of memory to the fore: *cold stones / the lit crack beneath a door / red boots / a fire / rhythmic speech–*

And then that, too, was gone.

But there was something small and shiny, under the bench.

My fingertips teased at the round smooth gleam, threatening to push it away for good. I sat back on my heels and reached for my hair, finding only fabric where my fingers had expected

44

hair-pins. But, I did have one pin. I found it in my pocket, bent it into a hook, and pulled the elusive circle out.

A gold ring, accompanied by a sharp hallucinatory odour of wet goat. It was not the one missing from my own hand, for it was big enough around to fit my thumb. A man's signet ring, very old and, judging from its weight and colour, very valuable. I held it to the lamp-light to study the worn design on its flat edge: a bird of some kind, a stork or pelican, standing on wavy lines that indicated water.

Not a thing one might expect to find in the shop of a brass-worker. But then, neither was it the sort of jewellery one might expect in the pocket of an amnesiac escaped circus performer.

But a pick-pocket? One who had run afoul of the police?

Or, did it belong to my missing husband?

I set the lamp on a clear patch of bench, and emptied my pockets down to the fluff.

I picked up the embroidered purse, noting that the clasp was still shut – the ring could not have fallen from there. I poured its contents out onto the age-old wood, coins and currency, all relatively new. BANQUE D'ETAT DU MAROC, they said, CINQ FRANCS; the coins were stamped with EMPIRE CHERIFIEN, 1 FRANC and 50 CENTIMES. One marked 25 CENTIMES had a hole in its centre.

So: Morocco.

I corrected myself: More exactly, this purse had been filled in Morocco. Still, it was evidence enough to be going on.

45

And the Arabic numbers, along with the spectacles and the modern rifles the soldiers had carried, suggested the twentieth century rather than the nineteenth – or the thirteenth.

Absently, I rubbed the currency about on the filthy wood, then crumpled it before returning it to my pocket: unlikely that someone with my current appearance would possess crisp, new bills.

In addition to the bits and bobs I had appropriated the day before, I found the following:

In the trouser pockets, grains of coarse yellow sand.

In the left-hand pocket, a chalky stone the size of a flattened walnut.

From the right-hand pocket I took a length of twine, snugly bound, and an object wrapped in a handkerchief. I unwound the worn muslin to reveal a length of copper pipe, four inches long and an inch across. The handkerchief was permeated with sand. Beneath the creases I made out the crisp lines of a long-ago ironing, but there were no convenient monograms or laundry marks. I examined the pipe; it contained only air. But when I wrapped it back in the cloth, then laid the bundle across the fingers of my right hand, they closed comfortably around it.

My left hand remembered all too vividly the sensation of driving a knife through flesh. My right hand, it would seem, provided the support of brute weight.

So: a pick-pocket accustomed to nasty fighting.

Had I killed a man to steal his ring?

I dropped the primitive knuckle-duster into its pocket, then took a closer look at the quartz-like

46

stone. Other than being of sedimentary origin, and vaguely reminding me of building material although it was of a size that more invited the hand to throw, it told me nothing – my store of odd knowledge apparently did not include petrology.

The stone and everything else went into the pockets they had come from, with the exception of a handful of dried fruit, the decorative knife, the empty purse, the scissors, and the ring. The fruit I ate; the empty purse I tossed onto the brazier coals, pushing it down with a stick; the rusted scissors, which had jabbed me continuously the previous day, I abandoned on a high shelf; the ring I sat and studied.

The problem was, everything I took from my pockets had seemed possessed of immense mystery and import, as if the stone, the pipe-length, the grains of sand were whispering a message just beneath my ability to hear. When everything meant nothing, it would appear, even meaningless objects became numinous with Meaning. The date pip I spat into my palm positively throbbed with significance.

It was damned irritating.

Another donkey went past, a reminder that daylight could not be far away. I had to leave this place, lest I be driven to make use of that pipe-cosh and the stolen knife.

First, I rescued a length of leather from a stack of the same – polishing rags, it would seem – and fashioned a rough wrist-scabbard for the stolen knife. I took a last look at the ring, sitting by itself on the workbench, then caught it up and dropped it into my breast pocket.

47

My hand stopped. Breast pocket: I'd forgotten I had one.

It was the size of my palm, with a flap, currently missing a button.

I fished around inside, feeling its emptiness – and then a faintly non-cloth sensation brushed my fingers. I drew out a tiny scrap of paper, smashed flat by having been slept upon.

I picked it open. The paper was near-translucent onionskin, and had been wet at some point, but I managed to get it flat with only a small tear: the corner of a larger page, a triangle three and a half inches high and two and a bit wide. There were a series of pencil squiggles on it, lines as pregnant with meaning as the grains of sand and the date pip:

It looked like a capital A drawn by a small child or the victim of a stroke, although oddly precise. Probably it was the result of a piece of paper and a stub of pencil riding together in a pocket.

I turned the scrap over. Then rotated it.

At first glance, the string of interconnected curves seemed as devoid of meaning as the accidental A on the reverse. But I knew they held some intent beyond mere idiotic self-importance, and indeed, once I shifted the direction of my gaze to read from right to left, the pencil scribble became words, in crude, even childish Arabic

48

writing: *the clock of the sorcerer.*

I sighed.

Pressing the scrap into my purloined note-book, I put it and the ring into the breast pocket, stitching the flap shut with the ever-useful hairpin. I arranged the cushions as I had found them, pushed the purse's metal clasp deeper into the coals, and blew out the small lamp. When I had let myself out, I padlocked the door and walked into the *suq* in search of a sorcerer and his clock.

I found many things during the course of the day. My first goal was food and drink, followed by thick stockings and a heavy woollen burnoose to keep out the penetrating cold. As I walked, the chorus of muezzins woke the town, and soon the streets burst into life, shutters opening to displays of colour and enticing aromas – not the least of which was the damp soap-smell that wafted from a *hammam,* a place I dared not even think of entering, no matter how much the pores of my skin craved a scrub-brush.

By mid-morning, I was warm, fed, and gaining in confidence: I had negotiated several transactions without arousing suspicions, I had passed two more pairs of patrolling armed soldiers, and my tongue was producing a reasonable facsimile of the local accent. Yes, a restoration of memory would be nice, but as the immediate needs of survival became less pressing, the *suq* provided an endless variety of distractions, for all the senses: I saw tailors and carpenters, carpet-makers and silk-weavers, book-binders and jewellers, purveyors of leather footwear and ceramic pots and elaborate wedding head-dresses, men embroidering the fronts of robes or trimming the beards of reclining customers. My nostrils were teased by the odours of frying onions and baking bread and the cloud of aromas from the spice merchants, in between being repelled by the miasma from butchers' shops and malfunctioning sewers, entertained by the sharpened-pencil smell of fresh cedar and the musk of sandalwood, caught by the clean reek of fresh leather or the dark richness of roasting coffee beans, and educated by the contrasts of wet plaster with crushed mint, donkey's droppings overlaid by fresh lavender. My ears similarly passed from one aural environment to another: a chorus of school-boys from over the walls of a *madrassa* and the sound of a grain mill grinding below street level; the rhythm of soft-soled footwear against compacted dirt beside the ceaseless, many-noted *ting* of brass hammers from a dark den; a pure voice raised in song giving way to the rasp of small saws from an inner courtyard.

The populace ran the spectrum from African black to Mediterranean olive, with the occasional Nordic features and even blue eyes looking out of Arab brown skin. Jews, Arabs, Europeans, Sufis, each in a different form of dress. Transportation was mostly tiny sweet-faced donkeys and sullen mules, but I also saw a few horses, a handful of wheel-barrows, two camels (at a distance, not within the *suq* streets), and one heavy-laden, flat-tyred bicycle being used to deliver lengths of bamboo.

And the wares on offer! One street held shops displaying tall cones of varicoloured powder, from the deep red of paprika to brilliant yellow turmeric, interspersed with vendors selling bags of sticks, leaves, seeds, and what appeared to be sand, bowls of dusty blue chunks of indigo, and carefully arranged hillocks of mice skulls and desiccated lizards. One shop displayed hundreds of prayer beads on its three walls – ivory and amber, lapis and coral, sandalwood and ebony. Its neighbour held teetering stacks of cylindrical *tarbooshes,* or *fezzes,* mostly red, with tassels of every colour imaginable.

Few of the shops had signs. I took care to read any that did, and once spotted the word *horloge* on a display of timepieces near a gate at the southern edge of the *suq,* but there was no mention of sorcerers.

Apart from the absence of magicians' time-pieces, the town held a richness of sensory stimulation and information, when a person had nothing to do but wander and listen. And as the morning wore on, I found that the previous day's sense of confusion had settled considerably.

I was, I determined, in Fez, a walled Moroccan town built where the hills meet the plains. Water was all around; wherever I walked I could hear a rush or a trickle, and decorative fountains in various states of repair and cleanliness were on many corners. Now that daily life was under way again, the flow of traffic (all either pedestrian or four-legged) led me from one neighbourhood to another, each centre composed of a mosque and its attendant religious buildings, food markets, a baker's oven, and the ever-tempting *hammam* baths. Specialised craftsmen clustered in given areas. As I made my way north out of the central mosque district, I found that even the more general tradesmen – grocers, tailors – tended to gather together, interspersed with stretches that were largely residential.

Some of the streets were packed with furious activity – men bearing loads, women haggling for greens, and artisans creating tools for daily life; other streets stood in a state of suspended animation, with nothing more lively than a sleeping cat (I saw no dogs, but then, this was a Moslem country). Earlier, the rooftops had brought to mind a honeycomb; now, the streets around me evoked the life within a hive, some corners almost deserted, others bustling with the same sense of incomprehensible purpose.

I continued north until I came to the city walls, and another gate. There I spooned up a bowl of *harira* that tasted entirely different from yesterday's, followed it with a bowl of spicy fava beans swimming in oil, made my dessert out of three sugary dried figs, then bought a handful of pistachios and perched on a bit of collapsing wall in front of a Moroccan druggist's shop, tossing away the shells and watching the French guards.

Sitting before the gates brought an odd sensation. I did not think that I had ever been there before – certainly there was no sense of memory attached to the scene – yet it was deeply familiar: the wall, the gate, and the guards; the aged olive tree overhead, under which women sat with their children and rested before carrying their burdens to homes outside the walls. A water-seller with tiny tinkling bells filled cups with water from a swollen goatskin slung across his shoulder (the sight stimulated another sensory rush: *taste of metal / mouth filled with warm and musty water / two dark companions* and then it was gone). A fortune-teller drowsed on one side of the gate, waiting for customers; on the other side, a blind storyteller sat in a patch of sun against the wall with a dozen children at his feet. The storyteller was too far away to hear, but still a voice seemed to murmur in my ears, in another language...

Hebrew. *In the square before the Water Gate ... those who sit at the gate ... at the threshing floor by the entrance to the Samarian gate ... in the gateways of the city, Wisdom makes speech.*

I found myself smiling at this transferred image of city gates where, since time immemorial, the people of a town gathered, for news and flirtation, sanctuary and entertainment, food, drink, and the dispensation of justice, all under the close watch of the guard.

And these guards were attentive, give them that. The soldiers eyed every person going in or out. Those with loads, on their heads or strapped to beasts, were examined more closely. A man with a donkey laden high with greenery from the fields – at least, I assumed there was a donkey beneath the green mountain, though all I could see were hooves and an ear – had to pull bits off before he was permitted to drive his beast onward. The only time the guards relented was when a weary and travel-stained family came to the gate: a pregnant woman, her mother, and a very old man, with three children, the oldest a boy of perhaps ten. The ancient man was balanced on a donkey that looked as old as he; the family's worldly goods were carried in ragged bundles by even the youngest, a child no more than three. This group of travellers the guards treated gently, with a nod of respect for the ten-year-old head of the family, a pat on the head-scarf of the little girl. The family went by, their eyes locked into the faraway stare of those who have watched more than they could take in. Refugees?

After a time, as I sat shelling and chewing and watching the crowds, I became aware of a nearby conversation in French. Four young men, Moroccans in European clothing, were drinking coffee outside a nearby café. Two of the three facing my direction bore on their foreheads the distinctive dark circle indicating regular prayer, but apart from that, their dress, their manufactured cigarettes, and their attitude of studied indolence declared them representatives of the local intellectual class. The hive drones, as it were. They did not care much for the French soldiers, although French writers, artists, and philosophers seemed to be acceptable. Short of joining them at their table, I could not overhear all they said, but I heard enough to suggest a degree of political turmoil, even anger, amongst the Fasi intelligentsia.

The word *reef* (rif?) was used, the names Abd el-Krim and Lyautey, the Sherif and the Sultan: *Lyautey* was said with scorn (though lowered voices suggested a degree of authority there) and *the Sultan* with caution, while *the Sherif* and *Abd el-Krim* seemed equally divided between support and doubt.

One of the quartet in particular was growing

increasingly hot under the collar. It came to a head when one of the others said something I did not hear, and he slapped his glass down on the table and made a loud declaration in which the only clear word was *Raisuni*.

The others instantly hushed him, glancing towards the gate. When they saw one of the soldiers looking their way, the four made haste to toss down some coins, and the little salon faded away into the city.

Political intrigue amongst the Mediaeval stone-work

I finished my pistachios, and watched a trio of donkeys laden high with brightly coloured hides leave the city, as laden donkeys had been leaving cities for thousands of years. I studied the glimpse of land through the gate. There was no reason to believe that any French soldier cared a *sou* for my existence; on the other hand, walking through that carved archway might prove my final act as a free woman. Best to feel my way around the *suq* a while longer.

My clockwise route along the city walls was hit and miss, the public routes often losing sight of them entirely. As I turned south, the air began to smell less and less salubrious; indeed, had it not been for the studied nonchalance of the locals, the stench would have tempted me to cover my face.

It was a tannery, built along the river. A trio of peculiar-looking women went by, under the care of a French-speaking Moroccan, and only when they had passed did the reason for their bizarre appearance occur to me: They were Europeans. I turned immediately to follow, meandering along in their wake, where I thus learned that the stink was indeed a tannery, the source of all that gorgeously coloured Moroccan leather, and the reason for its stink was the pigeon droppings used as part of the process.

Or so the guide claimed.

But then, he also claimed that his very brother was the shopkeeper selling leather goods, and that the prices were especially low just for his clients, and that the Prince of Wales had bought a cigar-case of precisely that design, Madame.

But I ambled along within hearing for two reasons. First, their language. Since coming to this place, I had heard several tongues. Some were a closed book to me. My Arabic had been rusty, although it was improving rapidly, and in French I was relatively fluent. But the language these ladies spoke amongst themselves slid over me like a well-worn glove: English.

The other reason was a pair of names one of the ladies said after a couple of aeroplanes flew noisily over our heads, headed north like a pair of worker bees tracking a source of nectar.

'Oh look!' the stout grey-haired lady exclaimed. 'It's the French RAF!'

'Ivy,' the tallest of the trio said, 'I don't believe the French have a royal anything.'

'Oh, you know what I mean. Are they bombing someone?' she asked the guide. The tall one translated, then gave Ivy his answer. 'He says, they're not bombing yet, just watching. What they call "aerial surveillance".'

'Oh, is it Raisuli?'

'No, Ivy, it'll be that Krim fellow. Now, what do you say we ask the fellow to take us to lunch?'

'Here in the medina? Do we dare?'

'We should go back to the hotel, where we know it's safe,' the third one worried.

But I did not listen to the debate. I wanted to seize the tall one and demand further information: the name Raisuli – or Raisuni – made the guide as uncomfortable as it had the three cafe intellectuals. But since physical assault on an Englishwoman was not a good idea, I had to make do with following – close enough to hear, but distant enough not to alert their guide.

Fortunately, they turned back towards the crowded parts, pushing past the big mosque and *madrassa* that swelled into the myriad of tiny lanes like a pair of queen cells distorting the rigid lines of the comb – I caught my thoughts. What was this fascination my poor brain had with bees?

In any event, the mosque was banned to the three Unbelievers (indeed, even I would not care to risk an entrance, despite my present dress), although all three went past as slowly as possible, craning their heads at the forbidden land. While in those crowded lanes I decided that I had probably not in fact been a pick-pocket – or if so, a raw amateur at the game. Surely an experienced professional would not have been able to resist the rich pickings available, literally brushing her fingertips?

But I came out of these tightly-packed alleys with nothing more than one withered apple.

The trio, on the other hand, came out more than a little flustered. The worried one seemed not far from tears, and even the tall one was short-tempered. Time, she demanded, for luncheon.

The guide jollied them along to the establishment of a cousin, which turned out to be in a sort of plaza where two roads came together, very near the first gate I had seen on the previous afternoon. I thought, by the expressions on his clients' faces, that his cut from the 'cousin's' business would have to be large to make up for the gratuity these three were no longer going to give him, but they entered the white-clothed café with the air of travellers lost for weeks amidst desert dunes, and the maitre d' clucked over them like a broody hen.

I looked down at what I wore, and the state of my once-new yellow slippers, and knew that there was not a chance in hell that I should be allowed inside.

Still, I was loath to part entirely with such a valuable source of information. In an hour, maybe two, they might be sufficiently restored to their British indomitability, ready to plunge again into the fray, dropping nuggets of Intelligence behind them.

I wandered off, bought and ate various foodstuffs that, I was sure, were far tastier (and probably more hygienic) than the pseudo-French dishes my three countrywomen were being fed. I even dared to sit for a time, parked just inside one tiny establishment, eating scraps of spiced chicken from a skewer while the two men beside me argued politics in Arabic (neither the name Raisuli nor Krim came up, and the men seemed divided on the benefits of the French on trade).

When I moved to an equally diminutive tea shop down the way, a similar argument held sway. And a leisurely purchase of some salted almonds gave me insight into the views of the two shopkeepers on opposite sides of the 'street,' separated by ten feet of roadway and ten miles of opinion.

Yes, I found many things in the course of that day wandering the Fez *suq* – or rather, if the ladies were correct, medina. I found sights and smells and a world I'd never have guessed existed. I found enough distraction to make me forget for minutes at a time my impossible situation and even, occasionally, my headache. I found a Mediaeval city being whirled headlong towards the twentieth century, yet secure enough in its identity not to be frightened by that speed. I found a tight-knit and age-old community that opened affectionate arms to outsiders. I discovered patterns in its confusion, humour in its voices, beauty in its decay.

And dark trouble at its edges.

What the refugee family and quartet of intellectuals had made me wonder and the vigilance of the soldiers had underscored, what the opinions of the shopkeepers confirmed and the military aeroplanes emphasised – and the English ladies nearly stated aloud – was confirmed by that lunchtime hour amidst the hurly-burly of the medina.

Morocco was, it seemed, a country feeling the ugly stirrings of civil war.

With the Front just to the north of Fez.

CHAPTER FOUR

I wandered back towards the white-draped restaurant, pausing to take on a supply of sweetened almonds and dried mulberries, drinking another glass of mint tea, adding a small pen-knife to my arsenal, and a cheap cotton handkerchief. My path described a circle, and as I drew near the French café, a means of lingering occurred to me. I stopped at a fruiterer's stand to buy five oranges. Across from the café was a deserted doorway with a step. I evicted a sleeping goat, spread the handkerchief before my feet, put two 25 centime coins in it, took out the oranges, and began to juggle. Three oranges became four, and then five – to my astonishment, a couple of white-draped ladies added coins – and then, when the stir at the front of the café proved to be the foreign trio, I dropped one, and the act collapsed. My audience, composed of one muleteer, a swathed lady, and three filthy children, dispersed as well, leaving me my coins but snatching two of the oranges.

I hastily gathered the remaining fruit and the money, and followed the ladies – who, as I'd anticipated, were restored and ready for more.

I listened to the English conversation drifting back – the café's food, a trip outside the city they were considering – and felt as if I'd stepped inside my own home. My headache even receded.

'–do not think it advisable,' the worried one was fretting.

'But the driver said we'd be quite all right.' This was the tallest, horsey in type and in face.

'Ethel, he's French.'

'Ivy, even the French don't like to put paying customers in the path of danger. The Front is considerably farther north.'

'But the roads will be filled with soldiers. And you know how they can be.'

'I think we should go south instead,' Miss Worry insisted. 'We might even have enough time to go to Erfoud, and see the dunes.'

'You and your sheikhs,' Ethel scoffed.

She pronounced it *sheeks,* but I hardly noticed, because when her friend said the word *Erfoud,* it had set off an echo, reverberating through my skull.

Erfoud: *blonde curls / the grit of sand / 'Action!' / the dust-smell of baking canvas / vast blue sky–*

Then it was gone, leaving me pounding on the closed door of memory.

I must have stood for half a minute, staring at nothing, before the urgent cries of *'Bâlek! Bâlek!'* penetrated, causing me to shift to the side an instant before the laden donkey shoved past. I hastened after it until I reached the ladies – but this time the guide caught sight of me. He frowned. I turned away, fishing one of the oranges from my pocket, and leant against a wall to peel it, to give a reason for dawdling.

The three continued to debate the advisability of visiting the outskirts of what my morning's eavesdropping had convinced me was, if not a

61

Front, at least the buildup to one. France, unhappy with the incursions of mountain rebels into the areas it controlled, seemed to be drawing a line in the sand – or rather, across the mountains. Fighting was sporadic, but the medina was certain that outright war was not far away.

Granted, those had been people who spoke in the same breath of spirits – *afrits* – and of the miracles of the itinerant holy men called *marabouts;* perhaps I should not be too certain of their judgment.

Then the ladies' guide spoke a word that made me drop half my orange: *horloge.*

Clock.

Nothing about sorcerers, but it caught my attention, and I waited impatiently as the women crept through the lanes at an escargot's pace.

When he gathered their wandering attention and directed it upward, I had to wonder if perhaps my assurance with French was misguided. On the wall overhead was a series of thirteen protruding beams, each of which held a low, wide bowl. A clock?

I drew out a second orange as he launched into an explanation that made it instantly clear that he had no idea what the object overlooking this scrap of bazaar was: Tradition claimed it was some elaborate Arabic waterclock, and thus it was known, throughout the ages, despite having neither mechanism nor display.

Ethel was not convinced, either. After she'd listened to his incoherent explanation, she pulled a face and said, 'It looks more like a series of door-bells to me.'

62

Then Ivy noticed that the object brushing her shoulder was the lower lip of a camel's skinned head, hanging before a butcher's shop. The doorbell-clock was instantly forgotten, and the guide made haste to lead them towards a nearby *madrassa* – here it was pronounced *madersa* – that was open to English ladies. As they went past him, he shot me a hard glance. From here on out, following them would require a great deal more effort.

It was the middle of the afternoon, and I would have given half of all I possessed – which, granted, was not much – to be permitted to curl up quietly for a few hours. The slippers did nothing to cushion my feet from the hard stones, my various bruises were clamouring, my head had begun to feel somewhat detached. I wasn't particularly hungry, but I needed to sit. I did not have to stand and wait for them to emerge from the *madrassa*.

I was folding the last-but-one segment of the orange into my mouth, preparatory to walking up the street to a stall selling various juices, when I became aware of a hand, thrust in my direction.

It came as something of a surprise, since the few beggars I had seen were old or leprous.

The importuning hand was small and dirty, as was the child to which it was attached. It was also stubborn.

As, judging by the expression on his face, was the child.

I put the final orange segment on the grubby palm. It vanished; the child did not.

'Be gone,' I ordered, an Arabic phrase that came readily to my lips.

To my amazement, instead of retreating or thrusting the open palm back at me, he reached to grab my hand.

I snatched it back. 'No! Go away.'

He took a backwards step, then another. He was a handsome child, with black hair, light brown eyes, white teeth, and a face so open and innocent, I was filled with suspicion. The expression his appealing features wore seemed oddly expectant. I glanced behind me, wary of some partner in thievery, but none approached; when I looked back, he had not dashed forward to snatch my worldly goods. Now he tipped his head, as if inviting me to follow him.

So I turned and walked in the other direction. To my astonishment, four steps away the small hand insinuated itself into mine. I whirled around, lifting the hand in a threat.

'Child, no. Leave me.'

He looked, if anything, puzzled. His finger went up, pointing ... at the series of bowls mounted on the wall.

At the so-called clock.

I felt the mechanism of my brain turning, more cumbersome than any thirteen-bowled timepiece. 'Clock?' I asked in Arabic. 'Sorcerer's clock?'

He nodded.

I worked my hand inside my *djellaba*, loosened the hair-pin on my breast pocket, and dug around until I found the tiny scrap of onionskin. The child came forward to see what I had, and then looked up and granted me an expression of wide approval. He patted his narrow chest and pointed at the paper, then held out his hand in a

64

gesture clearly meaning, '*Now*, will you come, please?'

However, if he had been responsible for the written Arabic, then he could speak it. 'Where do you want me to go?' I asked him.

His light brown eyes slowly blinked; his hand remained raised.

I thought about it, thought about the lack of shelter and the coming night. What choice had I? To join the acrobats and snake-charmers at the city gate? I took a breath, and placed my hand in his.

I had, it seemed, acquired a guide.

CHAPTER FIVE

THIRTEEN DAYS EARLIER

Sherlock Holmes watched the slender brown hands pour the thick coffee and arrange the silver spoons, then fold themselves against the woollen robe in a semblance of a bow. When Youssef had been assured they needed nothing else, and his dark eyes had surveyed the room as if commanding the objects there to behave themselves in his absence, he left. Holmes took an appreciative slurp from his cup, stretched his feet towards the glowing brazier, and told his companion, 'I thought I'd hire a guide in Marrakech.'

'Be certain that he has a functional rifle.'

'It's still unsettled down there?'

'"Unsettled". That's an understatement. One of the more distasteful tasks of my position is arranging for ransoms. That, and funerals.'

'I see. Well, for your sake, I shall specify arms.'

'At least you're not going north.'

'You've worked a miracle in this country.' They were speaking French; the pronoun Holmes had used was neither plural nor formal, but the *tu* of intimates. The older man on the other side of the brazier, dressed in a blue uniform with seven stars on its sleeve that even at this hour looked morning-crisp, was Morocco's Resident General, Louis Hubert Gonzalve Lyautey. The Maréchal was, oddly enough, a blood relation. Of course, most minor European gentry could locate common blood if they looked deeply enough, but in the case of Holmes and Lyautey, they were fifth cousins on their mothers' sides. The two men had met by accident thirty-one years before, when, during the usual stilted dinner conversation of fellow passengers on a Mediterranean crossing, Holmes happened to mention that he was related to a French artist by the name of Vernet.

The two had seen each other but a handful of times in the intervening decades, and Holmes hesitated, on finding himself in Morocco, to inflict familial duties on someone with as much pressing business as Lyautey. However, he had discovered in this distant cousin a complex and intriguing mind, and the alternative was to remain under the jurisdiction of Randolph Fflytte and his band of merry film-makers, forced to carry out a prolonged act of imbecility. So, he wrote to the Maréchal (using the surname Vernet) and the Maréchal wrote back immediately, to say that the turmoil on the Protectorate's northern border was keeping him in Fez, but he was well pleased to have a house-guest, if the guest did not mind a host who was somewhat *préoccupé*.

Holmes seized this opportunity, and five days ago he had made a coward's exit from Rabat, abandoning his wife to her task. In truth, Russell had been looking forward to the experience of emoting before the cameras, although she would never have admitted it, and certainly not to Holmes.

Or so he told himself.

Morocco had come under French control twelve years earlier. A land of Islamic feudalism, a country with neither railroads nor telegraph lines, its roads were the tracks of camel caravans, its only wheeled vehicles the toys of children. The 1912 treaty had divided the country between Spain in the north and France in the south, and within weeks, native troops in Fez rose up and massacred their French officers. European shops and offices were ransacked, the Jewish quarter was in ruins, the Sultan locked himself inside the palace, for fear of being rescued by his supporters. When Lyautey dismounted at the gates of Fez, in May 1912, tribal gunmen were inside the walls, and the new Resident General was greeted by the news that all was lost.

Lyautey's response had been to walk without hesitation into the medina, to the house that had been set aside for his use, and dress for the formal reception.

On the surface, a blue-blood cavalry officer would seem a most unlikely choice for escorting a Mediaeval country into the modern world, but whether through accident or intent, the appointment of Hubert Lyautey had been a stroke of genius. Even as the Great War approached Europe, he had seized the Moroccan problem as one would a fractious young horse, taking its reins in a grip both iron-like and respectful.

Unlike Spain to the north.

'A miracle is called for,' Lyautey now told his English cousin, 'to negotiate a path between Spain and the Rif rebels.'

'Have they put someone sensible in charge of

those negotiations, at least?'

'That's not for me to say, although I try.'

'You?'

'Me. France appointed the current Sultan; France controls Fez and the major portion of Morocco; therefore, France is responsible for any foreign negotiations the Sultan might wish to make. *Et la France? C'est moi.*'

Resident General, military commander, governor of the state, and foreign minister. No wonder the man was looking his age.

'I heard rumours about the Rif while I was in Rabat, but little hard fact,' Holmes remarked.

'Extraordinary, is it not, how disconnected the parts of Morocco are? Always has been – the Sultans have never really controlled the Atlas mountains, or even the Rif. *Rif* means "edge", did you know? As in sharp. Of course you know that. Very appropriate. No, identity in this country is tribal, not national. The north is in a riot of bloodthirsty savagery; while down in Rabat, French ladies sip their *tisanes* in sidewalk cafés. Morocco is like a man walking his dog while his hat is in flames.'

Holmes' mouth twitched at the image. 'Forgive me, but I have spent most of the past year travelling in places where news is sporadic, inaccurate, and maddeningly out of date. I understand that Spain is having little luck in quelling the Rif Revolt?'

'The Spanish have combined wholesale corruption with abject stupidity, and now de Rivera – you know that Spain has become a military dictatorship?'

'That I did hear.'

'Primo de Rivera. A dictator determined to replicate the catastrophic decisions and attitudes of his predecessors. As we speak, men are dying. You heard of Annual?'

'A town, and a battle.'

'A catastrophe, for the Spanish. From childhood, the Berbers of the Rif are taught violence and blood. They scorn a man who has not killed before his marriage. Three years ago, in the summer of 1921, some five or six thousand Rifi tribesmen bearing antiquated rifles came down from the mountains against fifty thousand Spaniards armed with everything from machine guns to aeroplanes, and slaughtered them. Twenty *thousand* Spanish soldiers and civilians died. A Moroccan Verdun – and the Rifi picked up all that equipment as they left. Tens of thousands of rifles, hundreds of machine guns, artillery – enough to furnish an army. Which is what they now have. They're calling it a war for independence. And thanks to the Spaniards, it's on my doorstep.'

'Sounds remarkably effective, for tribal warfare.'

'The two brothers at its head – Mohammed and M'hammed bin Abd el-Krim – are a clerk and an engineer of mines. The Rif has enormous mineral potential. Iron, phosphates – you'll recall that The Great War nearly broke out in 1911 over the Agadir mines?'

'Gunboat diplomacy at its most flagrant.'

'And if the response dissuaded the Germans from colonial claims here, it didn't stop them from economic colonisation. They were happily bur-

70

rowed into one of the world's largest iron deposits, just south of Melilla, when the rebellion came down and smashed everything to pieces. The mine, the port, the equipment, all now in rebel hands.

'Extraordinary country; this,' Lyautey mused. 'Terrible and beautiful. A gem. And like a gem, hard, multi-faceted, and tough to hold on to. The hills rich with minerals, the central plains as fertile as anything in Europe, the people lively and intelligent, located in a place vital to world trade. If we can bring to bear what I like to call our *"arsenal pacifique"* – medicine, education, and hygiene – if we can nurture the social framework here instead of the usual mindless European destruction that leads to resentment and anarchy, we have a chance to witness the birth of a vibrant and beautiful new nation. Yes, the only thing Morocco lacks is natural harbours, and once we've built a couple of sea-ports, this land will blossom.'

'Assuming the rebellion doesn't spill over to the French side.'

'As you say. These brothers Abd el-Krim, I don't know what to make of them. They're modern. And somehow, they have managed to unite tribes across the Rif into one fighting force – they even have Arab and Berber fighting side by side, unheard of in this land. As we speak, a major battle is going on, scarcely 150 kilometres to the north. More problematic for us, reports indicate that Rifi troops are moving in along the boundary, which is only a day's ride from here. Ah, but come, you're not interested in matters military, my dear cousin.'

'To the contrary;' Holmes said. 'It makes a refreshing change from moving pictures. That is, if you are willing...?'

'Very well, if you like. Ah, Youssef, how did you know that I was thinking my coffee needed a drop of brandy? The man's a mind-reader,' he said to Holmes. 'Would you like some in yours, *cher cousin?* No? In a glass, then, Youssef, and that will be all. Lift your glass, my English friend, that you might drink to the stupidity of your fellow man.

'To the north of here,' the Maréchal began, 'deep in the Rif mountains, lies a town called Chaouen. It is a sacred town built by Moors expelled from Spain – I am told it resembles Granada – with a multiplicity of mosques and shrines, a town to which previously (so legend has it) only three Europeans had ever come; two of them, in heavy disguise, left safely; the third, a missionary, died from poison.

'Four years ago, a Spanish general by the name of Castro Girona talked his way into Chaouen to tell the city leaders that they ought to surrender.

'Incredibly enough, they did – and equally incredibly, the Spaniards marked this triumph by stabling horses in the mosques and abusing the ladies of the town. Offensive behaviour, so short-sighted.

'This past summer, Spain had to draw back, stranding some three or four thousand troops in Chaouen. In September, they moved several divisions – Intelligence reports say forty thousand men – to Tetuán, some fifty kilometres off, and sent them to Chaouen's relief.

72

'The Spanish troops reached Chaouen around the first of October, having lost far more men along the way than the number they were relieving. And six *weeks* later, just in time for the heavy rains, they began their retreat. Through mountainous terrain. With no proper roads for their artillery and armoured cars, while a whole nation of skilled and well-armed guerrillas lay among the rocks like shadows. The Rifi waited until the last Spaniard was free of the town – their Foreign Legion brought up the rear, under a young madman by the name of Franco – and fell on them like wolves.

'I can't imagine what is going on up there now – no, I can imagine. Every Rif male has a gun and a reason to hate the Spanish. Thousands will be dying. Tens of thousands.'

'Under Mohammed and M'hammed ibn Abd el-Krim.'

'The two brothers. Their names are about all we know of them, other than the older one having a limp. Their only photographs could be any man in Fez. The younger one, the Revolt's strategist, was educated in Spain as a mine engineer – they were born to the Beni Urriaguel, whose land holds most of Morocco's iron deposits. The elder brother – Mohammed, the Emir of the Rif Republic – worked as a Spanish journalist and native affairs officer until he was gaoled during the war – his limp is from an escape attempt. Both bear long witness to the insults, corruption, harassment, and general contempt with which the Spanish treat their Moroccan possession.

'And yet, if you'd told me five years ago that

73

there would be a rebellion, I'd have wagered that it would have Sherif Raisuli at its head.'

Holmes stirred. 'Raisuli as in "Perdicaris free or Raisuli dead"? Brutal and corrupt Raisuli, the last of the Barbary pirates? The man has made a career out of kidnapping Europeans – Perdicaris and Varley, Harris, Maclean. I wonder how much he's made altogether from his various extortion schemes?'

'Raisuli lives in considerable luxury – more to the point, he pays his men well. But it's not just ransoming prisoners, or selling them as slaves. The Sherif's a master in the art of playing European countries against one another. During the War, he took German money to foment a tribal revolt against us. More recently, I'm told that he's tried to collect their bounty on Abd el-Krim – the Germans are determined to get their iron mines back. He's even made a couple of attempts on my life – he has his eye on the Moroccan throne. Claims to be of the blood.

'He's given the Spanish merry hell for years, although of late he's quieted down towards them – Abd el-Krim has forced him to choose sides. Given a choice between Spanish pesetas and the threat of an enemy's Republic, Raisuli went with Spain.'

'Spain must have mixed feelings about that.'

'They can't afford to be fastidious about their allies. The Sherif may be ruthless and corrupt, but to his followers he is blessed – *baraka* – and can do no wrong. Buying peace with him secures Spain's western flank.'

'For the time.'

'True. As you say, for a pair of office workers, the brothers Abd el-Krim have proved unexpectedly adept at guerrilla tactics. No one but Raisuli has been able to resist them – and once they run out of Spaniards to pick off, they're sure to turn their sights on him.'

While to the south, Holmes reflected, moving picture companies and adventurous tourists moved freely across new French roads and on new French railways. And one more or less retired English consulting detective sat before a brazier with his distant cousin, in one of the most intriguing towns he had ever laid eyes upon.

'Will the Emir Abd el-Krim win?' he asked.

'Only if he can avoid a confrontation with France.' Lyautey took out his cigar, frowning at the end of it. 'The problem is, the border between the French and Spanish Protectorates was drawn in haste, with little attention paid to tribal boundaries. The Werghal River made for a convenient line, but as Spain withdraws, the Rifi move in. I have asked for reinforcements; however, Paris tells me our troops are heavily committed in the Rhineland and the Ottoman mandates. They'll change their mind once Abd el-Krim forces the issue. His Berber are magnificent fighters – independent, ruthless, and absolutely fearless. But – to answer your question – when he does attack us, it will be the end of him. If he tries to fight a war on two fronts, with tribal warriors, he will lose.'

And when Paris does send your reinforcments, Holmes wondered, *how far north will you push?* It was not a question he could ask, even of a friendly cousin. Still, faced with Spain's dangerous incompetence, any military man worth his salt would be sorely tempted to redraw the equation by – treaties be damned – simply sweeping across the mountains and tucking all of Morocco under French rule. Let the politicians sort it out.

As an Englishman, Holmes knew he should be concerned. Twenty years ago, Britain had let France have Morocco under the firm condition that the northern strip remain Spanish. It was one thing to have a moribund power like Spain in charge of land a cannon's shot from Gibraltar; it would be quite another if France, a strong country with whom England had a not always easy history, took over the coastline.

Holmes wondered if this Abd el-Krim understood the delicate balance of power his revolt was threatening – and the danger that awaited, should he venture south of the Rif mountains. 'Interesting, is it not,' he mused, 'how often the fate of nations comes down to personalities? Like Colonel Lawrence: one little man who has changed the entire shape of the Middle East.'

'I have heard of Colonel Lawrence. I do not know that I would have wished him under my command.'

'Most of his superior officers would have said the same. But don't be led astray by the Lowell Thomas portrayal. Lawrence was a singularly effective officer, for his time and place.'

'I should like to meet him,' Lyautey admitted.

'I should like to introduce you.'

'You know him?'

'We met in Jerusalem, just after the War. My ... Russell and I were in Palestine for some weeks.

Living as Bedouin, in fact – you'd have been amused to see it.'

Lyautey reached for the decanter and demanded the story. Holmes lifted his glass, considering. The tale concerned British espionage, some details of which were unsuitable for French ears. Too, Lawrence had been broken – in heart, and nearly in mind – by his own government's ruthless abandonment of the Arab cause, a betrayal that had left him standing alone, a liar to his friends. But the distasteful particulars of that power-play might be avoided, and the events themselves were five years old – there were details he could adjust to resemble a police investigation rather than an Intelligence one.

Yes, he could tell his cousin the story. If nothing else, it would offer a brief distraction from the man's huge burden of responsibility. Small enough payment for Lyautey's gift of this jewel of a city, where the air was a thousand years old and smelt of Arabia and Andalusia.

'In the early months of 1919, it happened that Russell – she was then my apprentice – and I needed to be out of Britain for a time. We ended up in Palestine, along with a pair of Bedouins named Ali and Mahmoud Hazr, who took us under their cloaks as they wandered about the desert. At any rate, we thought they were Bedu. However...'

It was a lengthy tale, and Holmes permitted himself considerable embroidery to an already ornate story. It was late, the decanter well down, another flask of strong coffee brought and drunk, by the time he described the meeting in the

Government House drawing room, with General Allenby (yet another remarkable figure, an English Lyautey – as Palestine was in many ways a British Morocco) lifting Russell's filthy hand to his lips before introducing them to the small yellow-haired man with the piercing blue eyes and dazzling white robes, Lieutenant Colonel Thomas Edward Lawrence.

Lyautey chuckled and shook his head, his aristocratic fingers folding the stub end of his cigar into the intricately pieced ash-tray. 'Yes, governments flourish upon the colourful exploits of individuals such as Lawrence, and your Hazr brothers. But governments also, eventually, crush them underfoot. In a fair world, Colonel Lawrence would be crowned.'

'Not that he would care much for that. I understand that he is currently working happily as a mechanic in the tank corps. While your Abd el-Krim is headed for a precipice.'

'I wonder if I will ever be given the chance to meet him, before I leave here,' Lyautey reflected.

'If the Spanish catch him first, they will tear him to pieces.'

'As a soldier, I can understand the impulse. Well, my old friend and cousin, work awaits, and tomorrow I must put on a patient face before a delegation of worthies.'

'While I turn south, to Marrakech.'

'As I said, if you venture into the High Atlas, make certain to examine your guide's rifle yourself. And if time permits, do bring this apprentice-turned-wife of yours to Fez. At the very least, you must bring her to France, once they permit me to retire.'

The Maréchal stood, betrayed by a faint stiffness, and drained the last swallow from his glass. But that did not mean that the man was going to bed: Lyautey awake was Lyautey at work – Lyautey, and his men. The Maréchal was speaking before the door had shut, to an assistant who waited in the courtyard below. 'François, you sent a message to Madame to say that I would sleep here tonight? Good. Tell Youssef I'll have more coffee. So. François, have we answered that absurd request from the archaeologists, *l'affaire Natale?* I suppose that we could spare a tent, and–'

His vigorous voice faded, leaving Holmes with a smile of admiration on his face: One o'clock in the morning, and the indefatigable Maréchal was summoning men to work. At least it sounded as if he intended to stop here the night, rather than walk back to the official Residence – or indeed, climb into a motorcar and set off for Marrakech or Casablanca.

Holmes took his glass to the window, standing for a time looking across the neighbouring roof-tops. The moon was waxing towards full; with the night's stillness, he could hear the constant splash of a fountain. The scent of orange blossoms sweetened the frigid air. He had never been one for the purposeless travel of mere sight-seeing; on the other hand, Russell would appreciate both Fez and its Resident General. The man's palpable love and respect for the country that had been placed in his hands might even restore one's faith in the colonial system.

Perhaps he and Russell could delay their departure for home, just a day or two. After all, this might prove the final opportunity for a pair of Europeans to do so: If the Revolt to the north managed to join hands with the uncontrolled tribes to the south, the French would be squeezed out in no time at all.

He latched the tiny window, dropped his cigarette stub into the low-burnt coals, and went to bed.

CHAPTER SIX

In the morning, there was a tap at the door.

'Come!' Holmes called. He was at the window again, his breath making clouds in the cold air, attempting an analysis of the neighbourhood's geometry. He crossed the room, rubbing his hands into circulation, and his nostrils flared at the aroma. '*Salaam aleikum,* Youssef,' he said.

'*As salaamu aleik,* Monsieur,' the servant replied. 'Monsieur's coffee.'

'I shall miss your daily visits,' Holmes said. 'The aroma alone could wake the dead.'

From the moment he entered Dar Mnehbi, six days earlier, Holmes had seen that Youssef was no mere servant. The man was, rather, the steward of this diminutive medina palace, and while he occasionally held sway over the official Residency as well – a considerably grander palace, in one wing of which Lyautey and his wife lived, closer to the city walls – for the most part, the Residency was a place where silk-robed, white-gloved servants waited on men in European clothing, while Dar Mnehbi was for the homespun supplicant at home in the medina.

Lyautey, truth to tell, seemed to prefer his medina dwelling as well, and often used the excuse of late nights to sleep in his simple rooms here.

Dar Mnehbi was, in fact, a complex of linked buildings, since the original palace was too small

81

until the neighbouring *dar* was taken over and converted into a combination guard house and guest quarters. It was now connected to Dar Mnehbi proper by a corridor and steps, its rooms adapted for the peculiar requirements of Europeans: the house hammam turned into a bathroom with a geyser tank, windows brutally punched through external walls, internal doorways converting individual salons into suites, with beds from France and the light-weight, decorative salon doors replaced by sturdy bolted wood. It did still have the central courtyard with fountain, cobalt-and-cream tiles, and a *halka* overhead, open to the sky.

Youssef had run the Dar Mnehbi complex for a decade, in charge of everything from the choice of flowers in the library to the brewing of such superb coffee in the kitchen. He was a tall, dignified Berber who wore his trim turban and striped *djellaba* with the air of a Roman Senator, and if Youssef chose to deliver food and drink himself, Holmes thought it was more as host than as servant.

'Black as hell, thick as death,' Holmes muttered in Arabic, watching the slim hands pour the liquid into the miniature cup.

The dark eyes looked up in surprise, then Youssef ventured the first humour Holmes had been able to tease out of him. 'If Monsieur wishes his coffee sweet as love, I shall need to bring more sugar.'

Holmes laughed. 'Thank you, my brother, I will take it bitter.'

The man set the cup before Holmes, and said,

'Few Europeans enjoy their coffee in this manner.'

'It is a preparation better suited to walking over the desert than driving in a motorcar,' Holmes agreed.

The Moroccan adjusted the spoon a fraction, tugged the trays cloth a centimetre, then left. In all the days of Holmes' stay here, it was the most Youssef had said in his hearing.

When the tiny cup was empty but for the grit, Holmes' nerves felt as if they had been connected to a low-voltage wall socket, but he felt vaguely dissatisfied until he spotted the carafe of drinking water on the side table. Water after coffee: another desert habit learned from the Hazr brothers.

Despite its Western-style renovations, Dar Mnehbi was a touch old-fashioned, a sumptuous expanse of tile and carpets with cramped private quarters, shared bath-rooms, few windows, and fewer fireplaces. The Residency, a short uphill stroll away, was an impressive, light-filled palace where guests could arrive in motorcars and be provided with taps that gushed hot water. Dar Mnehbi, deep inside the ancient walls of the medina, provided the French with a very different set of resources and messages. The Residency displayed power and flash; Dar Mnehbi made a clear statement of ferocious intent: The Resident General was an integral part of Fez, and he was here to stay.

Offered rooms in either place, Holmes had chosen to stop here rather than in the Residency, and had spent the past few days happily wandering the tangled streets that were equal parts Granada and Cairo, and wholly their own. Fez was the centre of Morocco, its heart and soul, rich and clever and lovely, and deadly as a Miniago stiletto. And its Resident General, manly and open with no taste for intrigue, was both unsuited for the task and the best hope of the country.

Yes, Holmes decided, he would return here with Russell before they sailed back to England. Having spent the past year in foreign parts, once they reached home, he doubted he'd prise her away from Oxford for a long time.

He coaxed a hot bath from the geyser (his last, he suspected, for some days), then packed his bag and left Dar Mnehbi, heading for the railway station.

Eleven days after leaving Fez – days filled to overflowing with sand, remote hills, the Arabic language, the Islamic world, and rather more excitement than Maréchal Lyautey would approve of his country having given one of its visitors – Holmes stepped off the train in Rabat, drawing a deep breath of the fresh sea breeze.

It was jarring, to go from a time spent far from motorcars and telephones, beds and newspapers, into the modern European bustle of Rabat. Holmes looked down at his travel-stained garments. He'd bundled away his disreputable *djellaba,* but in truth, the European trousers and jacket were not much of an improvement. He needed a bath, and a shave.

Rabat was enough of a European centre that, as he'd suspected, Fridays were less scrupulously observed than elsewhere in the Moslem world. Outside the train station, he brushed aside the mid-day clamour of hotel-boys and taxi drivers and headed to the portion given over to native trade. He picked out a cart with wheels that appeared to have seen grease in the past decade, addressing the startled driver in Arabic.

'*Salaam aleikum.* Do you know the Hotel de Lyons? Near the waterfront?'

'*A'salaamu aleik,*' the driver replied automatically. 'Yes, of course. But–'

'Good.' Holmes threw his case into the back, and, after a murmured *Bismillah,* climbed in beside it.

The bemused fellow looked at his horse, at Holmes, and followed him up.

When Holmes had left Russell, seventeen days before, they'd agreed to meet on Friday the nineteenth, at the hotel where Fflytte Films was ensconced. He rather hoped she would be out when he arrived; no need to inflict his present disarray on her. And (here he fingered a neat circle near the hem of his jacket, wondering if he could contrive to make it look less like a bullet hole) no need to point out that he'd had a more interesting time than she.

Seventeen days before, there had seemed little point to him cooling his heels while she finished with her cinema project. And since he'd found a replacement for his role in the moving picture (a corpulent ex-headmaster who looked the very image of a modern Major-General – far more than Holmes ever did), he had packed a bag and merrily left his wife behind, to pay his respects to a distant cousin and explore a country he'd never seen.

He turned his attention to his driver, engaging him in fluent Arabic while absorbing the man's gestures and the distinctive manner of driving (one never knew when one would need to act the part of a Moroccan horse-cart driver) and noting the details of the town around him. He saw more European faces on the short drive to the hotel than he'd seen the entire previous week – strolling the pavements, eyeing the windows, sipping coffee along sidewalk cafés. He had to agree with the Maréchal: A person would never believe that bloody rebellion seethed just 125 miles away.

They arrived at the hotel, which was run-down enough that a doorman did not instantly appear to order the cart and its passenger back into the street. Indeed, there was no doorman. Holmes climbed down, haggled cheerfully with the driver, and carried his own bag inside.

He recognised the figure at the desk, a Moroccan who pretended to be French; only after he had spoken to the man in that language did the man recognise him.

'Monsieur ... 'Olmes?'

'The very same. Is my wife in?'

'Monsieur, your wife left us, long ago.'

Holmes' arm checked; there was surely no reason for the cold sensation trickling into his chest. The film crew she was assisting had been delayed, that was all.

'When is the crew expected back?'

'Oh, Monsieur, the others, they returned three – *pardon*, two days past. Late on Wednesday. They remained here for one day, then early this morning – before dawn, even – they all boarded the sailing boat. To do the filming, you know? But they will be back tonight. *Insh'Allah.*'

His hesitation before adding the final word had the sound of an ominous afterthought. Holmes gazed at the man, who shifted the desk register between them, as if a display of its names would assuage this glaring customer.

Russell must have decided to change hotels again. To more comfortable rooms. 'Did she leave a message?'

'She did not. Her bags are here, of course. As is your–'

'Bags?' he said sharply. 'She left her bags here?'

'One she left, the other was brought back.'

'She abandoned her things?'

Either the desk man was remarkably perceptive, or the creeping panic Holmes felt was visible in his face, or his voice.

'Monsieur, please, there is no cause for concern. *Bismillah.* Her friends – if I may be blunt for a moment, I should say they were irritated, but not at all worried. She simply did not come back with them.'

'My wife walked away from all her possessions, and none of the company was concerned?'

'Put like that, it does sound remarkable, Monsieur, I agree. But I can only say again, they did not seem in the least troubled. They merely left her bag with me, rather than having it clutter the room of one of the others. Clearly, they expect her to return.'

Holmes took a breath. 'My wife had left one of her cases with you, you say?'

'When they went off to the desert, the motor-

87

cars were very full of equipment. M. Fflytte asked his company to leave any excess luggage here. The others have retrieved theirs, of course. Your wife's remains. With, as I said, the one brought back in her absence.'

'Let me have them both.'

'Certainly, Monsieur. Oh – stupid man that I am, I forgot – a gentleman left a message for you.'

Aha – it was Russell, in disguise. But when Holmes looked at the envelope, in hotel stationery and the same ink as that in the register, one eyebrow rose. He ripped the envelope open, and read, in beautiful Arabic script:

My brother, if you are available to assist in a grave matter, you will come to Fez and drink coffee at the shop nearest the train station, when they open in the morning or before they shut at night.

At the look in Holmes' eyes, the desk man immediately recalled the need for the two bags from the storage-room. He placed them on the floor, hastily retreating behind the solid desk again. 'Will, er, Monsieur be requiring a room?'

'No – yes. Good idea.' He needed to go through Russell's things, and it would give him a chance to clean up a little: In his current state, he would intimidate no one into parting with information. He held out his hand for the hastily proffered key, then asked, 'Are there any of the film crew who didn't go on the ship today?'

'Only two or three of the local men, Monsieur, who were not needed.'

'Where are they?'

'I am not certain, Monsieur.'

'They live in town?'

'Yes, Monsieur. Or so I presume.'

Holmes eyed him: That addendum had been too hurried, and his look of innocence too open.

However, bags and bath were more urgent than pinning down whatever mild chicanery the desk man might be hiding. And in any event, the local help were less likely to know what had happened to Russell than the crew itself. Without a word, he caught up the bags and headed for the stairs.

He went through every centimetre of both bags. One contained garments and equipment she had not thought necessary for a week's filming in the desert. The other bag's garments were less precisely folded and had sand in them. He strewed the room with the contents, and when the bags were empty, prodded the seams for hidden pockets, ripping apart one of the handles that felt lumpy.

He found neither passport nor revolver. Nor was the small leather valise she used inside the larger bags. The absences were reassuring, suggesting that her disappearance was deliberate, the lack of word merely an oversight or mislaid letter.

The water from the taps was actually warm; the water in the bath when he climbed out was opaque. He opened his shaving kit, squinted at the reflection in the spotted glass, and closed it again. Shaving could wait until he was certain that a beard would not be required.

He shoved his young wife's clothing any which way into the bags, did the same with his own, and returned to the lobby.

89

'Where do I find those local crew members?' he demanded.

'Monsieur, I have no idea, I–'

Holmes put both hands on the desk, leaning forward until the man drew back. 'I see that there is money involved. Some minor crime. I am not interested. I merely require to speak with the crew.'

'I ... that is... Yes, Monsieur.' The desk man wrote an address on a piece of paper, and pushed it across the wood.

Holmes took it without looking, then said, 'The gentleman who left the envelope for me. When was he here?'

'Monday.'

'What, four days ago?'

'Yes, Monsieur, in the afternoon. Not a European, Monsieur; a big man with–'

But Holmes turned on his heel and made for the door. He knew what the man looked like.

With his hand on the door, he whirled to see the desk man's face. The Moroccan looked relieved, but it was not the queasy relief that comes from getting away with a profound wrongdoing. Whatever scam the man had going on with this crew of locals, it did not touch on Russell's safety.

It took a couple of hours to run the crewmen to earth. They were not at the medina coffee house whose address Holmes had been given, nor at the home where he was directed next, but in a warehouse of sorts clear across town, not far from the hotel where he'd begun.

Four men looked around as he pushed open the door. All wore beards, turbans, and *djellabas*;

three of them had the build of stevedores; one of them was six feet tall, an extraordinary height here. The youngest man, a slim figure whose beard was precisely trimmed and whose robe was more neatly tailored, spoke up, in French.

'You are in the wrong place, Monsieur.'

'I think not,' Holmes replied, then changed to Arabic. 'I need to ask about one of the moving picture crew. You are just returned from the desert, I think?'

'The picture crew is off working on a boat,' the man said, sticking to French.

Holmes shifted back to that tongue, since the others were Berbers, and to at least one of them, Arabic appeared to be a closed book.

'My wife, Mary Russell, was with them when I left Rabat, but at the hotel, they tell me that she did not return with the others.' He slid his hand into his jacket, drawing out his note-case. He opened it, and removed several franc notes, which he tucked beneath the handle of a hammer that lay on the packing case by his side. He looked at them, and said simply, 'I am concerned.'

The four men consulted in silence for a moment. One of the heavily bearded individuals said something in a language Holmes recognised, although he only spoke a few words of it. Thamazigth was the language of the Berbers of North Africa, and of an intriguing structure. One day, he intended to study it properly. Today he merely required communication.

'Do you know the person I mean? Tall, blonde, she wears spectacles.'

'A lady with ... much assurance.'

91

'That's a diplomatic way to phrase it. Did she go with the company to the desert?'

The slim young man's eyes gave the briefest flick over the money, before he lifted himself onto a crate and took out a cigarette.

When he got it going – Holmes blamed the picture industry, for making every man a dramatist – he blew out a smoke cloud and answered, 'Yes, she went along. But she did not come back.'

Patience, Holmes.

'Tell me what happened.'

'We were at Erg Chebbi, near Erfoud. You know Erfoud?'

'I know where it is. Past the *bled* and over the mountains to the Sahara proper.'

'Precisely. And that is why M. Fflytte took everyone there, because he wished to film the sand dunes for his picture. We warned him, there are few *sheikhs* in Erfoud.' He chuckled; two of the others did as well; the big man just stared.

'Such was the plan before I left,' Holmes said. 'Why did she not come back with the others?'

'It was Tuesday night,' the dapper man persisted. 'The filming was all but finished, although Monsieur Fflytte planned to spend the following day filming scenes he thought he might want. That were not written into the script, you understand?'

'Yes.'

'So.' The man examined the end of his cigarette, flicking the ash until he was satisfied with its shape; the only thing that kept Holmes from going after him with the hammer was the knowledge that it would cause even more of a delay. 'We had a very full day, on Tuesday, from before sunrise – M. Fflytte wished to capture the sunrise – to sunset, which he also desired to film. We had fallen upon our dinners like hyenas (How those pretty blonde English girls can eat!) and the younger ones had gone to their tents, while some of the others, as this would be their last night in the desert, lingered around the fire with cognac.

'Not the crew, you understand – not those of us who carried things and made arrangements with the local people. We had another fire, and were sitting there.

'So we were the only ones to see your Mademoiselle – rather, *Madame* – Russell – go away. She had gone to her tent,' he explained – Holmes' hand twitched, craving the hammer handle – 'before the other ladies, and a boy came to speak with her.'

'A boy? A young man?'

The Moroccan laughed, thinking he perceived the underlying question. 'No, Monsieur, you need not be concerned with your wife's virtue. No more than any European husband needs to be concerned, that is. He was young – one of many such who wandered in and out of the camp, you understand, selling small items, begging for coins. Occasionally stealing perhaps – we hired guards from the town, which helps to keep thievery down. In any case, the boy came to her tent, and they spoke.'

One of the others made a remark. The two talked back and forth for a minute in Thamazigth, then the spokesman returned to his narrative. 'I am sorry, Monsieur, but Massim here says that it was not so much a case of the two speaking, as it was her asking questions.'

'You mean, the lad didn't answer?'

'Not that Massim heard. And Massim's hearing is very good, *Bismillah.*'

Massim looked at Holmes, and for the first time smiled, displaying a mouth like a smashed fence.

'So she asked the boy questions, but he didn't understand her.' Which was unexpected: A young man accustomed to the camps of foreigners should speak either Arabic or French, in both of which Russell was fluent.

But the crewman shook his head. 'Oh, he seemed to understand. Merely did not answer.'

'Did not, or could not?'

The three men consulted without speech. Massim gave a tiny shrug; the slim man admitted, 'Perhaps could not. He seemed friendly enough towards her. And after all, they went off hand in hand.'

'Did they now?' The man's face gave a little twist of chagrin, that he had been distracted into a premature revelation of the tale's dénouement, but Holmes did not give him the chance to regain the floor. 'When the boy came that night, did he loiter about for a time? Speaking with the young girls perhaps?'

'We did not notice him. He was Berber, not a desert-dweller, so he stood out a little. The first we saw of him, he was scratching at the door of Madame's tent. The two talked – or, she talked – and they went inside for a time. When they came out, she was wearing the heavy *djellaba* she had bought in the village – a man's *djellaba*,' he added disapprovingly.

'The two of them walked away together, into the night. In the morning, she was not in her bed.'

'Had you seen the lad around the crew, before that night?'

The men agreed, no. 'We thought he was one of the village urchins, even though the dunes are quite a walk from the town.'

'Wait – urchin? How old was he?'

'Oh, young. As I said, too young to be interested in the girls.'

'A child? Russell went off with a *child?*'

'Put her hand in his and walked away into the desert.'

'But he must have said something to her, or given her a message of some kind.'

The other short man spoke up, his French ungrammatical and heavily accented. 'He gave her a thing. Not letter, just small, I don't know. She looked at it, very–' He said something to the other, who translated.

'Very interested.'

'What did she do with it? Did she hand it back to him?'

The man shrugged. 'They went in tent. I don't see, after.'

'She did not take a valise away with her?'

'Not that was told, Monsieur.'

'And she did not return, once she and the lad had left?'

'Again, Monsieur, who knows?'

The more fluent one commented, 'But she must have expected to be away.'

I shall murder this fellow, Holmes thought. 'Why do you say that?'

'Because she left a note. And her passport was missing.'

'None of her other possessions?'

'Who knows? One of the other girls packed Madame's things and brought them back.'

With a jolt, Holmes remembered the presence among the Fflytte crew of Annie, one of Mycroft's agents. That redoubtable young lady spy would surely know what had happened.

'What did the note say?'

'"I have to go to Fez, I will come to Rabat later." In English, naturally. In any event, that is what I was told.'

'Did no one think it odd?'

'M'sieur Fflytte was irate, because as I said, he wanted to do a few more scenes the next day, but none of them were of importance, and in truth, he was finished with her. If it had been one of the girls who disappeared, we would have been concerned, but Miss – Mrs – Russell? The lady is *formidable*. Who could worry?'

Indeed. And yet, Sherlock Holmes worried.

The big man seemed to have the brains of a tortoise, but at Holmes' expression, even he was beginning to look alarmed.

Holmes drew a calming breath, and started again. 'So she left her tent that night. After dark.'

'*Oui, Monsieur.*'

'And was still gone the next day.'

'*Oui, Monsieur.*'

96

'She spoke to no one, merely left a brief note to say that she was going to Fez.'

The man nodded.

'The filming ended. The rest of you came back here. No one thought this odd. And all you have to say is that my wife was last seen walking into the desert in the company of a child. Three days ago.'

Four faces stared back at him, unable to respond.

'Who brought her bag back from Erfoud?'

'One bag, and a small valise. It was the oldest of the yellow-haired girls.'

Annie.

Holmes left the notes beneath the hammer, and went to find a taxi.

CHAPTER SEVEN

Holmes' thoughts raced in front of the trotting horse. The sun was low. He badly wanted a conversation with Annie (a young lady with a background almost as interesting as her skills) but her late return would keep him from reaching Fez tonight, and he was needed there – or he had been needed, on Monday.

Would that conversation justify another day's delay? Russell had only disappeared on Tuesday – in England, after three days he'd have scarcely noticed her absence. But in an unknown place, accompanying an unknown person, leaving no notice? And, considering the note left on Monday...

True, Annie might have some answers. But that competent and persistent lady Intelligence agent would insist on accompanying him, and shaking her from his tail would not be a quick matter.

Back in the hotel, he used the desk pen to write a message to Annie, telling her that he had gone through Russell's things. He handed the note to the desk clerk, noted the slot into which the note went, and then walked upstairs to apply his lock picks to the door of that room.

The first thing he saw was Russell's leather valise, sitting openly atop the room's wardrobe. It contained a thick folder of moving-picture notes, her favourite fountain pen, three books, a couple of expensive scarves, and a necklace that looked as if it had come from a Moroccan bazaar. The bag had grains of sand in all its corners, as might be expected.

And in its hidden bottom compartment, which Annie may or may not have discovered, a passport and a gold ring.

Holmes sat on the side of the bed, looking from one to the other. It was Russell's usual passport, and he did not think she had brought another. The ring he'd had made four years ago, when his wife-to-be had admitted, in a shocking display of sentimentality, that she rather thought she might wear a wedding band, if he gave her one.

'Russell,' he muttered. 'What the devil are you up to?'

He told himself that finding these objects in the valise should be reassuring, rather than worrisome. That their presence here suggested she'd not been drugged, or dragged, from the tent. But the ring might have sat in the secret compartment for some time, since she would not have worn a gold band during the filming. And she could have left the passport with it, guarding against desert sneak-thieves.

In any event, even if she had left both items behind, it would make for a clear statement that she anticipated being in a situation where British identity papers and a wedding ring – even one worn around her neck – would be vulnerable, or would make its wearer vulnerable.

Not knowledge to put a man's mind to rest.

When he was satisfied that there were no messages concealed among the papers or books, he pushed everything but the passport and ring back into the valise, then turned to Annie's possessions, making no attempt to hide the signs of his search.

The only things of interest were half a box of bullets and a very new passport.

He stood, fiddling with the ring, feeling its etched design. The windows had gone dark; the others would return any minute. Wait for Annie?

No: She would be more liability than assistance.

Holmes left the hotel carrying only a small rucksack, heading in the direction of the train station. He hailed a passing horse-cab, and paid the man for a gallop, but the last train had left.

He spent the night in a flea-ridden hotel near the station, and caught the first train north in the morning, heading for many cups of Fez coffee, and for – *insh'Allah* – some word of Russell.

The train reached Fez just before noon.

Holmes walked directly to the first coffee house he saw, bustling with Saturday traffic.

Two hours and far too much coffee later, he went to find the facilities.

An hour after that, a young boy stepped inside, swept his brown eyes across the clientele, and walked over to Holmes' tiny table.

A light-eyed Berber, *too young to be interested in the girls.*

'May I help you?' Holmes asked, in Arabic, then French.

The boy held out his hand – but it was curled slightly inwards: an invitation, not a beggar's request. Holmes' eyes narrowed.

'Do you understand me?' he asked.

The boy blinked an affirmative.

'Have you been in Erfoud?'

A smile.

'Are you capable of speech?'

This time, a brief shake.

'You wish me to come with you.'

The lad stood back, and dropped his hand.

Holmes laid some coins on the table and followed him out the door, onto the street, up to the town, and through the streets of Fez el-Jdid ('New' Fez, a mere seven centuries old, as opposed to the twelve-hundred-year-old medina) between the Sultan's palace and the Jewish quarters, before plunging once again into the incredible hotchpotch of tiny pathways that was Fez el-Bali – packed to bursting with all the human types of North Africa.

Holmes had spent five days meandering through the city on his previous visit, so he knew the primary routes. Just inside the Bou Jeloud gate, the main paths diverged, to join again near the city's main mosque. The Dar Mnehbi complex was along the more southern track, Talaa Seghira. Now, however, at the Fasi equivalent of the village green where the ways split, the mute lad led him to the left, along the more northern Talaa Kebira.

Much of this area was covered by the rush matting that made the streets cool in the summer, but did nothing to warm them in the winter. The ways were dim and crowded, and Holmes would not have been surprised to feel a pick-pocket's fingers, dipping into this foreign prey being led deep into the medina.

No thieves made a try at his pockets, but as they went, Holmes came to two conclusions. First, despite taking him the wrong way, the lad knew the city like the inside of his teeth. And second, he was looking for someone.

Twice, the boy paused to scramble onto a box or a step, peering along the heads or down an adjoining lane before hopping back down to the cobbles and pressing on. He repeated the act a third time just under the so-called waterclock, a puzzling structure of protruding beams and brass bowls made all the more enigmatic by the local insistence that it had, at one time, been an actual clock.

But whatever – or whomever – the lad was looking for, he did not find it, diving back into the street and leading on, ever on.

Then he stopped, looked around him, and seemed to realise that he had overshot his goal. He turned south, wriggling through several by-ways so small, Holmes would have taken them for inadvertent gaps between the buildings, before finally popping back out onto the street a few doors up from Dar Mnehbi. The boy marched up to the broad double doors, banged on them with a small fist, then turned to give Holmes a cheery grin. The door opened; Youssef looked out, first at the boy, who seemed to surprise him, then at Holmes. He came to attention.

'Monsieur,' he said. 'You have returned.'

'So it would seem,' Holmes said. 'My young friend here– Wait! Stop!'

But the lad had taken off, sprinting into a crowd of ladies. By the time Holmes had struggled through the shocked and giggling women-folk, the boy was nowhere in sight.

Back at the entrance to Dar Mnehbi, Holmes looked at Youssef. 'It would appear that I am to remain here until the young man returns for me. If you don't mind?'

He was returned to the arms of the Resident General's household as if he had never left, given the same rooms, brought a tray of the same excellent coffee, offered luncheon.

'I'd better use the bath first, and rid myself of these clothes. I shouldn't wish to introduce fleas into Dar Mnehbi.'

He took his time, coaxing a quantity of very hot water out of the geyser. Again, he considered his beard in the looking-glass, and again decided to retain it. He wrapped his previous night's clothing in the damp towel, to lock any wildlife inside, and rang to let Youssef know he was ready for his meal.

The quiet man was there in minutes, uncovering the tray, laying out a cloth, replacing the empty carafe of coffee with a fresh one. He had the good servant's skill of efficient invisibility, with smooth motions that got the job done while attracting no attention. Quick, yet unobtrusive.

Holmes appreciated professionalism, in any profession.

As he tucked into a most pleasant couscous of spiced lamb and chickpeas, clean and warm before the room's glowing brazier, the sounds of another arrival were a reminder of Lyautey's manifold responsibilities. He must let the Maréchal know that a second round of entertaining this stray English relation was not required: He intended to leave, once he'd figured out why the boy had stashed him here.

When he had finished, he took his coffee over to the window. Windows in traditional Arabic architecture were primarily shuttered openings that faced inward, onto the central courtyard, to provide a basic amount of light and ventilation. Here, the French had breached the external walls of the *dar's* upstairs guest-rooms with hinged windows. The sacrifice of security and privacy was well worth it, from Holmes' European eyes, and the tantalising glimpses of gardens, streets, and rooftop terraces had proved the most desirable quality of the rooms during his stay.

Now, he flung the glass open and planted his shoulder against the frame, his cup balanced on the tiled sill. The town's noise obscured the splash of the courtyard fountain, but the air was still fragrant. Somewhere, a canary trilled. He took out his tobacco, torn between simple pleasure and waspish impatience.

He would give Russell until the morning, before he turned the town upside-down.

He knew that she was almost without a doubt the author of her own absence. Had it not been for two things, he might have thought that she had decided to, as the Australian aboriginal peoples called it, 'go walkabout' – that the memory of those weeks in Palestine with Ali and Mahmoud, living in their goat's-hair tents and drinking coffee as strong as that in his cup now, had tempted her to the romance of the dunes. Her version of his own sojourn in the southern High Atlas, but among the Tuaregs.

Except that the letter left for him in Rabat five days ago suggested, and the appearance of a mute boy that morning confirmed, a quite different scenario than a light-hearted holiday. The letter, and its author, opened the door to an alternative explanation that was both reassuring and yet, in the longer term, troubling; one that—

'*Salaam aleikum,* Holmes.' The lisping voice from the adjoining window startled Holmes, but it did not surprise him. He leaned out, past the burning cigarette resting between his fingers on the window's sill, and looked into a pair of black eyes above a faint smile that revealed a gap in the front teeth.

Holmes' grin was considerably wider. 'I thought as much! *Aleikum es-salaam,* Ali Hazr.'

CHAPTER EIGHT

'I wondered if I mightn't see you, before long,' Holmes said to Ali. They were settled before the brazier in Holmes' room, speaking in the habitual low tones of men on whom heavy secrets often rest: A *dar's* architecture allowed for little privacy. 'Did my brother, Mycroft, tell you we were here, in Morocco?'

'He sent word last month, but his letter only reached us ten days ago. We have been in remote parts. As my brother no doubt told you.'

'I have not seen Mahmoud. He left a letter for me in Rabat.'

Ali lifted his eyes from the process of dribbling tobacco into cigarette paper. 'A letter?'

Holmes took out his note-case and gave Ali the page. 'I know his hand well enough, there was no need for a signature.'

Holmes watched his eyes skip over the sheet. The younger man was more conservatively dressed than he had been in Palestine, where brilliant colours and beaded plaits had given him the look of a Bedouin pirate. Now, his clothes were chosen with care, but he wore no scent, and his dark eyes showed no trace of kohl.

'How is Mahmoud?' It was not an idle question: Trapped in England the previous year, Ali's partner had suffered – and Ali with him.

'He is well. Nearly himself.'

'Nearly?'

'There are ... uncomfortable elements to our task here. We shall both be glad to go home.'

He did not mean England.

Ali scowled at the brief message, holding it up to check for hidden marks. There were none – Holmes had looked, but retained the page in case he had missed something. Now, the writer's partner replaced the note in its envelope, and dropped both onto the glowing coals.

'He left it at the hotel on Monday,' Holmes told him. 'I've been travelling in the Atlas, and only returned to Rabat yesterday. Where I found a letter from an old friend-in-arms, and discovered that Russell had last been seen walking away from an encampment near Erfoud on Tuesday. You and I both seem to have mislaid our partners. Experience suggests that the two events are connected.'

Ali, frowning into the flames, muttered, *'Insh'Allah.'*

Holmes narrowed his eyes. 'That sounded remarkably like a prayer.'

The younger man woke to the unlit cigarette resting between his fingers. When he had it going, he pulled his long, wickedly sharp knife from its decorated scabbard and drew a scrap of wood from his pocket. Ali thought best with a knife in his hand.

'A year ago,' Ali began, 'Mahmoud and I left England, fully intending to return to Palestine for good. We took our time, stopping two weeks in Paris. Mahmoud – Marsh – wanted to talk with Iris. He thought it possible they would not meet again, and he had business with her over the boy.'

Ali and Mahmoud Hazr were also Ali and 'Marsh' Hughenfort, with a complex and high-born English history they had worked hard to leave behind. Iris was Marsh's wife; 'the boy', their grandson. A very young duke.

'We nearly made it. We were waiting at the docks in Marseilles when Mycroft's telegram caught us up, and sent us to Morocco instead.

'You will know, by now, of the rebellion in the Rif?' Ali asked.

'Even in the peaceable corners of the country, talk is of Abd el-Krim.'

'A remarkable man.'

'You have met him?'

'I have fought beside him. But let me begin in the early months of the year, that you can follow the path that brings you and me together.'

'Any army requires guns,' Ali said, frowning at the object beneath his knife, 'even one that has conquered well-supplied enemy strongholds. More than medical supplies, or horses, or food even, an army requires arms. So in February of this year, Mahmoud and I saddled a pair of fine horses and headed up into the Rif out of Tangier, to sell some guns.

'Our first concern was to keep out of the hands of Raisuli. You know Raisuli?'

'A brigand and general opportunist, who claims the throne of Morocco. I have heard him called "the last Barbary pirate."'

'Raisuli is the blood enemy of Abd el-Krim. Selling guns to the Emir would declare us

Raisuli's enemies as well. Since Mahmoud and I did not wish to end our days nailed to a tree while the vultures feasted on our entrails, we took care to avoid him.

'It took us until the end of February to reach Abd el-Krim. He was fighting eighty miles or so down from Ceuta, trying to use some captured artillery against a Spanish warship lying off the coast. Mahmoud offered them advice, and the ship moved away in a hurry.

'It was a piece of good fortune, and it opened a door that might have taken some time otherwise. We joined with him for a few weeks, and saw enough fighting to prove that we were men. The Berber are a simple people. Like the Bedu, in many ways.'

'Brutal?'

'Clear-minded. Practical. We were not blood – would never be blood – but we had demonstrated our backbone and our skill, and that counted for a great deal. Plus that, our guns were good.'

'You actually sold them guns?' No need to ask what else they were doing: The two brothers were spies, after all.

'It is what gun-sellers do.'

'Agents of His Majesty; selling guns to be used against two European countries.'

'You begin to see why Mahmoud and I are keeping our heads down.'

'Who knows?'

'You.'

'Lyautey?'

'I have met the Resident General briefly, twice. He knows me as a representative of Abd el-Krim, nothing more.'

Holmes watched the nimble hands for a moment, then: 'What do you need?'

The knife peeled a paper-thin curl of wood from the small block, shaping legs. 'I believe you are friends with Maréchal Lyautey?'

'He's a distant cousin.' He explained the link to the surprised Ali. 'So I have known him for years, even though my visit here earlier this month was the longest conversation we've had.'

'Your brother's letter merely said that you would count yourself the man's friend. The Maréchal has been here for twelve years, and has forged considerable respect. He is known to be a man of iron decisions. He stands firm against the wishes of Paris, yet when it comes to the voices of subordinates, Lyautey not only listens, he actively requests advice. He is an aristocrat who seems to understand the lives of working men. He is a Christian with great respect for Islam. He is often in pain, such that he must work from his bed, yet he does not permit infirmity to keep him from rising and riding into the hills when need demands.'

'I have seen no sign of infirmities,' Holmes interrupted.

'He has been to France twice this year for surgical operations. He returned from one such just last month. He would have retired by now, but for Abd el-Krim.'

Holmes said nothing. Ali glanced up from his whittling.

'He is also known as a man whose word is as iron as his will. During the War, even when he was called back to France as Minister of War, his

Moroccan programs continued. The men of the Rif see Lyautey as a man who would bleed himself dry before betraying an oath.

'So, that is your Maréchal Lyautey. In the meantime, Mahmoud has become as close to Abd el-Krim as a man who is not of the Beni Urriaguel can ever be. Do I need to tell you about the Emir?'

'I have been hearing about Abd el-Krim for weeks now, mostly stories. He is Robin Hood, he is a brilliant tactician, he is a murderer, he is a power-mad tribal leader out for revenge against the Spanish, he is a greedy man aiming to control the Rif mining interests.'

Ali did not deny any of the descriptions. 'Abd el-Krim is a man in his early forties, educated in the Fez *madersa,* whom fate gave a path, and who found the courage to step onto it. Precisely speaking, the Emir did not begin the Rif Rebellion, but he was the man who bound the rebelling tribes together, who took over a dozen small revolts and Raisuli's self-serving brigandry and forged them into an independence movement. It is true that the Germans would give almost anything to regain their mines near Melilla – one suspects Deutschmarks behind the seven million American dollars the Spanish offered him.'

'Seven million? For what?'

'Seven million dollars – plus arms to use against the French – if the Emir would permit them to reoccupy the area around the mines.'

'He turned them down?'

'The bay is the only place along the Mediterranean coast where large numbers of troops may

111

be gathered. Ceding it to Spain would mean holding a knife to the throat of the entire Rif.'

'Raisuli would have taken the money – and then gone back on his word.'

'You see the difference between the two men.'

'Yet Raisuli is not without his followers.'

'There are those who would die for Raisuli because of who he is, who care nothing for his sins because the blood of the Prophet runs in his veins. For them, it is a world of black and white: Compromise is weakness, victory is proof of divine approval, crimes are not crimes if they are in the service of the Most High. When religious fanaticism enters the realm of politics, the mix is extremely volatile. Spain does its best to stir the pot – they believe that Raisuli's victory would be to their benefit.'

'Why then does Raisuli deny the rightful Sultan of Morocco? Surely that is a God-given position if ever there was one.'

'Raisuli is also of the house of Alaouite, Morocco's ruling family for three centuries. He regards himself as a more rightful ruler than Sultan Yusef. Abd el-Krim, on the other hand, denies the Sultan because Yusef is under the control of France. A political viewpoint, rather than the visceral religion of Raisuli – just as Abd el-Krim is attempting to fight a war of independence rather than a *jihad* against the Christian world. The Emir walks a razor's edge every day.'

'The traditionalists do not like Abd el-Krim?'

'They like him less. He is a modernist, who would bring the country into the new era. For example, he has little patience for local *mara-*

bouts, shrinekeepers, whom he regards as dangerously mired in the past. He attended the Fez *madersa* and is a Believer, but he does not speak the language of the holy men.'

'And this is the man your brother has befriended.'

'Mahmoud's advice has proved good, his commitment to the Rifian cause solid. This means that now, after ten months, he is in a position to say a word into the ear of Abd el-Krim, and it will be heard.'

'And what is the word that Mahmoud has said?' By now, the two men were speaking in low murmurs.

Ali paused to set the rough creature on the table for a moment, to check that it stood firm on its four legs. Then he resumed. 'My brother says that the head of the Rif Republic and the Sultan's foreign minister should meet, face to face, without the presence of Spain. That we need to bring together Emir Mohammed Abd el-Krim and Maréchal Hubert Lyautey.'

'Moroccan soldiers mutinied in 1912 when they thought France was controlling the Sultan. Why wouldn't the whole country go up in flames over this?'

'It would. Were it known.'

'A secret meeting, then. Abd el-Krim would come, despite the risk of arrest?'

'Once we saw that Chaouen was all but won, we put the question before the Emir. He agreed, and a message was carried to the Maréchal, asking if he would be willing to meet.

'It was the following day that your brother's

letter reached us, giving your location in Rabat. It seemed a possible solution to the problem of how to permit Lyautey a guard without risking knowledge of the meeting getting out. Plus, you might be needed to talk him into it.

'We received Lyautey's tentative acceptance eight days ago – on the twelfth. Mahmoud left the next day, both to find you and to confirm that the site we had thought of would be adequate.

'We requested a neutral place, to the north of Fez, even though if the Emir wished, he could walk into Fez through the Bab Bou Jeloud and no man would be the wiser. A handful of teachers at the *madersa* might recognise the man from the boy he was, but outside of them, his face is known only to those who have fought at his side. Abd el-Krim walks in the shadows.'

'So long as his name is not said aloud.'

'As you say. He would not come to Fez knowing that a potential enemy could be waiting, *Allah ystor.*'

'Why do you need me?'

'Your cousin has made preliminary agreement to come and speak with the Emir. He may be less willing when he finds that it will take him away from Fez for a day, and that it renders him vulnerable. Only a brave man would ride alone to such a meeting, but only a stupid man would do so without being certain it was no trap. Lyautey is a brave man. He is not a stupid one.'

Holmes studied the side of his companion's face. Ali remained intent on the figurine. After a while, the older man got to his feet, walking to the little window to stare unseeing at the rooftops.

A chain of links, strung across a chasm: Lyautey, Holmes, two British spies, and a rebel leader, on which the perilous future of a country rested – and Morocco's future was only a part of the picture. If such a meeting went wrong, if Lyautey was shot or taken prisoner and England's hand in his fate came to light, French outrage would have artillery pointing north across the Channel.

'Why?' he asked, his back to the room. 'What are you after?'

'Till now, the Rif Rebellion has pushed exclusively north, against Spain. If it matters at all to this discussion, Mahmoud and I happen to believe that the Rifi have a right to their land, but opinion notwithstanding, the Emir is on the brink of forcing Spain to the negotiating table. By spring, when the Spanish people have buried their dead and filled their eyes with newspaper images of the Spanish retreat from Chaouen, after the government have patched their wounded and added up the cost of what they left behind, Spain may well begin to feel that narrowing their Protectorate down to the countryside around Ceuta – as Britain has the country around Gibraltar – would be of benefit. And the brothers Abd el-Krim would be a powerful presence across a negotiating table. They may ride on horseback and dress in handspun robes, but do not make the mistake of picturing them as tribal barbarians. They are educated men with subtle minds, who would give their lives for the sake of their Republic.'

'And you wish to convince both Lyautey and Abd el-Krim that they need not be enemies?'

'I – we – wish fervently to at least delay any confrontation.'

'But the Rifi are moving south into the Werghal Valley.'

'How do you know this?' Ali's voice said that it was no surprise to him.

Holmes turned. 'The Maréchal told me. He also said that, militarily speaking, the Rifi had little choice.'

'As I said, a wise man. It is true that, as things stand, there appears no alternative. The French border divides families. The brothers of those families must ride to their support. Their manhood demands it.'

'While French authority equally demands that it defend the borders it has been given, even when those borders are nonsensical.'

'Two men alone can stop it, *insh'Allah*.'

'I do see that.' Holmes pushed his shoulder off the glass and walked back to the fire. And you wish me to convince the Resident General of Morocco that he can trust the word of his sworn enemy. That he can place his life and the future of the country in the hands of a man who can only wish him, and all other French, dead.'

'He can, because Mahmoud and I have said so.'

'Two more men he has no reason to believe.'

'If Lyautey trusts you, he will trust us.' Ali glanced up from incising tiny textures into the creature's neck.

Holmes held the other man's eyes. 'The odd thing is, you are probably right.'

'But it must be soon. Abd el-Krim has agreed – in general terms – to be within a day's ride of here on Monday, *insh'Allah.*'

'What, in two days? Impossible!'

'Once the French Christmas is over, troops from Fez will begin to move into the Werghal.'

'How do you know all these– No, don't tell me.' With the number of factions here, spies would be thick on the ground.

'I suggest that Abd el-Krim be permitted two men: Mahmoud and me. And that Lyautey be allowed the same number. One of whom, I hope, will be you, Holmes.'

He blew off the tiny carving, and set it onto the small table: a pony, two inches high, with an arch to its neck that promised mischief. 'There remain two problems,' he added.

Holmes gave a cough of laughter. 'Only two?'

'Primarily two. First, the French mission is permeated with spies. If Abd el-Krim has an ear into the Maréchal's business, it should be assumed that everyone from the Sultan to the Spanish do as well.'

'So the other member of Lyautey's party must be chosen with care. And the second problem?'

'A common tongue. The Emir speaks Spanish and Arabic but little French. I would suspect the reverse is true of Lyautey?'

'There'd be no reason for him to know more than a smattering of Spanish, although he might surprise me. He has taught himself some Arabic, but it is more formal and theoretical than practical.'

'Classical Arabic and that spoken in the Rif are indeed separated by more than miles. What about you? How is your Spanish?'

'Basic. Very basic.'

'For his other man, Lyautey may wish to choose someone fluent in Spanish, to permit mutual translations in any direction. If there is someone he trusts who– You smile. Why do you smile?'

'I may know just the man. Or rather, woman.'

'Wom– No. Miri?' In Palestine, he'd called her *'Amir'* – *Prince* – but evidently she had outgrown the joke.

'Russell, yes. She's fluent in all three languages.'

'But, a woman.'

'Not just any woman.'

'And young.'

'Russell? She's never been young.'

'And Jewish.'

'It didn't get in her way in Palestine. In any event, a feminine presence has been known to disarm male aggression. Unless your man Abd el-Krim is too... traditional to do business with a female?'

'I might ask the same of your Lyautey.'

'I think my cousin would be fascinated at the prospect.'

Ali frowned. 'If Miri were a Moroccan woman, the Emir would not permit it, even though he is a Berber – Berber women do not cover their faces,' he explained. 'But, a foreigner?'

'If Gertrude Bell can sit down with Arabs in Mesopotamia, why not Russell in the Rif?'

Holmes took out his cigarette case, watching with amusement while Ali embarked on his own bout of silent wrestling: the deep and automatic refusal to bring a woman into danger, balanced

118

against the woman herself. When he saw the man's thumb travel across the long, thin scar that Russell's knife had sliced in his arm in 1919, he knew that agreement had been reached.

'Miri may be just the man for the job. But where is she?'

'We have two days to figure that out. As I told you, she was last seen walking into the desert, hand in hand with a young boy who did not speak. By a rather striking coincidence, I was met at the train station coffee house this morning by a young mute boy, who led me through the town to the door of the Dar Mnehbi and ran off.'

At mention of the boy, Ali's face lightened. 'I am glad to hear he is safe. 'The lad is called "Idir". He was found wandering half-naked through one of the early battlefields in 1921, a child of six or seven, it was decided. No one knew what happened to the rest of his family, but he attached himself to some of the camp-followers and made himself useful, and he's been with the Revolt ever since. He has a tongue, but he's never used it, not that anyone has heard. Mahmoud thinks he's older than he looks – and he's certainly bright enough. He learned to read with very little instruction, and he can even write, after a fashion.'

Holmes suspected there was more to the story than Ali was giving, but the man had never been one to reveal any softer side, and taking a mute orphan under his wing would definitely be considered soft.

'He appears to know Fez well. Has he spent time here?'

'Not that I have heard. But the boy does have a remarkable gift for finding his way around even a strange patch of countryside.'

'He's trustworthy?'

Ali shrugged. 'Who else does he have, but us? Mahmoud uses him to run messages from time to time, and couldn't see any reason not to bring him along when he came south.'

'So what have the two of them done with Russell?'

Ali just shook his head.

'What about Mahmoud? Why are you here, and not him?'

'We planned to meet here. My brother left the mountains for Rabat on the thirteenth, as the last Spanish troops retreated from Chaouen. His French is better than mine, so he came here while I stayed with Abd el-Krim, trying to keep him from getting killed, and, during any lulls in fighting, reminding him that a talk with Lyautey was in his best interest. Mahmoud's plan was to find you, and ask that you present the same argument to Lyautey, or if he couldn't find you, to come to Fez himself and speak with the Maréchal.'

'Any idea why he didn't wait for me – or, us?'

'No.'

'Since I doubt that Mahmoud would have sent a child, even one gifted at finding his way, all the way to Erfoud to fetch Russell, we may assume that Mahmoud and Russell left the desert together.'

'And came here to Fez, leaving Idir to watch for you in the café, while my brother went ... where?'

'The boy will know. Certainly, he appeared to

be looking for someone as we came through the medina. What if we go back to the railway café and see if he is there?'

'That's as good an idea as any,' Ali agreed. 'We might also ask the Maréchal if our partners, as you call them, are in custody somewhere in the city.'

Holmes gave a wry smile. 'The gaol hasn't been built that could hold those two for long. What if we–'

But Ali was not to know what Holmes was about to propose, because the older man went still at the sound of another group of arrivals, outside the room. Voices rose from the *dar* courtyard, loud and troubled voices, familiar voices. One in particular–

Holmes dropped his cigarette into the coals and made rapidly for the door. Ali was at his heels.

CHAPTER NINE

On the *dar's* balcony over the courtyard, the two men moved towards the argument that was echoing out of the enclosed corner stairway. In a moment, figures began to appear: a small boy in a dirt-coloured *djellaba;* behind him – being physically pulled up the uneven stone steps by the lad – a slim young person with blue eyes, wearing a similarly rough and grubby *djellaba;* behind the boy and his unwilling charge came Youssef, looking displeased at the invasion.

'–might be better if we were to remain below and wait to be claimed,' the slim young person was saying – in English, oddly enough, and with an attitude of musing aloud rather than conversation. 'Seems to me this poor chap has been very forgiving of our intrusion, and in a moment that soldier will come after us and– Oh, *pardon,*' the voice broke off, switching to French. 'I'm sorry to disturb you gentlemen, truth to tell I'm not sure what I'm doing here. Perhaps one of you could–'

'Russell, don't tell me you've lost your spectacles again!' Before she could notice Ali and give him away with an exclamation, Holmes stepped smartly forward to seize his wife's elbow. 'Come along, you'll find it brighter–' he began to say.

But there followed a series of fast and confusing motions that left the slim young person standing

122

alone and bristling at the top of the steps, the child who'd been at the fore of the procession glued up against one wall, Ali Hazr taking a step back in astonishment, and Holmes sprawled against the iron railings amidst the remains of a vase of flowers.

Youssef looked at the child, saw that he was safe, and fled down the steps for reinforcements.

Holmes gasped for breath. 'Russell, what is wrong with you? You've seen me in a beard before!'

The newcomer's hood had fallen back, revealing what looked less like a turban than a head bandage. From beneath it peeped wisps of yellow hair.

The blue eyes beneath the bandage narrowed, then shot a quick glance at the swarthier man, standing farther down the balcony. Assured that he was not about to attack, the slim figure took a step forward. 'Do you know me, sir?'

The prostrate figure's grey eyes stretched wide; after a moment, he turned his head, to meet the other man's equally alarmed, dark eyes.

Ali Hazr pursed his bearded lips. 'We may have a problem.'

CHAPTER TEN

It was my mute young guide who convinced me that the two strangers were friends – or at least, that they were not my immediate enemies. Once past the first shock that my defensive reaction had caused, the lad trotted past me and took hold of the younger man's hand, holding it and patting it, smiling at me by way of illustration.

My head gave a mighty pound; the resulting sway of my body brought a look of alarm to the face of the man on the floor. I let my fists unclench, and said to him, 'I'm sorry, Monsieur, you startled me. I hope I haven't hurt you.'

He scrambled to his feet, agile for a man with that much grey in his beard. 'Russell, I–'

He broke off at the same instant I leapt around to put the unoccupied stretch of balcony at my back: Soldiers came pounding up the twisting steps, the servant close behind. The man I had thrown across the balcony moved to intercept, holding up a pair of pacifying hands, assuring them that it had been a mistake, that everything was fine, that we – *we!* – were sorry to have alarmed poor Youssef.

The guards took some convincing, but once the older fellow had plucked the flowers from his damp shoulder and run his hands over his head, they lowered their rifles and turned to me.

'This man should never have been permitted

124

entrance,' one of them declared, but before they could question me, or take me into custody, my victim moved between us like a dog separating a sheep from a flock. (Where, I vaguely wondered, had that rural image come from?) He put out his arm, taking care not to make physical contact, gathering me past the soldiers and along the balcony, talking all the while in an almost accent-free French.

'This is a friend, a person Maréchal Lyautey will want to speak with later. We won't disturb the Maréchal just yet, we shall permit my friend here to have a rest and perhaps something to eat. Youssef, might we have another tray of the couscous? And perhaps a large pot of mint tea? Oh yes, and some of your excellent coffee as well would be a good idea.'

Then we were inside a room – the two men, the boy, and me – and he shut the door in the soldiers' faces.

The four of us held our collective breath, waiting for the soldiers to assault the door. Instead, they retreated, growling commands at the servant. I cleared my throat.

'So,' I said. 'That's my name? Russell?'

The older man's face betrayed no reaction, yet I seemed to feel a shudder run through his body. 'Your surname,' he replied. 'Your first name is Mary. You've had a head injury?'

'My skull certainly aches. I haven't dared look.'

'Perhaps that is where we should begin. Would you like to sit before the fire, while I investigate?'

It was odd – odder than any of the long string of peculiarities that had happened since I woke in that small upper room, nearly twenty-four hours before – but despite being an absolute stranger to my eyes, my bones seemed to respond to him. He could be trusted, with my scalp and with my life. I was still utterly lost, and yet I was home.

Tears came to my eyes, and again I swayed. This time, I did not hit out when he gently grasped my arm, but allowed him to lead me to a chair before a most welcome brazier. I sat with my eyes closed, that I could not see the room spinning around me. Deft fingers explored my bandage-turban, locating the end and starting gently to undo it. After several turns, the cloth stuck.

I heard him move around in front of me. I opened my eyes. He slid one hand inside his garments, drawing out a folding knife. He displayed it on his palm. 'I don't have scissors, and I need to cut the cloth.'

'I trust you,' I said. Again, I felt his internal reaction to the statement, but he simply unfolded the knife and returned to my side, pulling at the clotted fabric, sawing gently.

The younger man, who had been standing in place all this time, moved now, gathering up a glass bowl of flowers and carrying it out of the room. When he came back, the flowers had been replaced by a face-cloth and the bowl's water was steaming.

He set it onto a large, centuries-old inlaid trunk pushed against the wall near my knee, and took the other chair. I felt his eyes on me, dark and disapproving but not without a degree of concern. The mute boy had found a small wooden

126

toy on the trunk, and had taken it over to the table, where he was now picking over a tray of cold food.

'I'll have to cut some of your hair,' said the man at my side.

'That may be the least of my worries,' I told him, and winced at the tug on whatever injury lay beneath.

The water in the bowl was red-brown when he lifted the final pieces of fabric away. His fingers parted the remaining hair, then stopped moving.

'What do you see?' I asked, imagining some gaping bits of bone that had been revealed.

'This has been treated. Someone put in stitches. The wound itself is healing.'

Well, that was something, anyway.

'You don't remember who nursed you?'

'I woke in a room, somewhere in the *suq*. Or, medina. Soldiers came, so I left.'

He started to ask something, then stopped. 'When you are clean, fed, and rested, we can talk about what you remember and what you do not.'

But the other man had waited long enough. 'What of Mahmoud?' he demanded – and I realised that we were speaking English, although he appeared Moroccan.

'An injury like this only becomes more intractable under pressure,' the older man warned. 'Let her rest, the memories will slip back.'

The swarthy fellow did not like it, but I found the words immensely reassuring. This damnable fog I was moving through was an injury, and it would heal. *Hold that to yourself, Russell.* Yes, that was my name: progress! 'I should very much like to bath,' I agreed.

'Shall I–' the older man began, then immediately caught himself. 'No, probably not.'

'What were you about to ask?'

'I was going to suggest that I might help you clean your hair, since it would not be a good idea to get too much soap and water in that wound, but I doubt in your current state you would care for that.'

'I should think not,' I said with indignation, then paused. 'Er, were I not in my current state, would I permit your assistance in the bath?'

'It has been known. Russell, I am your husband.'

The room was very still. Even the boy, who had followed none of this, glanced up from his snack. 'Well. So you say. Perhaps I ought to ask your name?'

'Sherlock Holmes. You call me Holmes.'

The name had a distinct ring of familiarity to it, and I tipped my head as if it might encourage my scattered thoughts to roll back into place. But no, if anything the name sounded like a story, and I'd had enough of unreality for a while. I looked at the other man.

'Ali Hazr,' he said. Recognition seemed to be expected, but at least he did not claim to be my brother, or a second husband. I looked more closely, confirming that the man's slight lisp was caused by a pair of missing front teeth – but what is normally a humorous, even endearing speech flaw had in this man a sinister air. One's mind lingered on the blow that had caused it.

'Mr Hazr, Mr – er, Holmes. I should appreciate

128

the use of your bath. Although I believe I shall make do without your assistance, for the present.'

'It is the first room to your right. Latch the door, if it makes you feel better,' he said. 'I'll have Youssef leave a change of clothing for you, and one of the female staff can help cleanse your hair once you're dressed. Or I can. Oh, and I found these in your – you left these behind.'

He crossed the room and came back with an object in each hand. The first was a passport, very battered. I glanced at the pages, tracing what appeared to be my travels: a lot of borders crossed in the past twelve months. The other was a small object, pinched between his thumb and forefinger. I stretched out my palm and drew back a ring, gold like the other. This one was a wedding band.

It breathed out familiarity, as the stone in my pocket and the writing on the scrap of onionskin had. Which could mean everything, or nothing at all.

I thanked him and was moving towards the door, then stopped when I noticed a subtle design etched into the ring's surface: a pattern of fine, interwoven hexagons circling the ring. Almost like a honeycomb.

Bees, yet again. The persistent hallucinatory odour of honey. The hive images that had kept coming to me in the medina. And when I looked up into the grey eyes, I realised that I did, in fact, know him: The face before me had appeared in a brief flash the previous day, surrounded by fog. 'Are you by any chance a beekeeper, sir?'

'I am. Among other things.'

I nodded, and slipped the ring onto my finger. It fit perfectly. I knew it would.

The hot water was utter Paradise. I scrubbed my filthy skin, nose to toe, even managing to get at the undamaged side of my head. Then I filled the large porcelain tub a second time, with water that was considerably cooler, and sank in it to my chin, safe behind the locked door.

For ten delicious minutes, I lay without thought or concern. I was aware of voices and movement outside, aware even of anger there, but that was another world, and I did not care.

Since the clipaclop of donkey's hooves had wakened me in the brass-maker's shop, snips and flashes of my past had come to me at odd moments. I had the clear memory of a room, for example, crowded with furniture, presided over by a stern white-haired lady who smelt of lavender. And the ocean – I remembered sitting on a cliff over the ocean, looking across at a distant smudge of land, ships in between.

And beehives, redolent with the summer-smell of honey.

All in all, I felt distinctly more real, now that I had a body and not simply multiple layers of rough drapes. I raised my arm from the water, trying to read my skin's history.

The hands were brown, but above the elbows, I was pale, suggesting that I had spent some weeks in the sun, dressed in short sleeves and without the ring. There were many old scars, including what could only be a bullet hole in my right shoulder, but the more recent injuries were mostly contusions. Multiple bruises explained the tenderness I felt in my right hip and shoulder, my left knee, both elbows – all over, really. They were mostly the same degree of black, indicating that whatever herd of bison had run me down, it had been about two days before.

The day before I woke up.

A different kind of pain came from the back of my left biceps, which I craned to see: a neat slice, sharp but not deep, about three inches long.

Again came the disquieting sensation of a knife in my hand, and I shivered in the cooling water. I could sense the knowledge of what those bruises meant, what that slice came from, resting just at the edges of my mind.

It was reassuring, really, if still maddening. When the man who claimed to be my husband (he did not look like someone who fit the word *husband*) said my name, faint reverberations had gone down my spine, stirring – not so much memories as the shadow of memories. As if I were outside of a library (libraries – those I remembered!) anticipating the treasures within.

I considered the taps, and decided that I had soaked enough. I splashed my face again, tugged out the stopper, and heaved my aches out of the French-manufactured porcelain.

As I moved towards the towels, my eye caught on the strange person in the elaborate brass-rimmed looking-glass. She had my blue eyes, my lanky build, but what happened to my hair? I lifted a hand to the blonde crop, and was brushed by another odd sense of dissonance: My eyes did not know the short hair, but my hand seemed to.

131

I took a face flannel and worked at the matted locks around the wound, and at the end of it I had clean hair and a tentative acceptance of the woman in the glass. Mary Russell.

With a towel wrapped securely around me, I snaked one arm out the door to draw in a stack of garments. They were, as before, those of a Moroccan man, but a richer fabric, tawny brown with dark chocolate trim. The slice on my biceps had opened in the bath, but the ooze was not serious, so I just wrapped a hand-towel around my upper arm before I dressed. I took a final glance in the looking-glass, grateful that the bruising seemed to have by-passed my face, then ran my fingers up the ridge of my nose.

At the reminder, I squatted by my discarded garments, emptying the pockets.

The match-box and fruit I dropped into the waste-bin. The knife and its makeshift sheath I strapped back on my arm. The spectacles needed repairs lest that shaky and irreplaceable right lens drop to the tile floor, so I pushed them into a pocket along with the mysterious ring, the crimson note-book, and the rest of my worldly goods. Then with a deep breath (*husband?*) I went down the balcony to the first room.

Three sets of eyes met me.

'May I ask for another moment of your nursing skills?' I asked Mr Holmes. 'Just a small plaster – I'd do it myself, but it's awkwardly placed, and I hate to get any blood on this nice robe.'

By answer, he picked up the roll of gauze. When I had wrestled my arm out of the garment and pulled away the stained hand-towel, he gazed at my arm in silence.

'You have been in a knife-fight.'

'I've been in a lot more than that,' I replied. 'My epidermis appears to have been bounced down a rocky hillside.'

His hands slowly resumed their motion, wrapping a neat bandage around my arm. As I stood there, feeling his unexpectedly strong fingers at work, my attention was drawn by the laden tray on the table; my stomach rumbled. To distract myself, I asked where, and what, this place was.

'This is the guard-room and guest quarters attached to Dar Mnehbi, the headquarters of the French Resident General, in the Fez medina. Dar Mnehbi is where Maréchal Lyautey holds meetings, houses the occasional guest, and keeps his finger on the pulse of the city – and thus, the country.'

'He doesn't live here?' Passing through the ornate building next door, it had seemed small to me, and decidedly non-European.

'The Maréchal and Madame have quarters in a larger palace a quarter mile away. He keeps rooms here, to use when he has been working late. Which seems to be most nights.'

That explained the formality of the main portion and the more cramped quarters we had veered into before coming up the steps. It also explained the new-looking European elements, such as external windows and internal doorways.

The man – *Holmes* – finished binding me up, gesturing at the table.

I hesitated no more, but applied myself with enthusiasm.

Holmes poured out some of the sweet mint tea, setting the gold-rimmed Venetian glass by my plate. 'Have you lost your spectacles, Russell?'

By way of answer, as my mouth was otherwise occupied, I dug a hand into my pocket and dumped the resulting fistful of my earthly possessions onto the table. 'Broken,' I managed indistinctly. He stared down at the tumble of objects; the boy looked at the pile, too, his eyes for some reason going wide; but it was the other man's reaction that had my chair flying over and me scrambling backwards with the stolen dagger in my hand.

Hazr had been at the window with a glass of the tea, looking down at the city. He glanced around at the sound of metal hitting wood, and then he was in urgent motion, leaping across the room to snatch at – not the damaged spectacles, but the heavy gold signet ring caught up in the earpiece. He shook the spectacles free, sending the loose lens skittering down the table, and thrust the ring towards me.

'Where is he? Where is Mahmoud?'

'I don't know!' He stared, breathing heavily, and now I saw that he was not angry – or, not just angry. He was afraid. 'Who is this Mahmoud? What does he look like?'

'Like me. Shorter, heavier. He has a scar on his face.'

A peculiar sensation, like a mental tickle, passed through my thoughts. 'Scar?'

'Not as dramatic as that of Captain De la Rocha,' said Holmes.

'Who is– Oh, never mind, I don't know either

of them. And I'm very sorry, but I don't know why I have that ring or where it came from.'

Hazr looked near to exploding, an expression that made his face slightly more familiar.

'I am sorry, Mr Hazr. If I knew, I would tell you.'

'Ali,' Holmes said, 'let her finish her meal. Shouting won't bring her memory back any faster.'

I pulled my attention away from the angry man at last, and met the other man's eyes. They were intriguing eyes, grey and calm and sure and very, very intelligent.

I hoped to God this man actually was a friend. If he was my enemy, I was in grave trouble.

CHAPTER ELEVEN

Food helped.

So did having this Hazr fellow's furious gaze turned away from me. He watched me put away the weapon and gingerly reclaim my chair and plate, then lowered his attention on the boy.

Interviewing someone who lacks speech is a slow business, particularly when the mute person is only vaguely literate. Granted, it kept Ali's attention occupied while I put away the meal, but it did not make him any less irritable. His questions were put in a combination of Arabic and the language I had heard in the medina. The boys answers took the form of nods, negative shakes, waves of the hand, and the occasional laborious scripting of answers. Which, since the only alphabet he knew was Arabic even if the words were in the other tongue, caused Ali a great deal of puzzling.

Trying to follow their conversation brought my headache back, so I closed my ears as best I could, and concentrated on the sensation of being clean, warm, and fed.

And, apparently, safe, for at some point, I closed my eyes, to be startled back into the room by the closing of a door.

The boy was gone, the nearby sound of running water explaining his absence.

Ali sat, tugging at his beard as he studied the

boy's scratches on the page. The robe he wore, I thought, was subtly different from those I had seen in the medina – rather, the robe itself was the same, but the way he wore it was not. On other Moroccans, the *djellaba* was a shapeless hooded garment that opened far down the sternum, like a large feed sack with a hood stitched on. When the men sat, one side or the other tended to fall off the shoulders entirely, revealing the shirt beneath. Ali's, on the other hand, was pulled neatly to his collar line. The turban he wore – snug and high on the head, in the Moroccan fashion, but lacking the common plait – was a darker shade of the rich *café au lait* colour of his robe. The shirt beneath it was crisp white.

The man was a dandy.

'Idir and Mahmoud arrived in Rabat after two nights on the road,' he told me, 'which, as you say, puts it on Monday, in the afternoon. They'd spent Sunday night in Fez, then took the train to Rabat, where they went to the hotel where Mycroft had said you would be.'

I'd been listening with interest to his accent – upper-class central English with long years of Middle Eastern Arabic laid over it – but now I interrupted. 'Would you be so good as to tell me who all these people are.

The two men exchanged another glance; I was beginning to grow tired of that look.

'He is Idir.' Ali gestured with his thumb at the adjoining room. 'Mahmoud is my brother. By blood a cousin, but we are as brothers.'

'And Mycroft?'

Holmes stirred. 'Mycroft is *my* brother. He is

head of a ... an Intelligence wing of the British government.'

'What – you two are *spies?*'

The sharp hiss Ali made was accompanied by a slice of the hand, telling me I had said the word too loudly. Was he concerned about ears from the balcony, or from the bath-room?

'Look,' I said, 'maybe I should just sleep for a while and leave you to your plans.'

Ali looked ready to agree, but Holmes did not. 'They are your plans, too, Russell.'

'Then God help you,' I said.

'Bismillah,' Ali muttered, as an echo.

'You were saying?' Holmes asked him.

'Yes. They went to the hotel in Rabat and found you both missing. Mahmoud asked for paper to write something, leaving it with the man at the desk. Then they went back to the station – Idir is very fond of trains – and took a train. Where to, I don't know, but when they got off, they got into a motorcar and drove through a lot of mountains and desert.'

'Someone was waiting for them with a motor?

'No. It would appear that Mahmoud ... com-mandeered a motor.'

Spies and motorcar thieves. Good companions for a pick-pocketing tight-rope walker like me.

'They drove until dark. Then, after a village, they left the motor and walked for a time into the dunes. Mahmoud gave the lad instructions on how to locate you among the moving picture crew, and gave Idir a note to hand to you. And he gave the lad his ring, by way of proof.'

'Mahmoud did not want to approach the en-

campment himself because of the guards?'
Holmes asked.

'Perhaps. In any gathering of foreigners, there
are children all over, but a man would be stopped
and questioned.'

Not a circus: a moving picture encampment.
Although I imagined the distinction to be a small
one.

'Does Idir know what the note said? Holmes
asked.

'No, he couldn't read it, but it must have told
her simply to come, because she took him inside
just long enough to put on her shoes and coat.
Later, after she and Mahmoud talked, she
returned to the tent to get some things and leave
a note.'

'And the ring?'

'She returned it to Mahmoud. The boy is clear
on that. When she came back, all three of them
set off the way he and Mahmoud had come, by
foot, then motor, and then train, arriving in Fez
on Thursday.'

'That's, what, 250 miles? More? Quite a lot of
rough road to cover, for one driver.'

'Miri drove part of the time. Idir was quite
impressed with her driving.'

'I can imagine,' Holmes said drily. 'Where did
they go, when they got to Fez?'

'They took beds in a small *funduq* – that's the
local *caravanserai* – near the city walls. They had
coffee, and Mahmoud gave Idir enough money
to gorge himself on sweets, and then Mahmoud
and Idir went to the *hammam* – Idir likes baths,
as you can hear.'

'Unusual child,' I remarked.

'He's lived his whole life among soldiers. He may never have seen a private bath before today – most people use the *hammam*. The bath house,' he added for my benefit, although I knew the word.

Holmes was growing impatient with the side remarks. 'So, the three of them took lodgings in Fez, and Russell was forced to forgo a bath lest she reveal her gender. What next?'

'Mahmoud and Idir went into the medina, and bought clothing for Miri – what she brought was incomplete enough to attract attention. Mahmoud sent the clothes back to the funduq with the boy, saying he had some business in the town. Idir does not know where Mahmoud went, but he came back after a couple of hours, and they all went out for a meal. The two of them talked a great deal, although the only word Idir understood was *aeroplane*.'

I twitched at the word: What sounded like a truly unspeakable motoring experience left me with no reaction at all, but the idea of flying carried with it a load of discomfort and a stir of cold terror. Ali did not notice.

'When they returned to the *funduq* at dusk, there was a message. Later that night, Mahmoud and Miri left. He ordered Idir to stay behind. Naturally, the boy followed. But once they left the medina – through Bab Guissa, at the north – he was forced to lag behind, since even at night the ground is too exposed to follow unseen.'

'But he is certain that Mahmoud and Russell were together when they left the city?' Holmes asked.

Ali made a face. 'He would like to be certain. He swears it was so. But he would have me believe that he never took his eyes off Mahmoud, that my brother's disappearance is not his fault. So ... I would say that chances are about equal that Mahmoud was with Miri, or that Miri left the city alone – possibly with a man of a similar build to Mahmoud.

'Once the pair left the city to climb the hill out of town, the boy admits that he does not know what happened, since as I said, he was far behind them, and the night was dark. All he knows is that there was shouting, and a single gunshot, and he was running up the hill with a stick when a motor-car's engine roared, and nearly ran him down.

'When he got to where the motor had been, he found Miri, trying to crawl up from the hillside below the road. A cart-man with a lamp was standing over her, and Idir beat at him with the stick until the man took it away and cuffed him. When he then climbed down the hill to help Miri, Idir realised that he was not one of those from the motorcar. I should imagine, in fact, that the man just happened to be coming along the road when the assailants saw him and fled, taking Mahmoud but leaving Miri.

'Her head was bleeding and she was babbling, but Idir knew Mahmoud would want him to help her, so he didn't run after the motor. Instead, he spotted her knife and revolver and put them into her boot and pocket, then helped the man get her onto the cart, and kept her steady as they went downhill. Only at the bottom did the boy decide that Mahmoud might also be lying off the road

141

rather than in the motorcar, so he jumped off and ran up the hill again. The cart-man shouted, to ask where Miri lived, but since Idir couldn't answer him anyway, he just kept running. He did, I should say, look back to make sure the man didn't just abandon you on the side of the road.

'He didn't find Mahmoud. I'm not sure where he spent the night – possibly among the tombs – but the next morning he searched the ground carefully, and found nothing.

'He returned to the *funduq*, hoping to find Mahmoud, but the owner said that some bad men were looking for him, so he did not stay.

'He spent the afternoon searching the medina, then decided that Mahmoud's absence did not change the task he had been given: namely, to meet a tall, thin foreigner drinking coffee at the café nearest the train station, either first thing in the morning or last thing at night, and deliver him to Dar Mnehbi. So he went to the station, and waited there until it shut for the night.

'Again, he wouldn't say where he slept, probably in a doorway, but this morning he alternated between the café and the medina until he found you, Holmes. Once he'd brought you here, he went for another look in the medina and discovered Miri as well. The lad feels quite proud of himself. He intended to go back out and look for Mahmoud, until I convinced him the task was now our responsibility.'

As Ali talked, I had progressed from wolfing food from the tray to a leisurely sampling of the crumbs. As at a signal, both men turned to look at me.

I straightened. 'You believe all that?'

'I see no reason to discount the lad's testimony,' Holmes answered.

'No reason apart from his age, his inability to communicate, and his wish to please adults, you mean?' To say nothing of the boy's face: Never trust a look of innocence.

I was doubly dubious about this information, since Ali was the only one who claimed to make sense of the boy's scratchings, and what was Ali to me?

'In any event, I don't remember. All I know is that I woke yesterday morning in an upstairs room, which I left when soldiers came.'

But it was time for detail. Holmes led me through my last twenty-four hours, from waking in the dim, whitewashed room to being dragged through the doors of Dar Mnehbi. He was gentle, but thorough. Ali said nothing the entire time. He sat, down the table from me. After a minute, he stretched to retrieve the wayward spectacles lens, then its frame. I eyed the big knife he drew out, but he did not look up, merely applying its scalpel-thin point to the tiny screw as the first in a series of precise adjustments to the wonky steel.

'I had ... there was blood on my hands. Dried blood. Quite a bit.'

Ali's fingers faltered, then resumed.

'Tell me again about the two people who came onto the rooftop, after the soldiers had gone,' Holmes ordered.

My headache had returned, with a vengeance. I wanted to find a heap of something very soft, lower my skull onto it, and leave it there for a

143

long, long time.

'A man and a woman. They looked Moroccan. At any rate, they were wearing Moroccan dress.'

'Tell me your impression of the pair. Married couple? The house's owners? Servants?'

'How should I know? Servants. Maybe. My head feels as if there is a red-hot poker through it.'

'Was the woman wearing a head-covering?'

'Of course. No.' I considered, head in hands. 'They didn't match.'

'How do you mean?'

'I mean they were together, but not intimates. And she was in charge. That seems unlikely, doesn't it? They were consulting. Her skin was lighter than his. She ... she was older.'

'As if he was her long-time employee?'

I raised my head to meet his eyes. 'Exactly.'

He smiled, and for the first time, I *knew* his face. Not his history or who he was to me – but that he was a part of me, I no longer doubted. I came near to weeping, at the relief of having a companion in this lost world.

His expression shifted, to one of concern. 'You must sleep.'

I did not exactly require his help to stand, but I did permit it. He led me to the adjoining room, which held a pair of beds. He even pulled back the bed-clothes for me. 'There is a lock, if you wish, although following a concussion, a locked door may not be the best of ideas. You will be safe here.'

When he had left me, I looked at the key in the door, then poured myself onto the soft mattress, where I stayed until the sun had left the sky.

CHAPTER TWELVE

The sound of men's voices slowly wormed its way into sleep's cocoon. I felt my breathing change. I could smell bread baking, somewhere near. And coffee.

As if in response, my body turned onto its back for a hard stretch. The odours suggested morning, but it felt more like night. I raised my head to blink at the dimly lit room: A lamp was burning low; brighter light came from around the doorway, but not from the window.

I threw back the coverings, then remembered the dangers of motion. More cautiously, I sat upright on the side of the bed, but my head's pain had changed, to a localised ache over the right ear; the previous day's terrible throb of pressure did not come with the change in elevation. My fingers made gentle exploration of the tender spot, feeling the stiff thread of the stitches and the dried scab, but no fresh blood.

You may survive, Russell, I thought.

Russell: yes. It was what Holmes called me – and with his name, several large pieces of myself came tumbling into place.

Mary Judith Russell, child – orphaned child – of a Boston Brahmin and a rabbi's daughter. Apprentice-turned-partner of one Sherlock Holmes, survivor of motorcar smashes, bullets, knife-fights, and furious theological debates.

Mycroft Holmes was now a person, the source of countless intricate machinations on the stage of international politics. I could even recall the outlines of Ali Hazr, if not the specifics – he seemed to inhabit the hazier edges of what I knew.

But I remembered his brother, Mahmoud, a man I'd once compared to an amused stone. Solid and dark beside Ali's colour and energy, Mahmoud Hazr had taken us into their small band, forced me to learn the ways of the desert, led me to the beauty of the Qur'an. We had fought side by side. Together, we had rescued Holmes from a terrible death. The four of us had saved a nation from catastrophe.

Perhaps it was the aroma coming in from the other room that brought me a vivid image of Mahmoud's hand dribbling a fistful of green coffee beans into a shallow roasting pan; the regular twitch of his wrist to keep them turning; the graceful motion as he poured the oily black mass of beans into the mortar for grinding.

The humour, deep within his all-seeing eyes. The powerful effect of his approval on me.

But that had been Palestine – an earlier waking with blood on my hands – and confusion in my mind, come to think of it – in an attic room with a sloping roof. For some reason, Mahmoud had come to Morocco. And he was now missing.

Apart from the phenomenon that I seemed to have married my teacher, I wondered what else I was supposed to know. Morocco itself was lost in the haze, although the impression of boats near a lighthouse seemed recent – *feluccas*, they were called, with high pointed sails. I had no more idea

146

what I was doing here than I'd had the previous day, and the concept of an encampment of moving picture persons was still just as incomprehensible.

However, the thawing of one portion of my frozen past came as a huge relief. More would come, I told myself: patience.

Someone had been in the room while I slept. The lamp was burning and my spectacles lay neatly folded on the bed-side table. I picked them up, finding them as straight and true as ever they had been. My scalp gave a sharp protest as the earpiece passed over its tender portion, then subsided. Experimentally, I got to my feet, and aimed myself at the door.

Everything worked. And despite a hard wince at the brighter lights in the sitting room, the headache stayed away.

The room now held three men and the boy. The stranger shot to his feet, a tall, pale-eyed gentleman as straight and flexible as a tree, whose age showed only in his close-cropped white hair and greying moustache that tapered to sharp points. The other two men looked at each other, then rose as well. The boy, who had been drawing on a paper, gaped in puzzlement.

Holmes spoke up, in French. 'Russell, this is Maréchal Lyautey, Morocco's Resident General and currently your host. Cousin Hubert, my wife, Mary Russell.'

'Good evening.' I held out my hand.

'*Enchanté, Madame,*' Lyautey said, bending over the fingers with a military bow.

The near-kiss startled a laugh out of me. 'The formality of generals! Your British counterpart in

Jerusalem did just that – and when I was dressed in similar clothing.'

Ali made an exclamation. Holmes said, 'You remember!'

'Not all, but pieces. May I apologise for tossing you over my head, Holmes?'

'You are welcome to throw me about anytime you have amnesia, Russell. Take a seat. The Maréchal was inviting us for dinner, but I expect that you will claim you lack the proper clothing.'

'I even lack the proper men's clothing,' I noted, looking down at the garments Holmes had found for me – less rough than the first set I had ruined, but not what a lady, or indeed a gentleman, would wear to dine with Morocco's Resident General.

'Unfortunately,' Lyautey said, 'I have other guests tonight in the Residency – a family of tedious Americans, I regret to say – or I would join you *en déshabillé* here over a tray. Consider yourself fortunate that you have escaped my obligation. I shall attempt to excuse myself early, and rejoin you. If nothing else, Madame, I look forward to meeting you properly, before my cousin spirits you away.'

With a click of his heels, he was gone. I turned to Holmes. 'Cousin?'

'Oddly enough, yes.'

'Have I met him before?'

'You have not.'

At least there was something for which my delinquent brain was not responsible.

Holmes poured me a glass of tea from the pot warming before the brazier. 'How much has returned?'

'I seem to remember everything about some things. Although, how would I know if I did not? Various years of childhood seem to be there, sailing to England after my family was killed, moving to Sussex. I distinctly recall meeting you. And spending some weeks in Palestine, with Ali and Mahmoud.'

Ali was sitting near the warmth. After Lyautey left, he had pulled out the wicked blade with which he fixed my spectacles, and started to whittle on a chunk of wood. The boy sat at his feet, watching the process closely. Now Ali snorted. 'Amnesia! We seem to have entered an Ethel Dell novel.'

'You don't believe me?' I demanded.

Holmes said, 'You must admit, Russell, amnesia is more commonly found in fiction than it is in real life. And to have you of all people living out a lady's—'

'Damn it, Holmes, there's nothing funny about this!'

'Now, *that* sounded more like Miri,' Ali remarked. A perfect curl of pale wood dropped into the boy's outstretched hand.

'Indeed it did,' Holmes agreed.

'Irritability is one symptom of concussion.'

'And, I should think, a natural consequence,' I said.

'Irritation would also appear to act as an *aide-mémoire*,' Ali noted.

'Perhaps we merely need to keep her irritated?'

'I wouldn't recommend it,' I growled.

'Perhaps not,' Holmes agreed. 'How far does your memory go? Do you remember seeing Ali and Mahmoud in England a year ago? At Justice Hall? The Hughenfort family?'

I slowly shook my head. 'There's a sort of an echo, like ... like a tuning fork under a blanket. But not active memory. And what's there is not continuous. There was... Someone came to our house.'

'Ali.'

'No, a woman. We'd met her in Palestine, at a dig.'

'Dorothy Ruskin.'

'Right! She came to visit, and she brought me, what was it? A box, a little decorative box. When was that?'

'Seventeen months ago.'

I stared at him. 'A year and a *half* ago? I've lost a year and a half?'

'In the last ten hours you regained twenty-two and a half years, Russell. I shouldn't give up on the remainder yet.'

He was right, I knew he was. And yet, I'd have sworn that I'd only met Miss Ruskin a few days before.

I shivered, and hastened to swallow some of the tea.

'The Maréchal did not send soldiers into the medina on Friday,' Holmes said. 'He is making enquiries into who might have done so, but as soldiers are often used to supplement the local police – it is his policy not to inflict a French *gendarmerie* on a colony – the answer may take some time. However, I did find the place where you woke up.'

'Really? How clever of you. Where was it?'

'More to the point is *what* it was. When you

described the two people as being familiar, yet not intimate, as if he was her long-time employee, I knew it was unlikely to be a traditional Moroccan household. And when I considered that you were, as the boy told Ali, "babbling", you might well have been doing so in English. Assuming your rescuer recognised the tongue, where would an injured English speaker be taken, but to an English nurse in the medina?'

'Is there such a thing?'

'There is. And you were. To Miss Peg Taylor, who is as much missionary as nurse – the sort of missionary who serves rather than self-serves. When I spoke with Miss Taylor this afternoon, she was relieved to hear that you were well. Oh, and she sent a few things you left behind. These, for one.' Holmes reached under his chair and pulled out a pair of much-abused boots. They were mine – I'd had them made in London, what felt like a few months before – but it was as if a friend had aged a decade overnight: mismatched laces, worn toes, one of the metal grommets missing, the brass lace-hooks at the tops worn thin. I slipped my fingers inside the top, and smiled as I drew the throwing knife from its hidden sheath.

Not enemies, then.

'Did Miss Taylor also give you a revolver?'

'It's in the desk drawer, over there. You remember having it?'

'Not really. My hand did.'

My fingers wrapped around the familiar steel, searching for memories. After a moment, my eyes went to Ali's arm. He shook back the sleeve on his right wrist: This knife had sliced that scar. By accident, of course.

'Was there blood on the knife?'

'There was blood all over your upper garments, but she couldn't tell if it was yours or someone else's. She had a message, at about half past ten on Thursday night, that she was needed at the nearest gate. There she found a farmer with you on his cart. She claims he was a stranger, although I don't know that I believe her, but in any event, he helped transport you to her door. When she had stitched your head and cleaned you up, she put you to bed, and she or one of her servants checked on you every hour. Later on Friday morning, when your condition seemed to be improving, she sent a message to the authorities.'

'Which authorities?'

'Unfortunately, her message went both to the Fasi police and to Dar Mnehbi. Hence the difficulty in finding who sent soldiers. I will say, it is fortunate the lady decided not to notify them immediately you arrived on her doorstep. Had they come to your rescue then and there, it might have killed you.'

To my rescue? I wondered. Or to take me for interrogation?

'Thank you, Nurse Taylor.'

'She salvaged everything from your pockets – and, since you came to her wearing a boy's tunic, she felt she ought to duplicate it. Excepting, of course, the bloodstains.'

'Could she describe them? The stains?'

My question brought a quick smile of approval, as if he'd been concerned that my brains were scrambled into utter uselessness. 'There was blood on the right shoulder from your head wound, and on the left sleeve from shoulder to wrist. Also on the knife.'

I was left-handed. Some of the latter had come from the slice in my arm, but again I was visited by the queasy sensation of knife parting flesh. I pushed it away: no reason to believe I'd killed a man. And in any event, it was self-defence. Had to have been. 'That suggests that I used it. And put it away afterwards. Any other stains?'

'Various spatters in the front, she could not be certain where. And some on your boots, which was why they'd taken them away for cleaning. The garments were also damaged: the slice at your left arm, a large tear at the right hip, a number of smaller rips, and a great deal of dirt. The sort of damage that might be expected from someone rolling down a hillside. Unfortunately, the tunic and *djellaba* had already been given to the rag-pickers. I told her I would pay for their return, but I don't have much hope.'

'So, the boy's story holds up to an extent. At least we can be relatively certain that at some point on Thursday I became separated from Mahmoud, got into a fight where I used my knife against another knife, and I was hit in the head – possibly all at the same time. Were there any–'

'–reports of such a battle? Yes. At sundown, three men were caught attempting to sabotage the aeroplanes. One soldier was killed, two injured – and before you ask, yes, one with a knife. One of the intruders was killed – not,' he hastened to say, 'a man with a scar on his face. The

153

other two escaped into the night. A soldier thought he might have hit one of the intruders with a bullet.'

At least I hadn't killed a soldier with that knife-thrust.

Ali spoke up, frowning at the tip of his blade as it worked some fine detail into the wooden object, which was so tiny, it was hidden by his fingers. 'I went to all the city's hospitals and surgeries. And the morgues. My brother is not there.'

'The military base,' Holmes told me, 'is to the south of the city. You left and returned through the northern gate.'

'There was also confirmation from the *funduq*,' Ali said. 'The three of you came in Thursday afternoon. The boy and the bearded man left. The boy returned after a time with a bundle, then left again. Later in the afternoon, he and the man came back and you all three went out. While you were away – according to Idir's story, taking a meal in the medina – a man the owner did not know came with a message, to be given on your return. You left after dark, the boy following behind, and did not return that night. The next morning, two rough men came asking for you. The *funduq* owner did not know them, and when he refused to turn over to them the possessions you had left behind, one of them hit him. The other man stopped the beating before it could go too far, and they left. When Idir arrived, looking for you or Mahmoud, the owner told him to leave over the back wall, and not to return.'

He sat back at last, sliding his blade into the decorated scabbard he wore, and held the figure out to the boy. When it sat upon a flattened palm, I could see it was a cat, less than an inch tall.

'What did he say about these "rough men"?' Holmes asked.

'They were not from here. He thought, from the way they spoke, that they were Jibali.'

'What is that?' I asked.

'The Jebala is the north-western part of the Spanish Protectorate. The Rif is the eastern portion.'

'The Spanish Protectorate? What about—' But Holmes overrode my quest for knowledge.

'Raisuli's?' he asked Ali.

'Not all Jibali follow Raisuli.'

'Still, he's popping up rather too often to ignore.'

'Who— Oh, never mind,' I muttered.

A knock came at the door, and the man Youssef entered with dinner trays. He supervised a trio of lesser minions, correcting one as to the placement of a spoon, another in the distribution of glasses.

He lingered behind Idir, who looked up, saw the servant, and held out the tiny wooden cat to show him. Youssef gave the lad a fond smile, then asked, 'Would you prefer for the boy to eat in the kitchen?'

'He's fine with us,' Ali said.

'Very well. *Bon appétit, Messieurs,*' he said, reaching out to ruffle Idir's head as he went past. I watched him warily, lest the dignified retainer decide that my head was that of a lad requiring ruffling as well, but he only swept past, and closed the door silently.

It was reassuring to know that my male disguise

155

would fool a Moroccan.

Talk of gunshots and morgues was suspended while we ate, and we had just settled to our syrupy tea when Lyautey returned – he must have rushed his Americans through their main course and abandoned dessert entirely.

He rubbed his hands as he took the empty chair before the brazier, and accepted a glass of tea from Holmes. 'Now, my good Sirs and Madame, you will tell me again why you propose to deliver my neck into the hands of this ruffian in the hills, M. Abd el-Krim.'

CHAPTER THIRTEEN

As the conversation went on, my interest in this French officer grew. A direct gaze and a subtle mind were a rare but valuable combination, and his manly openness and well-concealed suggestion of humour were remarkably suited for his current situation. He might prove a little fastidious for some of the acts required of a Resident General, but he had been a military man long enough to suppress his distaste. And one assumed that he had in his service men more gifted than he at the arts of deviousness.

Lyautey agreed in theory that parley was a good idea; he was less easily convinced that to place the high commander out of reach of his soldiers would be to Morocco's best interest.

Interestingly enough, it was Ali he listened to. Ali spoke his language – not Arabic, of which Lyautey's was more literary than practical – but the language of soldiers, of troops and politics, of valour and responsibility.

In effect, Ali attempted to paint a picture of the Rifi leader, Abd el-Krim, that would speak to a cavalry Maréchal and Resident General of the French presence in Morocco. He began by describing the man's background and attitudes, but Lyautey soon had him giving detailed accounts of actual battles.

Holmes smoked pipe after pipe. Ali drank many

cups of black coffee, replenished by visits from the silent Youssef. Lyautey sat straight-backed and listened closely, interrupting from time to time with a request for some detail or other.

Some of the vocabulary the two men used was too technical for my French.

'The partner with whom I came,' Ali was saying, 'could give you that information, when he returns.'

'When will that be?'

Ali's eyes went sideways, to Holmes, who sat abruptly forward, pipe forgotten in his hands. 'I don't suppose he's been here already?' he asked the Frenchman. 'A stocky man of average height, black hair and dark eyes, a scar down the side of his face.'

Lyautey listened to this vague description with no sign of recognition, until Holmes got to the scar.

'Oh yes. Monsieur Hassan. He was here on Thursday.'

The sleepiness that had been taking over my body vanished; Ali snapped upright in his chair. All three of us started to speak, but Holmes' voice came out on top.

'–the details of the meeting?'

'Intriguing fellow. He came here, without an appointment, just after mid-day, I think it was. That's right, my secretary was attending a luncheon and Youssef brought the man's card in. Mohammed Hassan, Moroccan of course, but with excellent French. Wanted to talk about setting up schools.'

'Schools?' Holmes said.

'Yes, that's where we started, though we ended

up speaking about any number of things, from the education of Moslem women to Arabic poetry to my time in Algeria. A curious conversation, all in all. He seemed quite learned and was interested in what we were doing here, how he might help. We talked for over an hour, before Youssef interrupted to remind me of an appointment at the palace.'

Ali was frowning, either in concentration or in befuddlement. 'How did he seem, when he left you?'

'Seem? Well, yes, that was odd. I had the impression that something we had been saying touched on some preoccupation of his. He was most thoughtful when he left.'

'What had you been talking about?

'As I said, all manner of things. When Youssef came in, I believe we were discussing the characteristics of Berber and Arab horses.'

Ali took out his cigarette papers, Holmes his pipe, Lyautey a cigar. The snoring boy had long since been carried off to a divan in Ali's quarters, and at the thought of the cloud of smoke about to engulf the room, my own exhaustion tugged at my arm.

'If you gentlemen will excuse me,' I said, 'I think I shall call it an evening.'

Lyautey stood when I rose, distractedly wished me a good night, then returned to the point under discussion before Holmes' question about Mahmoud, namely how, lacking telegraph lines, Abd el-Krim had communicated with his men on the opposite side of the Front eighteen months before, and why he did not make use of...

I shed various garments on the floor beside the narrow bed, and barely managed to pull the covers over me before I fell asleep.

Some time later, a sound woke me. I sat up in alarm: A man stood in the doorway.

'I apologise,' he said, remaining where he was. 'I should have retrieved my things earlier.'

My *husband*.

'I've taken your room,' I said.

'This–' He stopped.

'Ah,' I said slowly. 'This was intended to be *our* room.'

'If I may take some blankets from the other bed, I shall be quite comfortable on the divan.'

The divan was a foot shorter than he, and stuffed with a combination of horse-hair and rocks. 'You'll be crippled, come morning. Take the bed.'

'Are you certain?'

I was far from certain. 'Of course.'

He came in, lit the lamp, and began to remove various garments. I lay with my eyes closed, following the sounds with some trepidation. How far did he intend to undress?

The answer was, not far.

At the sound of weight settling onto the other bed, I shot a quick glance sideways and saw the thinning top of his head as he bent to undo his shoes – saw, too, that he had removed his *djellaba,* but retained the trousers and long tunic he wore underneath. Once the shoes had slid beneath the bed, the sound of him standing up made me look again, but he was merely bending over the lamp. In the dark room, I listened to the vigorous rustle of bedclothes, the image of his lamp-lit profile fading before my eyes. Suddenly, the ridiculousness of the situation struck me.

At the noise I made, he went still. 'What?'

I turned onto my side in his direction, feeling an unaccustomed lift to my facial features. 'I was reflecting how, after the business at the top of the stairs, it may be a while before you approach me without a qualm.'

'My dear Russell, never have I approached you without a qualm.'

Extraordinary, how it can hurt to laugh, yet also heal.

On Sunday morning, I woke to the thought of the onionskin pellet in the chest pocket of my shirt: a shirt long since dispatched to the laundry. But surely I had not left the scrap there? I had taken the ring from that pocket, so...

Aha: the crimson book, empty but for this torn-off corner of so-thin paper.

I carried it out to the next room, where Ali and Holmes were sitting with a collection of outdated English newspapers. Ali's face held a peculiar sour look, and he glanced up as I approached, giving the offending paper a shake.

'*The Times* reports on Abd el-Krim taking Chaouen: "It will be curious to see what the Moors will make of these elements of civiliation." Do they imagine the Emir fights with spears and muskets? That the Rifi heal sickness with incantations and leeches?'

I thought it not the time to mention the sellers of dried lizards in the medina.

161

Ali flung the paper to the floor in disgust and looked at my hand. 'What is that?'

I gave him the scrap of onionskin. 'Is this your young friend's writing?'

By way of answer, he said a few words in the Berber tongue. Idir looked over from his plate (for a small child, he seemed always to be eating) and nodded. Ali switched to Arabic. 'When did you give this to her?'

Then he had to get up and dig some paper and a pen from the room's desk. Idir wiped his hands on his shirt, and began the process of transcribing his thoughts, chewing his lower lip in concentration.

'How do you feel today?' Holmes asked me.

'Better. I remember our – well, wedding, I suppose, and portions of that spring. And around the gaps, the memories seem more substantial. Detailed.' It was as well that I now recalled events matrimonial – that glaring failure might cause even a sensible man to feel a degree of affront. However, the newfound clarity was not in all ways a good thing. The death of Dorothy Ruskin, the Holy Land archaeologist, was a fresh grief, while the reality of Mahmoud's disappearance had taken on urgency: He was a friend, and I feared for him.

With half a dozen lines on the Dar Mnehbi stationery and ink blotches across both page and lower lip, Idir dropped the instrument (another blotch on the page) and returned to his bread.

Ali puzzled over the writing, then asked, 'But why?'

This necessitated a repeat performance, even

162

longer and messier than the first. Finally Ali sat back with the stained pages, translating for us.

'When the three of you ate in the medina on Thursday, Mahmoud said that if you were for some reason separated, you should return to that same café. He then tore the corner off a letter he carried and had the boy write the location, so you would know what to ask for.'

'Why didn't Mahmoud write it?' I asked.

Ali looked at me as if I had said something remarkably stupid. 'How will the boy become literate, if he does not practice?'

'Of course. I wonder why I kept the paper.'

'Tidiness?'

I shrugged, and put the red book away in my pocket, reaching instead for the coffee. 'What now?'

'If there is to be a meeting between Abd el-Krim and Lyautey, I must return to the hills today.'

'But, Mahmoud–' I started to protest.

'–will have to wait.' Ali spoke as if it was no concern of his, but I remembered enough of the two men to see the swell of apprehension beneath the surface.

Holmes said, As you said, there are two possibilities: that he was taken away in the motor on Thursday night, as the boy tells us, or the lad is lying, and Mahmoud left the city earlier.'

'The only thing that would have caused Mahmoud to leave on his own,' Ali said slowly, 'would be an urgent message from the Emir. We may find that he has already returned to the Rif.'

'Wouldn't he have told the boy?' I asked.

163

'Not if he'd wanted Idir to wait here for me. If he'd said where he was going, Idir would have followed.'

'But surely he would have left a message *somewhere*,' I objected.

'Perhaps,' Ali said pointedly, 'he left the message with *you*.'

Ridiculous, to feel guilty at having been injured, yet I did. 'Yes, of course.'

Holmes intervened. 'In any event, unless one wishes to entertain some vastly improbable theory – such as Mahmoud Hazr being the victim of a completely random, run-of-the-mill crime, or sitting in a quiet corner of the medina eating bonbons – it points to the conclusion that some enemy knew of Mahmoud's presence, and knew either where to find him, or how to tempt him out. The question being, What enemy? An opponent of Abd el-Krim? Another gun-runner, fighting off encroachment?'

'It could even be some old foe who recognised him from Palestine,' Ali remarked.

'The boy has no idea what Mahmoud and I were doing that night?' I asked.

'None.' Ali stood up. 'I must leave the solution of this to you two. If I do not leave now, I will not reach the Emir tomorrow. We will meet you on Monday.'

'Mahmoud will turn up,' Holmes told him.

'*Insh'Allah*,' Ali said, not sounding at all confident of God's will.

In ten minutes, Ali was gone and Holmes was preparing to set off into the city. I fetched my oddly ancient boots from beneath the table and started to put them on.

'You are staying here,' Holmes said.

'Mahmoud is my friend, too,' I protested. 'You're not going in search of him without me.'

'Russell, you have had a severe head injury. A normal woman would be in hospital.'

'I'm fine!'

'You're not fine.' He finished adjusting his turban and stood, facing me. 'Can you honestly say that your presence will not distract me? Will not slow me down?'

I did not answer. He retrieved a heavy bur-nouse from the wardrobe and dropped it over his head. 'I intend to return by dark. If I'm not back by midnight, you have my full permission to ask Lyautey to turn the city inside-out. Come, Idir.'

And they were gone.

Moments later, a rap at the door heralded Youssef, come to remove the coffee things. It was the first time I'd paid much heed to the servant, an immensely dignified Moroccan of around sixty with skin like warmed chocolate and eyes that saw everything. His *djellaba* and underlying shirt were pristine, his almond finger-nails spot-less. He came and went with a manner that slipped just under one's awareness, as if one of the delicate French end tables had become diffi-dently animated, for the convenience of the residents.

'Does ... Madame wish anything else?' he asked. I smiled at the hesitation: Since the previous night, he'd learnt that the yellow-haired guest was a woman, appearances to the contrary.

'No– Oh, but wait. Is there a library here in Dar Mnehbi?'

'But of course, Madame, there is a fine library.'

A hunt for information can, after all, take many forms.

The library opened off the grand central courtyard of the main *dar*, where an ornate expanse of tile echoed with the music of falling water and cushioned banquettes lay against the walls. The *halka* grid was directly overhead, indicating that this part of Dar Mnehbi was but a single storey high. I could see why it had been necessary to take over the adjoining *dar* – most of the doors opening onto this ornate courtyard stood open, revealing a series of formal salons. It took Youssef some time to lead me to the correct doorway, my steps being slowed by my attempts to take it all in. I goggled, frankly, at the intricate texture of the *zellij* tiles and carved plaster, *zellij* and water, *zellij* and painted wood, *zellij* and coloured glass. It was a space both intimate and intimidating: lavish to the point of majestic, yet clearly designed as a place to welcome guests.

The patient servant, having stopped me first from walking into the fountain and then from tumbling over a charcoal brazier, finally led me to one of the intricately painted doors off to one side.

It would originally have been a salon, but was now the library. The room was larger than it seemed from the courtyard, incorporating the corner space as well, and it was clearly a working room, not merely a collection of decorative leather spines among which the ladies took tea

166

and the men their cognac and cigars.

For one thing, there was a much-hammered type-writing machine on a desk against the wall. For another, a gentleman's gathering would have been considerably inconvenienced by the large wooden table that dominated the centre of the library. Lamps were spaced down the table's surface; wide, shallow drawers slid out from its top; comfortable work chairs stretched down its sides.

The room was silent. It smelt of books and ink. I felt my muscles relax, as if the odour had the power to transport me to my faraway home. I turned my back on Youssef, lest he see my face, and thanked him. The fade of the splashing fountain was the only sound as he shut the door.

I made a circuit of the room, running my eyes over the shelves, sliding open a few of the drawers under the long table – the wider ones in the middle held maps; those on the ends held stationery, envelopes, note-pads, writing implements.

Lyautey had lived here for a dozen years now, and appeared to have every book on Morocco ever published, from the report on a 1721 ransom expedition to Mequinez to a war-time Edith Wharton travelogue (of which there were eleven copies – explained by its dedication to the Resident General and his wife). I put one of those onto the table, then a volume on Old Morocco, and half a dozen others. I was leafing through an unbound box-file of Victorian photographs when the door startled me by rattling open.

The young man in the doorway looked as nonplussed as I – dark hair and eyes, but not Moroccan, his hair parted in the middle, a thin moustache that might have been pencilled onto his upper lip. He was dressed in a handsome suit of Italian wool. His eyes darted into the room, pausing on the table, before returning to me.

His French was impeccably Parisian. 'Pardon, Monsieur. I did not realise anyone was here.'

'I was merely looking for some reading material,' I told him.

His gaze sharpened, rising from my men's clothing to the sticking plaster on my scalp. 'You are perhaps *Madame* Russell?'

'More or less,' I said, which rather confused him.

He crossed the room with his hand out. 'François Dulac, at your service. I am Mme Lyautey's secretary.'

His grip was light but pleasantly dry, and held not a hint of Gaulish flirtation.

'Good morning, M. Dulac. I have been ordered to pass a quiet day, so I thought I'd read up on the history of this country'

'Very good idea. Ah, I see you have chosen Madame Wharton's book. And Monsieur Andrews'. Perhaps you might be interested in this? And perhaps M. O'Connor?'

'Yes, thank you. You seem to have read a fair number of these.'

'It only seemed sensible, when I came here, to see what others had to say about the country'

'How long have you been here?'

'I came with Mme Lyautey a year or so after the Maréchal arrived. He did not care to bring her at the beginning, of course, when the country was in turmoil.'

'Of course.'

'Her being here presents more of a ... balanced face than that of a military leader alone.'

'A good idea.'

'What do you think of this one?' He held out a book for me.

As I paged through it, I asked him, 'What are your responsibilities here? That is to say, does Mme Lyautey perform official functions? I haven't met her.'

'She is in Casablanca at present, visiting friends. I assist in her appointments and correspondence, much of which might be termed "official". And of course, I make myself available to the Maréchal.'

'Yes, these look fine to begin with. And might I borrow a map?'

'A map?'

'Of Morocco.'

'But of course, Madame; the maps are in this drawer. However, the Maréchal makes use of them with some regularity, so it is requested that you not remove them from the room.'

The idea of my absconding with the cartography seemed to make him uncomfortable, so I assured him I was quite happy to leave them in place, which was especially true since so many of them were awkward sizes. Few of the maps were commercially printed, and those that were had been corrected by hand. Others were entirely hand-drawn, showing patches of close cartographic detail set against large areas of vagueness. South of

Fez and to the coastline, details were good, but to the north, beyond the Werghal River, it might as well have been labelled *Here be monsters.*

'Mapping the country is a work in progress, I see.'

'Indeed, Madame.'

'Well, the books should keep me occupied.'

He insisted on helping me, exchanging a greeting with a Moroccan as we crossed the tiled courtyard, following me up the guesthouse stairway with the books in his arms, carrying on the kind of light and charming conversation that is part of the personal secretary's profession. Were he a touch more handsome, I might have speculated about his services to Mme Lyautey, but by the time we reached my room, I had dismissed from my mind the possibility of a French liaison.

Dulac placed the books on the table, arranged some pieces of charcoal in the brazier, and said he would send Youssef up with tea. This time, I accepted.

I opened the Wharton book. Around me, I was dimly aware of activity; and after a bit I heard the dull clang of a small European-style church-bell. I stopped reading to listen. After a few minutes, the sounds of Dar Mnehbi slowed. Sunday morning: Somewhere on the grounds was a chapel.

My own reading was less spiritually refreshing. Considerably less. Every chapter seemed a reminder that I was a Jew and a woman in a land firmly rooted in Mediaeval Islam. The pirates of Salé and that town's ongoing simmering xenophobia. The sacking of Fez's Jewish quarter, twelve years before. A dance of fanatical self-mutilation

170

in the nearby town of Moulay Idriss. The jaw-dropping brutality with which a pretender to the throne was dispatched – and not in some distant and barbaric age, but here in Fez, a mere fifteen years before. The palaces of Mequinez, an African Versailles built by Sultan Moulay Ismaïl, a contemporary of Louis XIV and the very image of what happens when a mad ruler has no checks on his power and no end to his resources. Ismaïl solidified the hand of the Alaouite dynasty – still in power, two and a half centuries later – with a Black Guard of some 150,000 Africans, brought in from the other side of the Sahara. Ismaïl drove the English from Tangiers, forced peace onto the land, fathered hundreds of children, and built a vast and magnificent city, using tens of thousands of slaves captured by the far-ranging Salé Rovers, many of them Christians whose families were too poor for ransom. The slaves – forty thousand? sixty thousand? – were kept in a vast underground prison beneath Mequinez called *Habs Qara*, whence they were brought out to work on the mad sultan's projects. When a man died, he was simply walled up by his fellows, and the building continued – only to have much of Mequinez flattened in the massive earthquake of 1755. After that, the Alaouite dynasty shifted its centre to Fez. To a palace one mile from where I sat.

The reading was not conducive to the rest Holmes had assigned. I'm sure it did my blood pressure no good.

In the end, I carried the books back down to the library and searched for something less troubling. I hesitated at the title of the latest volume by M. Proust – *Le Prisonnière* – but decided that the coincidence was unlikely to extend to its subject matter. And indeed, the fictional tribulations of Albertine and her tedious companions proved the ideal soporific. I spent the remainder of the afternoon under the influence of that balm of hurt minds, sleep.

I woke just long enough before Holmes and the boy returned, to splash my face to wakefulness, but not long enough for my anxiety to build. When they came in, the lad was dragging, and even Holmes sagged a bit around the edges. They had spent a long and fruitless day scouring the narrow streets of the medina, trying without result to prise further information from the owner of the *funduq*, venturing into the burgeoning suburbs outside the walls, even making their way through the Mellah, the Jewish quarter tucked against the shelter of the Sultan's palace. They had asked shopkeepers and donkey-men, soldiers and *madrassa* students, but had found no trace of Mahmoud.

Who would have imagined that it would be a simple matter for a ducal Bedouin/English spy/arms dealer to vanish into thin air?

CHAPTER FOURTEEN

Before dawn on Monday, Holmes and I joined Lyautey in the silent Dar Mnehbi courtyard The Maréchal was wearing civilian riding clothes – jodhpurs and knee-high boots – and carrying a robe. His head was bare, the close-cropped white hair gleaming in the light of the single burning lamp.

He greeted us politely, then said, 'A response came to my enquiry about the soldiers at Nurse Taylor's door. It seems that the police did not summon them. I have ordered my assistant to continue the enquiry – the possibility that criminals might be impersonating soldiers is disturbing. But, Madame, how do you feel today?'

I did not meet Holmes' eyes. It had taken a while, the previous evening, to persuade him that a physical reminder of my emotional centre might assist the restoration of my intellectual faculties ... but I was not about to go into that, even with a Frenchman.

'Very well, thank you,' I said demurely.

My headache persisted and my bruised hip and shoulders were stiff, but I told myself that exercise would help.

He nodded, and said to Holmes, 'I have a *djellaba* and burnoose, as you suggested, but I won't put them on until we leave the city. Wouldn't you two prefer proper riding boots?'

'We'll be fine,' Holmes said.

The Maréchal led us out of the palace, startling the drowsing guard. Equally surprised were the soldiers at Bab Bou Jeloud, which was still closed for the night. But none of the men made protest: Clearly, the Resident General was well accustomed to going his own way, despite attempts on his life.

Holmes had told me that Lyautey often walked the streets accompanied only by an interpreter. He had also told me that today, that role was mine. I was not entirely clear why he or Ali could not perform the function, but I did not argue, since the other option seemed to be remaining behind with Idir.

The Maréchal's habit made things easier at the stables, when he simply walked into a box and led out a horse. Before he had the saddle-cloth smoothed, a pair of sleep-rumpled grooms were there to assist; by the time we rode out, half a dozen soldiers marked our exit, and although their sergeant offered armed accompaniment, they were not taken aback when the Maréchal refused.

The horses he had chosen were by no means the handsomest in the stables; all had long manes and the heavy coats of winter. Similarly, the saddles were not the highly polished trappings of cavalry officers, nor were the bridles of European style.

Something told me that the French were not unfamiliar with the business of looking like Moroccans. Strictly speaking, the horses were too well fed, well groomed, and well shod for native stock, but they would pass.

My cob was the roughest-looking of the three and had a mouth to match, but its gait was a surprise, smooth enough to preserve my tender skull from too much jostling. My body did not recall riding in a saddle quite this shape before, high fore and aft and with wide, flat stirrup hooks. The saddle would hold a corpse upright; coupled with its sturdy breastplate, I thought that my mount could climb mountains without tipping me off.

And it appeared that mountains might indeed be involved.

Away from the city walls, with the morning sun glowing behind the eastern hills, we stopped for Lyautey to don his Moroccan garb, and for Holmes and me to make adjustments to the unfamiliar saddles. Lyautey wore the garments in much the way he spoke Arabic, with more confidence than was fully justified. He looked like what he was: gentry in exotic costume.

All three of us carried revolvers.

As might have been expected from the city's numerous streams and fountains, Fez was built in a long valley where the sparsely-grown hills met the green and fertile plains of the *bled*. On this northern side of the walls, the city had no suburbs at all, merely a few scattered tombs and buildings set amidst olive groves and cactus, which soon gave way to wild ravines, dense thickets, and hidden caves in which sheltered – according to Lyautey – highwaymen, mad folk, and lepers. The morning was cold enough that our breath came in clouds, so still that we could hear the bell on a distant goat.

We were following, somewhat to my surprise, an actual metalled road, which looped back and forth out of the city towards the heights. When I commented on it, Lyautey, who was riding slightly to the fore, reined in so as to come between us.

'Roads are paramount, both for security and for civilisation,' he said. 'Think of the Romans – wherever they went, straight roads. Those and railways were the first things I commanded built when I came. If I have to move troops across the country, I can now do so. If I have to be in Casablanca or Marrakech, I can do that.'

'No more Rifi tribesmen infiltrating the city,' I remarked.

'Being welcomed in that manner was an embarrassment,' he acknowledged.

'You see where the other road goes past the tombs?' Holmes broke in. He pointed to a heap of rubble just becoming visible in the sunrise. 'That was where the lad found you, the other night.'

The only road along the ridge. I was wondering if it would be another embarrassment to ask why a patrol had not seen the motor, when Lyautey answered the unspoken question.

'I may need to reinstate guards along the heights,' he said. 'It is a balance between security and reducing our visible presence here.'

He shot a last glance at the offending spot, and kicked his horse back into motion.

I paused to survey the city before me, nestled in

the lap of the Middle Atlas. Fez was a *hortus conclusus* writ large, a garden walled around by hills, set about with a myriad of the fountains and streams that define luxury to a desert-dwelling people. A closed garden composed of ten thousand closed gardens; a mosaic of rooftops built out of a million mosaics; a palimpsest of history, layer upon layer of hidden life.

The first muezzin's dawn call echoed, eerie and faint, out of the valley below, as I turned my horse's head to follow the two men.

We were riding north-west to the meeting place with Abd el-Krim, a hard half-day's ride into the rough land between the Sabu and Werghal rivers. The Werghal was the age-old geographical boundary between tribes, even though the current political borders between the French and Spanish Protectorates lay well beyond it. The cause of much potential strife.

But from Lyautey's demeanour, we might have been on a family picnic. He embarked on a polite but comprehensive grilling of his cousin's wife, exploring my history, my family, my interest in things theological, the farm I had inherited in Sussex. His interest was genuine and wide-ranging, his ability to follow an idea to its conclusion remarkable, and I could soon see why Holmes responded to the man's supple and restless mind, his boundless energy, and his devotion to learning more than he taught.

We passed a tiny roadside shrine with its attendant *marabout*, and the Resident General asked me about the holy men of the Old Testament.

We moved aside to permit a troop of soldiers to

177

pass (all unknowing) their commanding officer, and he wondered how long it would take before a transplanted soldier of ancient Rome felt at home among them.

A pair of men working among a rocky grove of centuries-old olive trees led to a detailed lecture on how the pressings would fuel the kilns for Fez *zellij;* riding through a quiet village led to a discussion of dogs versus cats in Islam; a Persian wheel worked by a donkey sparked an exploration of the Archimedes Palimpsest; three unveiled women watching us pass from a streamside laundry had us discussing how Berber women could be devoutly Moslem, yet go unveiled and given free voice in village affairs.

The day woke, the sun warmed us. At mid-morning we stopped near a pink oleander, to climb numbly from the saddles and allow sensation to trickle back into our limbs. My aches had returned, my headache grumbled in the background, and I was grateful for the tea Holmes brewed over a small fire.

Then back onto our horses and on into the hills.

Ali's instructions had been to follow the French road to a certain small village, then turn due north on a well-marked path and watch for a hut with a tree growing through it. A secondary path led away from there, following a narrow *wadi* that might or might not have water in it. After three kilometres, we should come to a clearing where Abd el-Krim and Ali would meet us.

After our stop, Lyautey pressed on, head up, spine straight. He reminded me of the Lombardy poplars that line French roads, erect and watchful. Beside him, Holmes' pale robe formed precisely the same outline as Lyautey's striped one, their two heads tilted towards each other as they talked. I rode behind them, Holmes glancing back from time to time to see that I had not fallen off or gone astray.

Our tea break had succeeded in restoring feelings to my legs – unfortunately. The wide, high pommel chafed raw patches while the equally tall cantle dug into my spine. My cob required constant correction, since it was determined to take the lead over its companions. To distract my mind from the various pangs and irritations, I summoned my usual mental tasks. A review of Spanish vocabulary and verb forms took up half an hour, after which I translated a memorised sura of the Qur'an (*An-Nisa*) from Arabic to Spanish. When that ceased to amuse, I dismounted and first shambled, then trotted beside the bewildered horse for a kilometre or two. Back in the saddle, I patted at my pockets, to see if my disparate possessions might tell me anything today about my missing life.

The heavy signet ring was on a leather thong around my neck, along with my own, thinner wedding band. I had tried to give Mahmoud's ring to Ali, but he had refused, on the grounds that his partner must have had reason to leave it with me. So here it was, large and gold. It was a pelican, the heraldic charge of the Hughenforts. Why Mahmoud had it and not the young duke, Ali either could not, or would not, tell me.

I tucked the gold back under my shirt, and dug

out the chalky stone. I knew now why the stone had made me think of building material – the snug, solid little house I shared with Holmes (or had, up to the time my memory failed) was made from Sussex flint, although of pieces far larger than this one, which did not even fill the palm of my hand. I stretched out my arm, intending to drop the stone to the ground, but instead, my fingers returned it to the pocket. When one had so little, it seemed, even a rock could be a talisman.

Similarly, I retained the items stolen in the medina. The length of pipe and decorative dagger I had left behind (since I had two more work-man-like knives and the gun), along with the hair-pin, which had jabbed holes in both clothing and skin. Bit by bit, I looked through the posses-sions left me, glancing at my features in the little glass, snugging the ends of the twine. I felt a mild pang of guilt over the stolen money, but no other sensation of memory. With a sigh, I put it all away.

All but the red book. I let its cover fall open to that inscrutable corner of paper. Idir's barely legible writing looked up from my palm: *the clock of the sorcerer*. I smiled: Leave it to Mahmoud and Ali to find a Rifi Irregular with the wits not only to find his way around alien territory, but the persistence to locate a pair of straying foreigners. Poor child, he must have been in a fury this morning when he woke to find us missing, even though we had left him a large and prominent note to say that we would be back. And Youssef had promised to look after him in our absence.

I had no doubt: If Mahmoud was in Fez, Idir would locate him before we returned.

I went to close the small book over the onion-skin corner, then stopped to turn the scrap over. The uneven capital A now faced me top-side down: three squiggled lines, one from upper left to lower right, one nearly vertical on the right side, and a shorter, less steeply angled near-connector between the two.

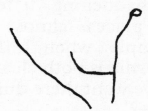

The right-hand squiggle had a sort of a loop at the top; its line then dropped straight down, nearly to meet the long angled line.

A pencil's random rub, no doubt, its very randomness serving to stimulate a brain desperately in search of meaning.

And yet, wouldn't a pencil point rubbing against a scrap of paper leave lines that were less ... precise?

'What are you looking at?'

The track had gone wide for a bit, permitting Holmes to fall back to my side. I let the booklet close and shoved it away. 'It's only that note Idir wrote – "sorcerer's clock". I was thinking that we should take the boy to see a proper doctor, to see if there is anything physically wrong with his tongue.'

'I'll ask Lyautey to arrange it, when we return.'

'An interesting man,' I said to Holmes, my eyes

on the steely spine before us.

'If the world had more of his design of mind, colonial lands would be well served. How is your skull faring?'

'Reasonably well. I'm grateful that the Maréchal picked a horse with a smooth gait for me. Although if you're asking if I got another chunk of my life back overnight, I don't think so. What I can remember does seem somewhat... firmer. But it's maddening. It feels like a wall, utterly solid in places, almost transparent in others. For example, when I think about my childhood, California is both clear memories and vague shadows. We went there during the missing months, didn't we?'

'Yes. Last spring.'

'I figured we had. Still, I couldn't tell you what we did. There was a man, a thin man whose hat flew off. Was he Chinese? Or a singer?'

'Those were three separate individuals.'

'It did seem an unlikely combination. And I gather that Ali and Mahmoud still work for your brother, Mycroft. Who runs a spy ring for the British government.'

'Mycroft isn't a spymaster so much as an ... instigator. He directs men and women like the Hazr brothers, true, but essentially he is looking at trends in the world, and at the means of, shall we say, nudging them in a direction beneficial to Britain.'

'What is he nudging here in Morocco?'

'I should imagine he aims to keep French interests in check.'

'By selling guns to the Rebellion?'

'Apparently.'

'Is that why we are here, too? Spying for him?'

'No. In fact, you and Mycroft are having a degree of feud.'

'Good heavens. Why?'

'It's complicated, and has nothing to do with the current situation. So, the summer before last remains your most recent memories?'

'There are odd jigsaw-puzzle bits that float to the surface – a burning aeroplane, and an elephant, and a heap of building wreckage in a street a bit like those in the medina, only not there. They're like that scrap of paper with Idir's writing on it: They make my brain itch with frustration.'

'It'll all come back.'

'And if it doesn't?'

'Then you'll have lost a year, which by the time you're my age, will seem of little importance.'

Small consolation. But he was right, and he'd also been right when he told Ali that pushing only made this particular wall grow stronger. Turn my eyes away from the memories, and let them slip in under their own inclination.

Resolutely, I changed the topic. 'Tell me about this Rif War, Holmes. The books I found yesterday had more to do with the seventeenth century than the twentieth.'

'Light-hearted reading, I imagine, that of Moulay Ismaïl and his captured slaves? It's as well Captain De la Rocha did not pattern himself on Sultan Ismaïl.'

'You mentioned him before – who is he?'

But he waved the name away: no doubt someone inhabiting the hole in my past. 'The Rif mountains across the north of Morocco are not particularly high, but they are wild and inhospitable, particularly this time of year. Its residents are Berbers rather than Arabs – a people every bit as fierce and inaccessible as the land itself.'

He described the long decades of tension along the north between Berber and European that threatened to wash through the gates of Fez. On paper, Morocco was a Protectorate, not a colony, but in fact this was a typical colonial conflict with European powers jostling for supremacy.

Most of what he told me sounded familiar, but I let his voice flow around me, talking about Umayyads and Almohads, Fatimids and Ottomans. The lecture was soothing. If nothing else, it distracted my mind from what it did not have, and my body from what it could not change.

Still, when we stopped at a tiny village in quest of a meal, I was more than ready.

The food, brought by a toothless crone and her imbecilic grandson, was appalling and fly-blown, and had my sense of smell remained as intense as when I first woke in the medina, I should have run from the threat. But our teeth were strong and it filled the stomach, with the inevitable mint tea afterwards to settle any gastric uneasiness. Following tobacco for the men, we rode on, watching for the designated track coming in from the right.

The track, when we found it, was little more than a goat's trail, narrow enough to force us into a single file, our right knees near to brushing the hill in places, the horses' left hooves a foot from catastrophe. I watched Holmes' back, with glimpses of Lyautey's at the fore, as the horses plodded up the *wadi*. After the recent rains, it held a noisy little river. This was a rocky area, with debris littering the path from the near-vertical wall to our right; flash floods had carved the canyon at our left. The bank across from us had a more forgiving angle to it, but appeared to be composed of a lethally crumbling rock – hence the goat-path worn into the right-hand side.

Without Holmes to distract me with his tales of bloodthirsty rebellion and European scheming, my various mental and physical complaints reasserted themselves. The skin on the front of my thighs felt nearly raw – probably the only time in my life I would wish for a side-saddle. The wool at the back of my neck was chafing. And my mind continued to scratch at its own internal itches. The Chinaman/chanteuse; the clear but inexplicable image of a sawn-off bolt; that damned scrap of onionskin with its Arabic writing. Its stroke-victim capital A on the obverse.

I shifted the reins into my right hand and worked the other into my pocket. The crimson book was no longer quite so pretty, having developed a curve to its covers from long residence against a seated body. I opened the cover, causing the snippet inside to flutter with the canyon breeze. I grabbed it, holding down the edge with my thumb.

The A gazed up at me, insolently proclaiming its importance. I was grateful that the irritating sense of Profound Meaning that had permeated everyday rubbish had begun to fade, as my battered brain subsided into a more normal state. However, this object stubbornly retained its numinous shine. With a sigh, I put the book away, raised my eyes to the men in front of me, and determinedly set about a review of Arabic verbs.

Five minutes later, I found that I was musing on the Indo-European roots of the letter A. It had probably originated as a pictogram of an ox, in Hebrew *'alp*. Its two horns had migrated from pointing to the right to downward, as the Roman alphabet has it today ... and here I was, thinking about the letter A again.

Arabic verbs were clearly insufficient distraction: I turned to the bones of the skeleton, beginning with the distal phalanges. I worked my way up to the temporal bone (mine may not have been cracked, simply bruised) and the various facial bones (my left zygomatic had also taken a knock, come to think of it) before turning downward. I made it through the cervical and thoracic vertebrae to the clavicle before getting distracted again: the scapula. Such an interesting shape, the scapula. Its flat surface linked the arms (or in birds and fish, the wings and fins) to the musculature of the upper torso. A broad bone, related to the Greek for *shovel*, it was what gave strength to the arms. When a man was strong as an ox (*'alp*) it was thanks to the way his A-shaped scapula–

There it was again, an image as persistent as the odour of honey had been.

This monotonous loop of thoughts threatened

186

to derange me entirely. It was all well and good for Holmes to urge perspective in the loss of a year, but he was not the one caught up in circular thinking. I glared at his back, wondering how I might approach matters were our positions reversed, if Holmes had been the one to–

Lightning jolted my entire body. It felt like that certainly, as electrifying as the time I'd grasped a live wire, only this charge entered not through my hand, but through my eyes.

As my gaze had lifted from my horse's ears to the backs of the two men, the shape of the approaching landscape nagged more and more stridently at my mind: to the right, the near-vertical cliff face with a large boulder balanced near its top; to the left, sloping terrain angled down to the river; in the distance, our goat-track curved around to the left, rising at an angle between those of the two valley sides.

In other words, a crooked, upside-down A with lines that did not quite touch.

A fresher or more skittish horse would have leapt into the abyss at my sudden jerk on the reins.

'Stop!' I cried. 'Oh God, stop!'

CHAPTER FIFTEEN

I don't remember getting down from the horse, nor do I recall seeing the two men dismount and edge past their own puzzled mounts to where I stood, staring desperately at the winding track ahead of us. I came to myself with Holmes' hand digging into my shoulder, and his urgent voice in my ear, with Lyautey's alarmed face looking past him.

'Russell, what is it?'

'An ambush. It has to be. *That* must be what the drawing was on the piece of paper. Here.' I dug into my pocket, talking all the while. 'Mahmoud did it, not a random pencil. I think. Yes – it *must* have been he. What I thought was a capital A was an *aide-memoir*, this exact spot. You see? Why else would he have drawn it?'

I held the crumpled bit of paper up to the view ahead of us, and indeed, it could be seen as a visual echo: cliff with boulder; sloping hillside; track.

Or, damn it, it could as easily be a still-fevered brain desperately grasping for sense in an accidental scribble.

I clutched my head, as if that might impose rationality. 'I said before, there's a sort of echo when you tell me something I feel I should know. Yes, it could be my imagination – this inability to be certain about *anything* may drive me insane!

188

But, when I looked up and saw that piece of hillside, it made an immediate connexion with the scribble on the piece of paper, a scribble I have been unable to get off my mind ever since I saw it. I *think* it is important. I *think* Mahmoud must have drawn it. And the only reason I can imagine for sketching this site would be as a warning, an illustration of where he knew danger lay. No, not even *knew* – if he'd known for sure, he would have cancelled the meeting. Say, he *suspected*. And he showed me where, in case he wasn't able to be with us.'

Holmes and Lyautey watched me with weirdly identical raised eyebrows. It was an agonising situation, feeling utterly convinced that I was right, at the same time knowing that I was probably just deluded.

Interestingly, it was Lyautey who moved first. He stepped to the very brink of the drop-off, craning his neck to see past the cliff-top to the teetering boulder. Shrubs and small trees covered the hillside above that point. Lyautey studied the hill, the route that boulder would take were it suddenly to come free, the quantity of debris that would surely follow in its path. When he turned back, his military mind had decided.

'We will assume that you are right. What, then, do you suggest?'

Silence. Then Holmes asked, 'Will the horses back up as far as the last wide place?'

'They will for me,' Lyautey said.

I objected. Granted, he was the cavalry officer, and should know what a horse could do, but it could take hours if each of the three would only obey his urging. 'It would be faster if Holmes and I circled back to climb the hill, to see if there is anyone waiting at the boulder.'

'Holmes and I will go,' Lyautey announced.

'If you do,' I told him bluntly, 'I can't guarantee you won't come back to find three horses lying dead in the river.'

He did not like it, but he was an officer to his bones, for whom delegation is vital. He took another survey of the track ahead – sorely tempted, I was sure, to risk a sudden, fast gallop up those two hundred yards – and then turned back, resignation on his face. He was opening his mouth to agree, when Holmes cut him off.

'Oh, damn,' my husband said.

Half a mile away, along the curve of track, two men with tall rifles were riding in our direction. The first man had his hood thrown back: Ali. The other, his hood sheltering his face, could only be Mohammed Abd el-Krim, Emir of the Rif Republic.

The three of us reacted according to our natures. Lyautey pushed his way past Holmes' horse with the clear intention of making a dash underneath the hanging danger. Holmes stepped forward and began to shout loudly, one hand spread out, the sound futile against the river. I pulled out my revolver and fired it into the air.

That last action stopped the distant pair's forward progress nicely. Unfortunately, I had not reckoned with the consequences of firing three shots in the vicinity of a guerrilla leader.

My horse, though accustomed to firearms,

nonetheless jerked and nearly went over the edge.

Holmes clapped a hand over one ear, which had been a foot away from my gun.

Lyautey pressed into the shelter of the cliff and whipped out his own revolver, waving it around as he looked for what I'd been firing at.

But worst of all was the reaction of the hooded figure up the *wadi*.

He was too far away to see that I had been aiming at the sky, but plenty close to hear the retorts. He vanished from his horse's back in an instant, sheltering behind the animal's bulk, invisible but for the hem of his *djellaba* – and the muzzle of his long rifle, aimed straight at Ali's back.

Ali's hands came off the reins and out from his body. His horse slowed to a halt; after a moment, our friend's body bent slowly forward in the saddle. My heart stopped, but Ali was not tipping lifeless to the ground; he was getting rid of his weapon. When he had done so, he sat upright again, both hands raised.

The turn of his head suggested that he was talking earnestly over his left shoulder. His right hand pointed in our direction; after a minute, a dark orange turban emerged above the second horse's neck.

At that signal, all three of us stepped forward, raising our hands to make exaggerated pushing-away gestures, shouting fruitlessly against the noise of the water.

The tableau held, while Abd el-Krim considered. Any sensible man would simply shoot

191

this potential traitor in the back and ride away to safety; that this man did not instantly do so suggested the superior quality of the brain beneath the colourful cloth.

Then Ali's hands came down. Moving with great deliberation, he dismounted, took a few steps forward, and stretched out on the ground. The other man darted forward into the shelter of Ali's horse, and stood with his rifle lowered on Ali.

'Now what?' I asked.

'I'll have to go up there,' Lyautey said. 'The man won't wait forever.'

'That's too much of a risk,' Holmes objected. 'I will go, and tell them what the problem is. Abd el-Krim is sure to know another route. I'll bring them around, and meet you two back along the track.'

Lyautey, being a man, objected to this plan, even though if ambush there was, he was the more likely target than Holmes or I. Not that I was in any way pleased with Holmes' offer to fling himself into danger, but rationally, I could see that it was less hazardous – for us all – than to send Lyautey forward along the track. One stick of dynamite – even a muscular man with a stout lever – would bring half the hillside down on us.

One considerable problem remained. 'I still don't think I can get this horse to walk backward all that way.'

'If I get him started, you should have less of a problem,' Lyautey told me.

There followed a jostling for position: Holmes

moving forward to take control of the Maréchal's horse, Lyautey coming back to assist me. And that was when the trap was sprung.

The flaw in my reasoning had been based on the ambush being explosive rather than munition-based. I – we all – had assumed that with a nice precarious boulder at the ready, any trap would make use of that. However, though their Bedu brothers might adore dynamite, Moroccans seemed to prefer guns. At least, the two men in the trees on the other side of the boulder preferred guns.

When they saw Lyautey appear to turn back, they opened fire.

The first volley took a chunk out of my horse's ear, which was too much even for a phlegmatic Army animal: It reared, made a mid-air *volte-face* that I would not have believed possible had its hooves not brushed my eyebrows in passing, and vanished down the trail. Holmes' horse bolted as well, in the opposite direction: The beast came within a hair of tumbling into the river as it attempted to push past Lyautey's, but then that one gave a scream of pain and leapt from standstill to full gallop. In moments, both were vanishing around the curve.

I had thrown myself down as my horse rose, and Holmes was merely lashed by his mount's tail as the creature made its lunge for freedom, but Lyautey was between Holmes' saddle and the cliff when the gunfire began, and the animal's weight drove the breath from his lungs. The Maréchal staggered away from the rock-face. Holmes and I both leapt to haul him back against the scant protection of the cliff. His face was alarming, although I'd had the wind knocked out of me enough to know that his lungs would remember how to draw air before he passed out. But perhaps not before he got in the way of a bullet.

We stood with our backs to the cliff-face, Lyautey between us, pistols drawn. Holmes had the disadvantage, being right-handed, but I aimed at the puff of gun-smoke above us and emptied first my gun, then his. Its third bullet hit something, because the gunfire suddenly stopped. At the same instant, Lyautey gave a great, ragged whoop of indrawn breath, then began to cough. Holmes pounded him between the shoulder blades while I helped myself to the Maréchal's revolver, and waited for a return of fire.

None came.

I risked a glance at the pair upriver. I knew there was little hope that Ali lived: One twitch on the trigger finger, one surprised reaction to the sudden volley of fire, and the long rifle would have punched a hole through our friend's spine.

I could not believe my eyes. The man with the gun had come out from behind the horse; at his feet, Ali was up on one elbow.

The rebel not only had brains, he possessed an astonishing degree of self-control.

I glanced at Holmes, who was as amazed, and as relieved, as I. When I looked upriver again, the two men were on the move. Ali's rifle was back in his grasp, and both were scrambling up the steep alley side, comrades in arms. Ali moved faster, and vanished into the trees while the stockier man was still labouring upward. But the Moroccan was determined, if not fleet of foot, and soon pushed into the scrub. Ali's horse lowered its head to pull at the sparse grass, then raised it again, startled, as our two came into view, their panicked run already slowed to a trot. Four sets of ears pricked upright, and in their simple way, our two forgot why they had been moving so fast. Before long, all four horses grazed in companionship, half a mile upriver.

'Should we go on?' I asked Holmes.

'Perhaps we ought to wait until they've cleared the hornet's nest,' he suggested. Again, Lyautey disliked the sensation of cowardice, but had to agree that it would be idiotic to step into an enemy's sights when the means to his end was coming up from behind.

So we waited. And in a quarter of an hour, we heard a shrill whistle. I ventured a peek, and saw Ali, waving at us from beside the boulder.

As one, Holmes and I looked at our companion, then at one another, and set about convincing Maréchal Lyautey that there was absolutely no need for him to climb the cliff-face.

Neither of us much cared for the picture of this white-haired, limping aristocrat tumbling into the river below.

We continued up the track on foot. In half an hour, we approached a small, neat camp-fire, where the leader of the Rif Rebellion was preparing to brew mint tea.

CHAPTER SIXTEEN

If Lyautey was Lombardy poplar, Mohammed Abd el-Krim was a piece of granite, his feet rooted in the mountainscape, his eyes the gaze of the Rif itself. Stocky, dark, intent – on the surface, he and the Maréchal ought to have nothing in common: One was a patrician military officer with the future of a country in his hands, the other an engineer from the hills with no military training and a tenuous grip on his fellow tribes. But when the dark Berber eyes and the blue French gaze met, there was a palpable click of connexion: two powerful, intelligent, and charismatic men who cared passionately about Morocco.

Holmes had other matters on his mind than diplomatic relations. Ali was just now scrambling down the hillside, sweating despite the cold day. 'Who were they?' Holmes demanded of Ali, in Arabic.

Ali ignored the question. His dark eyes searched us intently as he drew near. 'Were you hit? Any of you?'

'Only the horses,' Holmes replied. 'Were they Berber?'

But either Ali did not know, or did not care. He whirled, seeing the thin stream of already-dried blood on the neck of the Maréchal's horse. He stormed over to examine the wound – a minor one, clearly, although a handsbreadth lower would have been a different matter – before turning back, his face a peculiar mixture of anger and confusion.

'It is merely a nick,' Holmes pointed out.

Ali glared at him for a moment, then his face went closed. 'Come,' he said, as he led us towards the clear place where the first tendrils of smoke were rising.

Holmes asked again, 'Ali, do you know who they were?'

Ali responded, still in Arabic, 'Two men. One dead, the other gone, taking both rifles and the horses.'

'How many horses?'

'Just the two.'

'Not a kidnapping, then. Was there anything on the dead man?'

'Nothing.' Then he glanced at his companion, and corrected himself. 'Except these.' His hand came out of his garments with three coins: two of bronze, stamped with 5 and 10 CENTIMES, and a very worn silver 2 peseta coin. 'The Emir saw him as well. He ... thinks the man Jibali. Not Rifi.'

'From Raisuli?' Holmes asked.

But I interrupted with a more urgent concern. 'Did I kill him?' My voice was a touch shaky.

'You wounded him, in the hip. A knife killed him.' He saw my reaction, and gave a humourless smile. 'His companion did not wish him questioned.'

Lyautey cut in. 'What is he saying?'

His demand called to mind the apparent reason for my presence. I put aside investigation and turned to translation, telling him what had been

197

asked, and answered.

He nodded, and said, 'We are somewhat exposed here.'

I translated the statement – which was, I felt, a mild question – into Spanish. Abd el-Krim replied, 'He has run. You are safe enough here.'

When I put that into French, I thought it prudent to change the *you* into *we*.

Belatedly, Ali realised that our diplomatic mission had got off to a somewhat distracted start. He cleared his throat, and launched into formal introductions.

I translated. After a moment, Abd el-Krim stepped forward and put out his hand. Lyautey took it. The Rif leader did not bother with Holmes or me, but returned to the fire, dropping to his heels to pull a primitive tea-setting from a lumpy saddle-bag.

While he was doing that, Holmes turned to Ali. 'We've had no news of Mahmoud. And Lyautey has not seen him since the one meeting on Thursday. He suggests that an order be issued for his soldiers to watch for a man with a scar; I said to wait, for another day or two.'

With a brusque nod, Ali stalked off to gather an armful of branches from among the rocks.

Holmes and I unsaddled the horses and I carried their blankets to the fire. Lyautey and Abd el-Krim sat across from each other, with Holmes and me at the other points of the compass, but subtly back from the fire. Ali took a seat near his leader, but also back from the fire, drawing his knife and reaching for a scrap of the wood.

Abd el-Krim adjusted a blackened pan over the flames, and spoke, his voice low and firm. 'You are recovered from your illness, sir?'

Lyautey did not blink at the knowledge that the state of his health was known beyond the French borders. 'I am seventy years old. I should be sitting with my feet stretched out to my own fireplace.'

(My translation went slowly at first, and was cause for a number of apologies. But after a bit, either the two men slowed and simplified their words or my mind regained its fluency, because soon it became more or less automatic. Tiring, but automatic.)

'Yet here you are,' the Berber commented, 'sitting among the rocks, drinking tea with your enemy.'

Well, I thought, that was certainly getting right to the heart of the matter.

'Are you my enemy, sir?'

'I would like not to be, *Bismillah*. I am told that you show respect to my country and to its traditions. If we may call this love, then you and I have common ground.'

'I very much hope that we do,' Lyautey replied.

There was a faint smile around Abd el-Krim's eyes, reminding me of Mahmoud. And as Mahmoud had, this host returned to the heating water, drawing a mashed and wilted handful of mint from a pouch, folding it into an aluminium tea-pot that looked as if it had been used as a football. The leaves were followed by a hefty dose of crude sugar chunks that he measured onto his palm, then stirred in with a dusty stick. He poured the tea into a glass from a height, then dumped it back into the pot, repeating the ritual until he was satisfied, at which point he handed one frothy glass to Lyautey and kept one for himself. He left the pot within arm's reach of Holmes, to pour or not, as he wished. Holmes poured, handing a cup across the fire to Ali and another to me, the mere translator.

Following the rather pointed opening exchange, I expected to dive straight into the problem of French claims across the Werghal, but after a noisy slurp, Abd el-Krim asked Lyautey whether he had children.

'Alas, no,' the Frenchman replied. 'My life has not been suited to families. And you?'

'Three young sons,' he said.

'Allah's blessing upon them,' Lyautey said, in recognisable Arabic.

'*Bismillah*,' Abd el-Krim agreed.

The polite conversation that followed was the two men's way to get a sense of the other. The Moroccan's questions about Lyautey's home – burned to the ground in the first year of the War, along with all his possessions and papers, by occupying German forces seizing a convenient target for their resentments – told more about the Maréchal's history than about the building. The Frenchman's return questions established not only the rebel leader's own losses, but that among the Berber, Abd el-Krim might be considered the equivalent of minor aristocracy. The cups were refilled, *zellij* tile-work and Moroccan music discussed, and delicate queries about the future (skirting around the minor problems of

200

what the rebellion would mean) confirmed that Lyautey intended to return to France, with his wife. Abd el-Krim took this to mean the beginning of a family, and wished him many sons, but before the Frenchman could disappoint him (Madame being rather beyond childbearing years) he set down his tea and picked up our reason for being here.

'You are aware that the 1912 treaty was a bad one?'

'Not bad,' Lyautey corrected. 'Perhaps incomplete.'

'It was imposed upon us, without consultation.'

'The Sultan agreed to it. Indeed, Sultan Yusef agrees still.'

'The Sultan is a prisoner and a puppet of the French,' Abd el-Krim said.

'The Sultan is ... inexperienced, when it comes to international relations. It is a balancing act, to keep him informed and involved, while still... encouraging Morocco to join the twentieth century.'

'In the south perhaps, but here in the Rif? To Spain, we are a colony, open to be ravaged. Were it not for our minerals, the Rif would be left in peace.'

'I can understand that the Spanish are ... problematic.'

'The Spanish are brutal. They drop mustard gas on us. On our women and our children!'

'You understand, I have no control over what Spain does on their side of the Protectorate?'

'You are the foreign minister for the Sultan, and hence for all of Morocco.'

'I have no authority over the Spanish,' the Frenchman repeated.

Abd el-Krim's hand waved the question away. 'We will deal with Spain. 'What I need is a recognition that the 1904 treaty is invalid, and that the 1912 border – a paper border that cuts through tribes and even villages – was drawn by fools.'

'I cannot change a treaty.'

'And yet, I am told that the Resident General has before this day been struck by occasional blindness when faced with foolish orders. It is not inconceivable that he would also see his way to revisiting the question of boundaries by establishing a frontiers commission.'

Lyautey looked through the smoke at him, no doubt wondering where the man's information came from. Abd el-Krim's dark eyes crinkled in a smile that made his intelligence shine out. 'My people have friends in many parts of the world, Maréchal.'

Lyautey drew himself up to return fire. 'You claim that the boundary between the French and the Spanish Protectorates should be Wadi Werghal. And yet your incursions into the disputed area leave me with little choice but to defend the line I have been given. If you wish to redraw the boundary, you must address the issue through the proper channels.'

'Perhaps you would have me ride into Tetuán? To be shipped to General de Rivera, who would have me dangling from a rope in Madrid's Plaza Mayor? Sir, you well know that for some things, a proof of strength is the first step to negotiation.'

'You cannot win if you move against France.'

'The Spanish run from us, and die as they run.'

'France is not Spain.'

'From the Rif, all of Europe looks much the same.'

'One does not create a new nation by hiding in the Rif.' This sentence I changed, since a literal translation of Lyautey's *hiding* might have Abd el-Krim reaching for his rifle: 'One does not create a new nation without venturing out of the Rif.'

'Nor does one create a nation by placing its leader's head in a noose.'

Lyautey clearly decided that the preliminaries were out of the way, and that it was time for specifics. 'Two days ago, I received word that your men attacked an outpost. Two of my soldiers were wounded, one of yours was killed.'

'No Rifi soldier has crossed the frontier.' The dark gaze was even, the voice sure.

'Then who were they?'

'Every land has its outlaws. These were not mine.'

'And the men stealing telegraph lines?'

'Ah. That was a mistake. It was thought that they were Spanish lines.'

'In any case, I have no choice but to reinforce that post, as well as the line leading to it. You see that?'

'I see that you should not be there in the first place.'

'Yet I am. And being there, I must hold my position. Even the leader of a guerrilla campaign will agree that land claimed must be held. France cannot permit the shame of that retreat. We have enemies closer to home to whom our failure here would be a sign of weakness. I realise–'

Abd el-Krim interrupted. 'I have told my men that they are not to interfere with the French. I will repeat the order when I return.'

Lyautey nodded, as if the other man had made a formal concession, then picked up a stick, drawing a line in the ground, and another. 'The Werghal River; the Sabu,' he said. Marks for Fez, Chaouen, Tetuán, Tazrut; another line for the Mediterranean coast.

Lyautey then returned to the first lines, drawing from memory precise details of where each of the French border posts stood, how many men, the difficulties of supply and access. For forty minutes, he laid before the hill man exactly where the incursions had taken place, who had been injured, when local civilians had come in the way of the fighting. He even knew when livestock and crops had been destroyed, down to the olive trees felled as firewood by Abd el-Krim's men.

The Moroccan shifted, so as to examine the rough map, but said little beyond the occasional correction – in one place, a man had not died, merely been injured; in another, it had been a neighbour who stole the sheep, not the rebels.

Lyautey paused, letting his opponent study the map. Then he dropped the stick, and leant forward, this seventy-year-old man with a bad back and several recent operations – my own knees, considerably younger, were aching. 'I am forced to send for reinforcements. Multiple battalions of infantry and engineers. We will hold the line we were given, and keep your fighters occupied. Your northern forces will be stretched thin. You are already fighting on two fronts. Your people are hungry. If France enters to your south, you will lose. Your children will starve.'

The Moroccan gazed calmly at the lines in the dirt. 'If it is the will of Allah, we will win.'

'Is it Allah's will that you have a country, or prove your manhood?'

I hesitated, racking my brain for a way to soften that blunt question, but since bluntness was the point, I had to translate it as it stood.

Abd el-Krim's dark eyes flashed up, probing Lyautey's expression for any trace of scorn. The three of us braced for intervention; the air quivered with potential violence; Lyautey met the other man's eyes evenly – and then the Moroccan's broad face relaxed into a faint smile.

'A man must often wait, before he knows Allah's will.'

'And while waiting, must a man do nothing? The God I know may give a man a horse, but he requires that man to seize the reins. A clever leader may find good reason to avoid conflict, by approaching the battle from behind. I am led to believe that you – and your brother – may be clever leaders.'

'*Bismillah*, we do what we can.'

'As I, too, will do what I can, so as not to provoke open confrontation along the Werghal, but encourage the sorts of battles that shed words, not blood.'

'And yet, my people are locked in by our enemies, who ravage our women and murder our sons, who want nothing better than to turn us into slaves to dig out our country's iron and coal and phosphates. Blood will be shed.'

'Not all neighbours are enemies. And it is possible that a door may become open. Perhaps one of your trusted men may be taken to Paris, to speak to those in power. A man such as your brother?'

The dark and appraising gaze slid sideways to Ali, then returned to the Resident General. 'Do you know?'

My translation stumbled, but the phrase was clear.

'Do I know what?' Lyautey asked.

'No, I think you do not. My brother did go to Paris. Your countrymen would not speak with him.'

'Really? When was that?'

'Last spring. He went ... quietly.'

'If I arranged a visit, he would be listened to.'

'My brother would make a powerful hostage.'

'I understand. Trust would be required.'

'The people of the Rif have seen their trust rewarded with death.'

'Again, you speak of Spain.'

Abd el-Krim tugged at his moustaches for a while, considering, before something caught his eye, back the way we had come. We turned and saw a horse, trotting along the track underneath the hanging boulder. My horse – but it looked as if it had grown taller since fleeing. Then my eyes focussed more closely on the proportions of the rider, and saw that it was not a grown man.

Idir.

CHAPTER SEVENTEEN

'The lad stole a donkey and followed you from Fez this morning,' Ali told Holmes and me, in English. Idir was hunched by the fire shoving bread down his throat, to the amusement of both Lyautey and Abd el-Krim, who had rumpled the boy's head with the familiarity of a father. 'He reached the last village at the same time a horse with an empty saddle trotted down from the *wadi* track, and the boy did not hesitate to change mounts. I suppose he figured that even if the beast wasn't yours, it would still be faster than the donkey.'

'I thought you said he would go searching for Mahmoud,' I complained.

'I thought he would.'

'A most determined young person,' Holmes said.

'Have we ever met a passive child?' I lamented.

Ali ignored my grumble. 'We must finish here, or we will be caught by night.'

'But they've come to no agreement.' My protest surprised him.

'Did you anticipate they would?'

'Wasn't that why we came?'

'That would have been icing on the cake.' The English simile sounded peculiar coming from that bearded mouth. 'The point was to have the two men speak directly, and to see that the other

207

was a man to respect, not a faceless threat. No: This has been a good day's work.'

The three of us looked over at the trio near the fire: rebel leader, French blueblood, and mute urchin. Abd el-Krim poured the dregs from the pot into his tin mug, and set it before the boy, sharing a glance with Lyautey at the eagerness of the filthy little hands. Lyautey took out a cigarette case and offered it to the Moroccan, who chose one, pulling a twig from the fire to light first the Frenchman's, then his own.

It is remarkable, how symbolic an act the sharing of tobacco can be.

Ali had finished his latest carving – a hawk in flight – and tossed it to the boy, then caught up one of the blankets and set Idir to saddling the horses. The shadows were growing longer; if we did not leave here in the next hour, we would be travelling that narrow, cliffside track in the dark. Or huddling here in our saddle blankets until dawn.

Abd el-Krim crumbled out the end of his cigarette, putting half of it away in a pocket. 'I will consider what you say,' he told Lyautey.

'My great hope is that we can forge a union,' the Frenchman replied, 'one that can only make both our people stronger.'

'I cannot draw back from pushing the Spanish to the sea.'

'I understand that. In your position, I would do the same. I only hope, for the sake of the soldiers themselves, that your own men show some mercy.'

Abd el-Krim did not reply; the purse of his lips was perhaps answer enough.

'The world will be watching,' Lyautey reminded him. 'Newspaper men are everywhere.'

'Them!' Abd el-Krim said, a noise of dismissal.

'They are a tool, which a wise man uses like any other,' the Frenchman suggested. 'In this century, international eyes are becoming a powerful force. Think of your compatriot, Raisuli, when he–'

'He is not my compatriot.'

'I understand. Even if those were not his men shooting at us just now, it has long been clear that Raisuli's only loyalty is to Raisuli. But my point is, he well understands the value of the international press. He may enslave or murder lesser prisoners, but his kidnapping of Walter Harris bore the face of a gentleman's affair. When he did the same with the Perdicaris family, he played the rage of the American president into a position of considerable authority. Even the Maclean kidnapping was friendly enough.'

'You wish *me* to follow the lesson of *Raisuli?*'

'He is a terrible man, I know, capable of the foulest of atrocities. But to the outside world, he takes pains to appear a brigand-hero.'

'It is a face some of his own believe as well,' the Moroccan admitted.

'A century and a half ago, Morocco was the first nation to recognise the United States of America. If you wish to see the reverse happen, to have America formally recognise the Rif Republic, you must take care to appear as gentlemen. Leaving a mountain of slaughtered Spaniards for the cameras is not the way to do that.'

Abd el-Krim tipped his head thoughtfully. 'You

speak almost as if you wish to see our rebellion succeed.'

'Officially, I regard you as in dispute with the Sultan of Morocco, the political and religious head of your state, for whom I am resident general and foreign minister. But, in fact, do I care if you defeat the Spanish to the north? Why should I? The French Protectorate has problems enough without having to take you troublesome Berbers in hand.'

It was beautifully judged: After a brief touch of outrage, the Moroccan burst into laughter.

As if the sound were an agreed-to signal, Ali picked up the tea-pot and dashed out the leaves. 'If the Maréchal does not return,' he said to Abd el-Krim, 'they will send soldiers after him.'

'And I must join my brother,' Abd el-Krim agreed. Still, he remained seated, watching Ali pack away the tea paraphernalia. 'Today my brother has sent el-Raisuli an ultimatum,' he told Lyautey. 'The Sherif is the only barrier to the north, now that we have removed the Spanish from Chaouen. My brother will wish to discuss what we are to do when the man turns us down.'

'I am told that Raisuli is ill. Too ill to travel, even.'

'Then we shall carry him.'

'Raisuli has no power left him, not in the face of the modern world.'

'Raisuli is a Sherif, descended from the Prophet, blessed be his name. While he has breath, Raisuli is a flag to be followed. And, he has a son who is old enough to call the tribes together.'

'A child,' Lyautey said sharply.

210

'Fifteen, sixteen years? A man. But before you protest, no, I have no intention of harming the boy, no more than I wish harm to the father. I have little respect for Raisuli, but I will respect his blood. As for the son, he is less than nothing. Without the father, he is empty.'

At that, the rebel leader got to his feet. Lyautey rose, too, moving stiffly as he stepped to one side of the fire, facing the shorter man. His spine went straight, then he bent and put his heels together, a formal salute. When he extended his hand, Abd el-Krim grasped the Frenchman's fingers for a moment, then touched his fingertips to his lips in the Berber gesture of respect.

'Maréchal Lyautey, I shall ponder all that you have said.'

'I hope that we may meet again, under better circumstances,' Lyautey replied.

'*Bismillah*,' the Emir of the Rif Republic murmured, and turned to snug up the saddle on his horse.

Ali dug around in his saddle-bag, coming out with an ancient tube of ointment. He tossed it to Idir. 'Put the salve onto the Maréchal's horse,' he ordered the boy. Then to my surprise, he swung into the saddle, clearly intending to ride with Abd el-Krim.

'You're not coming with us?' I asked – in Arabic, for the Emir's sake.

'I am needed in the north.'

'But what about–'

'Mahmoud? I trust you will not rest until you find his boot-prints.'

'Ali – trusting us? Impossible. 'What do–'

211

I stopped, at a grip on my elbow: I was not seeing something, but Holmes was. I changed my protest into a question. 'Where do you suggest we pick up our enquiries?'

'There are but two places to ask: the medina and the road where last Idir saw him.'

'We've asked. *You* have asked.'

Abd el-Krim spoke up. 'Perhaps the wrong people were asked.'

I opened my mouth to snap at the inane remark – clearly we'd asked the wrong people; had we asked the correct people, we'd have found Mahmoud. But it was one of those drearily obvious statements that yet reverberate in the mind, and shift around, until it became: Perhaps the wrong people were asking.

It was crystal clear, the moment the thought occurred: In the intimate quarters of the medina, there could be few secrets. The dawn tremble of a web at Bab Bou Jeloud would ripple across the city, to arrive at Bab Guissa well before mid-day.

But no stranger's eyes would notice it.

And it had been strangers who had been looking.

I looked up at All, perched in the high Moorish saddle. 'We will find him.'

'*Insh'Allah*,' he said, his voice fervent, before wheeling his horse and kicking it into a gallop.

CHAPTER EIGHTEEN

With three horses and four people, the natural distribution of weight would have put me and the child together. However, the Maréchal was meditating on his conversation with the rebel – his only remark had been, 'Shrewd fellow, that' – and I wanted a private conversation with Holmes. So we started back along the narrow track with Lyautey in the lead, followed by Idir, with me perched behind Holmes, my arms around his waist.

The last time I could recall riding with Holmes on a horse, he had been barely conscious, while I was both thoroughly terrified and terrifyingly young. That had been 1919; this was (so I had been told) 1924. I was no longer his young apprentice. I was his wife.

I felt Holmes' hand briefly on mine, as if he had shared the thought, and I pulled myself closer against my husband's back.

'Why did you stop me from asking Ali about returning to Fez with us?' I asked him.

'I did not wish him forced to admit openly that he was standing surety with the Rifi. It's all very well for a pair of gun-runners to come and go, but after one of them has been witness to a secret meeting? And permitted a would-be assassin to escape? By staying with Abd el-Krim, Ali comforts the leader's mind.'

'I see.' Which meant that at that very moment, if Abd el-Krim had studied the back riding up the trail before him and decided Ali was not worthy of his trust, our friend could be lying on the ground with a bullet in his brain. With an effort, I pulled my mind off that image. 'As to secrecy, it appears that both sides have a plenitude of spies.'

'All sides watch the others, always. The Spanish have eyes in the Sultan's court, the French have ears in the Spanish headquarters, both slip money to men within the rebellion. And you can be certain that Abd el-Krim has men close to Raisuli as well as Lyautey.'

'Tell me about this Raisuli character.'

'Sherif Mulai Ahmed er Raisuni has spent a long career of cruelty and corruption. He began as a cattle thief. After spending four years chained to a dungeon wall, he blossomed into real brutality. He has tortured and beheaded, played the Spanish for all they are worth, taken various foreign visitors prisoner – men who considered themselves his friends, even after their experiences – and demanded huge ransoms.'

'The slogan "Perdicaris alive or Raisuli dead" re-elected President Roosevelt,' I remarked – and why would my memory cough up that bit of trivia?

'Voters do love the image of warships steaming to the rescue of an innocent. In point of fact, Perdicaris had rescinded his American citizenship. Plus, he was a wholehearted admirer of Raisuli – called him a patriot. And far from "Raisuli dead", the Sherif came out of it with $70,000 and–'

214

'Seventy *thousand* dollars?'

'*And* dual positions as district governor and pasha of Tangier. Brief positions; he was thrown out a year later because, as he put it, Europeans objected to a few heads stuck on the walls.'

'Raisuli seems to have studied at the feet of Sultan Moulay Ismaïl.'

'To whom he is related.'

'Ismaïl fathered nine hundred children – I'd imagine most of Morocco is related to him.'

'But most of the country would not claim to be its rightful Sultan.'

'Why haven't Raisuli's people quietly put him into a hole?' I grumbled.

It was the sort of question Holmes enjoyed, an opening to both knowledge and opinion: Raisuli as an upholder of the Faith, a Moroccan Robin Hood, in a land where brutality is expected and softness in a leader can be a fatal mistake. And yes, the same applied to that educated Berber gentleman who had just made us tea, the Emir Mohammed Abd el-Krim. As Holmes put it, 'European soldiers have been known to commit suicide, rather than be taken prisoner by a Rifi.'

From the history of Sherif Raisuli, this husband of mine wandered off into the political hinterlands of our situation: the drive to war and Morocco's long history of conflict; Arab and Berber; the conquest of Spain by Hannibal (a Berber). The building of Alhambra and Alcazar. Spain's expulsion of the Moors, their return to the Rif mountains.

It had been a long day. My energies were at a low ebb, and the warmth of my companion's back and the ceaseless rumble of his voice against my ear were soothing. I may not have followed all the details of his extended lecture, but I was not asleep. Although it did take a moment for his accusation to register.

'–and why do I go on when you are not listening?' he ended.

I sat up. 'I am,' I protested. 'To every word.'

'Then what was I saying?'

'You were talking about the six factions fighting over this one scrap of country,' I replied promptly. 'Four of them are European: The French want peace and progress, the Spanish want revenge on the Moors, the Germans want iron, and the English want the status quo. Internally, there are two: Abd el-Krim wants a Republic, and Raisuli wants to be Sultan. And every faction has legal rights, a long history here, and a full complement of spies and informants. Did I miss anything?'

'Hmm. Mycroft, I suppose.'

'Mycroft is a nation unto himself.'

'True.'

'Holmes, have we today diverted even in the slightest the drive to war?'

'Oh, I shouldn't think so,' he said. 'The best any individual can hope for is to establish a degree of mutual respect between the principals.'

'In hopes that, when hell breaks loose, they remember they once shook hands?' I said dubiously.

'In hopes they remember that the other man was open to conversation.'

'Have you any reason to think Morocco will be more sensible than Palestine – or Europe?'

He did not reply. I shifted, to return circulation to my nether anatomy, then asked in a lower voice, 'Holmes, what was that attack about?'

'Assassination.'

'Not abduction – or simple robbery?'

'The bullet missed the Resident General by inches. It was not a random shot.'

'How did they know where he would be?'

'More to the point, why did they choose here rather than one of a hundred other opportunities? The Maréchal does not exactly hide himself away.'

'Perhaps they're unfamiliar with Fez?' I wondered.

'It's possible. It does suggest that their information came from within the camp of Abd el-Krim, rather than Lyautey's own.'

'I don't know that I'd agree. It seems to me that any smart spy would take care not to use inside knowledge that could give him away.' Holmes gave a pleased nod, as if I had passed one of his little tests. 'Though I agree, it's probably a Rifi. Lyautey's circle of intimates is small enough, he'd have spotted a spy long before this.'

'Not, as you say, if the man is sufficiently skilled. An effective spy is a man of the shadows. A person both seen and overlooked. Someone who knows much and says little. Those with information to sell are always such.'

'Sounds like Mahmoud.'

'Precisely.'

'Holmes! You don't think–'

'That Mahmoud Hazr sells information? No. But he is missing, and someone set men to shoot

217

at Lyautey. The two facts are related. We must find him.'

'How?'

His reply was oblique. 'What were you thinking of, when Abd el-Krim suggested that we were asking the wrong people in Fez?'

'It occurred to me that yesterday, when you were making enquiries about Mahmoud, you were there as a foreigner. The Fez medina is a warren, all inter-connected and on top of itself. A beehive. I can't believe that its people don't know what's going on in the next house.'

Interesting, that I knew this man well enough to tell thoughtful consideration from scepticism by the back of his neck.

'You propose that going undercover would result in information?' he asked after a time.

'I was thinking more of locating someone who had an ear in the market-place, who would yet speak freely with us.'

'And yet...'

When he did not complete his thought, I encouraged him with, 'And yet what?'

He muttered an Arabic phrase that sounded like, *A nugget of truth often sleeps, deep in a tangled web of lies.*

'What a dreadfully mixed metaphor,' I complained. 'Who said that?'

'I did.'

Interesting, too, that I knew this man well enough to be certain he would not answer further until he had chewed over all the possible considerations of whatever scenario I had inadvertently planted in his mind.

I sighed, and tried to make myself comfortable on the horse's rump.

Afternoon wore on towards evening, and the narrow, *wadi*-side trail joined the wider track which led to the actual road. It was a relief, to have navigated the worst part of the journey before darkness made it life-threatening. It also meant that we no longer had to ride single-file.

To my surprise, rather than urge our mount up beside Lyautey, Holmes reined in and worked his off leg over the shaggy neck, dropping to the ground.

'What are you doing?' I asked. 'Let me get up with Idir, if you think we're too heavy for this beast.'

'I need to make a few changes to my garments. Better to do so now, that I might become accustomed to them.'

'What is going on?' the Maréchal asked before I could.

'Mahmoud Hazr is neither a common nor a vulnerable person,' Holmes explained, his hands busy pulling at his turban. 'If he was abducted by motorcar on Thursday night, it means that someone provided information, and that several men were available to lay a trap. Witnesses will have noticed where the motor went. Russell has kindly pointed out the obvious to me, that a person may not see far into the shadows while he stands in a bright light. When I made enquiries about Mahmoud, I was standing beneath a spotlight. I shall take more care, as I repeat my questions outside of the city.'

'If you wish people questioned, I need only give an order,' Lyautey pointed out.

'And you will receive answers every bit as helpful as those I received.'

'Do you think so?'

'I know so.'

'What do you propose?'

'I propose to become a creature of the twilight. Beginning here and now.'

He meant it literally: His hands were already at work, adjusting his turban to bear some subtle message I did not immediately see, patting the ground to transfer dust to his limbs and clothing, scuffing at his boots, cutting one boot-lace and knotting it, mended and frayed. It wasn't until he had pulled a set of prayer beads from some inner recess that I was sure what he was after. With a sigh, I dug out the little pot of kohl and handed him that.

Lyautey remained baffled. *Cher cousin,* what are you about?'

In response, Holmes began to recite, in flawless Arabic, an early Sura of the Qur'an, while his hands played over the worn beads.

'Is this why you haven't shaved your beard?' I asked him.

He shifted into English. 'Not specifically. I merely reflected that facial hair might come in useful. As often happens, I was correct.'

I shook my head, and turned to the Maréchal. 'What do you see before you?'

'An Englishman in fancy dress.'

'But if you were motoring along and saw this figure beside the road saying his prayers, what would you think?'

The pale eyes grew wide: 'A *marabout!*'

A holy man, one of Islam's everyday saints: Educated or insane, a charlatan or a learned scholar of Qur'an and Hadith, a *marabout* could also be a wandering pilgrim. A less likely identity for Sherlock Holmes would be difficult to imagine. A nun perhaps. 'You don't need Idir, Holmes. I'll go with you.'

'Russell, you must concentrate on Fez. You need to find the man who brought you to Miss Taylor – he might remember some detail about the motor. And perhaps those in the vicinity of the *funduq* have an idea what you and Mahmoud did, during those times when the boy was not with you. You have an advantage over me: Apart from one morning when you juggled a few oranges, there is no reason for the people there to remember your face, whereas Idir and I spent most of the day quartering the city, asking after Mahmoud.'

'But surely a mute child would be a fairly distinctive companion?' My protest was not about the child, but about the hard twinge of desperation I felt: I'd just got most of my life back, and now...

Holmes' gentle response, too, was less argument than apology. 'In the mountains, he may be known, but not in the *bled,* where even the Emir Mohammed bin Abd el-Krim can pass unrecognised.'

I looked at the boy, then at the setting sun. 'You are placing a great deal of trust in the suggestion of a person with half her brain frozen solid.'

'Russell, I would trust you in any state short of catatonia.'

There was really no way to respond to that, except turn again towards Fez.

So we did, riding until the night wrapped around us.

When the bowl of light that was Fez came into view, everyone except Lyautey slipped to the ground. I held two sets of reins as Holmes tugged up his hood and pulled out his prayer beads. His eyes gleamed from the darkness beneath his hood, and his voice came with a cloud in the cold night air.

'My dear cousin,' he said, 'be so good as to permit your men to guard you, if only for a few days. It would not serve your country – either of your countries – to have you lie in state in the Fez palace.'

'You may be right,' the Maréchal admitted.

Holmes turned to me. 'Russell, I... That is...' He stopped and cleared his throat. 'I require your note-book and a writing implement.'

I fished through my pockets for the crimson book and pencil. 'Why do you need them?'

'Origami,' he replied.

Origami?

By the light of Lyautey's electric torch, Holmes ripped out a couple of pages on which I had scribbled notes, returning those to me. Then he rubbed the pad of his thumb against the pencil for a moment before transferring the stain to his forehead, imitating the mark of habitual prayer. Pencil and book went into his garments. 'It may take me until Wednesday night to work my way back to Fez. I shall circle the city walls. If I've heard nothing, I'll make for Mequinez, then Moulay-Idriss. You'll find me either on the road, or at the shrines. And, Russell?' On my name, his brisk recitation faltered. His left hand rose to grasp my shoulder, hard, and he leant forward to murmur in my ear, 'Watch your back.'

'And you, Holmes.'

His eyes glittered in the torch-light for a moment longer, then he turned and scuffled off, his stiff gait a marked contrast to that of the amiable child at his heels. I had gathered sufficient memory to feel that it was a common thing, for me to watch his retreat and wonder if it would be the last time.

At least this particular holy man was armed.

With no small reluctance, I climbed back into the saddle and followed the Maréchal around the walls to the stables.

We turned the horses over to the grooms. It was a short walk to the nearest city gates, which were closed, but not for Maréchal Lyautey.

One of the guards there fell in before him, carrying a lantern and a rifle. Neither were the city's heavy internal barriers closed to us. Sleepy gatekeepers brought out bundles of Mediaeval-looking wooden keys and inserted them into heavy wooden locks, giving us passage. I waited for a momentary distraction – in this case, two young boys dashing towards home – and slipped away into a dark lane. The Maréchal's voice briefly followed me; the soldier did not.

Holmes had been right: Protecting Lyautey was not my responsibility. Finding Mahmoud was.

CHAPTER NINETEEN

It was near the dark of the moon. The medina was a sea of shadows, the few open shops casting diffuse pools of yellow lamp-light against the damp cobblestones. In one respect, it was ideal – indeed, the ability to fade into the background was precisely why I had shed the good Maréchal. However, within minutes I knew it was a hopeless task, to trace my steps of Friday to the house where I woke with blood on my hands and a pounding inside my skull. I might wander all night and pass its very doorway a score of times, unknowing.

What I required was a very small and unobtrusive source of illumination, to light my way without drawing attention to myself.

I tugged my hood well up on my head, hoping it was enough to obscure any flash from my spectacles, and approached the next open store-front. It was, unusually for Fez, a shop of mixed goods, displaying a few sprouting onions and wilted greens, a teetering pyramid of mismatched tins with many dents but few labels, a bowl of straw-speckled eggs, rounds of bread that looked a day or three old, some copper bowls, a row of dusty glasses, and a few twists of paper spilling the deep orange of dried chilli peppers. The sort of place a desperate cook might turn for last-minute supplies – probably why it was still open.

I lowered the timbre of my voice to greet the

shopkeeper, then pushed a 25 centime piece across the counter and asked for bread, haggling until I had twice the amount he had originally offered. I pushed the rolls into the depths of my *djellaba,* and only then asked if he knew the English nurse, Miss Taylor. He shook his head, but I continued as if he had not replied.

'The wife of my cousin took their son to her for an infection of the eye, and Miss Taylor gave her an ointment that cured it, and now my brother's first son has the same infection, and my brother is worried that the boy will go blind and be unable to read, and he is such a bright boy, I said I would find her and ask her for the ointment.'

'You want ointment? I have ointment,' the fellow said, reaching under the counter to pull out a tea-chest so ancient, it retained the faint arms of the East India Company on its side. He began to rummage through its contents, drawing out a series of bottles, tubes, tins, and packets, all of which were half-used, several of which, like the food tins, lacked identifying labels.

'I told my brother that I would bring that of Miss Taylor. He loves his son. I would pay, if (*insh'Allah*) I could find a man who could guide me to her door.'

The shopkeeper ceased his archaeological burrowing to raise an eyebrow at the one-franc coin on the counter. 'When there were three of them, his head shifted minutely; at five, I paused, and made to draw them away.

He dropped his handful of pastille tins back into the wooden chest, swept aside the mound of dodgy medicaments, and locked up his shop for the night.

Perhaps if someone offered me enough francs, my own memory would improve?

My sense of direction is generally adequate, but in Fez, I seemed perpetually to have a magnet being waved past my internal needle. Maybe it was just the bang on the head. In any event, in a city without street-lamps, whose lanes are covered with woven ceilings that obscure the sky, and where even the thoroughfares are straight for no more than a few yards at a time, I was instantly lost. Mute as Idir, I followed my guide, who acknowledged half the men we passed with a word, a quick hand-clasp, or a raucous joke – confirming my suspicions that the citizens of the medina were a tightly woven lot. Even when we came to one of the internal gates between the neighbourhoods, which was closed for the night, its attendants let us slip though with only a small coin by way of acknowledgment.

Twenty minutes of twists and turns, during most of which I had a firm grasp on the knife on my forearm, finally brought us to a tiny lane with a blind kink in it. As I had a score of times already, I held back lest a gang of thieves wait around the corner; this time, I saw a brief stretch of alley with a door on either side and a third where the passageway came to an end. A small light shone down at the steps, and I saw at once that it was the very same patch of architecture that had so puzzled me when I woke, three and a half days earlier. Beside the Moroccan door, looking remarkably out of place, was an English bell-pull. My guide gave it a yank and stood to the side, giving me an expectant look. I moved forward into the light. In a moment, the door came open, and a round Moroccan gentleman looked out.

I told him in French, 'I am looking for Mademoiselle Peg Taylor.'

'Is it an emergency?'

'No. Yes. Well, it's hard to say.'

At my response, the shopkeeper looked less eager to depart, but I stood to the side and made the sort of gesture that in any language is a clear invitation to leave. Reluctantly, he exchanged a hand-clasp with me, then retreated down the stone passageway.

I turned to the other man. 'It is not a medical emergency, but it is urgent that I speak with her. Is she here?'

'Mademoiselle Taylor was called out to a sick bed. She will not be long. Will you come in?'

I stepped inside, finding myself in a dimly lit entranceway. He shut the door and led me through a brief version of the twisting lanes outside, including a second doorway, and finally into a much smaller and less decorative version of Dar Mnehbi: a small tiled courtyard with rooms opening off all four sides, part of its roof open to the stars. I pushed back my *djellaba's* hood, and the man's eyebrows went up, a variety of emotions playing over his face: surprise, relief, a touch of amusement, and something curiously like embarrassment. 'Ah – it is you! She will be glad to see you return.'

I knew him then – he was the man who had

come onto the roof, looking for me. Which indicated that the woman would be, as Holmes had suggested, Miss Taylor.

He settled me in one of the salons that opened off the tiled courtyard, this one an odd mixture of Moroccan architecture overlaid with English sensibilities: The banquettes were higher than those I had seen elsewhere, almost like sofas, with upholstered cushions of bright local fabric scattered with needlepoint throw-pillows of English roses; the table before the banquettes was a gigantic brass tray, but half the knickknacks on its surface came from British seaside resorts; the paintings on one wall were imitation Constables mounted in ornate Moroccan frames. The one distinctly non-Moroccan feature it exhibited was an actual stone fireplace built into one corner, cold at the moment but with wood arranged and ready.

'The hour is late,' he said, 'but will you have tea?'

'That would be most welcome,' I said with enthusiasm. His face creased into a smile, and he left me alone.

The wall opposite the paintings held photographs: One, very faded, showed a Victorian-era picnic on the Thames; beside it were three laughing Englishwomen on camels; a third, with more recent clothing, showed a party at – yes, that was Dar Mnehbi, with Maréchal Lyautey and several Moroccans, all of them holding glasses that did not appear to be tea. There was also an ageless picture of a man with a dog and a shotgun on a misty hillside, paired with an Arab-looking gentleman on a white horse, a falcon perched on his wrist. When the tea arrived, it was as bi-cultural as the room: A flowered pot suggested England and smelt of Lapsang, while a brass pot contributed the odour of mint. The disparate drinking vessels were included: porcelain cup and saucer alongside gilt-edged glass. A single small plate held slices of lemon, while the Moroccan bowl of sugar could perform for both countries.

But it was the platter of tit-bits that I particularly appreciated, where the delicate English tea-biscuits were overwhelmed by the considerably more substantial Moroccan delicacies. I fell on them with an urgency I had not realised, and only just managed to keep myself from licking the plates.

Miss Taylor was away longer than her ... butler? assistant? had anticipated. I was dozing among the cushions with a throw-rug wrapped around my shoulders when the sound of voices startled me awake, but managed to be on my feet when she came through the doorway.

Peg Taylor was a small figure dressed in the enveloping white garments of a Moslem woman. Her face was lined, but sweet, in the way of those who have spent a life in service to those they love, the sort of face that makes an ill person's aches diminish. It was also a face I knew: I had seen it before: *Faces would appear and make noises, then blow out the lamp and leave me alone.*

'I am very glad that you found your way back here,' she told me, taking my hands, looking into my face both in earnest affection, and to make an examination of my pupils, my body, and my head.

'I was quite worried when you disappeared from your room.'

She was speaking English: because Holmes had told her it was my native tongue, or because I had babbled in my delirium? If the latter, what else had I given away?

'I apologise for having left so abruptly,' I replied. 'I saw the soldiers arrive, and I thought they were coming to arrest me.'

She looked surprised. 'For what?'

'I didn't know. I still don't. I can't remember what happened. I've lost all memory of the past few months, in fact, although bits of it keep coming back.'

Her hands left mine. 'Amnesia?'

'Rare, I know, but it happens.'

'That must be remarkably disconcerting.'

The others had greeted my condition with emotions ranging from polite disbelief to open irritation; her sympathy took me aback. 'Er, yes, it is.'

'You should have remained here, resting. I trust you have spent the intervening days in a quiet state?' She stepped back, and began to unwrap various scarves from her person.

'Not exactly. In fact, I need to ask–'

'No business until you've eaten. And then I'll examine your injuries – William!' The small figure overrode my protests, ordering that a supper be brought, a hot bath readied.

Leading me across to the fireplace, she made *tsk*ing sounds as she took a box of the same matches I had carried away from here, and lit the laid fire. 'This is my one true luxury. Moroccans don't believe in heating a house, they think it

230

unhealthy, but even though I've lived here more than thirty years, after a long day I still find the cold absolutely penetrating. One wouldn't think an Englishwoman would–'

I seized her arm to interrupt her.

'This is urgent,' I said. 'A man is missing.'

She sat, but she did not rescind her orders. I frowned at the growing fire, and began to explain.

'The other night, I was brought here following some kind of a fight. The man I was with – at any rate, a man who I have reason to believe was with me – is an old friend. He has not been seen since then. I need to find him.'

Her man – William – came in with a basket of wood for the fire. When he was gone, she said, 'A young man whose wife I nursed back to health last year was bringing fire-wood from the family orchard, in the hills to the west of the city; when he noticed a motorcar stopped on the road ahead of him, its head-lamps pointing in the opposite direction, downhill. As he came near, there was shouting and what he thought was a gunshot, after which the motorcar raced away down the hill. He hesitated, but things seemed to have gone quiet, so he went forward, and heard noises to one side of the road. It was you. As he was trying to help you back to the road, a child came running up and started hitting him with a stick, although once he realised that you were being rescued, not assaulted, he helped the young man get you onto the cart and down to the city. The moment you came near the gate, the child turned and ran back up the hill, without a word of explanation or of thanks.

'Since you could not tell him where you belonged, the young man brought you to me.'

'Why? Why you and not a hospital?'

'You appeared to be a native, but you were muttering in a language he did not know. And he thought that if he reported a motorcar hitting you, he would have to go to the police and tell them what had happened. The people here are not fond of the police,' she explained. 'Instead, he sent a message into the city, asking me to come to the nearest gate. It was locked, the hour being late, but all the guards know me well, and thought nothing of my going in and out. I'm afraid that I did have to lie to them in order to bring you in. I told them you were the mad brother of one of my families – you appeared to be a man, and you were rather babbling – who had wandered off during the day.'

'I see.'

'William and I settled you into my surgery, where we began to examine you. You can imagine poor William's shock when you turned out to be a woman. Or perhaps you cannot?'

'I know Moslems, so yes, I can understand.'

'William and his wife converted to Christianity – it's not generally talked about – but he is still a Moroccan, so I excused him and brought in Fatima. She and I cleaned you up, dressed your wounds, and stitched the cut on your scalp. I had her find another tunic for you, and we emptied your pockets – which reminds me: Did your friend – your other friend – deliver your boots and that weapon?'

'He did, thank you.'

'Considering your state of mind, I thought the gun a poor companion, and the boots wanted cleaning. Your other possessions we left on the table – except for a ring, which seemed to me too valuable to leave sitting out. I trust the people who work for me, but there is no call to tempt them. Other than the ring, you had remarkably little. Not even any money. Were you robbed?' And before I could answer, she said, 'Of course, you wouldn't remember.

'In any event, I decided that further disturbance would be dangerous in your condition, so we carried you upstairs and left you to sleep, checking on you every hour. The next day you showed signs of waking, so I sent a message to the authorities. I was–'

'You sent the message both to Dar Mnehbi and to the police, is that right?'

'Yes, and I let the police know that I had done so. Someone might have reported you missing, and since the police have been known to exhibit a heavy hand when they suspect wrongdoing to a European, I did not wish to put off notifying them that you were safe. Bad enough to steal a car, but to kidnap a woman with it – I feared they might arrest some poor fellow and beat him for information,' she said baldly. Then she added, 'I did not expect them to respond with armed soldiers.'

We had got that far when William returned, asking, 'Will you take supper here?'

'The dining room will be like ice, so yes,' she said. Clearly, he had anticipated her response:

233

Before she finished the sentence, trays were coming in, to be arranged on a number of small decorative tables. Miss Taylor explained, 'I hope you don't mind this girls-school style of informality? I often take my supper in here, after a long day. It's the only proper fireplace in the house, and we go through far too, much firewood as it is.'

I assured her that warmth and informality were my own preferences, although I suspected that William did not fully approve. He settled us with tables across our laps, arranged the dishes within reach, filled our glasses, and left again.

Miss Taylor shot me an amused glance. 'I sometimes think William would prefer a starched collar in a grand house, poor fellow. He has worked for me these thirty-five years, and I never fail to disappoint him.'

'You work as a nurse, here in the medina?'

'Nurse, doctor, mid-wife, dispensing chemist, occasionally dentist. I once performed surgery on a donkey. And you? What brings you to Fez?

'I ... I am told that I came to Morocco in the company of a moving picture crew.'

'Really? I didn't know that a moving picture company was in town.'

'As far as I know, they're still in Rabat. I seem to have come to Fez with my missing friend. And before you ask, yes, we have checked all the obvious places where a dead or injured man might be taken. Except here.'

'I'm afraid that you were our only unconscious foreigner this week. Who is "we"?'

'The "other friend" whom you met on Saturday.'

'Oh yes, the pleasant older gentleman who spoke fluent French. You know, with all the foreign visitors I've met here, he is the first one who grew up in the same town as I. We couldn't come up with any common St Albans acquaintances, though.' Holmes had not grown up in St Albans. Which told me that he had invented a persona in order to ingratiate himself into her confidences.

'What a coincidence,' I remarked.

'*I* thought so,' she said. I glanced sharply to the side. She appeared to be nonchalantly picking her way through her plate of chicken.

Not perhaps a mind to underestimate: Missionary is not always a synonym for naïve.

'You gave him my boots and gun,' I said, 'but not the details of how I came to be here. Why not?'

She frowned as she worked a piece of meat from its bone. 'He seemed to know you, well enough to be trusted with a pair of very old boots and a weapon that, in any event, I preferred not to have in the house. But I have lived in Fez a long time. I was here before the French. And hard experience has taught me that things may not be as they appear. That a man who may be trusted with a person's footwear may not, in the end, prove worthy of that person's safety. I was glad to be told that you were well, but that did not mean I was about to give him information that could create problems for my well-meaning young friend with the cart.'

'But you will talk to me about it.'

'You have the right to know.'

'What did the man with the cart tell you about

235

where he found me? Did he say anything about the motorcar?'

'He said little more than what I've told you. I was more interested in saving your life than asking who had done it to you.'

'And I am very grateful, for all you did, but I now need to locate the motorcar. My friend may have been abducted in it.'

She lowered her fork and knife. *'Abducted? What nonsense is this?'*

'I told you, there was a fight, and–'

'Fight as in lovers' spat, or fight as in fisticuffs?'

'Definitely the latter. Although I suspect it was more knives than fists.'

Now she dropped her utensils entirely. 'Young lady, are you suggesting that you were in an actual *battle?* On the road outside of Fez?'

'What did you– Oh. You thought I'd been hit by the motor.'

'Weren't you?

'I was attacked. By men. Not that I remember, but the child says I was, and I have no reason to disbelieve him.'

She looked at me, and her eyes wandered across my garments. 'They thought you were a man,' she concluded.

'Perhaps. In any event, they left me concussed and bleeding, and seem to have taken my friend. I must find him.'

'This is ... most remarkable,' she murmured to her plate, then raised her eyes. 'Morocco may be a violent country, but it has little crime in that sense. We must report this.'

'No!' The threat of a combined French and

236

native bureaucracy would be more than I could face. 'Let me talk to the man with the cart first.'

'He may not answer your questions. Strangers are mistrusted here.'

'My Arabic is good,' I told her in that language.

'Even then.' But when I started to press her, she put up her hand. 'I do see that you need to follow that train of events, but there is little point in your rushing off to question him. For one thing, he is almost certainly abed, and would be greatly alarmed by an invasion. And for another, I would be happy to accompany you into the medina tomorrow, but not tonight. I cannot force you to stay, but I refuse to countenance a person in your condition racing headlong into further activity'

I watched her calmly resuming her fork, and her meal. 'You will help me, if I agree?'

'If you permit me to examine you and then put you to bed, yes.'

'First thing in the morning?'

'If you wish.'

I picked up my utensils, and obediently ate what was on my plate.

And when she had finished prodding my skull and reassuring herself that I had not ripped out her neat stitches, I used the hot bath and curled up in the same bed I had occupied before.

To dream of vague figures flitting through the doorways of empty tiled rooms, carrying with them the loneliness of ghosts.

CHAPTER TWENTY

Tuesday when I woke, the vague clamour of city noise trickled into the room. I lay listening for a time, then jerked upright as the significance hit me: If traffic in the medina had already reached that pitch, the hour was by no means early.

I threw on various pieces of clothing, shoved my glasses onto my nose, and scurried down the stairs.

Miss Taylor was seated over the remnants of her breakfast, going through a stack of letters. She took off her reading glasses and smiled at my dishevelment. 'Good morning, Miss Russell. Do sit down. Would you prefer tea or coffee?'

'You shouldn't have let me sleep in. Shall we go?'

'When you've had breakfast.'

'Miss Taylor, I appreciate your concern, but I have a friend who may be in danger.'

Her reading glasses went down atop the letters and she stood up. 'I will be just a few minutes. Help yourself to coffee.'

I heard her voice from another room, and a minute later, the cook came in with a basket of warm rolls.

'Thank you, Fatima,' I said. Only when I lifted the buttered and jammed roll to my lips did I realise what I had said.

I remembered coming here! Not the arrival

itself, but my early hours in this house. What before had been a vague sense of motion and warmth was now peopled with faces and voices: Miss Taylor, bent over me with professional concern, talking and explaining as she worked; William holding a steaming bowl for her to sponge off my face; a woman taking his place as the removal of garments revealed my unexpected gender: Fatima.

The shadows had drawn back from another piece of memory.

And yes – the desert, and a tent! I had gone from the sea to the sand, working on – oh Lord: the moving picture. I was *acting* in a moving picture? I pushed away the memory, and concentrated on the tent.

Idir, his eyes roaming over the canvas room and its peculiarly sumptuous fittings (hired from Morocco's Sultan; hired by me, in fact) as I prepared to join–

Mahmoud! Yes, Mahmoud Hazr had called me out of the desert, piled me into a rattletrap lorry – stolen? Could that be right? We had climbed into the lorry, which trailed great clouds of black smoke and slowed alarmingly with every hill – and blew a tyre – no, two tyres – on the way. But we had repaired them, and we had found a spring to fill the boiling radiator, and we had made it over the mountains and...

And there again, I came to shadows. There was dust, and a row of laden camels, and Idir's frightened face, and a sensation of fury and violence in the night, but the more I pushed at it, the harder I concentrated and tried to force it into focus, the thicker the shadows became. All it gave me was a headache.

'Miss Russell, are you ill?' Peg Taylor's voice came, sharp with concern.

Startled, I dropped the bread and jerked around. How long had I been staring off into the space between my ears? 'I'm fine, just thinking.'

'You do not look at all fine.'

I picked up the roll, wiping a smear of preserves from the table, and took a bite as if that might prove the excellence of my health. 'I was thinking,' I said around the mouthful, 'about what you said concerning the Fasi disinclination to talk freely with outsiders. I know that you have been here for a long time, but I fear that the sort of things I shall be asking are those that your admirers might wish to shield you from. It would be better if you were to introduce me as someone worthy of trust, then leave us to talk unheard.'

She did not care for the feeling that she would be abandoning me, but she agreed that an un-overheard conversation might be for the best. It took the better part of an hour to get out of her door, following consultation with William, and checking on a patient, and just as we were about to leave, the arrival of a woman with a child needing stitches on his foot.

We finally stepped out into the medina. My companion slid through the tortuous streets with the ease of a native, although somewhat inevitably we found that the cart man was already about his day's work. Miss Taylor insisted on accompanying me to the place where he had been going, a hillside tile-kiln outside the city

240

walls, but when we were then informed that he had gone on to a destination over the next hill, I turned to the little woman.

'I can take it from here. You have patients requiring you, and I now know the man's name and where he is going. I shall let you know what I find.'

In truth, I had no intention of letting her know anything, but I thought it would encourage her to leave me. And so it proved. Hesitantly, turning back twice to give me some forgotten piece of essential information about the man and his family, she finally retreated towards the city gates. I turned my face to the hills, in search of a man with a cart.

Few investigations follow direct lines, and this was no exception, but eventually I found the man, returning from a distant grove with three large canisters of olive oil and a tangle of fire-wood. I gave him greetings from Miss Taylor and engaged him in harmless conversation for a time, before asking him about the night he had found the wounded foreigner along the road.

He hesitated, but since I had established myself as a friend and nothing to do with the government, he agreed that he had found such a person, and helped him (as far as he knew, then and now, I was a him) down to the city gates.

'He was run down by the speeding motorcar, yes?'

'So it would seem. Some of the French drive so fast, it is a wonder any of us survive.'

'It was a French motor, then? Had you seen it before?'

'It was dark. I cannot be certain.'

'But something made you think it was a French motor. One you know.'

He chewed on his lip for a while.

'Your name will not come into it,' I assured him. 'I promised Miss Taylor.'

At the reminder of the author of his son's well-being, he reluctantly admitted that it was a motorcar he had seen before. 'I do not *know*, for certain. But I was close enough to hear its engine, when it speeded up and flew down the hill, and it sounded like a motorcar that I have heard before, on that road. A motor that is kept at the palace.'

'What, it belongs to the Sultan?'

'The Sultan owns everything in the country,' he said. I did not correct him. 'It is a handsome machine, very shiny. I have seen the Resident General in it. More than once. It is probably a different motor,' he said again.

I asked him for any identifying marks on the motor, hoping that perhaps it was missing a fender or had a crack across its wind-screen – something obvious enough for a farmer to notice. I did not hold out much hope.

'One-zero-zero-six-two-seven,' he recited. I stared at him in disbelief. 'The plate it wears. I like numbers,' he said simply.

I hastily removed the expression from my face, and turned the conversation to lesser matters. When the next road forked off to the south, I thanked him, wished his son long health, and took my leave.

The Royal Palace was in Fez el-Jdid, the newer

section of old Fez (as opposed to the upstart French Ville Nouvelle, where the streets were broad and the lights were electrical). I bought a handful of nuts in the Jewish quarter, amused at the queer pronunciation of Hebrew, then continued on towards the Bou Jeloud gardens, to sit beneath a tree and study the palace walls. This was a different city from that whose gate lay mere yards away. The medina was tight and secretive and Mediaeval, but here, two women in frocks were looking at the banner of a cinema house, while a man wearing suit, necktie, turban, and sunglasses stepped into a bank. Not that those in foreign dress weren't outnumbered by draped women and robed men, or that an approaching motorcar wasn't forced to thread its way around a donkey onto which were roped six European chairs, being driven by a child wielding a willow switch, then another donkey laden with a family of five or perhaps six – hard to tell, since they were all intertwined.

It was, all in all, not a bad place to wait, had I been in no hurry. However, time pressed on me, and I might have been forced to wait until darkness but for a works project, under French supervision, adjoining the palace. After a time I pocketed my snack and fell in with the queue of labourers, receiving my load of rough bricks, depositing them with the others, returning to the source.

Two trips in and out were sufficient to make my skull ache. Fortunately, they were also sufficient to tell me that the motorcar I was looking for was not in the section of the palace stables given over to the new age of transportation.

So I abandoned my unpaid hod-carrying and returned to my previous means of surveillance, perched atop a bit of wall, eating nuts and olives, longing for a cup of tea – but ingesting liquid while keeping lookout threatened to take a person from her post at a key moment.

Before dusk, my watch was successful. A pair of motorcars worked their way up the road and into the former stables. They pulled to a halt, but the people who climbed out looked nothing like Moroccan nobility. I stared, and realised that I was looking at the American family that had so irritated Lyautey the other evening. The motors might be royal possessions, but they were evidently used for many purposes, including the transport of day-tripping foreigners.

As they went past, their accents proclaimed their identities. The woman of the group, a New Yorker, was telling the others – a daughter and two young men – all about the coliseum in Rome. It seemed that my countrymen had spent the day at nearby Volubilis, the Roman ruins. I closed my ears to the stream of factual errors pouring from the grand dame, and watched two Moroccans come out from the stables to splash buckets of water over the dusty black metal before opening the doors and tossing out what seemed a remarkable quantity of debris.

The cleaners' haphazard methods gave me some hope, although I had to wait nearly an hour for confirmation. When they had tidied the floors and run rags over the front window-screens, they started the engines and moved the two motors inside. No closer attention was to be given them, because the men came out, closed the big doors, and walked off.

With the shadows growing long, I found a place where trees grew up to the stable walls and let myself in through a smaller door, walking along the deserted space until I reached the newly arrived vehicles: There remained light enough to read the registration plates: white letters on black, French flag on the left, and on one: yes, 100627.

The car was not quite as pristine as it had appeared at a distance. There were scratches on the bonnet and front fenders, a chip out of its wind-screen, and one head-lamp looked new – I had a brief vision of boys popping up from behind a low wall and pelting the passing motorcar with stones. Political turmoil in a country tended to affect the glass on shop-fronts and motorcars.

However, I was more interested in what the car had done than what had been done to it. And even without a magnifying glass, I could see that: two threads caught in the join of fender and running-board, and one hair trapped by a bolt of the folding roof.

A blonde hair.

How close I'd come to death. And one might have thought that remembering nothing about the event should have softened it, making it less immediate, but instead the internal images were worse. That one blonde hair, caught in the metal stub.

I shuddered, and fled.

Back in the city, darkness was falling. I felt cold, thirsty, tired, and desperately in need of a toilet suitable for female anatomy. My feet were tired, and the rest of me was both sore, from injuries just five days old, and shaken, by the significance of that pale strand. I was also out of money. I eyed a passing figure who had just slipped a laden note-case into his pocket, wondering how much a European-style hotel room would cost me. Or the *funduq*, where I needed to go in any event, to question the owner about the 'bad men' who had been asking after us. On the other hand, there was a familiar retreat not five minutes away, warm and secure, where I could satisfy all my needs without resorting to criminal behaviour. Just for a short time, before I returned to questioning the residents of Fez el-Jdid and the *funduq*.

Holmes had told me to watch my back. And there was no doubt, the Resident General's quarters could be as riddled with informants as any other institution in Morocco. But even if Dar Mnehbi was not completely safe, neither were the streets around me. At least under Lyautey's roof, no one would run me down, and if I was held under gun-point, someone might notice.

Dar Mnehbi's tall, dignified butler, coffee-man, and general factotum drew open the door at my knock, standing back with the Moroccan equivalent of a courtier's bow.

He didn't even cast a disapproving glance at my garments. 'Good evening, Madame,' he said in his lightly accented French.

'Good evening, Youssef,' I replied, stepping inside. 'I haven't come to stay, nor do I wish to disturb the Maréchal, but if I could sit for an hour or so in the library, it would refresh me greatly.'

But he insisted on ushering me to 'my' room, where he summoned life into the brazier and assured me, despite protests, that both drink and food would arrive. He even brought me a pair of leather slippers.

When I returned from the lavatory, I sank into the chair, revelling at the heat. A wave of exhaustion took me. I sat without moving, too limp even to lean forward and unlace my boots. I would do so. In just a minute.

Voices came from out in the *dar,* men in conversation, their words indistinct. They went sharp, then silence fell, for perhaps a minute. I had just roused sufficient energy to sit upright, aiming at removing my boots for a time, when a rap came on the door. Youssef entered.

'Your tea, Madame. I apologise for the delay, I fear it has gone cold.'

'You were very quick, thank you.'

'Shall I pour?' he asked, already doing so. 'Is it cold, Madame? Shall I take it away?'

I already had a cup in one hand and a fried savoury in the other, although with him standing at my side, I couldn't carry through and shove the morsel into my mouth. He hesitated, adjusting a spoon, then noticed that my laden hand was hovering.

Whatever he had been about to ask, he did not, merely gave a small bow and left, saying, 'Enjoy, Madame.'

I did.

A gratifyingly large plate occupied one side of

247

the tray, contributing a spicy odour to the mint of the tea. Even cool, the savoury pastries were a perfect counterpoint to the sweet, fragrant liquid, and I polished them off, leaving only one or two of the sweet tit-bits.

Satisfied, I poured another cup of the refreshing brew, and sat back with it. The room was warming nicely. Really, I thought, I should slip off my boots to rest my feet, just for a few minutes. And perhaps the *djellaba*, since the room was growing so warm. Though I mustn't get too settled. I had things to do. But the warmth of the room was lovely, so lovely, making me so relaxed, even drowsy. Oddly drowsy. Drowsy enough that the internal alarm seemed tiny and faraway. Not that it mattered. I was comfortable. Still, I mustn't fall asl

CHAPTER TWENTY-ONE

I dreamt.

It was dark, and there was a sound. I stopped to listen, hearing only the gabble of conversation near the camp-fire and the laughter of English girls.

It came again, as of a finger-nail scratching canvas. I glanced at the pillow on my camp-bed and decided against pulling out the revolver I had just secreted there: A robber was unlikely to knock – or, scratch – at my door.

I pulled aside the canvas, standing back so the bright light fell on my visitor, and looked out, then down. The late-night intruder was a winsome young urchin with brown skin and hair, light brown eyes, and gleaming white teeth, of which I could see nearly all due to his wide grin.

'No thank you,' I said in Arabic. The local inhabitants were ingenious when it came to sales techniques, and had quickly learnt to send their most attractive children to prise coins out of the Fflytte Film crew. Either children or parents decided early which of our members were easy targets, and had left me alone. This lad seemed not to have got the message.

I fastened the door on his winning smile and outstretched hand, and turned back to my beckoning sleeping roll.

The scratching came again. And again.

Bare-footed now and with my knife clearly displayed in my hand, I yanked away the canvas door. The smile disappeared; the eyes fixed on the blade; the small hand remained outstretched.

'Whatever it is you are selling, I do not wish one,' I snarled.

The boy shook his head vigorously, and pushed his grubby hand at me. I looked more closely, and saw there a piece of paper, folded in precise quarters. The moment I took it, the lad's hand dove back into his garments, coming out with something more solid. Not a weapon. Something the size of an acorn, with a gleam to it.

First things first. Taking a step back, lest he make a sudden grab for my person, I unfolded the paper.

Come with the boy.

I turned the page over, then back, but no more words appeared.

The clenched hand shot out again. I opened my palm. Onto it dropped a heavy gold ring.

And with that, I knew the writing. With recognition came pleasure and eagerness and apprehension, all together: The owner of this ring was a friend and colleague – a brother, even – whom I had never thought to see again, but whose sudden appearance was unlikely to be free of trouble.

'Where is he?' I asked. By answer, the lad stepped back, out of the light. 'No, come in for a moment, I need to put my shoes on.'

He ducked inside: So, he understood Arabic.

I sat on the camp-bed and reached underneath for my increasingly ragged old boots that, despite Fflytte's objections, had been my footwear for the past week. The boy stood in the centre of the canvas room, eyes wide at the fittings, which (unlike the footwear) were luxurious in appearance and occasionally even in comfort. He was particularly fascinated by the carbide lamp, bending to squint into its brilliance.

'Don't touch that,' I warned. 'It's hot.'

When he looked at me, he blinked furiously against the spots the lamp had etched into his vision, and the grin returned. I reached behind me to slide the revolver into the back of my waist-band, and donned a coat against the cold outside.

'What is your name, child?'

He just blinked again and grinned. Odd; he hadn't struck me as simple.

'Do you understand what I'm saying?' Vigorous nod, aimed to one side because of his temporary blindness. 'But you don't speak?' More nodding. Which could be seen as an ambiguous answer, but I decided it was response enough.

'Lead on,' I said, and he patted his way out the doorway and into the night beyond.

I dreamt.

It was dim, the sun obscured by clouds and the woven mats that covered the narrow streets. Mahmoud had given Idir a coin to buy sweets. The lad seemed to be taking a long time about the task.

Still, his absence gave us time to linger over our

coffee and catch up on life in the past year. It was a gift, to see Mahmoud restored to robes and Arabic after watching his painful transformation into an English gentleman the year before. He was solid again, the confidence returned to his hands, the authority to his glance – the only thing lacking was his habit of sprinkling his speech with aphorisms and quotes, most often from the Qur'an. I missed the depth it provided his thoughts, but perhaps its absence was due to the change in setting, and that Moroccans didn't appreciate the habit.

No matter what this favour of his cost me, it would be worth it, to have seen him like this once more.

He had been born an English earl, become a Bedouin spy, and for a brief time, worn a ducal coronet. Now he was … something else.

My teacher. An elder brother perhaps. A friend, no doubt.

In Mahmoud's presence, my Arabic seemed to go more smoothly. I told him about our time in India, the previous spring, and he had been talking about the unveiled women of the Rif when Idir came sauntering up to our tiny table, sucking his fingers, sticky to his ears.

'Happy now?' Mahmoud asked.

The boy nodded vigorously.

'Honey may be a drink of many colours, healing for men,' Mahmoud solemnly pronounced, 'but its presence necessitates a visit to the hammam this afternoon.' As he stood, gingerly pinching the boy's sleeve to draw him towards a wall-mounted fountain, I was pleased to realise that Mahmoud had come very close to giving one of his habitual quotes.

Once the boy was not a hazard to passers-by, we set off again through the bustling gloom of the medina.

Now it was dark, and I was walking up a hill. With Mahmoud. Precisely the companion one wants in a dark dream, solid and competent.

When the road turned, I saw below us a scattering of lights, climbing the slopes of the wide hollow. Some lights moved, suggesting the lamps of travellers in the medina. Off to the south was an area of greater, and stronger, lights: There, people had electricity.

Underfoot was a road, grit crunching under my boots. The sky had cleared, with the bright half-moon sufficient to keep us from walking off the cliffs. The moon – and the head-lamps of the un-moving motorcar, half a mile distant on the road above.

I had been asking Mahmoud about Lyautey, this French Maréchal we were about to meet, but he had seemed distracted. Now he stopped, studying the motionless beams for a moment. I heard a faint sound, as if he sighed. 'I will go forward. You wait here, out of the light. If there is trouble, I will need you.'

I slid my hand into my robes, on one side the comforting solidity of the revolver, on the other the weight of the knuckle-duster I had fashioned from a scrap of copper pipe found as we came through Fez el-Jdid earlier in the day. 'You expect trouble?'

His hand came up, following the scar that ran from left eye to beard. 'One always expects trouble,' he said absently.

'Who else would this be, but Lyautey?'

'Still. You have the paper?'

'The scrap? Of course.'

'Give it to me.'

'Mahmoud, what is going on?'

'Show me,' he insisted.

Impatiently, I dug around in various pockets until I came out with the bit of onionskin on which he had sketched a brief illustration earlier, to show me the place along the route where, if there was an ambush, it might be. He'd told me, he said over coffee, simply because it was foolish not to. One never knew when a brick would fall out of the sky or a soldier would decide to make an arrest.

This demand for reassurance suddenly placed a lot more weight on the possibility of his disappearance.

'Mahmoud, if this is a trap, let's stop right now.'

He said nothing, but there was sufficient brightness to see that his hand was out.

Asking to 'see' the paper scrap was somewhat pointless in the dark, but I pulled it out, flicking it back and forth to prove its existence. His hand came over mine, removing the little triangle, wrinkling it until he was satisfied that it was the correct one. Then he thrust it back into my pocket, and turned away.

'Stay here. I will call when I am sure it is safe.'

'Don't be long,' I said. 'I'm half-frozen.'

His footsteps went ahead of me, towards the

motorcar, not hesitating even as the light blinded him. It was, it would seem, the correct motor: Maréchal Lyautey, making a brief stop in his incredibly busy day for an appointment with a man he had met but once. I could hear Mahmoud's feet over the low idle of the engine. His black silhouette grew, robes tugged by the breeze coming up the hillside.

The wind made me shiver. I squatted down to give it less of a target. Listening to Mahmoud's footsteps recede, watching his long-stretched outline grow along the road and then disappear as he reached the motorcar, hearing his voice speak a question, my left hand held the revolver while the fingers of my right hand idly explored the ground at my feet, picked up a couple of conveniently-sized stones, and – without my thinking much about it – slipped them in the nearest pocket. Except that when I did so, there seemed to be one there already: a bump, where none had been before. My eyes watched the road while my fingers let go of the stones to explore this foreign object: a lump, with a crinkle around it – the scrap of paper, and...

I leapt upright, and my cry loosed an explosion. 'Mahmoud!' I screamed, and many things happened at once. The flash from his revolver imprinted a sense of struggling figures; voices began to shout. I ran, the revolver useless with Mahmoud up there and invisible. But before I had covered ten yards, the engine sound changed and the twin beams ahead of me swept over the road, splashing across me for a moment before they returned, seeking me out, blinding me as they drew rapidly closer.

Hand raised against the brilliance, I leapt behind a boulder just off the road, where the driver would have to risk flying off the mountainside if he wanted to run me down. Gun in one hand and knife in the other, I turned my head from the searing brightness, and waited for the impact.

Instead, a mad scuffle of hard braking made the motor veer wildly back and forth until it came to a halt, thirty feet away, its head-lamps shining at the opposite hillside. Voices, one of them sharp, commanding, even furious. After a moment came the sound of a man jumping down to the road. I crouched in silence, waiting for him, and for the dazzle to clear from my eyes.

Steady footsteps came down the roadway, on a line between me and the motor, forcing me to hold my fire. More harsh words came, in the language I did not understand. No response from the man on foot. The car stayed where it was, facing the upper hill, engine idling. Slowly, almost reluctantly, the man drew nearer.

The situation was perplexing: They must have guns – everyone in Morocco seemed to have one. Why not just pin me in the head-lamps and shoot me? Either they wanted to capture me alive, or they feared attracting attention: One or two gunshots might go overlooked, but not a blazing battle. Which meant that the man coming towards me either bore a silent weapon – against the gun they would assume I, too, carried – or he had been given the task of drawing me out. With a torch, perhaps, to guide the aim of a comrade at his back...

The threats of an angry commander with a rifle might also explain the reluctance of the footsteps – I might almost have suspected that the approaching man was a bound and gagged Mahmoud, were I not certain that he'd have contrived to give me a clue. No, this was a different kind of sacrificial goat – not a captive, but one of their own.

As my eyes cleared, the approaching figure's stance betrayed the weapon in his hand.

Moving with stealth, I laid down the revolver. The steps slowed, and stopped, twenty feet away. He listened for my breathing, then I heard the sound of fabric shifting, and I moved.

Half a second after the beam from his hand-torch came on, my rock knocked the torch to the ground.

But he'd had the torch in his left hand, and as I closed with him, his right hand came up fast.

I was lucky, both that he could not see well, and that he was not used to left-handed opponents. His blade sliced fire across my upper arm before I danced back, but my hand was alive with the awareness that my own knife had cut deep: I had done more damage than he.

He staggered away, calling out to the motorcar. Gears clashed and the beams drew back from the facing hillside, but the moment the head-lamps appeared, the first of my missiles clattered off the metal fender. The second went wide, but the third hit home, splintering one glass head-lamp into darkness while they pulled their wounded colleague inside. Then the engine roared as the driver realised the danger, and the remaining beam was rushing at me, swerving back and forth to avoid my stones. At the last instant, I threw myself to the side.

But either I'd left it too late, or a twitch on the steering wheel brought them a fraction too close. The front fender brushed beneath my arms like a bull under a toreador, and the running board slid past my legs, but as the metal body travelled down my garments, some portion reached out to snatch me, pulling me in and slamming my head a great blow.

I stepped into the dark, and was gone.

I woke, again. It was cold. I was thirsty.
This time, the darkness was absolute.

CHAPTER TWENTY-TWO

Sherlock Holmes did not look back. One would think, he reflected, that a person could grow accustomed to walking away from a wife who might be headed towards danger (Russell? *Might?*) but after nearly four years of marriage, he had yet to learn indifference. Although considering her general state, the last thing he wished was for her to accompany him. He'd end up with her collapsed on the road, and having to purchase a donkey across which to sling her.

Still, in her stead he had been given an almost ideal travelling companion, one who would not interrupt with questions that were either imbecilic (at the one extreme) or overly perceptive (at the other), one whose very passivity was a strength. One for whom there was no distracting attachment: no hostage to fortune, no emotional grit in the machinery.

'Do you know how to whistle?' he asked the boy. The voiceless lad glanced at him without comprehension, so Holmes repeated the question – and in case his Arabic vocabulary was faulty, he followed with a brief demonstration.

In response, Idir pursed his lips and blew, with no result.

So as they walked, Holmes demonstrated first simple tunes, then the piercing blare made by a pair of fingers. Idir's were filthy, but efficient, and he soon mastered both a breathy warble of notes and a short blast.

'Very good,' Holmes said. 'Now you have a means of attracting attention. Your next task is to find us a place to sleep for the night. Preferably with a roof.'

The boy gave him a sideways glance, then gestured at his mouth with pinched-together fingers.

'By all means, we must have a meal.'

The fingers rubbed together, the universal symbol for cash.

'I have a little money, yes.'

The child was of an age when responsibility came as a gift; he walked on with a bounce in his step and a whistle on his lips.

Holmes' plan was simple: to talk, and to listen. The fabric of social interactions in this country was closely woven, and if a group of men had lingered in the vicinity of a motorcar, waiting for a message that would send them to an abduction, elements of that series of events would make them stand out: access to a motorcar, a means of receiving a message (be it by hand, telegraph, or telephone), and a place where a minimum of three men might wait for that message.

A town was the most obvious place to find all three elements. In this part of the country, that meant either the outskirts of Fez, the growing town of Mequinez, or the hillside town of Moulay Idriss. If their opponents were followers of Raisuli, it suggested a degree of religious conservatism that might feel more at home in the last of those.

Fez itself he would leave to Russell: As he'd told

her, he and the boy were too liable to be recognised there. And if his veteran beekeeper's mind persisted in its vision of a hive turning to attack an invader, well, there was little he could do about it now except trust to Russell's skills.

The route he and the boy would follow took them beyond Russell's spheres of Fez el-Bali and Fez el-Jdid. As he had seen from the train, clusters of buildings lay along the road between Fez and Mequinez, each too small to be considered a village but incorporating the occasional garage, café, and telegraph connexion. Beyond Mequinez, one could describe a circle back to Fez through Moulay Idriss, but the final leg of that route sounded little better than a mule-track; it was not impossible that the motorcar had originated in the mountain fastness of Idriss, but unlikely.

In any event, taking the slower southern way would let him pick up a few accoutrements – an inexpensive leather bag to sling across his chest, a worn prayer rug, a bright embroidered cap the boy eyed with envy – and to polish his role. It would also permit the local bush telegraph system to lay the ground before he faced the more demanding audience of Moulay Idriss.

But that would be tomorrow. Frankly – although he'd never say as much to Russell – he ached. It had been a long day in the saddle. And walking, which had begun as a relief, held little appeal with more than thirty miles before him.

Whatever his young companion's background, the lad was well versed on the ways of the road. Within the hour, they were tucking into a greasy lamb *tagine* at a roadside eatery, the proprietor somewhat reassured by the appearance of coins on the table: Holy men were all well and good, but one didn't give a wandering *marabout* a place by the fire and the choicer bits of meat if he wasn't paying for it.

A Moroccan *marabout* could be anything from a highly respected *madrassa* teacher to the keeper of a scruffy roadside shrine (the word even meant the shrine itself). In the south, where the temperature was less deadly for those forced to sleep rough, Holmes had seen a number of raving madmen who were thought touched by God. His own form of *marabout* was that of an itinerant pilgrim, on a tour of holy places to honour a vow made when a grandson's life was spared. And to give him an excuse to engage the locals in conversation, he would produce amulets for them, Qur'anic verses written on paper, folded into shapes he had learnt in Japan.

'Do they not look at camels, how they are made?' was folded into a vestigial face with a long neck. 'And your Lord inspired the bee, from whose bellies comes a healing drink, a sign for all who give thought' became a quite recognisable honeybee. And for a patron so loud and stupid, one might have thought alcohol was being served, he folded the verse 'He who claims to worship Allah but does not follow His Law is like the donkey laden with books, who does not understand the wisdom' inside a long face with two ears.

At first, the men in the ramshackle wayside café were wary, receiving the small paper figures with bewilderment. But when he showed no indications of greater lunacy than giving away what he claimed were amulets, and was amiable in conversation, they slowly relaxed, and their tongues as well.

Talk was of the French soldiers, being drawn from all over Morocco to the encampment south of the city. Soon, they would march into the Rif. In the meantime, there was the thrill of the aeroplanes that rose and disappeared out over the mountains, to return to earth on the flat strip the French had caused to be laid. The younger men were eager for the fighting to begin; the older men (a man here was truly old at fifty) had a pang for the planting season, but all agreed that Abd el-Krim was sure to turn his once-Spanish guns on the French before long.

Holmes permitted the talk to run for a time on what were clearly well-worn grooves, before giving tiny nudges. Many Unbelievers must have come with the French, he supposed. Yes, they were indeed curious, he had seen that himself. But in his own village (vague, to the east, somewhere) when the Unbelievers came, it seemed to open the door to other strange men. Small groups of men, who asked odd and urgent questions. Men who seemed in a hurry. Men who were there, and gone. And their motorcars – roaring through villages at all hours, threatening life and livestock.

The very opposite of this amiable pilgrim, who was in no hurry to do anything but press into the hand of every person in the room a scrap of Arabic-inscribed paper folded into the shape of a bird or a tree or, once, the frog whose verse – 'We sent a flood, and locusts and lice, frogs and blood, as signs, but they were an arrogant and criminal people' – had sparked the discussion of an influx of criminal types.

Nor was the pilgrim in a hurry to leave. He drained his final glass of tea, laid a few more coins on the low table, and wrapped his burnoose snugly around him. When the proprietor gave a final glance into his café, he saw the aged *marabout*, his long fingers playing along the beads of his *tasbih*, staring into the embers of the low-burning brazier.

Ah well, thought Holmes: Not every cast hooks a winner. These men had neither been questioned by intruders searching for Mahmoud Hazr, nor had they taken note of a fleeing motorcar, late on Thursday night.

An enemy scarcely required formal spies here, he reflected, not with half the populace in and out of the homes, offices, and military bases. And perhaps he was too near Fez for the residents of this hamlet to take note of an evening motorcar. Ten years ago, yes, but in this fast-moving world of 1924, even rural villagers were technological sophisticates.

In the morning, he and Idir were on their way again. They walked along the dusty road towards Mequinez, the only likely route for a motor abduction, stopping regularly for tea and talk, venturing a mile or two down likely side-roads. Whenever he heard a distant reminder from a muezzin, he paused to take out his scrap of carpet and say his prayers.

Idir took these for granted. As a child, he was not required to join in, but he watched with

264

interest the first few times, and after that, accepted it as part of the day's routine.

The lad reminded Holmes of the young street Arabs he had paid to act as Irregulars in his Baker Street days. And like those lads, one could only speculate about this one's history and inner life. The boy was intelligent, no doubt of that. And while he seemed content to stay with this adult to whom he had been assigned, he also seemed to have his own private matters to attend to. It was a bit like walking a business-like and energetic retriever who spent more time casting to and fro in the shrubs and by-ways than at heel. Fortunately, again like the retriever, Idir had an instinct for when his companion was about to change direction, and the bright cap would come trotting back into view.

It proved a congenial way to travel, permitting Holmes adequate time for meditation over what he found during the course of the day: a garage that sold petrol, run by a wizened shopkeeper and his six grandsons; a car hire agency, run by a Jewish woman in trousers; a dozen shops with public telephones; countless small cafés where men might have waited for darkness; and any number of narrow roads that would have performed the same function.

Nowhere did his understated questions about men in motorcars strike an answer.

Very well: They had originated in a centre of greater population, where men waiting in motors were too commonplace to notice. Therefore, what was required were more specific, and hence more dangerous, questions.

Darkness and Mequinez approached simultaneously. Mequinez had been a small backwater town until the opening of a railway station, when modern life began to pump in energy. The town's disproportionately vast ruins traced the palaces and mosques, stables and pavilions of terrible old Sultan Moulay Ismaïl, who had fought off Turk and European alike, wrapped an iron fist around the country with his army of Black Guards, entertained himself by acts of extreme cruelty, and employed Christian slaves as either beasts of burden or sources of income. Now it had the beginnings of industry and the drawing room salons of an expatriate European community.

More immediately, it had facilities for native (and seemingly native) travellers. He hired beds at a *funduq*, wishing it had been a British inn built above a public house with a good claret, and took his footsore self down the road to an eating establishment, asking his increasingly tedious questions over glasses of cloying mint tea, skewers of overspiced chicken, and plates of dry couscous. At the end of the fruitless exercise, he and Idir returned to their hired beds and curled up in their *djellabas*. He hoped they didn't catch some loathsome malady from the cushions.

By noon, he was well finished with Mequinez. As they walked north, a mule-cart came rattling behind them, and the driver called out to see if the pilgrim would like a ride.

He was a burly, one-eyed farmer who had seen Holmes and Idir in the market that morning, where he had gone to deliver a load of reeds. Holmes glanced thoughtfully at the road ahead of them, noting its almost complete lack of garages, cafés, or shops containing public telephones, and tossed the boy onto the cart's flat back. He climbed up beside the man, who whipped his mule into a bone-jarring trot and launched into a monologue about reeds, mules, wives, children, and the state of the country. Holmes rode along, nodding at appropriate spots, idly folding a piece of paper while smoking one of the farmer's hand-rolled cigarettes – a tobacco so powerful it made his tongue go numb. Idir sat watching the road roll out behind them, his feet dangling free, practising his whistles.

When the man paused for breath, Holmes handed him the amulet, then managed to slip in a question about motorcars. But though the farmer had much to say about them, he had no specific knowledge.

The man was heading more or less in the direction of Moulay Idriss. The road turned north, bringing into view an unlikely piece of architecture, away in the distance.

'Is that the ancient city of the Romans?' he asked the man.

The man followed Holmes' eyes to what could only be a triumphal arch and began a detailed story about the time his wife had got it into her head that what their farmyard needed was a stone entranceway and how much time he'd had to spend hauling blocks out of the place until she was satisfied.

Clearly, not a student of archaeology.

On the other hand, the arch piqued Idir's curiosity. When they were on the ground and the man had whipped his mule back into a trot, Idir tugged at Holmes' sleeve, looking a question at him.

Holmes glanced at the sun, and at the distance to the white city of Moulay Idriss. They'd made better time than he had reckoned, and after two days of pointless questioning he doubted he would strike gold here; so why not permit the boy some entertainment?

He nodded, and Idir skipped ahead in pleasure. Fifty metres down the road he bent to pick up something; when Holmes caught up, he saw the boy scowling in mighty disapproval, working to smooth a wadded bit of paper back into shape.

Holmes' amulet for the cart driver had been a mule.

'Do you know what this is?' Holmes addressed the lad.

Idir waggled both hands on the sides of his head.

'Not the amulet, the buildings. They're Roman.'

A quick lift of one eyebrow indicated that the lad was listening.

'Hundreds and hundreds of years ago, even before the birth of the Prophet Mohammed (blessed be he), there was a great empire sprung from the city of Rome, in Italy. You know Italy?'

A shrug.

'The empire stretched across the known world, from England to India, and across the north of Africa to here. Here, and a town down near Rabat, were the empire's south-western boundaries.'

He told the lad stories of Roman emperors for

a time, and soon they were craning their necks at the stone arch topped by a stork's untidy nest, a monument that would surely collapse at the next minor tremor. Volubilis was a vast tract of scattered blocks and broken columns, with but a portion of the city under archaeological excavation. The miracle was that any portion of the original remained to be studied: for centuries, local building projects had made use of all this conveniently prehewn rock as a quarry. Much of Mequinez had been built of Volubilis stone – Holmes had spotted the odd block and column along the road, discarded by grateful slaves upon news of the old Sultan's death. More recently, a small-scale railway had been driven through the site, to speed the pillaging.

Holmes sat down on a block that had thus far remained in situ, smoking a cigarette while Idir scuffed at some grass from a bit of mosaic pavement, squatting to prise up a few of the stones.

The curator's house, surrounded by gardens, terraces, and decorative pergolas, was currently a centre of activity. A cluster of Europeans including three women consulted with several Army officers. Holmes watched, but stayed where he was, not wishing to be driven away with a stick or arrested for permitting the boy to rob the site. When his cigarette was finished, he dusted his clothing and turned back to the road, prayer beads in hand, making for the splash of white buildings surmounting the pair of hill-tops above.

The town of Moulay Idriss was *haram* – sacred, or forbidden, a holy place suited for mystics. It contained the tomb of Sultan Idris I, a direct descendent of the Prophet, who came to Morocco in the year 789, married a local woman, and laid the foundations of Fez. The little town was conservative to the point of xenophobia, welcome home to extremists and fanatics; only very recently had foreigners even been permitted entrance. The shrine was a natural goal for any Moslem pilgrim; it was also a place where an unmasked European might expect to meet harsh hands.

Idir caught him up, chewing on an apple he had either begged or stolen from the Europeans.

'We need to take care in this place,' Holmes told him. 'They are very proud, and not loving of strangers.'

The lad looked at him sideways, clearly understanding all too well what that meant. The enthusiasm went out of him as they drew near the town, the sun beginning to throw their shadows ahead on the steep road. He stayed close by Holmes' side for a time as they followed the flow of bodies towards the central square. But when the inhabitants did not instantly leap on them with cudgels, and when Holmes settled into a native café under one of the main square's arcades, where the air was rich with the odour of grilling meat, some of the tension left the lad. After a few moments fidgeting on a bench, he wandered off to study the wares of the fruit merchant, then stood watching the sawdust flying from a hand-drill as old as civilisation, but he kept one eye on Holmes, and trotted back as soon as the food appeared.

When their plates were empty and the glass of tea had been refilled, Holmes drew out his pencil and the paper again. For the next three hours he produced a series of origami shapes with Arabic script at their hearts, and never had to pay for his own refill of tea. He made it clear that he was no beggar – he did not accept coins for his paper amulets – but in the end, the café's customers paid in gossip. Idir's initial trepidation gave way to boredom, and he wandered in and out, as was his habit.

Holmes did not expect to hear news of a motor-car racing through Moulay Idriss, considering the state of the back road to Fez. However, to catch the scent of a politically-based abduction, a town of fanatics seemed as good a place to begin as any.

Love for Lyautey and his French Protectorate was thin on the ground here, despite general agreement that the French trade fairs were worthy additions to the country's festivities, and that French roads simplified travel to market, and the medical clinics had saved the lives of their sons. When Holmes dropped gentle mention of the northern rebellion, as he had suspected, there proved to be mixed affection for Abd el-Krim: The Emir took a satisfyingly strong stand against the foreign oppressor, but he was both a commoner, and from a tribe that was already too powerful for their neighbours' comfort.

Raisuli, though...

'I am told that the Sherif is ill,' Holmes commented as he wrote a careful verse.

A pool of quiet spread around him. When he

271

finished the line, he looked up to find the men around him studying their finger-nails and gazing into their glasses.

So: Raisuli had friends here. And even those who loved him not hesitated to venture a criticism. Clearly he, or his son, or perhaps merely his followers, were a force to be reckoned with.

'It was merely a rumour I heard in Fez,' he said. 'It may be untrue, *insh'Allah.*'

The chorus of agreement confirmed the tenor of their support.

'I was also told that the Resident General has been ill. Although when he was pointed out to me in the medina, he looked quite hearty.'

This took the conversation neatly sideways for a time, into wide-ranging speculation as to who might replace the Maréchal and what difference it would bring. Only when the conversation had looped around to the changes in village life under the French did Holmes drop in his question about dangerous motorcars and inquisitive strangers.

Being a town with an important shrine, strangers were commonplace. It took some time before a laconic argument between two men – partially in Arabic, fortunately, rather than entirely in Thamazigth – told Holmes that there had indeed been such a trio, and that they had left in the direction of Mequinez. Whether this had been three days before or seven, he could not contrive a way of finding out without raising suspicions.

Originally, Holmes had intended to stop the night here. The sun was near to setting outside, but the longer he sat, the less pleased he was with the idea of staying. When the evening call to prayer came and the plaza emptied, he abruptly folded away his dwindling supply of paper and looked around for Idir.

The town was prickling the hair on the back of his neck. An apparently irrational judgment, but he had not got to his age by ignoring his body's reaction to threats too subtle to see. He had the uneasy sensation that information here was going both directions, and his presence would not go long unnoticed – and unreported.

So: He would not risk more questions, and certainly not chance settling down for the night. As soon as Idir came back, they would leave.

But Idir did not return.

It was the first time his faithful retriever had not anticipated him. Holmes took a slow turn around the square, expecting the lad to pop into existence as he had every ten or thirty minutes during the afternoon.

He sat and smoked a cigarette.

He studied the dwindling crowds in the square, waiting for something wrong to come to the fore, some pattern of motion unlike the others, some face watching him with untoward intensity.

He waited, and Idir did not come.

He had given the lad a few coins, insufficient for anything more time-consuming than haggling over a handful of walnuts. Perhaps he'd talked – or signalled – his way into a bath. Holmes slung his bag across his shoulder and made enquiries as to the nearest *hammam*.

Once beyond the central square, the ill-lit streets of Moulay Idriss were narrow and twisting, often steep enough to become a flight of uneven steps, slick with centuries of use. It did nothing to assuage the feeling on the back of his neck, and his questions to the few shopkeepers and beggars still out – if they had seen a lad with an embroidered cap – grew ever more urgent.

They had not seen him. Nor had the attendants of the *hammam*.

The sky was black overhead when he returned to the square. The arched arcades, bustling with vendors and craftsmen during the day, were mostly shuttered now.

It made the waiting figure very easy to see.

A lamp sat on the ground before the man, whose face was covered by a fold of his turban, in the style of a desert-dweller. But Holmes barely looked at the seated figure. His eyes were drawn by the embroidered cap, arranged so the lamp-light fell directly on it.

Holmes stayed in the deep shadow of one of the entranceways to the square. The space was by no means deserted, and there were others sitting beneath the arcades, most of whom were either smoking or talking with friends.

The seated figure's hand came up to adjust the tuck of his turban. His hands were empty. After another close survey of the square, Holmes decided the man was alone. He was also seated in a position that made it impossible to come up behind him.

Holmes blew out a breath, considering his options.

There might be no emotional attachment to this Moroccan Irregular, but there was responsibility. And in truth, even knowing that the mute lad's 'personal business' could be with Raisuli's men and his disappearance a part of a trap, the cap made it difficult for Holmes to turn his back

In any event, Mahmoud and Ali were bound to the lad, and that was all the debt he required. Surely Russell would agree.

He stepped out of the darkness, pacing evenly across the square towards the seated man.

He was pleasantly surprised when no one shot him.

The man stood as he approached, his hood going back to reveal a clean-shaven face.

'Where is the boy?' Holmes asked.

'We have him.'

'Yes,' he said impatiently. 'Where?'

'You will come.'

'Then lead.'

And incredibly, the man did. Holmes stared at the exposed back, then bent to snatch up the cap before following. Across the square, under the dim arcades, past the shuttered shop-fronts and through residential areas, wary at every step of the darker shadows.

At the end of the city, the road that came down from the hills and ran along the edges of Moulay Idriss turned sharply away. There the man, as seemingly oblivious of a danger at his back as he had been for the previous ten minutes, came out from the city and continued down the sloping road towards a parked motorcar.

Beyond the motorcar and the faintly visible figures, a glow of acetylene lights rose from the Roman ruins, a mile or so away. Impossible, not to pause for a moment's reflection on the symbolic and unreachable brilliance of the French authority – then Holmes shook off the thought, to consider what lay before him.

It was no later than ten o'clock, but the roadway was deserted other than the motorcar and its cluster of figures, half-illuminated by the headlamps. Three men, including the one he had followed, stood staring back at the city walls. But it was the fourth figure who interested him. The small one whose shoulder was in the grip of a man's hand.

Holmes cupped his hands to shout, 'Idir, if you are well, raise your arm.'

The boy's head shot up, followed by both hands. They appeared to be bound – and proved so as the lad made a lunge for freedom, then gave an inarticulate cry as he was snagged back. Not only bound, but leashed to his captor.

The man yanked the boy cruelly towards him, and his arm went up.

'No!' Holmes' sharp command surprised himself as much as it did the man. It would appear that he had made up his mind. Cursing under his breath at the wandering of retrievers and the inevitability of emotional grit in the machinery, Holmes accepted the responsibility laid upon him. 'If you hurt the boy, you will not get what you want.'

The tableau held, then the beardless man called, 'What do you imagine we want?'

'You want me.' Not that he could see why, precisely. Still, the ransom was sure to be either political or monetary. If they'd simply wanted him dead, they'd had sufficient opportunity.

'You will trade yourself for the boy?'

'You let him go, I will come out.'

'You come out first.'

Holmes walked out of the darkness, covering a third of the distance before he stopped.

'You are armed?' the man asked.

'Yes.'

'Lay your gun down.'

'Not until the boy is free.'

The sound that came made his skin go cold: the working of a rifle bolt, as the third man readied to fire. He forced his voice under control, to say, 'You may take one of us alive, not both. And what harm can he do you? He can't talk.'

The conversation that followed was too low for him to hear, but after a minute, the large man leashed to Idir moved. There came a dull flash of metal, but the knife was low – and in an instant Idir was running up the road.

The boy skidded to a halt in front of him. Holmes stepped around so the motorcar's head-lamps were not blinding him, face on. He pulled the embroidered cap from his pocket, then bent down to meet the child's eyes.

'You must not let these men take you again,' he said. 'Make your way to Fez and tell Russell – tell Miri what happened here. She will help you. Understand?'

The half-lit, half-shadowed face nodded, then the boy snatched the cap and shoved it onto his unkempt hair.

'Run,' Holmes told him. 'Run like the wind, and do not let them capture you – now, run!'

And the boy flew – up the road and around the corner, and was gone. Holmes straightened slowly, aware of a thin trail of longing that followed the small figure. Still, the lad's safety simplified what was to come – and would provide Russell with a scent of where her husband had gone.

He was left with two options. Simple flight was not one of them: He had committed himself too far into the road for that. He could straighten his arm and empty his revolver at the men, trusting to their startled scramble for shelter to cover his retreat into the town. His other choice was to go with them.

Long before Raisuli, kidnapping for ransom had been a time-honoured profession here in the Maghreb. And while kidnappers were not gentle to their victims, they rarely murdered them outright. Also, captivity by its nature bore the possibility of escape, particularly with Mary Russell and Ali Hazr in pursuit. Who knew – he might even find Mahmoud.

For he had no doubt at all that this shiny motor sitting before him was the same one that had taken Mahmoud, nearly killing Russell in the process.

But he would not think about that just yet. Anger was incompatible with clear thinking.

'Your gun,' prompted the man.

'If I lay it down, you will shoot me,' he answered.

'If you do *not* lay it down, we will shoot you.'

'If you're going to shoot me either way, why shouldn't I want to take you with me?' It was an

278

idiotic conversation, about an idiotic topic – what an ignominious episode for an otherwise superb career, to be snagged by unimaginative thugs on a dusty road in a distant country. But the longer he kept them talking, the farther the boy could run.

'If you come with us, we will not shoot you.'

'A knife, then.' One minor blessing was that Russell didn't have to overhear this supremely pointless conversation.

'We will not kill you.'

'You don't imagine I believe that?'

But to his astonishment, the man swore an oath – using the Divine name – that neither he nor his companions would kill Holmes, if he laid down his gun and came with them: *immediately.*

It was an oath no true believer would break. As Holmes considered where the oath's loopholes might lie, the man's voice made it clear that his time was at an end.

'Do *not* make me shoot you.'

'I wouldn't think of it,' Holmes answered.

Laying his revolver on the ground, he straightened and took two steps to the side. And waited.

CHAPTER TWENTY-THREE

My world was black. Tar black. Feel-your-eye-lids-to-see-if-they're-open black. Blinded black.

It smelt of dust. Not the baked dust of a summer's day, dust bleached clean by the sun's heat, but a dust that was old and vile, dust that was the crumbling of bones and subterranean spaces. Dust that had collected for centuries, without a glimpse of the sky.

Once before, I had awakened in a black cellar, an experience that still haunted my dreams. For an instant, I thought this another nightmare, but the smell was wrong: The cellar had smelt of damp, this of dry. That tiny difference not only convinced me I was awake, it kept me from stepping instantly into panic.

Instead, I sneezed, which generated three reactions: First, my skull screamed at me that I really mustn't do that again, for a very long time, if ever. Second, chains rattled in a most un-friendly fashion. And third, I heard a voice.

Or, I thought I did, underneath my own groan at the flare of pain. I lay still, breathing through my open mouth, eyes straining at the darkness. It came again, a hoarse whisper.

'Miri?'

The surge of emotion that swept through me was both powerful and absurd. Given that he had to be as much a prisoner here as I, the sensation that my flailing hand had just encountered a solid raft in a vast ocean was unjustified.

But that is what I felt.

'Mahmoud!' I said. 'Is that you?'

My voice slithered unpleasantly into the blackness, stirring echoes; belatedly, I realised that perhaps I should have kept my voice down.

But the sound he'd made had been faint not through a fear of being overheard or because it was far off, but due to a quality I would never have associated with Mahmoud Hazr.

Weakness.

A murmur arose, a sound like a distant engine that took me a while to realise was coming from my companion in the darkness. He paused to draw breath, before the thready voice came again, this time in words rather than a mumble. 'How long?'

'How long have you been here, do you mean? It's five or six days since they drove off with you.' Was this still Tuesday night? 'Where are we?'

He drew breath, and spoke on the exhale. 'Habs Qara.'

For a moment, the words meant nothing. Then the combination of hiss and guttural descended like a fist: Habs Qara, the vast underground prison built by the tyrannical sultan Moulay Ismaïl to house his foreign slaves. Some fifty thousand of them. Those who did not die and become construction material. I sat up, feeling metal bite my left ankle as I did so. 'No! Why?'

His breath wheezed in and out for a few moments before his laborious answer came. 'El-Raisuli. Is of the Alaouite. Dynasty.'

I bit back my initial response of *Huh?* for fear of making too great a demand on his strength. While my thoughts fumbled with his words, my fingers explored the metal on my ankle: shackles, rough but sturdy; padlock, ditto; chains extending out in both directions, flat against the floor. The whole lot rattled as I worked myself around to lean against stone – a pillar, judging by the chains, rather than a wall. I scratched my head – bare; pushed up my spectacles – gone; and tried to pull my burnoose tight against the cold, only to find it missing as well. Why they hadn't stripped me entirely, I did not know.

Very well: I still had my brain.

As I told myself that, I discovered it was true: The frozen grip on my memories had loosed. The dream that had brought me awake was no dream: the motorcar, the fight, the stone in my pocket. All real.

I made a noise, which sounded like pain even though it began as a kind of laughter, at the hideous irony: Light had dawned in the utter darkness.

I ripped myself away from that pointless spiral, and started thinking aloud.

'Raisuli is of– Oh, and by the way, Ali is fine. He went back into the Rif with Abd el-Krim after the meeting with Lyautey, which was apparently successful, although I can't see that much of an agreement was reached. However: Raisuli. As you say, he is of the house of Alaouite, and claims to be the rightful heir to the Moroccan throne. Being a descendent of Moulay Ismaïl (frankly, I should think it's hard to find a Moroccan who isn't), that would make Ismaïl's capital city a potent symbol. And Ismaïl's dungeon for foreigners doubly so, it being under the very noses of the foreign intruders.'

I waited for a response. When none came, I went on. 'Lyautey and your friend Abd el-Krim agree that Raisuli himself is very ill, which makes it unlikely that he was actively involved in putting us here. If you think he is behind this, it would, rather, be his supporters, striking a blow against France and the Rif Republic at the same time.'

I interpreted the small noise my fellow prisoner emitted as approval, however vague. I continued. 'I'm not going to ask how you got here or what you imagine they have in mind for us, since I can tell that you're finding speech difficult. More immediately, we need to free ourselves before they come back. Let me know if they left you with anything that might be of use – I have no spectacles, robe, or turban, though they did leave me my trousers, shirt, boots, and– What was that?'

I went quiet so he could repeat his short phrase. When he did, I heard the words but the meaning escaped me. At first. When they finally took hold in my mind, the darkness grew so very cold.

'What do you mean, "not coming"?' I demanded. 'Raisuli's made a career out of selling back foreign prisoners. Once Lyautey pays the ransom, we'll be out of here.'

No answer came.

I pushed the silence away. 'I suppose that if his followers see Raisuli as the heir of Moulay Ismaïl, kidnapping Europeans comes naturally to mind when their purse runs empty. And Raisuli seems to treat his captives better than Moulay Ismaïl did. The important ones, anyway. Like Perdicaris and Maclean. And us.'

Silence. Raisuli perhaps, but his followers?

'I have to say, it's awfully cold in here. Did they give you a blanket or robe of some kind?'

Either he did not answer, or his response was too low for me to hear. 'What about food? I don't imagine it's anything to write home about, but how often do they bring it?'

He did not reply.

'Mahmoud, can you hear me?'

His answer was long in coming. When it came, I wished it had not done so.

'No food.'

The cold and dark seized my very bones. 'No food?' It was my turn to whisper. 'What about drink? Surely at least they bring water?'

No answer came. Which from Mahmoud was answer enough.

'You've been here for five days with no food or water?'

The appalled silence that fell was a palpable entity, a huge, infinitely heavy thing that drifted over a pair of tiny heartbeats, faltering lungs, weak fingers. The other time I had woken in blackness, my imagination had peopled that prison with an enemy capable of utter silence, invisible at my side, readying a knife for my throat. Here, I was in a dungeon that had known the implacable death of a thousand like me – ten thousand, suffering and abandoned beneath the ground, the living bound up with those who rotted in their chains, while above, the world went on.

I have known fear before. This was terror. It hollowed my strength and brought a whimper to my throat, and with it an almost overpowering urge to fling myself to the reaches of my shackles and scream until my voice failed.

Almost. Had Mahmoud not been there, had the memory of his sardonic gaze not been more immediate than the present reality of a man barely conscious, the wave of despair would have broken over me. But he needed me – *Mahmoud*, needing *me* – and I could not afford the luxury of losing control. If any passer-by even heard my screams, they would be dismissed as the wind, or as a *jinn*. Just as Mahmoud's had been: He must have shouted to the limits of his strength. It was why he could barely speak.

And at that knowledge, my hollow limbs filled, my spine went stiff, my trembling mouth snapped shut. This proud and gifted man had given a lifetime of service to king and country, only to be reduced to screams for help in a deserted prison. Death in open battle was one thing; craven atrocity could not be permitted.

I would not permit it.

'Damn it, Mahmoud,' I shouted, 'Ali will have my guts for garters if I let you die here!'

I had been locked in a lightless cellar before, and survived. The experience had taught me that there are more ways to see than the one. It was hard, to force my mind away from emotion and into a cold analysis and assessment, but as I did

285

so, I began to suspect that our captors were more driven by ideological passions than methodical criminality: They had removed my burnoose and *djellaba,* but had not stripped me bare. They had found the bank-notes, coins, and folding knife in my pockets, but failed to notice the two thongs around my neck, both of them holding gold rings. They had removed my glasses – in any event, my glasses had disappeared – but left behind the flat stone, the scrap of onionskin, and a few bread crumbs. They had found the sturdy knife I had strapped to my right wrist, but–

Incredibly, they had left me my tired footwear. Including the slim throwing knife that rode there.

'Mahmoud, are you there?'

'…'

'I have a knife. I'm going to get us out of here. Don't you dare die on me.'

His response was indistinct, trailing away in echoes, but even so, I knew what he had said: *insh'Allah.* And I knew, too, that even now, there would have been a faint smile as he said it.

Rage warmed my fingers as they searched the shackles around my ankle. Fury pushed back the darkness, reducing it from a deadly threat to an exasperating inconvenience. The shackles were rough with rust, but not to the extent that they were weakened. The hasp was fastened with a padlock, which felt new. I had a brief picture of a man in a *djellaba* haggling with the medina equivalent of an ironmonger, and that stoked my outrage further.

I needed something to open the lock. A year ago, I'd have put my hand to my head and drawn

286

out a pair of hair-pins, but my hair was short now – I even recalled cutting it, eleven months ago in India – far too short to need pinning. My spectacles were gone. And the knife might be slim, but its point would not slip into the padlock's hole. I could try using it to prise the mechanism apart, but the lock felt solid, and I was loath to risk snapping my only weapon.

I sat against the pillar, finger-tips caressing the cool blade. The alternative was to conduct a detailed search of the ground within my reach, in hopes of finding an object that could be turned to picking a simple lock. A bit of metal, my trodden-on spectacles, a stout twig, even a bone – and my mind hastily turned away from the question *What kind of bone would you expect to find here?*

Before I started crawling about, I went again through the inventory of my possessions: stone, paper, crumbs. Half a dozen small buttons on my garments: What if I carved one down...? Too short.

The knife scabbard in the top of the boot was of leather, but it was stiff. Perhaps if I sliced away its softer portions...

The boot. With its old, worn, brass lace-hooks.

I drew up my right foot, and got to work.

'I'm assuming that you have nothing that could be used on these locks,' I said, 'or you'd have freed yourself long ago. But whoever brought me here was either in a hurry, or had been told that I was a woman, which made him loath to strip me properly. For whatever reason, he – they – left me my boots. Which have various bits of metal on them. And that should make matters easier.'

A throwing knife is a flat piece of steel whose handle is simply a continuation of the blade, cross-hatched to offer control. I keep mine sharp, and it took but a moment to separate one of the thinner brass lace-hooks from its leather. The knife's handle was too thick, so I slid the little loop over the blade, pulling at it to work it flat, and talking, so as to keep Mahmoud with me.

'I should tell you,' I said, my words pushing away the darkness that caressed my skin, 'I've had amnesia, since the night you and I were set upon outside of Fez. I took a knock on the head, but a farmer and your young friend Idir came to the rescue.' I told him the story, all of the past events from the time I had staggered away from the fleeing motorcar. Whether he was hearing me or not, I could not tell, but my fingers kept prying.

And then the knife slipped, slicing a chunk out of my finger and, far worse, flipping the metal snippet into the darkness. I cursed, and stuck my finger in my mouth. Should I conduct a search for the thing, or just start again?

I made mental note of the direction in which I thought it had flown, then picked up my boot and got to work on the next-thinnest hook – this time leaving it attached to the leather. I resumed the story, with Holmes, Lyautey, and me riding north out of Fez.

Lacking its key, a padlock may be opened in two ways. It can, of course, be picked like any other lock, a technique requiring both a pick and a companion wire to hold the sequence of manipulated pins in place. But a padlock may also be popped open with a shim: a thin, narrow strip of metal that, worked into the tiny gap between the lock's shaft and its body, releases the latch. That was what I was attempting to create.

It was a ridiculous task, one that I would have said impossible – one I would not even have attempted – but for two factors: First, I suspected that my captors had not invested in an expensive lock. And second, I had no choice.

If I did not free my ankle, Mahmoud Hazr and I would die here. Time, the story, and my skin, all wore on.

When this second hook was more or less flat, I cut it from the boot, then struggled around to face the pillar. The metal dug into my ankle, but the soft tile pillar stood atop a slab of rock hard enough to be a grind-stone. I worked away at the slip of brass, wearing it down, flattening it on the stone. My fingers grew raw. My hips ached, my ankle burned. I ripped various bits from my clothing to shield my skin from the blade. My conversation descended into babbling – snatched recollections about the night of his abduction; meeting Nurse Taylor; my reaction to finding his ring, first in my pocket that night with the head-lamps on me, then again beneath the brass-worker's bench on Saturday morning. I told him about throwing Holmes head-over-heels at the top of the stairs in Dar Mnehbi, and what Holmes had said about the shadowy person who possessed information about the secret meeting, and my own speculations about whether that man was within the ranks of the French

Protectorate or the Rif Republic. On and on.

I had not heard any reaction from my companion for at least an hour. Apart from my stream of words and the susurration of brass on stone, the only sound in the universe was one that added a note of vicious irony: a slow, regular drip of water into a small pool, thoroughly out of reach. And on I worked.

The knife blade had opened the hook to a gentle curve, taking pieces of my flesh as tribute for its task. A thousand blows from the knife handle now flattened the curve – even Mahmoud's ring came into play, the knife jammed through it to form a rolling-pin. Once the curve had opened, I set about reducing the metal hook to the thickness of paper by grinding it – and my finger-tips – against the stone slab.

As I said, it was a ludicrous plan. I did not actually believe it was going to work: The hook would not be long enough, it would never be thin enough, the padlock was sturdier than I hoped. But as my only other option was to curl up hopelessly on the filthy stones, I kept going: rubbing, resting my fingers, rubbing again.

The brass wore away, becoming sharp enough to contribute another set of slices to my finger-tips. My fingers were so numb, merely picking up the slip of metal risked losing it, much less trying to use it.

Ten, twenty times I slid the boot-hook down the shaft of the lock. Each time, one edge would go in, an eighth or a quarter of an inch, before the flatness of the hook and the curve of the lock shaft would reach a point of disagreement. Half a dozen times, I thought it irretrievably stuck; each time, repeated attempts freed it, and I sat with my hands tucked under my arms for a while, to rest them, warm them, and allow the blood to dry. Then I would try again.

For the hundredth time – the five hundredth? – I wiggled the little scrap of metal down the padlock shaft to the hole and pushed it in. This time it was thin enough. In fact, it was too thin: At first I thought it was merely the lack of sensation in my fingers that lost track of the sliver of brass against the rough steel, but no. The thin hook was gone, vanished into the body of the lock.

My heart stopped. Hours of labour, my only hope of escape, gone. The urge to fling myself to the ground and wail rose up, but I ruthlessly forced it down. Without moving my right hand on the lock, I splayed and clenched my left fingers to restore circulation, until I could pick up the knife. Closing my eyes (as if this might help me to see!), I rested the blade along the shaft and probed, blindly, ever so gently, hoping I might ease the minuscule brass sheet up. I could feel it, but short of turning the lock upside-down, it did not seem inclined to come out. I started to move my arm, to lay the knife down and turn the lock over, and then stopped.

Maybe it had caught on something. Something internal. A rough bit, or...

With a prayer to the gods of the open skies, I gave the knife a tiny jab.

Click.

I did not believe it. I had doubted for so long

that anything was going to happen – I had been so convinced that I would be found here, in a year or a century, a rust-clogged padlock nestled against the bones of my foot – that I did not trust my senses.

But the lock snicked. More than that, it moved: Cold metal pressed against my palm.

I fumbled and dropped it, then grabbed it with horror, convinced that it had relocked itself – but it had not. The padlock haft swung free. A quick twist and it was out of the ankle shackle, and the chain fell away.

I stifled the urge to leap for freedom. I did shove away the chain. And rested my head against the pillar. I may have wept, a little. And then I snatched up the padlock to throw it into the darkness...

And stopped.

I had spent hours rubbing metal on stone, but the metal had been brass. Brass does not participate in the chemistry of $Fe_2 + O_2 = Fe_2O_3 + heat$. The equation that iron and oxygen equals rust and heat has lit many a back-country camp-fire. In plain English, rust is the slow oxidation of iron; a spark happens when the oxidation is instantaneous.

A spark is merely a very rapid rust.

I had in my hand a million potential sparks, in the form of steel.

The necessary flint, however, was stuck beneath a massive mud-brick pillar.

As I sat forward to lace up my boot, a tiny *ting* drew my attention to the blessed scrap of brass. I retrieved it, folding it into my shirt pocket, then set off on a crawl around the pillar, using the point of my knife to explore the stone foundation slab for cracks. Three-fourths of the way around, I found one.

A corner of the stone the size of my palm rose up a fraction of an inch, suggesting an ancient crack. Digging it free would be laborious, but with the knife, not impossible. I opened my mouth to tell Mahmoud what I was doing.

Then I sat back on my heels.

God, I was being stupid.

I thrust my right hand into its pocket, then changed hands, finding in the left side the small, chalky stone I had picked up on the road on Thursday, that Nurse Taylor had preserved for me on Friday, that I had not been able to bring myself to drop by the wayside Monday.

Holding tight, I crawled back to where I had begun, felt around for the padlock, and prayed that the universal laws of physics held sway in this Mediaeval underworld.

The first try gave nothing but a dull scratching sound. The second, a clean tap, but no light. Was I, in fact, blind? Had this entire charade, from sneeze to crawl, been rooted in the delusion that the world was dark, when it was not? Raisuli was known for laying hot coins upon the eyes of displeasing messengers: Had his followers come up with some method of blinding that did not cause pain?

No – damn it, that was absurd. I palmed the stone and rubbed it about on the foundation-block for a minute, to scrape away the chalky surface, then grasped both objects as best I could, took aim, and slammed my hands together.

The fragile instant of light would have been invisible in a dim room; here, it was a miracle.

'Ehiy 'or!' I cried aloud. 'Let there be light!'

And it was good – though not much assistance in seeing, when the spark was directly before my eyes.

I got to my feet. Facing the direction where I thought Mahmoud's voice had come from, I held my iron-and-flint over my head, and cracked the pieces together.

The flash left an impression of great distance, a less impressive height, and rows of moth-eaten pillars radiating into the darkness. I took a step to the side, and bashed my primitive firestarter again, then again.

And saw a man's foot.

When I reached Mahmoud, I knelt in the darkness, laying my tools on the ground. My hands hesitated, fearful of what they might encounter, until I forced one to reach out and touch him. I found a corpse.

But the corpse reacted to my touch – or had it? Fumbling my way up his arm, I located the hollow of his neck, and pressed. I felt something … no, it was only my own pulse. I held the pose for a long time, my entire being focussed on the two fingers of my left hand, until at last I perceived a rhythm that was not my own. It was weak, and the motion of his chest was no deeper than a bird's, but he was alive. Barely.

I worked my way back down to his hand, taking it in mine, cradling my arms around the hard skin and broad fingers. The joints were flaccid and it was as cool as a corpse, but the skin on its back betrayed the greatest threat: so dehydrated, it had the texture of half-tanned leather.

'Don't you die, Mahmoud,' I commanded again, and sprang to my feet.

Each click gave me an instant of infinitesimal energy, so brief that only after many hours of darkness did it actually qualify as light. The sparks had the effect of a vastly slowed cinema projector, each one taking me a few steps closer to the sound of the drip. As I went, I scuffed a wide trail through the dust and fallen debris, terrified of losing my way. I had a bad moment when my tiny flare revealed what I thought was my own trail, running crosswise to my path. Several desperate sparks later, I realised that I had found the route of our captors. Towards the exit.

But I would investigate that path later. Now, I made for the steady sound, eventually rounding a pillar to find a dripping stalactite half as long as my arm. The pool at its base was small and malodorous, but when I had sopped my torn-off, cut-up, bloodstained sleeve in the water, I sucked up the result with more pleasure than I had ever taken from chilled water in a glass.

Although I could have done with the glass. Or a screw-top canteen. Even a medina water-seller's musty goatskin would have done nicely. Here, I could either see, or I could carry water – unless... Yes, my boots were old, but I had kept them oiled, which meant they were more or less waterproof. After soaking my swollen hands in the frigid pool, I managed to tie together the laces of one boot. With it dangling around my neck, I succeeded in transporting a good cupful of the precious liquid back to Mahmoud.

I vowed that if I ever got back to Sussex, I would make a shrine to those boots.

Working blind, I wrenched off a small scrap of the sleeve and dribbled some water into his slack mouth. I did it again, and again, and when at last he actually swallowed, I felt as if a chorus of angels had burst into song. I put down the cloth and picked up his hand, rubbing his extremities for a time before starting the process over again. It was probably an hour later that I squeezed the last of the water into him, and he gave a faint groan.

'Mahmoud?' I said. 'I've given you some water, there's more available, then we'll see what we can do about getting your–Ack! Stop!' My patient had gone from comatose to aggressive in an instant, his convulsive grab sending a bolt of pain up from my already throbbing hand. 'Mahmoud, *ow!*' but my other hand had already knocked loose his grip. His response was to bring his other arm around – only this time he fastened onto my knee, which was uncomfortable but not actively excruciating.

'It's all right,' I told him, 'you're not blind, you're not alone, you have water. I'm here. You're not alone.'

The grip on my leg seemed to pause. 'Miri?'

'Right. I got my shackles off and found a pool of water dripping out of the ceiling. When you're ready, I'll go fetch some more of it, and then we can see about getting you free as well.'

At the word *go,* his fingers clamped down to

keep me from carrying out the threat to walk away. I kept talking, as if I had not noticed. 'I managed to turn one of the brass hooks on my boots into a shim and opened the padlock. It took me a while, and I'm afraid my hands may be too swollen to repeat it on yours, but once you've had some more water, we can let you try. I can also see the direction we were brought in, so we won't have to wander around looking for the door.'

As I spoke, his grip lost its intensity, until, with an effort I could almost feel, he forced his fingers from my knee.

'Are you injured?' I asked him.

'No.' Which only meant that whatever had been done to him, it stopped short of broken bones.

'All right, I'm going back for some more water. Oh, but first—' I retrieved the larger of the two rings I wore around my neck and pressed it into his hand, folding his nerveless fingers around the warm gold. 'This is yours. I'm sorry it got a bit nicked; I needed it to flatten the boot hook.'

The ring had been in Mahmoud's family for three centuries. The newer ducal signet ring, created a mere two generations ago, remained with the child duke; this one Mahmoud had kept, his only possession from his former life.

With the boot around my neck again, I retraced my steps to the pool, drinking more myself, soothing my hands in the cold puddle, sopping up another cupful in my boot. Back at the pillar, Mahmoud was sitting up, and this time he could summon enough control to raise the sodden cloth to his lips and suck – taking his time, at my

297

urging. While he did so, I set out to quarter the immediate area, one spark at a time, in search of anything that might prove useful. A padlock key, for example. A keg of ship's biscuits. Surely this enormous space hadn't sat here for three centuries without drawing the attention of smugglers?

No key, but I did find the keg.

Well, not really a keg, and certainly no biscuits, but scraps of wood from what had once been some kind of a crate, half-buried under the collapse of a wall. I gathered them by touch, wary lest the rest of the wall come down, and secreted a doubled handful inside my garments. Enough to start a fire, pushing back the dark and cold, allowing me to cease this exhausting method of illumination before my agonised hands failed altogether.

Back at Mahmoud's pillar, I emptied my pockets of the wood, chose one piece that felt a fraction dryer than the rest, and drew my knife to carve it to slivers, cursing under my breath as splinters joined the accumulated damage to my half-numb fingers. When I had a handful of scraps, I sorted them by feel (more jabs) into fine below and very fine on top. A frayed snippet from my shirt-tail added fibres. I took out my flint and padlock again, wondering if this could possibly work – and then I laid them aside, and dug through my pockets.

The scrap of onionskin paper, Mahmoud's map and Idir's writing, was the driest thing I had. I crumpled it, laid it atop the fibres, and knelt over the would-be fire.

'Say a prayer, Mahmoud,' I told my companion, then: 'Sorry; what was that?' I leant forward, straining to hear his threadbare words.

'Truly,' he breathed, 'Allah has cursed the Unbelievers and prepared for them a blazing fire.'

I laughed aloud, in surprise but also in pleasure: His earlier mumble had not been wordless, after all. It had been Arabic, I thought, the beginning of *Al-Fatihah,* the Opener of the Qur'an – poetic phrases a Moslem recites numerous times every day, a song of God's greatness: 'In the name of God, the merciful, praise be to God, the Lord of all being, the beneficent, the merciful, Master of the Day of Judgment.'

Mahmoud had regained his habit of quotation.

I replied, 'Mahmoud, from your lips to God's ears.'

I struck a spark from my makeshift firestarter, then another, and half a dozen more.

The tenth try resulted in a brief thread of orange crawling across the paper, but it died before my breath could coax it to life. After a dozen attempts, I sat back on my heels.

'I need to rest my hands for a minute.'

'Shall I try?' came his voice, low, but stronger.

'Are your hands steady yet?'

'No.'

'We'll wait a bit, then. Have you any idea who put us here? Other than it being a supporter of Raisuli?'

'Someone within the Maréchal's camp.' A five-word sentence, with only one slight break in the middle: definitely an improvement.

'Yes, I agree. But how did *you* know about the ambush?'

299

'When I came–' His voice broke off with an audible shudder: He had retreated far enough from death to be feeling the cold. 'Ali and I came down the *wadi*. When we stopped–'

His teeth chattered, unable to finish the sentence. My hands had rested long enough. I bent back to work. This time, driven by the desperation of the man at my side, the sparks flew: directly onto the paper, which caught in a tiny dot – and this time my breath reached it in time to cause a flare. The paper burned; cotton fibre caught; the flame edged onto the small shreds of packing crate. I blew steadily, and the tinder reached greedily for the oxygen, spreading to the wood beneath. There was even a hint of a crackle – but no. The sound came not from the ground before me, but from the distance, off in the direction that the multiple foot-prints had led in.

I looked up to the firelight gleam of Mahmoud's eyes, my first clear sight since the Dar Mnehbi guest-room had faded the day before. He, too, heard the noise, and ill as he was, his reaction was faster than mine.

He dropped the damp cloth over the flames. It did not even create a hiss as our infant fire died.

CHAPTER TWENTY-FOUR

I snatched up the knife and padlock as Mahmoud fell forward across the dead fire, scraping the bits of firewood beneath him. I retreated towards my own pillar, given form by the light of an approaching lantern, and arranged myself across the slack chain.

Voices rang out, joking in the foreign language, and at least three sets of feet tramped across the beaten soil floor. The noise and dancing brightness were a shock. When they paused, about fifty feet away, there came the all-too-familiar rattle of chains.

I lay still.

As I suspected, when they had finished, they came to check on their earlier prisoners. Mahmoud's motionless form, the shackles clear on his ankle, was cause for amusement; one of them gave him a solid kick. He did not react – either that, or his exertions had made him pass out again – and they turned to me.

I lifted my dust-smeared face from the ground and snarled feebly; they laughed, but came no nearer.

When they were halfway to the entrance, I fell upon the trio.

The flattened-walnut stone I had been carrying all these days cracked off the unpadded top of one man's head. He stumbled, dropping his rifle, just as the clean-shaven man beside him went down with my thrown knife between his ribs. I followed the stone with the heavy padlock, and the first man collapsed.

That left the other bearded man with the lantern.

As I'd hoped, he was more terrified of the dark than he was of me, and took care to set the light down before grabbing for the gun in his belt – both with his left hand. As he turned, I saw the reason for his clumsiness: His right arm rode in a sling. The revolver was not clear of his belt when I hit him in the face, following the blow with a harder one to his exposed neck.

I stood over the three unconscious men, panting – with fury more than effort – and gloating over my arsenal and the undamaged lamp. Run me over and plunge me into confusion, would you? Kill my friend with darkness?

I stepped forward to rip the sling off the last man, pushing back his sleeve. Bloodstained bandages lay heavy about his upper arm; my left hand tingled with glad awareness.

But I had no key.

I searched their every pocket, turned out every pouch, even ran my fingers down their collars feeling for strings, finding an assortment of weapons, an odd variety of foodstuffs, and dirt. But no keys.

I retrieved my flat flint-stone – I was becoming quite attached to it – knotted the hem of the man who seemed closest to consciousness, and wedged one of the knives under the door. Then I gathered the considerable armful of weaponry and returned to my companions.

Halfway back, I discovered what they had done with the keys: a faint glint of reflection caught my eye. When I raised the lantern, a scrap of metal gleamed from the far end of a track dug into the dust of ages. Once a padlock went shut, the men had simply tossed its key into the dark. No doubt, I thought as I bent down awkwardly around my armload, another source of amusement.

I made my way to the new prisoner, who squinted warily against the approaching light.

'Hello, Holmes,' I said.

'Russell!' He cleared his throat to conceal the flare of relief. 'I thought I recognised those boots. I am most gratified to find you inside of them.'

'Not half as much as I was,' I replied. He took the lamp from my hand, freeing me to lay down three rifles, four handguns, and half a dozen daggers, all the while keeping a death grip on the key. 'Mahmoud is over there. I was just about to start on his shackles when we were interrupted. Where is Idir?'

'When I last saw him, he was racing off into the darkness. I trust he's too clever to have been recaptured. What shape is Mahmoud in?'

'Better than he was a couple of hours ago. And you?' He, too, had been left relatively clothed, apart from bare feet and lack of robes.

'My skull took a crack. Thank goodness for turbans. For the rest, contusions alone. How did they take you?'

'I was drugged. This key doesn't fit yours.'

'Where are we.

'Habs Qara, the Mequinez dungeon. Mahmoud has been here since Thursday, with nothing to eat or drink. I've given him water. I'll see if this key fits his shackles, then search those three more closely.'

'Are they dead?'

'Unconscious. One of them might not make it. Well, two. One is bleeding, and another I hit kind of ... hard.' With the admission, reaction tightened my chest. A living soul, dying, at my hand. Yes, they had left me little choice, but a life is a life, and there was a cost to be paid.

But not just now.

I tried the key in Mahmoud's lock, feeling the tension quivering through his body as my hands fumbled. At last, the mechanism clicked. In one convulsive movement, he snatched the steel shackles from his leg and threw them as far as he could manage. He sat panting for a moment before he spoke, again in Arabic: '"She removes from them their burden and the shackles that were upon them."'

I laughed. As the echoes faded, a groan came from the direction of my victims.

'I need to tie that man,' I told him. 'After that I'll bring you some more water and we'll get the fire going.'

'There may be others outside,' Holmes pointed out helpfully.

'There's nothing we can do about that just yet. And we have the guns. Once you're loose and Mahmoud is on his feet, we can go look.'

A closer search of the three men produced two more knives, tobacco, a handful of dried fruit, two fist-sized hunks of stale bread, a boiled egg, an orange, and five candied almonds. The edibles allowed me to resist the urge to kick them as I went.

Lighting the fire, now that we had an active flame, took but an instant. I brought more water, handed Mahmoud one of the rock-like and grubby dried figs I had taken from the groaning man (my third victim, the one I had simply hit), and fetched another handful of the smashed crate. Leaving Mahmoud gnawing the fig before the flames, I turned to the search for Holmes' key. Neither of us had heard the thing land, since the men had been making noise when they threw it, but beginning at Holmes' pillar, I quartered the area, finally spotting a track in the dust that ended at a slab of fallen ceiling plaster.

With Holmes quenching his thirst at the drip, I hunted farther afield. I discovered a scattering of wooden slats closer to the entrance, but the real treasure was a half-flat, rust-speckled tin I found in a corner. I set it beneath the drip, spread my sodden boot before the little fire, and settled down with my companions to a prison picnic.

Mahmoud was reviving more quickly than I would have imagined possible. Perhaps desert life and month-long Ramadan fasts accustomed a person to desiccation? And the familiarity of the setting now, evoking a thousand cook-fires around which he and Ali had set up their goat-hair tents, was no doubt restorative as well. Still, I went first with my tale, catching Holmes up on every detail of my fairly tumultuous Tuesday – it was, he interrupted to tell me, not yet midnight on Wednesday, which meant that I had been here a mere twenty hours. When I finished, he picked up his own portion of the story, taking us through two long days with Idir, the market rumours in Moulay Idriss, and his submission to abduction.

He took our silence, correctly, as surprise, and explained, 'It meant that the lad could escape, with news of what had happened. And they swore convincing oaths that they would not kill me. Which, strictly speaking, they did not. They do seem to have a fondness for clouting people on the head,' he reflected. 'For which one should perhaps be grateful, since the chances of recovery may be a fraction better than a knife under the ribs or a bullet to the chest. Still, waking to find oneself bound, hooded, and on the floor of a motorcar does not improve one's temper.'

'You are certain that Idir was an unwilling hostage?' I asked.

'Reasonably so,' Holmes agreed.

Mahmoud spoke. 'The boy is loyal.'

Holmes and I could hear the conviction in our companion's voice. However...

'If that is so,' Holmes said, 'it would support the thesis that these attacks come from men only thinly familiar with Abd el-Krim's situation. An insider would know that one of the Emir's close advisors had taken a mute lad under his wing, so that when a mute lad later surfaced at the side of a man dressed as a *marabout*, even a head-bashing fool would take care to keep him close at hand.'

'Which suggests that whoever gave us away is within Lyautey's camp, not Abd el-Krim's,' I concluded.

'It would appear so.'

'Mahmoud, you were about to tell me how you knew there would be an ambush on Lyautey.'

He shifted before the fire; a speech of any length required a summoning of energies. 'I did not know. I wondered. This is how it happened.

'Ali and I were in Chaouen, helping search for traps left by the Spanish, when Mycroft's letter came. We decided it was time to bring the Emir and the Maréchal together. Ali went north, to convince the Emir, while I made my way to Rabat to summon you, then take you to Fez to assist me with the Maréchal.' He paused to drink from the rusty tin; when it was empty, I went back to the drip to refill it.

Holmes called from near the entrance, 'Russell, give me a hand here.'

The groaning man was conscious now, though still securely bound. Between us, Holmes and I dragged him, bucking and shouting, over to my pillar, where Holmes snapped the shackles onto his ankle. When he began shouting, Holmes cocked a revolver at him.

The man went silent.

Back at the fire, I spoke before Mahmoud could resume.

'That man we just moved has a recent slice on his right arm, about where you might expect to see the wound from a left-handed person's knife. His bearded companion has a lot of scrapes and scratches on him, as if he'd pushed his way at speed through a wooded hillside. The third man – clean-shaven a few days ago – looks more like a clerk than someone who would casually knife a wounded comrade. He also looks remarkably like one of the men dressed as a French soldier who came to arrest me in Fez the day after you and I parted company.'

Mahmoud nodded, then picked up his tale. 'The roads in the Rif are little more than foot-paths. In the rain they become muddy streams. I did not hurry, since I thought it would take Ali far longer to reach the Emir than it would for me to reach you. As I went, I stopped often to rest the horses and to speak with the local people.'

Mahmoud being, after all, a spy.

'We had a site for the proposed meeting, half a day's ride from Fez, remote yet open enough to reveal a trap, to either side. When I had explored the immediate area and found it satisfactory, I continued down the track along the *wadi* until I met with the road. There I was told a story about two mad strangers seen on the cliffs above the river, hunting for goats. I laughed, and agreed they were mad, but I also located where they had been: a spot where a large boulder hung above a cliff, an object that Allah might one day choose to roll down on an unbeliever. It was a place where, on the track near the cliff, I had noticed a fresh branch lying, one belonging to a tree that grew considerably higher up the hillside. It looked like a kind of marker.'

A spy, and a man with the instincts of an Indian tracker.

'When we reached Fez on Sunday, I went to a *funduq* where we might leave the horses. The next morning, Idir and I took the train to Rabat – the boy had never been on a train before. He liked it

308

very much.

'In Rabat, I found your hotel, as Mycroft had told us, but I met your absence. As no-one had a clue where *you* might be,' he said to Holmes, 'I had little choice but to follow the moving picture crew. To one of the most inaccessible places in the country.'

'The director wanted sand dunes,' I said.

'Russell,' my husband interjected, 'I am most relieved to find that your memory continues to return.'

'Not all of it, but most.'

'There is little but sand in Erfoud,' Mahmoud continued. 'Barely a road. Certainly no railway. I considered abandoning the attempt and making do with just the two of us, but since I had five days to fill until Ali came to Fez, I thought I might as well fill them entertaining the lad, and seeing a part of the country with which I was not familiar.' Spying out that land, too. 'So we took another train – two trains – as far as we could get. And then we stole a lorry.

'When we located the encampment, I sent Idir in to fetch you.' His eyes flicked to mine. 'When you had heard me out, and brought some necessities from your tent, we drove north to the railway. I can only hope to return the child to the Rif before he is introduced to further sins – Idir is even more enamoured of motorcars than he is of trains, and now believes that all one need do to acquire one is to steal it.'

His words held another reassuring trace of humour, but I was distracted by an image of sheer terror: 'Did we nearly smash into a camel on the way?'

'We did, scarcely half an hour after we'd started. The beast must have wandered away from some camp-fire. Had we not still been on sand, we should have overturned, or broken a half-shaft. As it was, you and Idir screamed – he with pleasure, you with alarm – and the creature's tail slapped our wind-screen as we went past.'

Mahmoud reached stiffly out to the collection of food-stuffs I had laid onto the rock, and selected a date. Rubbing away the lint and twigs, he went on. 'We reached Fez at mid-day on Thursday. You and I took coffee near the clock while Idir bought sweets, and then we returned to the *funduq*. Later, I went with Idir to a *hammam*. When we were clean, I sent him back to the *funduq* with clothing for Miri, while I went to Dar Mnehbi.'

'Where you called yourself Monsieur Hassan,' Holmes provided. 'The Maréchal said that you were a man interested in establishing schools, and that you and he had an oddly wide-ranging conversation.'

'Yes, I was ... trying to get a feel for the man. One hears much about the Maréchal, but meeting him face to face was ... thought-provoking. I spent the afternoon drinking coffee in the medina and listening to street rumours, and decided that I needed a second, more specific conversation with the Maréchal. I left a message at Dar Mnehbi, requesting an appointment. That evening, when we returned to the *funduq* after dinner, there was a message from the Maréchal saying that he would be passing along the road above the

Merinid tombs, at nine o'clock that evening.'

'An odd venue.'

'Earlier, he had said that I happened to catch him at his one free hour of that day. And the man is known to work all hours, in all manner of places – setting a rendezvous along his route would not be unlike him.'

'Was the message in his writing?' Holmes asked.

'I would not have known, if it were. But the note was written on a typing machine.'

'Ah.'

'Yes. Yet it was on Dar Mnehbi stationery, and in the message I had left that afternoon, I told the Maréchal that I required privacy. In addition, Miri and I were armed. So we went.'

'Leaving Idir behind.'

'He is a child, and this was adult business. And he is resourceful: If we became separated, he knew when Ali was returning, and he knew where our rendezvous place was to be.'

'The sorcerer's clock?' I asked.

'So it is called,' Mahmoud said.

'You had him write it for me, on that scrap of paper. While we ate dinner.'

'I thought that having him tell you where the rendezvous was might reinforce its importance to him, since the lad tends to wander and lose track of the time. I also thought having *him* write it for *you* would make him feel less overlooked when we left him behind.' He closed his eyes for a moment, summoning strength. I took over his tale.

'As I told you, I've spent the past few days with a very faulty memory. Most of it seems to be

311

returning, but that night is still … dreamlike. As I recall, you and I walked through the medina and left out of the Bab Guissa, on the north. That's when you told me about the possible ambush site, wasn't it?'

'I thought it best if I was not the only one to know. I used that same scrap of paper–'

'–to show me how the site with the hanging boulder would look, coming from the south. Then we climbed the hill towards the Tombs. After a time, we saw motorcar head-lamps, pointing down the road towards us. That was when, under the ruse of checking to be sure I had the scrap of paper, you tucked your ring into my pocket.'

'Yes.'

'Why?'

He took a minute to answer, as if reading his answer in the flames before him. 'Fez is unfamiliar territory. Had I known the land better, I might have seen earlier how unlikely a place that was to meet. But Lyautey being famous for unconventional work habits, I did not see the trap until we were too deeply inside it to escape. There was no way for both of us to avoid capture, but I had given you the warning. Leaving you behind was the only way I could see to keep the Maréchal from an ambush of his own.'

And coincidentally, to preserve a scrap of golden family history.

'Miri had her revolver out, and she was positioned out of the lights – if they shot me, she was as ready as she could be. The instant I passed the head-lamps I drew my own weapon. I saw

312

that the man in the back was wearing a French officer's cap, then the front door flew open into me – there wasn't much room, between the motor and the hillside – and my gun went off, but before I could even attempt to aim it, there were three men on top of me.

'They were practiced at abduction, no doubt of that. Gag in my mouth, hands bound behind my back, shoved onto the floor of the motor. Couldn't have taken more than twenty seconds.'

He looked up with an apologetic glance – at Holmes, not at me. 'And all I could do was lie there and listen to them attack Miri.'

'One of them approached me,' I told him, 'armed only with a hand-torch and a knife – his job seemed to be locating me, so one of the others could shoot me.'

'Or take you hostage,' Mahmoud added. 'He was not pleased at his assigned role.'

'Did they not imagine I might have a gun?'

'They asked me if you did. I said no.'

'And they believed you?'

'Not entirely. But they had a knife at my throat. Men like that generally imagine threat to guarantee the truth.'

'Oh. Well, I couldn't understand what they were saying, but when the fellow switched on the torch, I knocked it out of his hand, and managed to cut him on the arm. The motor started moving, and I got one of the head-lamps with a rock, but before I could smash the second, there was a lot of shouting, and they dragged my attacker inside and sped away.'

'They saw someone coming,' Mahmoud said.

'Who? Idir?'

'We'd left the boy at the *funduq*.' Apparently he'd been unconscious during my rambles earlier.

'He followed.'

'I might have known. But the voice said, "Someone's behind us." Which would be on the uphill side.'

'A mathematical farmer,' I provided. 'He's lucky your abductors were so agitated. They could have just shot him down if they hadn't panicked. And me as well.'

'They seemed to imagine that villagers were closing in, particularly when they then passed another person coming up the hill. Idir, as you say. With one of them lying on top of me bleeding and the other two shouting at the driver, they had no intention of stopping again until we arrived here. I apologise,' he said. 'The entire show was a display of exceeding incompetence.'

Imagine, I thought: Mahmoud Hazr bested by a mere quartet of armed attackers.

Holmes spoke up. 'What did you learn of them?'

'Four men, two of them large and with rough hands, two more educated. They spoke Thamazigth, some of it too fast to follow. The driver was the most frightened of the four. His voice squeaked when he realised that one of his comrades was bleeding all over the seats. He wanted to eject the man, and when the others wouldn't have it, he stopped a few minutes down the road and forced them to bind up the wound.'

'If he cared about the state of the Sultan's motorcar,' Holmes said, 'we may assume that there is a tie there which leads back to him.'

'No doubt. We drove for perhaps an hour before the paving under our tyres changed. When we stopped, they dragged me out, stripped me of my outer garments, did a most thorough search of my person, then chained me here.

'During the entire time, they only gave away two things of interest. First, one of the men in the back – those with rough hands – began to ask about instructions from Fez, and one of the others ordered him to be silent. Which suggests that they are not amateurs, letting talk run free before they have finished their task. And second, a thing one of them said as they left me. "May all enemies of the house of Alaouite rot into nothing in the dark."'

'Raisuli's men,' Holmes remarked.

'Almost certainly.'

'But what threat are we to them?' I asked. 'I had barely heard of Raisuli before this week, much less declared myself his enemy.'

'You and I saved the Maréchal, and Mahmoud wished to speak with him about Abd el-Krim. Perhaps those acts were declaration enough.'

'A rather extreme reaction,' I said, 'with a rather extreme punishment.'

'"And man says, When I am dead, will I yet be brought forth alive?"' mused Mahmoud. 'I knew that if there was a force capable of imposing human will onto what had been ordained, it would be Miri.'

A taciturn man, capable of phrases that made one willing to die for him.

As indeed was Holmes.

I sat and looked at the two men, both of whom had more or less volunteered to be abducted. Unlike me. I'd just been stupid.

Holmes stirred. 'One can only hope that your young companion has also emerged unscathed.'

'He is a most resourceful individual,' Mahmoud said.

His words might have been a signal: The murky air was split by a sharp, high sound; for a bizarre moment, I was on a London street while a taxi was summoned.

A piercing, two-finger whistle, like the one Holmes had taught me, many years before.

CHAPTER TWENTY-FIVE

The boy was resourceful, I had to agree. And persistent.

At the sound of the whistle, Holmes' head lifted. 'Idir,' he told us, and put his fingers to his mouth to echo the shrill sound. I went to remove the knife-chock from beneath the heavy door; the lad strode past, looking justifiably proud, as I risked a glance outside, into the blessed open air. No waiting assailants attacked, no bullets flew. But I wedged the door shut again, in case.

When the small figure drew near to the fire and spotted the men beside it, his cockerel strut turned into a sprint. He flung himself at Mahmoud, who grunted with the impact but returned the child's embrace. For the first time, I heard the child make a sound, a sort of crooning noise as he patted the man's bearded cheeks with both hands, tears in his eyes.

If Mahmoud had not been so dehydrated, I think his eyes might have gone misty as well.

'Oh, worthy child!' he said in Arabic. 'How did you find us?'

The boy leapt to his feet to pantomime an answer. Pointing to Holmes, he threw up his hands: *the man, gone!* A churning of hands and legs showed him running, running – then he stopped in surprise, pointed off into the dungeon to represent a discovery, and grabbed the air with

317

both hands, bending over with a lesser churning of extremities.

'You stole a *bicycle?*' Mahmoud asked. A cheeky grin was his answer. 'Where on earth did you find one of those – and when did you learn to ride it?' There were few enough of them in the country; and I could well imagine that such fragile forms of transportation were even less common in the rough mountains of Abd el-Krim.

Idir did not attempt to answer the first question, but to the second, he drew back a sleeve to reveal a nasty sequence of scrapes and embedded gravel. He did the same with his left leg, which was raw from ankle to knee. The wounds were shallow and seemed the source more of pride than of pain, so we rewarded him further with loud admirations of the blood he had shed for the cause.

But the lad was not finished. Either he had decided that he would never catch the retreating motorcar, or (more likely) he had ruined his two-wheeled transport in the fall, because now he held up a finger and repeated the expression of surprise. Tip-toeing a few steps, he drew open a door and climbed inside. One hand mimicked the release of a brake handle, then joined the other in a grasp of a steering wheel. The slight forward to-and-fro was a driver urging a motorcar into motion on a hill-top. His forefingers began to circle around each other, slowly, then less slowly, and finally rapidly enough for the hands to return to the steering wheel stance.

As one, Holmes and I looked at Mahmoud. He shrugged. 'Yes, he knows how to steal a motor,

318

especially if it's left on a hill. He's a clever lad.'

The two fists moved, mimicking driving; the boy leant forward, peering – then one hand came up to shade his eyes for a moment before shooting out to point into the dungeon. When he turned to us, his eyes gleamed in triumph.

Could the lad have simply driven around Mequinez until he spotted the motorcar?

That was one of a load of unanswered questions – how he happened to find an unattended motorcar on the road, how on earth he hadn't wrecked the thing or killed the engine, or himself – but without writing materials, his responses would take forever. In any event, it was time to move.

I gathered our arsenal and the lantern, while Holmes helped Mahmoud to his feet. He stood, swaying but resolute. Then he straightened, one hand on Holmes' shoulder.

'Miri, you and the boy go ahead. We will join you in a few minutes.'

I started to ask why, then glanced at the darkness and closed my mouth. Handing the lad one of the rifles, I steered him across the cavern towards the doorway and out into the cold, star-spangled night, where I took care to push the door to behind me.

The boy did not need to hear whatever sounds came from within. When we were well clear of the door, I laid the rifles on the ground, and held the lantern high.

Prominently parked, where head-lamps from the nearby road might rake it, was a large and shiny motorcar – rather, what had been a large and shiny motorcar. It was now somewhat ... compressed.

Its back end bore the imprint of the rhinoceros-like nose of an Army transport lorry, massive and implacable. The motorcar's head-lamps lay embedded in a dangerously bulging stone wall, while the lorry had drifted backwards a few feet after the impact, as if to admire its work. Its front end appeared unscathed.

The lorry's sides were a different story. Half the canvas had been ripped free, the paint appeared to have been raked by huge claws, the tool-box beneath the bed lay dangling open and empty. The machine looked ravaged by dinosaurs. By some miracle, the visible tyres seemed to be intact, but the stink of a dangerously overheated engine block filled the air, and even a quarter hour after the boy had abandoned it, the click of cooling metal was rapid-fire.

I held out the lantern to my small companion. 'Idir, I need you to hold this up so I can see where I'm going. If there's a petrol leak, the flame would make it explode. Can you do that?'

The lamp went as high as his arm could stretch. Cautiously, I approached the wreckage.

The smell of petrol was unmistakable, but not powerful. Gingerly, I worked the motorcar's back-door handle, and looked in. There was a figure behind the wheel, staring up at the roof, but the dark glisten of his clean-shaven face and the lack of breathing sounds told me that he was beyond worrying about the state of the Sultan's motor. A bundle on the floor turned out to be Holmes' robe, sitting atop his boots; a metallic reflection from the door-pocket proved to be a flask – left behind by one of the Americans? A dim shape on the opposite side tempted me across the seat, and rewarded me with a hand-torch.

I carried the clothing back to Idir, and went for a circuit of the lorry. The torch revealed that all the wheels were inflated, the tool compartment on the far side was intact, and the cab held the usual complement of steering wheels and gear levers. There was no windscreen, but then, there never had been.

I wrestled open the tool compartment and found the starting handle. With mixed feelings, I pulled it out and walked around the back of the lorry.

To my surprise, I heard the scrape of the dungeon door. Idir turned, casting lamp-light onto the two men, Mahmoud's arm over Holmes' shoulders. His golden ring signet flashed in the darkness.

They'd been alone with the captives for less than five minutes.

A cry followed them out of the door, cut off when it shut.

'The threat of abandonment alone proved sufficient to stimulate his conversation,' Holmes remarked.

'He knew nothing,' Mahmoud growled.

'He knew little,' Holmes amended. 'We were correct that they are followers of Raisuli, but they are by no means committed believers. Rather, they are hired ruffians whose professional and personal lives happen to coincide. The one we

321

questioned is new to the task, brought in a year ago by the one you concussed with the padlock. He says that the gang has done occasional jobs for seven or eight years now, including one on Friday for which the concussed one and their driver – both of whom are fluent in French – were given the uniforms of French soldiers, ordered to shave and have their hair cut in the European style, and sent to arrest you at a house in the medina. Their employer is an anonymous person in Fez. They have a contact address in Fez el-Jdid, but from the sound of it, there are several layers of protection. It will take some time to peel them away. Oh, and speaking of which, Russell, here is your knife. The gentleman had no further need of it.'

I looked at his outstretched hand with distaste. I had used the weapon in the heat of combat, but prising it from a man's living back had been more than I could bear. Holmes had cleaned it, but only of the blood itself. However, with both men watching, waiting for me to accept it, I had little choice. I slid the blade rapidly away into its boot-top sheath, then made haste to resume the previous subject.

'Their employer must be one of Lyautey's close associates.'

'Agreed,' Mahmoud grunted.

'In Fez itself? Or down at the military camp?' Fez el-Jdid, being outside the medina, was easily accessible to both.

'Fez,' Holmes answered. 'Either the Residency or Dar Mnehbi. I suggest we begin with the latter.'

'Holmes, do I take it that you propose a direct confrontation? Rather than laying the evidence before Lyautey and letting him carry out the investigation?'

'When the motor and the four hirelings fail to return, our quarry will flee.'

'Very well,' I said. 'Your boots are in the pile.'

I traded shoulders with him, and helped Mahmoud towards the lorry. 'Your young protégé seems to have paid more attention to the starter than the gear lever,' I remarked.

'So the smell would suggest,' Mahmoud admitted.

'That motorcar is going nowhere, but the lorry may be drivable,' I said. If the engine hadn't fused entirely.

Idir and I between us got Mahmoud into the cab. Leaving the boy to puzzle over the canvas leg-covers, I went back to help retrieve the armaments.

Holmes rose from lacing his boots, and held something out to me.

'My spectacles!'

'And your *djellaba*,' he said. 'They were wrapped inside mine.'

He'd even managed to catch the glasses before they hit the ground, for which I was very grateful. I put them on, and the world came into focus. And became warmer, with the second layer of clothing.

'Everything in the lorry seems to be in place,' I told Holmes. 'Shall we try it?'

By answer, he picked up the starter handle. 'Can you manage the controls?'

'God knows.'

'Just be certain it's in neutral,' he said, walking towards the front end.

'And you take care how you work that thing,' I retorted. 'When it catches, this engine could rip your arm off.'

But it did not. And if twice I was not fast enough with the adjustments of the unfamiliar throttle and choke, on the third time the engine roared into life. Giving Holmes a moment to get clear, I located the switch for the big guide-lamp above the bonnet – fender-mounted head-lamps being too vulnerable for this lorry – and turned it on. The flattened back end of the motor jumped into view – along with a dangling registration plate: 100627. In reaction to the blow, of noise or light, the plate dropped to the ground; an instant later, the bulging wall collapsed – fortunately showing nothing but open space, rather than the interior of a house filled with shocked and bleeding inhabitants.

Holmes trotted towards the back of the lorry. I ground the shifting lever horribly before locating a reverse gear, and we lurched backwards twenty yards before Holmes' palm hammered against the side, at which signal I clashed the gears some more. Holmes scrambled onboard. We lunged forward, a motion that to my astonishment neither killed the motor nor attracted a volley of gunshots.

'Does anyone know where we are going?' I shouted at the men squeezed onto the seat beside me.

'Fez,' Holmes replied helpfully.

'I was rather hoping one of you could suggest a direction.'

Mahmoud said something I didn't hear, and a small hand stretched past my ear. For lack of a more certain authority, I followed the direction of the pointing finger. In five minutes, we were on a road. Perhaps not the road to Fez, but it was a road.

Holmes played the powerful beam back and forth along the approaching track for a half-mile or so before he sat back, satisfied that we were going in the right direction. He showed Idir how to move the lamp about, then took up the hand-torch again.

'Back in a moment,' he shouted, and before I could ask what he intended, he had swung out of the side, pulling himself through the flapping canvas into the lorry's back. A minute later, pads and travelling rugs started landing on our heads. Idir grabbed the first few, swathing Mahmoud, me, and lastly himself. Holmes eventually reappeared with what looked like a tramp's bundle – a linen table-cloth, out of which he drew a feast.

'There was a party of some kind, at the Roman ruins,' he bellowed, handing me a stale bread-roll into which he had shoved a wedge of soft cheese. 'It seems that this lorry was being used to clear up afterwards. If you can think of any use for seven long tables, a hundred place-settings, and four acetylene lamps, we have those as well.'

There was even drink, a half-empty bottle of wine for us, some very fizzy lemonade for Mahmoud and the boy.

Warmth; food; transport. If the abused engine did not die completely and the lorry retained its wheels – *insh'Allah!* – we should cover the thirty miles or so to Fez in little more than an hour. I took a harder grip on the steering wheel (which vibration was adding loose shoulder sockets to my list of ailments) and stepped more firmly on the accelerator. The noise grew. I raised my voice. 'Do you believe our man is at Dar Mnehbi?'

Holmes said something. I asked him to repeat it, then a third time. 'Certainly, someone inside the staff is behind these attacks,' he bellowed in agreement.

I leant towards him. 'How will we get in the gates?' I shouted. 'You want to telephone to Lyautey?'

'Sorry?'

I took a deep breath and tried again. 'Telephone? Lyautey?'

'No!'

'Wait until morning?'

'Exactly!' he said. 'There must be another way.'

'What?'

'Another way ... to warn him!'

'*Warn* him? I said *morning.*'

I felt a hand then upon my juddering arm. The other two passengers had been communicating, Mahmoud's mouth to the boy's ear, the replies visible by the light from the head-beam. I tipped my head to the side, and felt as much as heard Mahmoud's words.

'Idir knows a way in.'

I glanced across the child at him. Mahmoud repeated the offer to Holmes, who looked at me for a long moment. We both shrugged. I gestured for Mahmoud to shift forward, then said into his ear, 'Where?'

He and the boy consulted for a couple of miles, ending with a vigorous nod of the young head. Mahmoud spoke against my hair. 'The north end of the town, near the tanneries.'

'Lord, I hope we don't have to wade through them!' I exclaimed, recalling all too vividly the stink.

'What was that?'

But I shook my head, and drove.

CHAPTER TWENTY-SIX

Fez was dark, apart from a few lights in the new quarter.

I steered along the city's north-facing walls, pausing for Holmes to get Mahmoud and the boy out, then continued on a mile into the hills before aiming the lorry off the road and letting the brakes kill the engine.

With a cough, silence returned to the night (so far as I could tell over the ringing in my ears). I cradled my aching arms for a moment, then kicked open the door, hitched up my *djellaba,* and trotted back along the road, abandoning tables, silver, and acetylene lamps to the resident thieves and lepers.

Limited by Mahmoud's pace, the three had barely reached the wall when I came up to them. There was a lot of débris out here, and we settled Mahmoud cautiously onto a trunk-sized hunk of fallen wall, trusting that the rest of the structure wasn't about to come down on us.

Holmes handed me the torch, which now had an obscuring handkerchief around its beam, and drew a pair of empty lemonade bottles from his robes. 'Idir, take these and see if you can find a fountain.' His voice was low, but fortunately, the ringing in my ears was subsiding.

Mahmoud protested that he was fine to go on, but Idir was already trotting off. We all knew that it would be an arduous trip across the city to Dar Mnehbi. Apart from which:

'We're looking at Youssef, right?' I asked.

'I don't believe we are,' Holmes said.

'Holmes, the man brought me a drugged meal! And he's the very definition of a shadowy presence. He's everywhere in the house, overhears everything, no one questions him.'

'Yes, Youssef *brought* you the meal.'

'What – you think the cook was responsible?'

'You said that there was a delay while someone spoke with Youssef outside of the door on Tuesday evening.'

'Yes, Youssef apologised for letting the meal go cool, although it wasn't actually–'

'Whose voice was it?'

'I couldn't hear.'

'What was your impression?'

'Holmes, are you asking me to *guess?*'

'Your impression.'

'I suppose I'd have said it was François Dulac, Madame Lyautey's secretary.'

'Exactly.'

'But he's a secretary – and not even Lyautey's secretary.'

'Did he tell you that?'

'Yes. Why? Isn't it true?'

'It is true that originally he was hired for Madame la Maréchale, and that he still handles her appointments schedule and official correspondence. However, the major part of what he does now is for the Maréchal.'

'But strictly speaking, he may regard himself as working for Madame Lyautey?'

For the first time, Mahmoud spoke up. 'A man's pride would drive the lie in the opposite direction.'

I opened my mouth to object that it was not a lie, but he had a point: A lady's secretary might claim to work for the husband, but it was unlikely the claim would go the other way without a reason.

'You just don't want it to be Youssef because of his coffee,' I grumbled.

'An investigation of the link between slipshod work and a more profound breach of trust would indeed make for an interesting monograph,' he mused, 'but I doubt that the reverse would prove true: that pride in one aspect of an employee's life warrants—'

I interrupted, before Idir could return and find us bogged down in a debate over responsibility and ethics. 'If Dulac deliberately misled me, it would suggest that he knew who I was – who we both were. Did he know your name, when you came to visit?'

'I did not use my name, and my cousin knows to make use of whatever pseudonym I may be employing. In this case, Vernet.'

'But the Maréchal would not keep your identity from Madame,' I pointed out.

'True. And,' he went on before I could, 'she might have found it so amusing – the idea of having the one and only *Shairlock 'Olmes* in her house – that she could not resist passing it on.'

'–in the hearing of either servant or secretary,' I concluded. 'Would he also have mentioned Mycroft?'

'That would be unlikely. My brother is not a public figure.'

'That would make it less likely that international politics has entered in, which is a relief. If the matter is domestic, then, and the man we're after could be either Youssef or Dulac, how do you wish to proceed? Secure them both and let your cousin sort it out?'

'My cousin maybe a gifted social tactician, but he has an insufficiently devious mind for unsnarling this kind of knot. He might require evidence before taking action against one of his own servants.'

'So what are you suggesting? That we break into the Resident General's house, search the rooms of not one, but two men, and locate evidence without alerting the guards? Simple.' We probably weren't even going to make it across the city without being caught.

'We have guns,' Mahmoud spoke up. 'You and Holmes can bring both men – and anyone else who wakes – to the library. I will keep them there while you search their rooms.'

I took off my spectacles and rubbed my tired eyes, visions of bloody gun-fights and international incidents playing out across my mind. 'And if we find nothing? If we keep an entire household under gunpoint, and whoever it is already got rid of all evidence? Not even Mycroft would be able to talk us out of that.' I could all but feel the noose around my neck.

'You could stay here,' Mahmoud said.

I put my spectacles back on. 'Sure. I can always do that.' I glanced in the direction the child had gone. 'Isn't it taking the boy a long time to find water? This city has a fountain on every– Ah, there he is.'

With a rattle of loose tiles, a patch of the night took substance, and Idir was there, pressing one of the bottles at Mahmoud, the other at Holmes. We left the empty bottles among the fallen masonry, picking our way after the boy into the medina.

Our noses alone might have led us inside, considering the almost tangible solidity of the air oozing through the wall's narrow gap. The tannery stink grew, and an interminable time later, receded, leaving a marvellous freshness to the remaining odours of mildew, urine, damp plaster, and rotting vegetables.

Silently, we passed through the sleeping city, our way lit by the cloth-muffled torch. I had no sure idea of the time, but it had to be a couple of hours past midnight. Even the perpetually-labouring Resident General might have taken to his bed by now.

Twice, late-night pedestrians approached down the lanes, their ways lit by bobbing lanterns held by servants. Both times, Mahmoud and Idir at the fore had ample warning, and we pressed back into corners and invisibility.

The ground rose; street after street of shuttered buildings, windowless houses, skittish cats – but fortunately, few dogs. Dozens of times, we turned left or right or through a ruined building, and after a while, I realised that somehow the lad was managing to circumvent the city's internal gates.

How did he know Fez so well?

Holmes and I followed the pair ahead, our progress slowing as the child took more and more of Mahmoud's weight. But we did not want to risk coming upon trouble with only a single gun, and putting Holmes under Mahmoud's arm would leave me the only one able to respond.

So the child bore the weight, and the child led the way.

Until we came to a junction I knew.

'Wait,' I whispered.

My three companions came to a halt, Mahmoud staggering to put his shoulder against a wall. 'I know where we are,' I said in English. 'We should go left, not right.'

Mahmoud translated for the boy, who nodded and pointed to the right.

'No,' I said, in Arabic this time. 'That way leads up to the Kebira. It's a long way around.'

But the boy was adamant: to the right. He tugged at Mahmoud's robe, to underscore his certainty.

Holmes raised the torch until its diffuse light shone on Idir's face. 'Do you know a back entrance to Dar Mnehbi?'

Another set of nods, even more emphatic.

I could hear the precise echo of my own thought running through Holmes' mind: *Just how had this lad come to learn so much about Fez in so few days?* I could feel his decision, identical to my own, in the way he stood back with the light, waving the boy towards Mahmoud again. And I knew, as we moved up the road to the right, that he would surreptitiously adjust the rifle he carried across his shoulder, making it ready for instant use.

The lanes grew ever narrower, from the width of a laden donkey to a passage unsuitable for two men side by side, to a crack between buildings that required us to edge sideways. Mahmoud pulled himself along, unable to conceal his laboured breath. Holmes came next, torch in one hand, rifle in the other. I held back, my own gun at my shoulder, waiting.

A scratching noise came from ahead, and the procession stopped. The sound was repeated, twice, and then a door opened. Lamp-light poured into the ridiculously thin passageway.

Youssef looked out.

And Idir stepped forward to embrace him.

CHAPTER TWENTY-SEVEN

I am not certain how Holmes bundled Mahmoud into the lighted room as quickly as he did – I expect he more or less lifted him bodily. But within seconds of the servant's appearing in the doorway, three Europeans and two rifles were in the room as well. Both rifles pointed straight at Youssef. The room was so small and the guns so long, the muzzle ends nearly brushed his chest.

The man's first move was to detach Idir's arms from his waist and put the boy behind him. Pale beneath his brown skin, he looked from Holmes to me and then to Mahmoud.

'Monsieur, what–?'

'Who are you?' Holmes demanded.

'Monsieur, I am Youssef.'

'Of what tribe?'

'Ah.' A degree of comprehension dawned on his features, and something that looked like chagrin. 'I am of the Beni Urriaguel.'

'And the child?'

'Also of the Urriaguel.'

'Mahmoud, did you know of this?'

'I did not.'

'*You* are Sayyid Mahmoud?' Youssef asked in surprise, but Holmes overran the question.

'What relation are the two of you to Abd el-Krim?'

'No relation, not by blood. I...'

335

Youssef paused, looking around the room. It was very full of human beings. The tiny space was irregular, typical of a room fitted into an odd gap between buildings. Both doors were only adequate for someone Idir's height, and the ceiling was a bare handsbreadth over Holmes' head. But everything was scrupulously clean and tidy: A low cushioned divan was pushed against one wall, with a trunk at one end and a stool at the other; a small chest of drawers, holding a water jug and bowl, stood near the door. A pair of long shelves mounted to the wall held Youssef's possessions, among them three framed photographs, a service of gilt-edged glasses, a comb and toothbrush, and a small leather box, on top of which sat the rosette of the *Légion d'honneur*.

And beside the box, a menagerie of carved wooden animals.

The eyes of Dar Mnehbi's steward lingered on the gilt glasses, as if he was about to offer tea before he told us his tale. Fortunately, he decided against it, and merely took a seat atop the trunk, gesturing with his hand in an offer of stool or divan.

Mahmoud, deciding it was better to admit weakness than to collapse, lowered himself onto the stool. When he saw that Holmes and I intended to remain on our feet, Youssef patted the divan cushion at his side, and the boy sat down.

'Mohammed ibn Abd el-Krim al-Khattabi was a student here in Fez,' he began, 'many years before the French came. He lived at the *madrassa*, of course, but because we were both from Ajdir, he often joined my family for dinner, and

336

for friendship. I became like an uncle to him. After he left Fez, to work in Melilla, we wrote from time to time.' He glanced down at the boy, then shifted to French, simple but clear.

'In the early days of the Revolt, my brother was killed, and his entire family but for this, his youngest son, *hamdallah*. When the Emir's men found him, the boy was silent, but the soldiers took him in, and when they returned to the mountains he went with them. They made him a – how do you say?' He said an Arabic phrase I did not know.

'Mascot,' Mahmoud supplied.

'A mascot. First one man, then another, would feed the lad and watch over him for a time. When that man was killed or went home to work his crops, another would take him.

'Not until winter did news reach me that one of my nephews had survived. I sent for him, and put him in a *madrassa,* here in the town. But the boy was a problem. He did not speak. He would not respond to his name, only to the name he had been given by the soldiers. Day after day, I would receive word that he had left the school and was somewhere in the city, and sooner or later we would find him on the road out of town. He was too young to be put to work here in Dar Mnehbi, too much of a problem to be given to others as an apprentice. He wanted nothing but to return to the mountains.

'My heart was heavy, for I have no sons of my own, but in the spring, I sat down and wrote to my old friend the Emir. And he came, himself, to Fez. We talked, he and I, and in the end it was decided that although the boy would not be safe up where the fighting was, neither was he safe on the roads or in the town. And so the Emir took my brother's son away with him. I think–'Youssef turned to ask the boy something, and saw that Idir had fallen asleep. He laid a hand on the dark head, but did not wake him. 'I was surprised to see him, a week ago. He came to my room first on the Sunday evening, arriving as he did tonight, and told me – he writes very well now – that he was travelling with a friend of the Emir whom he called Sayyid Mahmoud, but the Emir commanded that should he find himself among the French, he must say nothing of his relationship with me.

'This was the Emir's business, so I agreed. The lad told me that he and Sayyid Mahmoud were taking the train to Rabat the next day, but would return immediately to Fez. However, it was not until Thursday that I saw him again. He put a note under the door during the afternoon, to say that he was in Fez and would come to see me that night. And he did, but it was very late, almost the morning, when he did so.

'He was very upset. Crying, in fact. His travel companions had disappeared the night before – he wrote that Sayyid Mahmoud had been abducted and their other friend, a woman who looked like a man, had gone as well. It was hard to believe, but he was very disturbed. I told him that we would inform the Maréchal, who would help, but the idea made the boy come near to a panic. To calm him, I agreed to say nothing, and put him to bed. I decided to speak with the lad the next day, when he was calmer, and take him with me to the Maréchal. But in the morning, he was gone. And then in the afternoon, he came to Dar Mnehbi openly, first with Monsieur, then with another person, and finally with a third. And if none of them was named Mahmoud, one did,' he added with a glance at me, 'turn out to be a woman who looked like a man.

'Clearly, this was the Emir's business. When you returned, Madame, on Tuesday evening, I intended to present you with my questions, but you left before I could do so. And I thought, so much the better: When it comes to my old friend the Emir there are times when it is better not to enquire too closely.'

The apologetic smile he gave seemed to indicate an end to the story. As he had talked, first I and then Holmes had lowered our heavy guns to the floor. I cleared my throat.

'When I left on Tuesday, what happened?'

Youssef looked puzzled. 'You left. That is what I was told.'

'Who told you?'

'Monsieur Dulac. He said you had wished to see the Maréchal, but when the Maréchal did not return, you remembered other business in the city.'

'Did any men come here,' Holmes asked, 'before you returned to clear the tray?'

'No, Monsieur. Well, merely the three men come for the trunk.'

'A trunk? A large one?'

'Yes, very pretty, with inlay, but old. It has been in the guest-room for years – the room that you

339

were given – but Mme Lyautey has decided to decorate, and wished some articles removed.'

'Did Dulac tell you that?'

'Yes. Because I had not heard of the Madame's wishes, when the men came to remove it that night.'

Holmes said in English, 'Either the fellow's a superb liar, or he's not our man.'

Mahmoud signalled his agreement by standing and holding out his palm to Youssef. 'The key.'

'Monsieur?'

'To this back door.'

With reluctance, Youssef turned to the shelf beside the door, picking up a fist-sized chatelaine of keys. He would have removed one – laboriously – but Mahmoud said, 'We will take them all.'

The key to Dar Mnehbi's hidden exit, an exit given to the house steward to safeguard, was a piece of Mediaeval iron-work the length of my hand. But the lock was well maintained, and when the ornate black shaft was turned, it moved with ease. 'Is there one for Monsieur Dulac's room?' Mahmoud asked.

'*Oui, Monsieur.*' Youssef pointed out a key some three centuries younger than the first.

We left the sleeping Idir and his anxious uncle in the tiny room, pinned inside by the massive storage chest that Holmes and I wrestled into place against the door, and went in search of a traitor.

CHAPTER TWENTY-EIGHT

Dar Mnehbi was an ornate jewel-box better suited for meeting visitors than for housing foreign guests. Lyautey had rooms off the stairway tower, but Holmes and I had been housed in the neighbouring guard-room *dar,* where, according to Youssef, François Dulac slept tonight, up on the first floor, in a room with an external window.

In the cramped corridor outside Youssef's barricaded door, we considered the best approach. We had two options: Wake first Lyautey, then the guards, working to convince a series of sleepy men that they needed rapidly to obey us, hoping that nothing panicked Dulac; or, we could take the direct approach.

Need I say which we chose?

The corridor was a plastered mole-tunnel that wound a surprising distance before entering the staircase tower connecting Dar Mnehbi's ground floor to its rooftop terrace. We eased down the steps to the courtyard. A shaft of soft light came from the entranceway, casting shadows and gleams across the *zellij*.

We waited there, straining to hear above the perpetual splash from the fountain, until we were certain where the guards were – or, as it turned out, guard, the source of snoring that overrode the splashes. Mahmoud slipped into the courtyard, leading to the right: By skirting around the sides, past the decorative inner doors and windows of the public salons and the library; any rustle of garments or scuff of feet would be concealed by the fountain.

The guard-*dar* was mostly asleep as well, although light came from one of the ground-floor salons, with the low sound of conversation from the guards on duty. They did not hear footsteps creeping up the stone stairs, or moving across the railed balcony.

Youssef had said that Dulac's door did not have a bolt, merely the keyed lock.

And it was true, there was no bolt.

Unfortunately, there was a sturdy wedge.

The key slid in, the mechanism turned smoothly, Holmes' shoulder went against the door, and nothing happened.

Except for inside the room. A light came on beneath the door, followed by a flurry of thumps and motion from within as the occupant tumbled from his bed, jerked on trousers, stepped into shoes, and scrabbled for his hidden stash of valuables before yanking open the window to his roof-top escape.

Only to stop at the sight of a revolver barrel, inches from his nose.

His hands went up.

'Drop what you're carrying,' I said. 'Now move away, slowly.'

When he was on the other side of the little room, near the rhythmically thumping door, I told him to turn his back to me, leaving his hands in the air. 'M. Dulac, if you turn around, if you reach for that pistol in your belt, I will shoot you.'

Fortunately, he believed me. He stood motionless as I struggled through the window. I plucked the gun from his waist-band and kicked the wedge from beneath the door just as the guards came up the stairs.

Holmes and Mahmoud tumbled in, slamming the door and turning the key.

Louder pounding ensued, breaking off only when Holmes identified himself. When the guards proved unwilling to accept his name as sufficient authority, I told Dulac to send them away.

He did, although I did not imagine they would retreat altogether.

Holmes began an immediate circuit of the room, emptying drawers, prodding wood-work, unscrewing the cap ends of the bed, getting down on his knees to examine the boards. Handing Mahmoud my revolver, I retrieved the object Dulac had been in the process of shoving into his shirt-front when he ran into the end of my gun.

It was a washed-leather bag about the size of my fist, very heavy, securely knotted. I picked open the ties, and looked inside: francs, sovereigns, pesetas, and two American double-eagles, but mostly Deutschmarks. Gold, all of them.

'Treachery appears lucrative, here in the French Protectorate,' I remarked.

'What do you mean?' Dulac seized upon bluster as a shield, and drew himself up to make the most of it. 'What are you doing?' he demanded of Holmes, who had lifted the curtain-rod from the little window and let the fabric slide to the floor. 'What is the meaning of this invasion? I thought

343

we were being attacked by town ruffians. I was about to go out of the window to hide my life savings.'

I glanced sideways at Mahmoud. 'Quick thinker, this.'

'A bit late for that.'

'Who is *this* fellow?' Dulac demanded, gazing down his nose at the admittedly scruffy figure of Mahmoud. 'If you don't let the guards in at once, I'll–'

Holmes dropped the curtain-rod, which bounced with a hollow metallic clatter, and held up a tightly furled paper tube. We waited politely for Dulac to complete his threat. We might be waiting still, but for voices outside the door.

'François? What is going on?' Lyautey's voice, as crisp as if he'd been up for hours.

But his secretary did not appear altogether reassured at the arrival of authority. His voice squeaked, just a little, with his answer. 'These ... individuals, Monsieur le Maréchal! They have invaded my rooms, stolen my goods, threatened my person. I demand–'

Holmes stepped to the door and turned the key. Lyautey stood in the doorway with three armed guards at his back. He cinched his dressing-gown, straightened his moustaches, and ran an eye over the room before cocking one eyebrow at Holmes. 'Would you care to tell me what this means?'

'Here?' Holmes asked.

Lyautey tilted his head, taking in the number of people and the size of the room. 'Perhaps the library,' he said.

CHAPTER TWENTY-NINE

We formed a parade: Lyautey at the fore as a commanding officer must, followed by a guard, Mahmoud, Holmes, Dulac, me, and two more guards. Holmes and Mahmoud had their weapons taken, but the soldiers looked at me, and let me pass. Foolish men.

The sleep-befuddled household – guests, guards, and servants – stood in doorways and at railings to watch us go, along the balcony, down the steps, through the corridor, and across the *zellij* courtyard of Dar Mnehbi. We filed into the library at the far corner, where a stout door and the muffling effects of carpets and books meant that if we kept our voices low, the entire city might not know our business by sunset. One of the guards lit the lamps and stirred up the brazier, then Lyautey told him to shut the door and stand away. Reluctantly, the soldier left.

When the five of us were alone in the room, the Maréchal fixed us, one at a time, with that aristocratic glare. When he got to Mahmoud, the gaze sharpened as he saw beneath the dirt and beard. 'You? What on earth are *you* doing here?'

Before any of us could respond, Francois Dulac raised his voice in complaint: that he had been sleeping in peace when some ruffians began to pound on his door, and when he would have escaped, that woman with her gun – Mahmoud kicked him, turning his tirade to a squeak, and I moved forward to separate them before Mahmoud's hand could grow a blade.

Holmes addressed his cousin, the Resident General. 'We have uncovered a problem in your security, Monsieur le Maréchal.'

Holmes clamped a hand on Dulac's shoulder and manoeuvred him into a chair at the long table. Mahmoud pulled another chair a few feet away, that he might keep an eye on the prisoner's every motion. Holmes took a seat across the table from Dulac, with Lyautey to his left at the table's head. The Maréchal caught my eye, since I was the only one still on her feet.

'We need coffee. Would you please find Youssef and tell him—'

Holmes interrupted. 'Youssef is ... otherwise occupied. This shouldn't take long. Monsieur Dulac, would you like to explain these items, which we found in your room?'

He laid the tightly furled tube of paper on the table, then set the bulging leather bag beside it. Lyautey picked that up first, stirring the coins with one long finger before he tugged the strings shut and reached for the paper.

It was a map, a copy of one that lay in the drawer of the table where we were seated, with the addition of neat pencilled annotations. Each of the French border posts on the original had numbers and letters beside them: *6/1/0/t; 9/4/2/nt; 5/3/1/t.*

Mahmoud got up long enough to tap this last annotation. 'When I went by that post some days ago, I saw three machine guns, one piece of light

346

artillery, and a telegraph line. It has, one would suppose, a permanent garrison of five?'

By way of answer, Lyautey lifted his gaze to his secretary.

'This is your writing, François.'

Dulac's pleas and protests might have been the burble of water in the Dar Mnehbi fountain, for all the impact they had on his employer.

The Maréchal shook his head, slowly, left then right, a motion that carried both personal regret and military condemnation. 'You have one very slim chance to save yourself from a firing squad. That is to tell me everything, now.'

And Dulac believed him. Like a lanced boil, corruption poured out: names and dates, money given and information passed on. At a gesture from Lyautey, Holmes pulled open the table's drawer and took out a pad and pen, writing down key points.

It had started in a small way during Dulac's third year in Morocco, 1916, when he moved the name of a Fasi builder to the top of a list of those being considered for renovations to Dar Mnehbi. That, after all, was how things were done here.

The secretary's private income grew, as he made 'recommendations' and provided inside information to everyone from village leaders to carpet-sellers. The building of Casablanca had proved especially lucrative. Business was good.

It became even better when the Germans arrived.

In 1921, the Rif Rebellion had swept across the iron mines leased to the Germans. Abd el-Krim's forces – at that time merely fellow tribesmen of

347

the Beni Urriaguel – destroyed every bit of equipment they could, and while the Rifi then withdrew, the mine owners dared not rebuild with the Revolt's stolen artillery on the hills above.

By the following spring, it was clear to the Germans that Spain was not about to regain control over the leased area in the near-future. So long as the rebellion flourished, one of the world's greatest iron deposits would simply sit there, the ravaged equipment rusting away. And the leaders of the rebellion proved strangely uninterested in receiving payment for a restoration of what was, by international treaty, German property. Abd el-Krim denounced their offer as a bribe and told the delegation that if they returned, he would permit his tribesmen to decorate the walls with some European heads.

So the Germans widened their scope, and one day a distinguished gentleman from Hamburg was seated across a restaurant table-cloth in Fez from François Dulac, suggesting a simple trade: the occasional gold coin, reassuringly stable compared to the post-War inflation of every currency under the sun, in exchange for any information that happened to come Dulac's way concerning the leader of the Rif Revolt.

'How many of the assassination attempts against Abd el-Krim had these Germans of yours behind them?' I demanded.

'None of them,' Dulac protested, then undermined his indignation by adding, 'that I know of.'

'A most convenient ignorance,' I said.

'You, a Frenchman, accepted money from

Germans?' This from Mahmoud, motionless in his chair.

'They are merely businessmen, international businessmen who happen to be based in Germany. Their claim to the ore is absolutely legal – it is no fault of theirs that Spain is incapable of keeping the peace in their Protectorate. In any event, I didn't sell them French secrets, only Rif ones.'

For the first time since his secretary had begun to talk, Lyautey lifted his gaze from the map. Under that icy glare, Dulac made a strangled noise, and said, 'Er, only small French secrets, completely unimportant pieces of information, such as when you were meeting with the Sultan, and your thoughts on the rebellion. And, er, your health.'

'Monsieur le Maréchal,' Holmes asked, 'how long has Monsieur Dulac been handling your correspondence?'

'For years, on and off. But more recently.'

'As you have become ... unwell. Often away in France?'

'I suppose.'

'Yes. And during that time, your secretary grew cocky.

'You began, Monsieur Dulac, as a seller of information. You were happy to work both sides of the medina, as it were, gleaning facts and selling them to whoever might be interested. By the time the Germans showed up, you not only maintained, but had expanded ties with the local criminals to make quite an efficient criminal organisation of your own. You did not take sides

– local villains or German industrialists, followers of Raisuli or supporters of the Revolt, it was all the same to you.

'I imagine that one day, a client required more than mere information. He needed a man to do a job. By this time you knew precisely where such men were to be found, on all sides of the political spectrum. You could indeed provide a man – for a price.

'And before you knew it, you were keeping all kinds of increasingly dangerous balls in the air: selling information both to and about Abd el-Krim; providing local assistance to Raisuli's followers while at the same time selling their names to Raisuli's enemies. You must surely have known how dangerous that could be, but once a man grasps a tiger's tail, it is impossible to let go without encountering the other end of the beast.

'You knew in your bones that sooner or later, one of them would notice, and you would encounter a blade.

'Then I came to visit – a grey-haired foreigner, distant relation of the Resident General, no particular concern of yours. But at some point in the days that followed, after I left for the south on December eighth but before these two arrived in Fez ten days later, you overheard something that made you fear your crimes were coming to light. My name perhaps? In an overheard conversation between the Maréchal and Madame?'

Dulac's sickly expression accompanied Lyautey's sounds of impending eruption. 'That time, no, not … not conversation. I saw it in … the Maréchal's journal.'

'My private journal!'

Holmes asked his cousin, 'Did you happen to mention my brother there as well?'

'Him? No, I certainly–'

Holmes cut him off, resuming his analysis of Dulac's crimes. After that, matters escalated. Sending fake soldiers to Nurse Taylor's door was dangerous enough, but to provide a motorcar for the purposes of abduction–'

'*Abduction?*' Lyautey exploded. 'Who's been abducted?'

'One moment,' Holmes told him. Pointing at Mahmoud, he asked Dulac, 'Do you know this gentleman?'

'I don't believe so,' the secretary replied.

'The Maréchal knows him as M. Hassan, a man who came to chat on Thursday last. Yes, I see you remember the name. You were away from Dar Mnehbi at the time?'

'I...'

'Speak!' Lyautey snarled.

'I was in the Ville Nouvelle, at a luncheon,' Dulac admitted.

'But you were back here by the time M. Hassan returned and left a message for your employer. Why did it alarm you so?'

'Of course it alarmed me. He wished to speak with the Maréchal about Abd el-Krim.'

Holmes turned a raised eyebrow at Mahmoud.

'I had little choice but to put it in writing,' Mahmoud explained. 'The Maréchal had said he was leaving for Rabat that night. Using the Emir's name ensured that he would make time to see me before he left.'

'Instead of which, M. Dulac intercepted the message and decided that you were working for me. Yes,' Holmes reflected, 'it can be a problem, having a recognised name. Those three syllables, and all the world begins to examine their sins. It is not so much coincidence, M. Dulac, as consequence: My presence was a catalyst for your guilt.

'Taken separately, the visit of a famous detective and a stranger's involvement with the Revolt would have meant nothing. Together, they convinced you that your treasonous acts were coming home to roost. That the great investigator Sherlock Holmes was onto you, and was busily insinuating his hirelings into your life.

'You had two options: to throw yourself on the mercy of Maréchal Lyautey, or to stamp us all out. We know what you decided. Tell me, your team of five: They were supporters of Sherif Raisuli, is that not so?'

'I ... it is possible.'

'You provided them with French uniforms, lent them the Sultan's motorcar, which the Resident General is given free leave to use, and sent them to capture "M. Hassan" and any of his companions. Did you know what your men would do with their captives?'

'I ... no.'

'You took care not to enquire. As you did not look too closely at how much they were using you for their own purposes, once your jobs were done. However, when your men only captured the one, you must have been furious. The following morning, you sent a pair to the *funduq,* where they threatened the owner – who described them as "rough men" – but missed the boy. Two others – fluent in French, wearing French uniforms, with French shaves and haircuts – were later dispatched to Nurse Taylor's surgery in the medina, after you received news of an injured foreigner brought to her during the night.'

'A woman,' Dulac blurted out, still astonished.

'Who escaped you. Again.

'Then on Saturday, the Maréchal's cousin returned, joined by another man, a woman, and a mute boy. These had to be the people you were seeking, yet you could hardly lay hands upon all four under the Maréchal's very roof.

'I imagine you spent a tense couple of days, watching us come and go, until Russell and I virtually walked into your hands. Russell presented herself here Tuesday night, when the rest of the household was preparing for the party at Volubilis. You drugged her' – Lyautey made a noise – 'stuffed her into a trunk' – Lyautey emitted a Gaulish oath –'and had her taken away. And finally, your men got wind of me and the boy in Moulay Idriss. Another journal entry?'

'A conversation. With Madame. They laughed, at the picture of you dressed as a *marabout* with–'

'Quite. At dusk last night, you gave them the Sultan's motor again, and they took me.'

By this time, Lyautey was staring open-mouthed between his cousin and his secretary. 'But *why?*' he said finally. 'To what purpose could this be?'

'Money,' said Holmes in disgust. 'Doesn't it always begin with greed? You said yourself, the Mannesmann corporation would give anything to get the iron flowing again. A bag of gold coins is nothing compared to what those mines are worth.'

'Treason,' Lyautey said, in a voice like tolling doom.

'No!' Dulac cried. 'I sold nothing to the German government – these were businessmen!'

'An interesting distinction, but ultimately meaningless,' Holmes said.

Mahmoud tugged at his beard. 'And yet he is right. Men like the Mannesmanns put profit over patriotism. They would happily underwrite the death of Abd el-Krim if it returned power to the Spanish, but they would be equally quick to throw Spain into the sea if they thought France gave them a better chance at the ore.'

Something in the argument had gone astray. It was akin to the sensation of Profound Meaning that had plagued me early in my time here, but this was more like Profound Wrong. The facts refused to fall into tidy array. Like one piece of a jigsaw puzzle that did not quite fit.

It made me uncomfortable. And eventually it pushed a question out of me. 'How subtle are their minds?'

Holmes narrowed his eyes at the tone of my voice, but Mahmoud merely asked, 'What do you mean?'

'Assassinating Abd el-Krim to undermine the Revolt would be an obvious move, but it's less apparent why the Germans would wish to heat up the Rif conflict with France. Would you say that these mine owners, having failed in their attempts to murder Abd el-Krim, could come up with a plan of using France – no friend of Germany – as a tool to get rid of him?'

My voice was taut. I could feel Holmes' gaze boring into my face, and wanted badly to look over at him, to ask why he wasn't jumping into this beside me – but I had to keep my eyes on Mahmoud, whose expression was no more revealing than ever.

After a moment, Holmes spoke. 'You are asking if the Mannesmanns are chess players, versed in the art of queen sacrifice? If they could craft a strategy that would lead to a buildup of the French presence in Morocco, even risk having France overrun Spanish territory entirely, because it appeared to be the only means of breaking the stalemate and ridding the country of the rebellion?'

Lyautey protested. 'France has no plans for "overrunning" the Spanish Protectorate. To do so would risk war.'

'Against whom? Spain?' Holmes asked. 'Spain is in no condition to fight France.'

'Every European country would be against us. We would be forced to back down.'

'Precisely,' I said. 'Even if you did decide that the only way to clear out the hornet's nest of the Rif Revolt was to trespass on Spain's region, France would–'

'I must object. I have no such intention.'

'Very well, then, your successor. But since it seems clear that France would have to withdraw from Spanish territory, the question remains: Do the Germans have minds that calculating?'

Lyautey grudgingly gave the question some

thought, lighting a cigarette over the table-top lamp. Dulac was too frightened to be anything other than confused; Mahmoud was glowering, and I could feel Holmes waiting.

Was I the only person to see this huge question, hovering over the room? Did no one else – not even Holmes – look past basic assumptions? Or had I finally veered into pure madness, and my suspicion was a consequence of delusion?

I felt as if I were sitting with a lit bomb in my lap, invisible to the others. I had no choice, but to go on.

'M. Dulac, you may be unaware that one of your Jibali hirelings was killed by a fellow conspirator, when his injuries threatened capture for both.'

'No, really? That is to say, I am sorry that–'

'You should be thankful that you fell into French hands, instead of theirs. One last question: How much were you paid for the information about Monday's meeting between the Maréchal and Abd el-Krim?'

'Is *that* where he went on Monday!' Dulac exclaimed. 'I knew that you three rode north, but you were gone before I could send men after you.'

The truth of his words rang starkly through the room.

As did the sound of a cocking trigger.

The rush of turmoil reached a crescendo in my ears, terror and uncertainty and the conviction that I had to act, even if lightning struck me dead. I spoke.

'Don't move, Mahmoud,' I said. 'Please, I beg you, do not move.'

CHAPTER THIRTY

Would I have dared, if the October revelations of Mycroft's cold-blooded schemes did not echo freshly in my memory? Would I have turned my gun on Mahmoud without that new and vivid awareness of what the British government and its agents were capable of? Would I have even envisioned the possibility that Mahmoud Hazr could be my enemy, had I not just rebuilt my mind from the ground up?

'Russell!' I did not often shock my husband, but I had now.

'Holmes, you can hear that Dulac is speaking the truth. He did not know where we went. Unless you wish to entertain the theory that we were set upon by random villains, that leaves Mahmoud and Ali.'

Mahmoud's fingers spread slightly, with care, to illustrate their emptiness. 'You would take the word of this traitor?'

'A traitor, yes, but no actor. Only you and Ali knew where the Maréchal was going. I suppose Holmes and I would have been unavoidable casualties of war.'

'I shouldn't like to try convincing his brother, Mycroft, of that.'

'Why were you sent here, to Morocco?'

'I told you—'

'That you were spying on the Revolt under the

357

guise of being arms dealers, I know. But what was your real assignment?'

There was a long pause. Dulac fidgeted. The coal shifted in the brazier, my hand on the gun throbbed, and finally under his breath Mahmoud muttered a brief Qur'anic phrase: 'To Him we surrender.' He lifted his eyes to mine. 'We were sent to kill the Emir Mohammed Abd el-Krim.'

Lyautey dropped his cigarette.

'Was this as a favour to the French?' I asked Mahmoud. 'Or to Spain?'

'It was thought that the Revolt threatened the stability of the region.'

'How is that Britain's responsibility?'

'Spain will never control its Protectorate without help. Even a year ago, it was clear that as the Revolt continued to win ground, sooner or later it would come up against France, and France would be forced to respond. And when it did so, the obvious military decision would be to continue north to the coast.

'Britain cannot afford to look across the Straits of Gibraltar at a French fortress. The Empire depends on easy access through the Mediterranean: Palestine, Egypt, India, Hong Kong. If shipping ceased, or even grew threatened, it would be catastrophic.'

'That being Whitehall's position,' I said. And, no doubt, that of his employer, my brother-in-law, the arch-manipulator Mycroft Holmes. A subtle mind – and a master of chess. 'But you and Ali have witnessed first-hand Britain's ruthless betrayal of the Arab cause. Like Colonel Lawrence, you must have felt stabbed in the back by your

358

own government. When did you decide that you couldn't stomach another round of it here in the Maghreb? That Abd el-Krim was right? That you needed to kill Maréchal Lyautey instead?

'Don't!' I cried at the motion of his right hand – although I could not have said which was the greater fear, what I was doing, or what he was. I, daring to hold a gun on Mahmoud Hazr!

'I did warn you, Miri, where the ambush would be,' Mahmoud pointed out. 'I drew you the location. How could I know that your injuries would turn it to mere pencil scratches?'

'Which only tells me that you changed your mind again once you found that Holmes and I would be at the meeting. That you couldn't quite bring yourself to murder two friends. It still leaves you a traitor, just not a cold-blooded one.'

His black eyes glittered across the room at me; even with my revolver pointed at him, I felt a strong urge to back away.

'Do you think me a stupid man, Miri?'

'I did not in the past.'

'Perhaps you imagine that living with primitive tribesmen has rotted my wits, made me believe that killing one man might frighten his country into retreat?'

'You and Ali have spent the past year fighting with the Revolt. Guerrilla fighters kill where and when they get the opportunity.'

'Ali and I have spent the past year with two of the subtlest military minds I have ever encountered. They are not terrorists, but insurgents, perceptive enough to know that assassination invites response, not retreat. And why kill the

Maréchal, who respects and honours the country he oversees?'

Lyautey spoke up. 'In any event, there are several men ready and able to replace me. No, France will stay in Morocco, with or without me.'

'You misunderstand,' I told Lyautey. 'He did not want to *stop* France from responding; he wanted to *ensure* it.'

'But why on earth–'

'France's response to your assassination, during a meeting with the head of the Rif Revolt, would have been immediate, massive, and military. In fact, Paris might well have decided for itself that the only solution was a clean sweep north, treaties be damned.'

'That would put France across from Gibraltar,' Lyautey countered. 'Do you suggest that this man, who evidently works for the British government, wants that? Would not his government see it as treason?'

'I am no traitor,' Mahmoud said, teeth clenched but hands motionless.

'You disobeyed orders,' I replied. 'You tried to murder the official representative of a British ally. What else does that make you?'

'We were–' He caught himself, and considered for a moment, before giving a tiny shake of his head. 'We were not trying to kill him.'

'Then who was?'

'We were trying to make it look like an attempt to kill him.'

I heard the sound of Holmes taking out his tobacco pouch, a sign of his need for concentrated thought. I said, 'Perhaps you ought to explain that.'

'The meeting was a ploy. There were two Jibali the Emir had used before – they may even originally have come through this ... person Dulac, ironically. The arrangement was for them to wait behind the boulder, and when the Maréchal appeared on the track, they were to shoot *into the air* – that was made *very* clear. Our goal was to build the tensions along the border so that, once fighting starts again in the spring, France would be determined to push hard into the Werghal Valley. If the Emir was present at the meeting, the attempt would be blamed on him – had he refused to come, we planned to bring another man of the Emir's build and hope the Maréchal had no accurate photographs.

'Then I came to Fez and spoke with you, sir. I expected a jingoistic administrator who paid lip-service to respecting the colonials. Instead I found a man with a deep affection for Islam and a willingness to twist the regulations to the break-ing point in order to further his goal of Morocco for the Moroccans.

'When I left Dar Mnehbi Thursday, I was uneasy. Ali and I had crafted the fake assassin-ation with care, and I was now thinking about discarding it, without consultation, for the sake of an irrational response to a Frenchman.

'When I sat down to coffee in the medina, my mind was in a turmoil. When I stood up again, the decision was made: We needed to bring the Maréchal and the Emir together in fact, not merely as a ruse.

'The original plan was, Ali would ride with the

Emir while I brought the Maréchal. As we approached the meeting place, shots would ring out. Ali and I would hustle our respective charges back home; both sides would be convinced of the untrustworthiness of the other, and firmly committed to war. However, Ali had more faith in the hired men than I. Men for hire are never to be fully trusted – and asking Moroccans, who take pride in their shooting, to deliberately miss a target may be foolish. However, he pointed out that the men in Fez had never let us down before. In the end, we agreed that he and I would take care to be in the fore of our parties, that we might "discover" the ambush and give warning.

'I expected to see Ali in Fez on Saturday, and tell him of the change – that he needed to cancel the arrangement with the two hirelings, and permit the meeting to go through. But as Miri and I were climbing the hill on the Thursday night, I thought of the men seen on the hillside near the boulder, and of the out-of-place branch on the track – yes, both those were the truth – and it occurred to me that such a degree of preparation was both unexpected and pointless. Unless another man's plans had overtaken our own.

'And although an actual ambush was nothing Ali and I couldn't handle between us, I decided that a degree of insurance was called for. So I gave Miri the vague outlines of the potential trap, knowing that if I was for some reason unable to speak with Ali, she would tell him, and he could make the decision, whether or not to go forward.

'I did not wish her to cancel entirely, merely to

ensure that she, Holmes, and Ali would be on the alert. So I told her that I was mildly apprehensive, and made a drawing of the place I judged the most logical site for a possible ambush.'

My eyes were alert for the least motion, but my mind was elsewhere. As, indeed, was Holmes'. I heard him jabbing meditatively at his pipe before he remarked, 'You are saying that you are not a failed assassin, merely a British traitor.'

At my accusations, Mahmoud had glared; at those of Holmes, he winced.

'I am neither,' he insisted in a cold voice.

'Explain.'

'To do so, I must go back to when Ali and I first came to the mountains. We were sent to kill Abd el-Krim, but it soon became apparent that removing the older brother alone would not stop the independence movement. And removing both brothers – if, as requested, it was to appear an accident – would be nearly impossible, since they are only rarely together.

'And then we met the Emir. He was a man, and a mind. He was a person who did not deserve the fate we would have brought him. Ali and I...'

'Became converts,' Holmes provided.

'I will not try to convince you of the rightness of the Rif cause. I will merely point out that Ali and I are well accustomed to carrying out distasteful tasks for our government. This was different.

'As we lived with the Rifi, we saw the implacable hatred that the Spanish have for them. Eight centuries of *Reconquista* mean that as far as Spain is concerned, there can be nothing for the

Moor but the heel of a boot. Nothing but poverty and abuse.

'And in October, as Ali and I watched the Spanish move to the relief of Chaouen, I thought, What if these were the French instead? What if the hand of France was pushed, forcing a show of strength against the Rif– the entire Rif, not just the portions of it south of the Werghal? The Revolt would be crushed, in no time at all. Of that we had no doubt.

'But afterwards, in the wake of defeat? Over the weeks of Chaouen, Ali and I had many long talks about this question, and could only see two possibilities. One was that France would stay over all of Morocco, shipping the Spanish troops home to their dictator. France does not hold 750 years of bitter struggle against the Moors, has no raw memories of twenty thousand slaughtered in-fantry rotting on the banks of the Mediterranean, no revenge-lust driving them to drop canisters of mustard gas over civilian villages. They have no reason to withhold mercy to the Rifi. Yes, the cost would be a threat to British shipping, but to be honest, was that sufficient justification? As you say, Ali and I had good reason to mistrust the colonial impulses of our country – seeing an em-pire from the bottom gives a different perspective. Going against our government's wishes might buy the Rifi a chance to enter the world with position and self-respect.

'But I say to you, this is not treason.' His black eyes bore across the table at Holmes. 'The men in Whitehall commit high treason daily – under-mining the crown, furthering their own positions.

By circumventing their schemes, Ali and I have been pursuing the greater loyalty.'

'You said you saw two possibilities, if the French annexed the north.'

'The other possibility would be that, as the Maréchal says, France would bow to international pressure and draw back south of the mountains. On the surface, this would appear a failure: The Revolt would be crushed, the Rif back under the boot-heel of Spain.'

He sat forward, and my hand tightened – but it was intensity that moved him, not threat.

'However, within this apparent failure lay the seeds of another possibility. A gamble.

'With the Revolt suppressed, and by a country with no long history against the Moors, we thought that the Rifi might at last achieve a voice in the court of public opinion. Particularly if Ali and I could convince either the Emir or his brother to leave the Protectorate before France returned it to Spain. You have seen the Emir's charisma; believe me when I tell you the younger brother has it, too. What if – and this was at the base of my change of heart that afternoon – what if the Resident General of Morocco had already spoken face to face with the Emir of the Revolt? What if the two men had cause to share a degree of mutual respect? Maréchal Lyautey, sir, you have drunk tea with the Emir. Has that changed the way you think about the Rifi? Changed how you will speak of him to your superiors in Paris?'

Lyautey did not answer, but was no doubt in thoughtful consideration. As was I.

Asking France to crush your pet rebellion in

order to clear the way for its distant victory was rather like setting alight the vegetation around a house when a wild-fire was approaching. A controlled burn was a huge risk, but sometimes it contained the only chance of salvaging the essentials.

I agreed that putting the Rif under a Lyautey Protectorate would be for the best. But it was common knowledge that Lyautey was on the edge of retirement. Plus, he had spent his entire career outside of Paris: His influence in the halls of power would be limited. Surely the Maréchal's usefulness for the Rif cause was drawing to an end?

Which suggested that Mahmoud might be lying: that Lyautey's actual death might have been of greater use than a staged threat.

Holmes made a sound of exhaling smoke that, even without seeing him, spoke eloquently of decision. 'Russell, think back to Ali's response at the *wadi*,' he said. 'What would you call it?'

'Ali took care to credit Abd el-Krim with saying the would-be assassin was one of Raisuli's, I remember that.'

'True, but after? When he saw the blood on the Maréchal's horse?'

'He was confused. Angry.' The urgent way Ali's eyes had searched us for wounds, his stormy reaction to the sight of the horse's bloodstained neck.

'Frightened?'

'Why would he be frightened?' I asked. Holmes did not answer. I thought for a minute. 'According to Mahmoud, Ali believed the ambush

366

was to be a fake, nothing more than a means of laying an explosive charge between the Rif Revolt and the French Protectorate. When Mahmoud disappeared, Ali either had to cancel, or do his best to play out the act alone. You are saying that he chose the latter. That he did not expect the attempt to be a real one. That his anger was genuine, when he found how close the bullets came to the Maréchal – and to us.'

After a moment, I permitted the gun to sag, pointing slightly to the side of Mahmoud's heart for the first time.

It would be a plan as tangled as the streets of the medina, a garment woven of lies and half-truths, of truths that look like lies, and lies that appear the truth. A garment suited to the half-light, its precise outlines impossible to discern.

Exactly what I would expect of one Mahmoud Hazr.

Or, indeed, of Mycroft Holmes.

The problem in turning independent thinkers loose on a matter is, they tend to go beyond the theoretical and seize the chance for independent action. Thus, two faithful servants of His Majesty who decide that the best way to serve their country is to betray it. Two faithful servants, or their employer back in London?

'An assassination that isn't,' I murmured. 'A defeat that conceals victory. High treason that embraces a greater loyalty. A spot-light on battle while the true struggle takes place in the shadows.'

I moved in my chair, reluctantly preparing to lay the revolver on the table, then stopped.

By describing all this, by revealing his labori-ously-laid plans to foment war, Mahmoud was voiding any chance of its success.

Or was he?

Lyautey, hearing the machinations of this pair of British agents, would take care to avoid the stepping stones they had laid out for him.

Or would he?

Would he, rather, take a hard look at their plot, and decide it dovetailed nicely with the interests of both France and Morocco?

Or – and this was the truly troubling bit – was that subtle chess-player still at work in the background, hiding these apparent revelations behind yet another layer of shadow? Was there a further plan behind this one? One built around our capture of a French traitor? If that was the case, it would call into question the role of Mah-moud's imprisonment in Habs Qara...

Shadow upon shadow, reflection upon reflec-tion.

I studied Mahmoud, inscrutable as ever, sitting with one knee over the other, both hands gathered on his leg. The gold of the ring was the brightest thing about him.

I narrowed my eyes. The ring.

When had he started wearing it? Idir gave it to me in Erfoud, to prove the authorship of the note summoning me into the desert. When I then returned it to Mahmoud, he looped it through a thong and dropped it inside his shirt: I pictured it clearly. He had not worn the ring openly, there in the desert or later in Fez.

Yet it was on his finger when he came out of

Habs Qara.

And something else.

'Mahmoud, tell me. Last week, before you were ... taken, your speech was different from when I first met you. More like how you spoke in England, stripped of reference to the Qur'an or even Ibn Khaldun. Why?'

He stared at me, unblinking. 'My brother Ali asked me that, too, some weeks past.'

'And how did you answer him?'

'I told him it was mere habit, and meant nothing. But I lied. He knew I lied. I could not speak those holy words because my mouth felt unclean.'

And now he could. He was finished with obedience to a government he mistrusted, finished with lies to his partner. Finished with shame.

I hesitated no longer, but laid the revolver on the table. Mahmoud sat, wearing his expression of hidden amusement. Which in itself was mildly alarming, but when it came to a choice between that face or the machinations of Whitehall, I had declared my loyalties.

My responsibilities in the world of international affairs were at an end.

Lyautey stood. '*Now* may we have coffee? And remove this ... secretary from my sight?'

'Both excellent ideas,' Holmes said.

As I got to my feet, to let in the guards and to go free Youssef, the familiar sound of the muezzin swelled over the city. Dawn, already? I pushed open the decorative door into the courtyard, bright enough now that I could see the complex design of the *zellij*. Yes, the sun was coming up.

Incredibly enough, a mere week after I had arrived. Thursday...

I paused. As I stood in the doorway, trying to recall the day's date, a hollow metallic clatter began to bash against the muezzin's song. It took my English ears a moment to identify the new racket as a church bell.

Darkness to light; sunrise in the depth of midwinter; a year's journey completing. Shadows giving way to clarity. I stepped back into the room, where three men had converged to bind the hands of the fourth. Holmes looked up, his eyes asking a question at my stillness. I smiled.

'"Peace on him on the day he was born",' I recited in Arabic, then switched to English. 'Gentlemen, may I be the first to wish you a very happy Christmas, and a peaceful new year.'

AUTHOR'S AFTERWORD

1925 was still young when Holmes and I rode out again from Fez. As we had the first time, we reined in to look across the beehive of tile roofs, the site of so much bustling intrigue.

We had waited to see François Dulac quietly dispatched to France, under guard, before leaving the city. Arrests had been made; more were pending.

'I feel as if I've helped remove a cancer,' I remarked.

'Thus permitting a war to live out its natural life,' replied the man at my side.

'Always cheerful, Holmes.'

Our other companion spoke up. '"God will not change a people, until they change themselves",' he quoted in Arabic, adding in English, 'One man may not prevent a war, but he may shift its path. Or one woman.'

I would make Mahmoud a feminist yet. 'And have we?' I asked. 'Did we change anything here?'

'Hubert Lyautey and Mohammed ibn Abd el-Krim are not the men they were a month ago. Their gaze is wider, their sense of the other man keener. They may continue to play out their roles, but they will also look past the immediate needs of war. Yes, we have turned the track, a little.'

'What shall I tell Mycroft?' Holmes asked him.

'By the time you see him, there will be little to tell.'

'He will not be happy.'

'My days of concerning myself with the happiness of London are over.' His voice, cold and hard, made me wonder – a touch uneasily – if perhaps the shared grievances of Mahmoud Hazr and Lieutenant Colonel T. E. Lawrence boded ill for the British Empire.

It would not altogether be a bad thing, for me personally, were that distraction to arise. Mycroft Holmes was sure to find some way to vent his wrath on me: This was the second time since summer that I had deliberately gone against him.

'You will remain with Abd el-Krim, until the end?' I asked.

'As long as he wants us,' said Mahmoud. 'Which I think will not be long.'

'And what then?'

The black amused eyes slid sideways to look at me. 'We shall think of something.'

The uneasiness stirred again. 'I imagine you will. But, Mahmoud? I am glad I didn't shoot you, the other day.'

'I would hate to have burdened you with that.'

My laughter attracted the attention of the lad on the pony, who, uninterested in the view, had ridden down the rough hillside to the remains of a fallen hut. At the sound, he yanked the beast's head up and urged him back to the road, eager to ride on.

'Idir,' I said, 'wait. I have a present for you.'

I pulled the paper-and-twine-wrapped parcel from my bag and handed it down to him. He undid the twine, folded it into a pocket, and opened the paper.

It was a belt strung with an ornate curved scabbard, its knife a miniature version of Ali's. I'd had it made in the medina. The boy pulled out the weapon, his eyes brighter than its metal blade. 'It's sharp,' I told him. 'Almost as sharp as Ali's. Try not to cut off any pieces of yourself.'

Mahmoud helped the child buckle the belt over his *djellaba*. The little hand patted it in delight, but when he looked up at me, his face took on a worried expression. He thrust his hands into his pockets, digging around with increasing desperation.

'No, Idir, it's a gift,' I reassured him. 'You don't need to give me anything in return.'

But he had come out with two handfuls of possessions, and was frowning at them. His right hand held three or four of Ali's wooden carvings – giraffe, dog, aeroplane. His left hand held a wad of lint and leaves that he'd had to peel from the pocket.

He looked at the right hand, and at the left, and then with a look of proud sacrifice, he held out his left hand to me.

Gingerly, I accepted the oozing wad, my nose finally identifying it as one of the honeyed pastries he'd so enjoyed in the medina, days and days before.

'Oh, Idir, you shouldn't have.'

'Time we were gone,' Mahmoud told us. Soon, the first troops would appear, bound for the coming Front, and we did not wish to be overcome by soldiers.

It was time for us to go our separate ways. Mahmoud edged his horse forward to clasp Holmes' hand. 'I thank you, my brother. You have done a good thing for Morocco.'

'Give my best to Ali,' Holmes replied.

Then the hand was held out to me, and although I was tempted to fill it with the honey sweet, instead I gave him my right hand. Our rings brushed together as our palms met. He held my hand, and my eyes, for a long moment.

'I hope our paths cross again, Miri,' he said.

'Insh'Allah, Mahmoud,' I replied. Then our hands parted, and he pulled his mount's head around and started uphill at a trot. Idir paused long enough to return the knife to its belt, then kicked his pony into a gallop and flew past him.

At a more leisurely pace, Holmes and I rode, shoulder to shoulder, around the east-bound road that led out of Morocco.

The odour of honey remained with us for a long time.

– MARY RUSSELL HOLMES

EDITOR'S NOTE

The Rif revolt was crushed in the spring of 1926, by combined French and Spanish forces that outnumbered the rebels approximately ten to one. The Abd el-Krim brothers surrendered – to the French. With their families, they were exiled to the island of Reunion – a French possession. In 1947, Mohammed Abd el-Krim, Emir of the short-lived Rif Republic, slipped away from a ship taking him to France itself and received asylum in Egypt, where he continued to work for Berber independence. He died in 1963, having lived to see the independence of Morocco and Algeria. In the brief existence of the Rif Republic, from September 1921 to May 1926, the Abd el-Krims forged the paradigm for colonial independence movements around the globe, while tens of thousands of Rifi civilians died by poison gas alone.

Mulai Ahmed er Raisuni was taken captive by the Abd el-Krim forces shortly after this story ends, in January 1925. He was ill, and died in April, of natural causes.

Maréchal Hubert Lyautey retired to France nine months after the events of this memoir. The French government gave him no escort, met him with no parades; Britain, on the other hand, provided an honor guard of two destroyers to see him through the Straits of Gibraltar. Lyautey's replacement in Morocco was Maréchal Pétain – First World War hero, Second World War collaborator and condemned traitor.

Mining continues throughout the Rif. A 1925 report by engineer Courtney DeKalb stated bluntly, 'Iron ore is the cause of the present trouble in Morocco.' This may reflect a geologist's bias; still, if one substitutes the word *oil* for *iron ore,* the statement may be applied to any number of countries throughout the region. The same month Lyautey retired, the Mannesmanns sold their Morocco holdings to an Anglo-American syndicate in a deal that newspapers called 'the biggest since the war': some £10,000,000 cash plus concessions in the Balkans. In current dollars, this would be approximately $500,000,000.

The December meeting between Hubert Lyautey and Mohammed ibn Abd el-Krim that is described in this volume of Miss Russell's memoirs remained a state secret, and appears in no contemporary account of the Revolt. Neither do public records reveal anything at all concerning the activities of Mahmoud and Ali Hazr in the Maghreb.

Both are precisely what one would expect the public records to show.

– LAURIE R. KING

ACKNOWLEDGEMENTS AND NOTES

Readers interested in Miss Russell's previous meetings with the Hazrs are referred to *O Jerusalem* and *Justice Hall*. For the volume of her memoirs describing the extraordinary events that brought her to Morocco in the first place, see *Pirate King*. Other volumes in her long and eventful life are described at www.laurierking.com.

Thanks are due to Mark Willenbrock, who welcomed me into his *dar* and made a gift to me of Fez and Morocco, his adopted home. Anyone looking to travel in Morocco would do well to consult www.madaboutmorocco.com.

The bit of poetry at the beginning of this novel comes from C. E. Andrews' *Old Morocco and the Forbidden Atlas,* attributed by him to the Persian mystic Rumi.

Much confusion exists as to where Maréchal Lyautey lived in Fez, but it would appear that Dar Mnehbi was used for official business, while the actual Residency was in the palace that is now Musée Batha, Moulay Idriss college, and the Palais des Hôtes. I have taken some liberties with the structure of Dar Mnehbi and the guard house next door; the Dar may still be seen on tours of the medina.

The 'Sherlockism' about the nugget of truth in

chapter eighteen was contributed by Priscilla Johnson. The nurse 'Peg Taylor' is based on Miss Sophie Denison, long-time resident of Fez, who wrote for *The Muslim World* on Moorish women. The nurse's present name was contributed by Meredith Taylor, drawn from a list of donors to the Laurie King fund-raiser for the writing project 826 Valencia.

ABOUT NAMES:

The name 'Abd el-Krim' (Abdelkrim, Abd al-Karim, Abdul Krim, etc.) is, strictly speaking, inaccurate when used for the two leaders of the Rif Revolt, since Abd el-Krim – 'servant of the Generous One' – was a title given their father. More correctly, two brothers would be Mohammed (or, Muhammed) and M'Hammed ibn Abd el-Karim al-Khattabi.

Similarly, 'Raisuli' (Rais Uni, Raisuni) is more completely Mulai Ahmed er-Raisuni.

ABOUT TRANSLITERATIONS:

Arabic, like Hebrew, is based upon consonants, with pronunciation and hence transliteration of words changing over time and depending on the language it is being translated into. Thus a *madrassa* in Morocco is a *madersa,* a *djellaba* a *galabiyyah,* and the Werghal River may be spelled Wergha, Wergal, Ouergha, or even Oureghla.

Similarly, the following:
Ghumara / Rhomarra
Jibala / Djebala
Mequinez / Meknez
Moslem / Muslim
Qur'an / Koran
Chaouen / Xaouen / Shawan / Sheshuan /
  Chefchaoen

GLOSSARY

Bab: gate

Bismillah: It is common in Morocco to evoke the Holy Name at the beginning of any task.

Dar: a house of one or three storeys, open to the sky, built around an inner courtyard on the ground floor

Djellaba: loose outer robe, in Morocco usually of striped cloth, with a hood, and knee- rather than ankle-length

Fasi: a resident of Fez

Funduq: a caravanserai for travellers and their livestock

Insh'Allah: 'If it is the will of Allah'

Madrassa: a Qur'an school, taught through recitations

Marabout: a holy man or a shrine

Riad: similar to a *dar*, but with a garden instead

of a courtyard

Rifi: someone from the Rif mountains

The publishers hope that this book has given you enjoyable reading. Large Print Books are especially designed to be as easy to see and hold as possible. If you wish a complete list of our books please ask at your local library or write directly to:

Magna Large Print Books
Magna House, Long Preston,
Skipton, North Yorkshire.
BD23 4ND

This Large Print Book for the partially sighted, who cannot read normal print, is published under the auspices of

THE ULVERSCROFT FOUNDATION